THE
SECRET
INTENSITY
OF
EVERYDAY
LIFE

◆

ALSO BY WILLIAM NICHOLSON

The Society of Others
The Trial of True Love
I Could Love You
Rich and Mad

THE
SECRET
INTENSITY
OF
EVERYDAY
LIFE

◆

WILLIAM NICHOLSON

First published in the UK in 2008 by Quercus Books PLC

Published in the United States in 2010 by

Soho Press, Inc.
853 Broadway
New York, NY 10003

Library of Congress Cataloging-in-Publication Data

Nicholson, William.
The secret intensity of everyday life / William Nicholson.
p. cm.
ISBN 978-1-56947-647-5
1. Middle class—England—Fiction. 2. Self-realization—Fiction.
3. Sussex (England)—Fiction. I. Title.
PR6064.I235S43 2010
823'.914—dc22
2010007769

Paperback ISBN 978-1-56947-956-8

Printed in the United States of America

10 9 8 7 6 5 4 3 2 1

'If we had a keen vision and feeling of all ordinary human life, it would be like hearing the grass grow and the squirrel's heart beat, and we should die of that roar which lies on the other side of silence.'

George Eliot, *Middlemarch*

The story takes place in Sussex over six days
in May 2000

1

She recognizes the handwriting on the envelope. She drinks from her mug of tea, looks across the kitchen table at Henry, sees him absorbed in the triage of the morning post. One pile for the bin, one pile for later, one for now. He uses a paper knife when opening letters. Not a kitchen knife, an actual slender, dull-edged blade made for the purpose. The children silent, reading. Rain outside the windows puckering the pond.

Laura wills the letter to remain unnoticed. It's been forwarded from her parents' address.

'You know Belinda Redknapp?' she says.

'Should I?' Henry inattentive.

'One of the school mothers. You rather fancied her. Husband like a frog.'

'They all have husbands like frogs.'

The bankers, lawyers, insurance company executives whose children are their children's friends, whose wealth makes Henry feel poor.

'Anyway, she wants to meet Aidan Massey.'

Henry looks up, surprised.

'Why?'

'She thinks he's sexy.'

Carrie pauses her absorbed scrutiny of the *Beano*.

'Who's sexy?'

'The man on Daddy's programme.'

'Oh.'

'He's an evil dwarf,' says Henry. 'I want to kill him.'

The letter lies by her plate, immense as a beach towel, shouting her unmarried name: Laura Kinross. She wants to muffle it, mute it, gag it. Pick up a section of the newspaper, glance at it, lay it down just so. But the desire inhibits the action. She's ashamed to discover that she means to leave the letter unopened until Henry has gone. So to mitigate the shame she makes no move to conceal the envelope, saying to Fate, See, I'm doing nothing. If I'm found out I'll accept the consequences.

Jack is interested in the proposal to kill Aidan Massey.

'How would you kill him, Daddy?'

'Hello, Jack. Good to have you with us.'

Laura frowns. She reaches out one hand to stop Jack smearing his sleeve in the butter. She hates it when Henry talks like that. Jack's too dreamy, he says.

'No, how?'

'Well.' Henry puts on the face he makes when summoning facts from his brain. He actually touches one finger to his brow, as if pressing a button. 'I'd tell the make-up girl to go on adding make-up until he couldn't breathe. Go on adding it until he's got no features left. Just smooth and round like a ball.'

Jack is awed silent by the detail.

Henry gathers up the pile of junk mail and takes it to the bin, which is already so full the lid won't close. He rams the wad of paper down hard. This action makes Laura flinch, because now it will be impossible to remove the bin bag without ripping it, but she says nothing. She is, it strikes her, lying low.

Henry reaches for his leather bag, which is bursting with printed matter.

'Oh, yes,' he tells Jack, suddenly remembering. 'I read your composition. I loved it.'

'Oh. Okay.'

'No. I did. I loved it.' He leans down for a kiss, Jack back reading *Tintin*. 'I'm off. Love you.'

Laura gets up. She moves slowly because she wants to move fast, to draw Henry out into the hall, out of sight of the letter. She squeezes between Carrie's chair and the dresser, remembering as she does so that last night Carrie had been in tears.

'Better now, darling?' she whispers as she passes.

'Yes,' says Carrie.

Laura knows her behaviour is undignified and unnecessary. Surely the past has lost its power. Twenty years ago almost, we're different people, I had long hair then. So did he.

'When will you be home?'

'Christ knows. I'll try to be on the 6.47.'

Rain streaking the flint wall. He kisses her in the open front doorway, a light brush of the lips. As he does so he murmurs, 'Love you.' This is habitual, but it has a purpose he once told her. Henry suffers from bursts of irrational anxiety about her and the children, that they'll be killed in a car crash, burned in a fire. He tells them he loves them every day as he leaves them because it may be the day of their death.

Recalling this, watching his familiar tall disjointed frame even as he steps out into the rain, Laura feels a quick stab of love.

'I think that letter may be from Nick,' she says.

'Nick?' His head turning back. Such a sweet funny face, droll as Stan Laurel, and that fuzz of soft sandy hair. 'Nick who?'

'Nick Crocker.'

She sees the name register. A family legend, or possibly ghost.

'Nick Crocker! Whatever happened to him?'

'I've no idea. I haven't opened the letter yet.'

'Oh, well.' Henry shakes open an umbrella. 'Got to rush. Tell me this evening.'

Nothing urgent in his curiosity. No intimation of danger. His footsteps depart over the pea-beach gravel towards the Golf, parked in front of the garage that is never used for cars. Laura goes back into the kitchen and harries the children into readiness for the school run. She's glad she told Henry, but the fact remains that she left the telling to the last minute. She had known it in the same moment that she had recognized the handwriting. She would open the letter alone.

A dull roar in the drive heralds the arrival of Alison Critchell's Land Cruiser. This immense vehicle parts the falling rain like an ocean liner. Laura stands under an umbrella by the driver window conferring with Alison on the endless variables of the run. Jack and Carrie clamber in the back.

'Angus is staying late for cricket coaching. Phoebe may be having a sleepover at the Johnsons. Assume it's on unless I call.' The litany of names that bound Laura's life. 'Assume the world hasn't ended unless you see flaming chariots in the sky.'

'What if they cancel the chariots?'

'The bastards. They would, too.'

The wry solidarity of school-run mothers. Laura confirms all she needs to know.

'So it's just my two at five.'

She waves as they drive off. Carrie is demanding about the waving. Laura must wave as long as they remain in sight. The car is so wide it creates a hissing wake through the spring verges, and the cow parsley rolls like surf. The drenched morning air smells keen, expectant. Who is it who loves the month of May? 'I measure the rest of my life by the number of Mays I will live to see.' Henry, of course, ever death-expectant. How could he have slipped so far from her mind?

Seated now at her work desk in what was once the dairy Laura Broad addresses the day ahead. Deliberate and unhurried, she makes a list of people she must call and things she must do. The letter lies unopened before her. This is how as a child she ate Maltesers. One by one she would nibble off the chocolate, leaving the whitish centres all in a row. Then pop, pop, pop, in they would go one on top of the other, in an orgy of delayed gratification. Even so it sometimes seemed to her as she tracked the precise moment of pleasure unleashed that there was a flicker of disappointment. Here I am, whispered the perfect moment. I am now. I am no longer to come.

She studies her list. 'Call Mummy about Glyndebourne.' Does being organized mean not being creative? 'Laura possesses the ability to achieve set tasks,' a teacher wrote when she was thirteen years old. Even then she had felt the implied criticism: a follower not a leader. A natural aptitude for cataloguing. Henry said once, 'You'd make a good fanatic.' He can be surprisingly perceptive. No, that's unfair. Henry is capable of great perception; only he isn't always looking. He never notices what I'm wearing.

'Tell me when you're wearing something special and I'll comment on it,' he says.

'But haven't you got eyes? Can't you see?'

Apparently not.

Back then she had bought her clothes in charity shops. It's easy when you're young.

She phones her mother.

'This weather!' her mother says. 'I'm praying it'll clear by Saturday. Diana says it's going to get worse.'

Saturday is the opening night of the Glyndebourne season. They're all going, Laura and Henry, her sister Diana and Roddy, courtesy of their loving parents.

'Don't listen to Diana, Mummy. You know she hates it when people are happy.'

This is true. Diana the ambitious one, Laura the pretty one. Some quirk in the sibling dynamic dictated from an early age that Diana takes life hard, and requires the world to reflect this. But she has her good moments, she can be loyal and generous. Never so loving as when Laura is miserable.

'We can picnic on the terrace, I suppose. What will you wear?'

'I don't know,' says Laura. 'I haven't thought.'

'Diana's bought something from a shop in St Christopher's Place. I forget where, but she sounds terrifically pleased with it.'

'How's Daddy's back?'

'Pretty hellish. I have to put his socks on for him in the morning. Doctors can't cure backs, you know. They just shrug their shoulders.'

What will I wear? Laura wonders as she puts down the phone. She reviews her wardrobe in her mind's eye. Her current favourite, a green Ghost dress, is too light for a chilly May evening. As for her beloved vintage Alaia, the truth is she no longer has the figure for it. Not bad for forty-two and two children, but there was a time when she could fit into anything.

Maybe I should zip up to London tomorrow.

This idea, suddenly planted, blossoms fiercely. There's barely time between school runs but it can be done. Glyndebourne opening night is a grand affair, and it's not often she gets a chance to dress up these days. There was a time when she turned heads.

She takes up the waiting letter and looks again at the handwriting that forms her name. A rapid careless scrawl in fine black fountain pen, effortlessly stylish. Every stroke premeditated, therefore the carelessness an illusion, an achieved effect. But she hadn't known that back then.

She opens the envelope. Headed letter paper, an unfamiliar address in London. No salutation. No Dear Laura, Dearest Laura, Darling Laura, nothing. As always.

Well, seems like I'm back in the old country for a few weeks. Drunk on England in spring. Walked yesterday in a bluebell wood so perfect it tempts my heathen soul to seek a Creator. How are you? Who are you? Shall we meet and compare notes on the vagaries of life's journey?

No signature, not even an initial. She smiles, shakes her head, both touched and irritated that he has changed so little. What right does he have to assume she remembers? And yet of course she remembers.

She opens the bottom left-hand drawer of her desk, the place where she keeps the family memorabilia. Birthday cards from the children, paintings they did in class long ago, letters from Henry. She fumbles all the way to the bottom, and there finds a sealed envelope she should have thrown away years ago, but has not. She takes it out and places it on the desk before her.

The envelope is addressed: 'For N.C., one day.'

She remembers writing it, but not the words she wrote. Ridiculous to have kept it for so long.

The flap of the envelope yields easily without tearing the paper. Inside is a thin red ribbon, a strip of four photo-booth pictures, a short note in Nick's handwriting, and her letter.

She gazes at the pictures. In the top one he's smiling at the camera, at her. In the bottom one he has his eyes closed.

She starts to read the letter. As she reads, tears come to her eyes.

Dear Nick. I'm writing this not long after you asked me to leave you. I'll give it to you when you ask me to come back.

The phone rings. Hurriedly, as if caught in a shameful act, she puts the envelope and its contents back in the desk drawer.

'So is it going to rain or isn't it?' Diana's phone conversations always begin in the middle. 'God, don't you hate England?'

2

She saw him coming down the carriage, swaying with the movement of the train, his eyes scanning left and right for an empty seat. She slid her canvas tote-bag over the table towards her, so creating a space that the stranger would feel permitted to occupy: an unthinking act of invitation which he accepted. His long body folded into the seat facing her. In the moment of glancing eye contact he smiled, making fine wrinkles round his eyes. He took out a book and opened it where a postcard marked his place. The book was a dark-bound library edition, and though she tried, she couldn't discover its title. The postcard, which lay on the table before her, was a painting of classical figures round a tomb. So he was a student like her.

She gazed out of the train window at the passing scene. The train entered a cutting. His reflection formed before her eyes, and she was free to look without restraint. He was handsome, his strong features framed and softened by a tangle of chestnut curls. He wore a denim jacket over a check long-sleeved shirt, the cuffs unbuttoned. Round his neck on a leather thong was a single mottled ceramic bead. He read intently, moving only to turn the page. She studied his hand in reflection, admiring the long fine fingers, noting the bitten nails.

He did not look at her. He seemed to be unaware of her. His indifference on this, their first encounter, won her respect.

She asked Katie O'Keefe later, 'Do you think that a man who wears a bead round his neck is gay?'

Katie screwed up her face to consider.

'One bead?'

'Quite a big one. Kind of tortoiseshell.'

'Bent as a poker,' said Hal Ashburnham.

'Pokers aren't bent.'

'It's all about where you put it, isn't it? In *here* it's straight. In *here*, it's bent.'

The following evening she went to a party given by Richard Clements in his college rooms. She had an essay to finish and worked long into the evening, so by the time she arrived the party was noisy and crowded. Felix Marks cornered her almost at once. He spoke to her intently but inaudibly while her eyes searched the room.

Richard had told Laura that Felix was in love with her, though how this could be, or even what it meant, Laura didn't know. Love that is offered but not returned is just words, surely, a nothingness, a whistle in the dark.

Why have I never been in love?

Nineteen years old and no shortage of offers. She caught sight of herself reflected in the uncurtained window panes, a shine of dark-blonde hair, a pale face, serious eyes. Why do I let Felix whisper secrets to me? Because I want to be liked. Liked but not loved. Admire me but don't touch me. No, not that. Touch me, love me, but only you, whoever you are, and only when I'm ready, whenever that may be.

Richard found her and rescued her.

'Someone you have to meet,' he said.

He had his back to her but she recognized him at once. He turned at Richard's touch and looked at Laura and smiled.

'We've met already.'

'You've met already?' Richard was hurt. 'No one told me.'

'Not exactly met,' said Laura.

So he had noticed her after all. He was smoking a Gitane, its acrid smell reaching her like a low growl. There was music playing behind the clatter of voices. Jackson Browne.

> Honey you really tempt me
> You know the way you look so kind
> I'd love to stick around but I'm running behind . . .

'Laura Kinross. This is Nick Crocker.'

3

Plumpton racecourse in the rain. White rails lonely without a crowd, just fields really. Woman reading *Vogue* has great legs. Catch Barry before the meeting, ask about changing the screen credit, written and directed by Henry Broad, it's called intellectual property, Barry. Not that I'm not grateful. Barry knows I took the job after eight months developing projects as they say, no one in television ever being out of work, merely unpaid. Though Jesus knows it's not as if even now they pay what they call in the City shed loads. You take a garden shed and fill it with twenties all the way up to the bituminous-felt-clad roof and you give it to a man like a frog as his reward for gambling with other people's money. The frog man buys a pretty young wife and a house in the country with a paddock for his pretty young daughter's pony, he takes the train to London every morning, he sits at his work station and fondles money, tosses money, jerks money until it spasms more money, on through the day, no lunch, into the evening hours. Daughter untucked, wife unfucked, shed reloaded.

Ah, sweet envy, balm of my soul. No, this isn't about money, Barry. This costs you nothing. This is about self-respect.

Woman reading *Vogue* has truly terrific legs. Can't see her face. Skirt with buttons up the front, one button missing, tights with a run on one side, not one of those glossy women you'd be afraid to touch. Rest my idle gaze on her crotch. Will she sense it? Play the mind game. Push up her skirt, reveal the let's say white triangle of her panties, white so much sexier than black or red. Translucent white fabric, dark crinkle of pubic hair. Look away. Down comes *Vogue*. Face worn and warm, rumpled, attractive. Tired eyes don't see me. Only a game. The secret life of commuters. They say men think of sex every seven seconds. Six seconds of rest, then.

Rain streaking on dirty windows. Look at it closely and it's got its own logic, pattern, form. They say you can see beauty in anything but then when everything is beautiful what's left to deliver the shock of beauty? A runnel of rain storming aslant this window bold and grey-gleaming to its disintegration and death. Yes I know, yes sometimes I catch it, the beauty lies not in the thing seen but in the quality of the seeing and that comes rarely, that charged intensity, and can't be willed. Takes a good night's sleep and a full stomach, or possibly starvation and exhaustion, but not vulgar busyness, the people's drug of choice, the trivial pursuit, the shrinking from thinking, the visceral dread of thought.

Me too, I'm no different. Later, I say, I'm busy. Then later, I say, I'm tired. And those big eyes watch without understanding as I pretend to read the paper. Daddy will you play a game with me? But I deserve my down time. Don't I do enough? Not enough never enough no never enough.

The train carriage is the old slam-door design, bought from British Rail by a consortium of former Southern Region managers and sold on at enormous profit to their successor, the French-owned railway company Connex. The seats are laid out in open stalls of four, twenty stalls to a coach, which gives a maximum capacity of eighty passengers. This morning as the train rolls through the grey rain-soaked light of the Sussex weald there are ninety-eight men and women packed into the one coach, because ever since the Hatfield crash the timetables have been in chaos and fewer trains have been running.

The early morning commuters, whether sitting or standing, read newspapers as they travel, the headlines offered outwards like credentials of rank. 'Cabinet falls out over cure for sterling.' 'Dame Liz pines for love of her life.' Only Henry Broad, unshielded by newspaper, magazine or book, sits exposed to the gaze of all, were any of the other travellers to have a mind to look at him: a tall, slender man in a brown denim jacket worn over a charcoal-grey crew-neck cotton jersey. He's in his mid-forties, his soft sandy hair cut fuzzy short, his face just a little too long to be handsome, a little too hesitant to be commanding, in the clumsy English fashion. Only his eyes might attract a second glance, because he alone in the carriage is looking about him. His eyes are hazel in colour, wide-set and striking, especially now as they move over the scene before him, animated by a lively nervous curiosity. He is sitting with his arms folded across his legs, his knee lightly touching the knee of the woman opposite, who is reading *Vogue*.

Yesterday evening Laura showed him a copy of a school composition written by his eleven-year-old son Jack. It was about a journey that takes place in a dream. The dreamer is walking along a path that turns into the top of a high wall, a wall so high that below it there are clouds.

When he woke this morning, Henry remembered that single page, those few lines, and experienced a wave of giddiness. He held the hard white edge of the bathroom basin and bowed his head, as the nausea passed through him. After a few moments he felt all right again, except his head seemed to be empty. What had happened? He interrogated himself as he shaved, seeking the source of the sudden sensation, which he recognised as misery. Why should Jack's composition make him miserable? Because once long ago he too had written stories that came to him like dreams, and were about journeys. Because there was a strangeness and a wonder in his son that had once been in him, and had become lost. Because he was not living the life he had meant to live.

My signature defect: indecisiveness. A tendency to see both sides of every question. Take iconoclasm. When Archbishop Laud speaks of 'the beauty of holiness' I say yes, the holy must be beautiful. God, being perfect, must be beautiful. But when William Dowsing leads his men into Pembroke College chapel and cries, 'Tear down the idols!', when his righteous hammer strikes the friable stone and the saint's face crumbles, I feel the excitement of the act, the outrage against superstition, the sheer bravado of defacement. This is original, no? Iconoclasts have had a bad press over the years. The evil dwarf Aidan Massey is not the author of this insight, for Christ's sake his special period is the Tudors, when it comes to the Civil War I know as much as him. So does Christina, one year out of Edinburgh University, three months' research and she's master of her subject. Mistress. But the professor gets the credit. The world turned upside down.

Where does an eleven-year-old boy get an idea like that? Walking on walls and below only clouds.

She's put her magazine down and closed her eyes. Such a sexy bruised face. Why these thoughts from a happily married man? My six seconds have expired. Things I want and haven't got. Hard to speak simple words. Why didn't I say more to Jack this morning? Breakfast the least serious time of day. And then there's Laura, sharer of my life, mother of my children. How come I daydream of sex with a stranger on a train? Fifteen years married and still a certain shyness, or a delicacy maybe. Not good form to love your wife and desire other women. Things I feel but can't admit. Suppose I were to say it. Hurt, lack of comprehension, perhaps even disgust. Driven out of the house like a dog with muddy paws.

The house Laura's father's money bought. The school fees Laura's father's money pays. And in this morning's post an insurance bill for over two thousand. Last month's credit cards not yet paid, oil for central heating running at four hundred a quarter, both cars due for servicing, even the water bill's a killer these days. And there's a tax bill coming up in two months that I do not have. But no, I'm not asking for more money, Barry. This isn't about money. Call it justice, if you like. Call it honourable behaviour. Call it an end to idolatry.

I must remember to ask Jack about his dream, maybe at the weekend when we've got time. A walk on the Downs on Sunday, maybe go into the secret valley, we could get as far as the lost monument if we give it enough time. The children always pull faces and say they hate walks.

You walk everywhere on the tops of walls, you can go anywhere you like, only don't fall because the walls are so high there's only clouds down there. And beneath the clouds? Ah, there's the question. A happy land of wine and roses. More clouds, more nothing. Or just falling, falling for ever.

Uncrossing her legs. Eyes closed but she won't be asleep. What makes one woman sexy and another not? Nothing to do with beauty. You can just feel it, or maybe it's a smell.

Beeble-beeble-beeble. Her phone.

'Hello? Yes. No, I can't do it, Tom. I wish, I wish. Ask Sally. I don't know.'

Here am I, inches away from her, and she's talking to someone invisible, someone far away. Her face makes expressions for her distant friend, but it's I, the close stranger, who witnesses them.

'I can't do your job for you, Tom. It's hard enough doing my own.'

Something in the fashion world? Not quite groomed enough. Could be publishing. Though Christ knows television has its share of dossers.

'Hi, Sally, it's Liz Dickinson, eight something Wednesday morning, just wanted to warn you Tom's on the scrounge. I'm out for lunch, catch you later.'

It's like being at the theatre, a one-woman play. The overheard life. *Rear Window* in audio. Maybe she's committed a murder.

'Jane? It's Liz. Look, huge apologies, I'm not going to be able to make it after all. I would, but I have to get back for Alice. She hates me leaving her with my mother.'

What makes her believe her phone calls are private? I'm listening and learning. Or at least guessing.

'No, I'm having lunch with Guy. Not a chance. No, I mean it. I keep in touch for Alice's sake, she needs a father, and he's the only one she's got, God help her.'

So she's a single mother. Someone wrote a whole book about picking up single mothers, the idea being that they're more up for it, though I don't see why. Not with me at least. Particularly as I'm married and even to think such thoughts is beyond the bounds of acceptable behaviour. What Jimmy Carter called 'adultery of the heart', which happens every day, every hour, and means nothing but is still a secret. How could I ever tell Laura? We're close, we talk, there's trust, but beyond the lamplight lies *terra incognita*, dark continents, the beauty of unholiness.

Do other husbands feel this way? If so, what a strange world we live in. Every man an almost-adulterer, constrained by decency, habit, squeamishness, lack of opportunity. No, there's more than that, there's something honourable, a refusal to inflict pain on one you love. But even so, the desire remains. The desire concealed. The secret carried in men's eyes, we recognize it in each other, but we don't speak the words.

'Because he's a two-timing bastard. Three-timing, ten-timing. He can't help himself. I don't blame him any more, that's just how some men are, it's not personal.'

Some men. But which men? Women know the worst about some men, but the man they love, the father of their children, he's the exception to the rule. He doesn't fantasize about sex with strangers on trains. Why would he need it when he has a good sex life with his wife at home?

Why indeed?

The train is passing over the Balcombe viaduct. Henry looks out through the rain-blurred windows at the green fields and woods. He likes this stretch of the journey, always watches out for it, the train raised high over the wide and peaceful scene. He has made something of a speciality of landscapes, you could say he collects views; and not views in isolation, views according to the time of day, the weather, the time of year. Thus his home view from Edenfield Hill looking towards Mount Caburn and the plain of the weald is at its most perfect on an early spring morning when there are high clouds in the sky and low sunlight spills over the land. He treasures his views precisely because they are not collectable, you catch them by chance, most days the light is too flat or the cloud cover too low. These days he rarely finds the time to go view-hunting because his hours at work are getting longer.

He pulls an orange paper file from the bag beneath his seat and settles down to prepare for his script meeting. Forty minutes or so still to go to Victoria. The rain seems to be passing.

It's very simple, Barry. What I'm asking for isn't a favour, it's a fundamental issue of justice. Also it happens to make me extremely angry.

He takes out a pencil and writes on the top of the script:

'Break something.'

4

The cars turn off the lane into Underhill School, follow each other nose to tail over the sleeping policemen down the rhododendron drive, swing left at the art classroom and past the dining hall, to pause, engines purring, between the gymnasium and the main school porch. Here Alan Strachan stands, idly calculating the accumulated value of the cars, while watching to see that no arriving children are run over. Toyota Landcruiser Amazon, W-reg, forty thousand new. Grand Voyager, X-reg, tinted windows, thirty thousand. Volvo V-70, T-reg, twenty-five. Mercedes SL300, Y-reg, forty. And these are the wives' cars, the nannies' cars, the little country runabouts. In Haywards Heath station car park even now there stand several million pounds worth of automobiles, the BMWs and Jaguars and Range Rovers that ferry their masters seven miles a day, not to mention the Sunday cars kept pristine in silent garages outside rectories and manor houses, the Aston Martin DB5, the Ferrari Testarossa, the Bentley Tourer built in 1935 when real men knew how to build real cars. Most mornings standing by the school drive you can pass the half-million mark in quarter of an hour.

'Morning sir.'

'Morning Richard. How's the cough?'

'Better sir.'

The young teacher wears brown cords, a mushroom-coloured jacket: his attempt at camouflage. On his pale and beautiful face there lingers a habitual smile, the outward form of an ironic view of the world. Alan Strachan is not embittered by the knowledge that any one of the arriving cars has cost more than his entire year's salary. He is amused. The absurdity of the world's rewards systems amuses him. The popular illusion that people get what they deserve amuses him.

Perhaps he would concede that in the long run justice is done, good work is honoured, poor work forgotten. But by then all concerned are dead.

No post yet this morning. It gets later and later. Maybe pop home in the lunch break to check. The letter should have come by now.

'Morning sir.'

'Morning Thomas.'

'Sir I'm off games today sir.'

'What's the problem?'

'Temperature sir.'

'Everyone has a temperature, Thomas. If you had no temperature you'd be dead. Or rather you'd have ceased to exist.'

'My mother says it's ninety-nine point two, sir.'

Save me from parents. Save me from the bored wives of rich men who work too hard. Save their children from them. This decent healthy kid, born into comfort and privilege, is being robbed daily of his natural resilience and vigour.

'Do you feel unwell?'

'Maybe a little sir.'

Feel unwell for Mummy, son. She'll love you more if you need her. Don't feel unwell for me.

'All right. Tell Matron.'

The boy stands back for Science, a door-wide form in the doorway.

'Morning Mrs Digby.'

'Good morning, Thomas. Alan, are you holding another of your rehearsals this afternoon?'

Note the anger in the pronoun. Not our rehearsal, or the school's rehearsal, but mine alone. Strachan's folly.

'Well, yes, Jane. Don't want the children to make fools of themselves in front of their adoring parents.'

'I'll release my class at three-fifteen as usual. Not one minute earlier. They have Common Entrance, you know.'

Cowplop of antimatter. Plughole of passion. Who cares about your arse-corker of an exam? Can't you see what happens to them on stage? They blossom. They grow strong and tall. They unfold. Feed their souls, inflame their dreams. We are the first stage of mighty rockets. We deliver the power that launches capsuled youth into the ecstasies of outer space. And then we drop unthanked away.

'The rehearsal starts at three as usual.'

Six compositions to mark. Fifteen minutes for lunch, five minutes to drive home, five minutes back, it'll take half the break, I should be handing the work back in fifth period, and there won't be a letter because the more you want something the less it comes. But it has to come soon so why not today? And if it does then I must open it and unfold the letter within and read the words typed by a secretary whose fingertips should have burned the keyboard but no doubt didn't.

Alan Strachan turns his head with an abrupt movement, only to gaze with a distant smile at the distant Downs. Prepare for all eventualities. Original writing requires original readers. *Moby Dick* a failure in Melville's lifetime. *Madame Bovary* scorned by the critics. Every creative act an act of will. The artist imposes his vision on the world. The familiar vision, the giver of comfort is embraced and welcomed, but the awkward, the indigestible, the strange in taste, causes the herd-mind to flinch from it and brush it aside, with unsent letters and unringing phones.

And yet, and yet. Byron was twenty-four when he woke up one morning and found himself famous. Scott Fitzgerald was twenty-three.

I'm late already.

Today perhaps is the day. Surely it must come. Why else the hard-won scholarship, the invisible years in a school that made me ashamed of my home but offered me no refuge? Why else this solitary exile?

Maybe the letter's already in the postman's van, toiling across Sussex, stopping at every house on the way. The verdict reached two days ago, committed to paper with warm breath, cooling in mail bags, on trains, in vans, seeping into the past, to reach me as history, an echo of a flicker in a filing cabinet in Portland Place. By opening the envelope I create a new present, a return of life, the verdict igniting like a letter bomb, exploding in my brain.

Yes I'll dash home after lunch.

'Morning sir.'

'Morning Jack.'

5

The taxi is an extravagance but Liz Dickinson is late and she's feeling nervous and maybe more to the point she's angry with herself. The piece on children's bedtimes isn't done yet. All she's got is a worked-up version of the American Psychological Association study which claims that seven to eleven year olds aren't getting enough sleep for their mental needs. She's rung all her friends to find a child who stays up late and can't concentrate in class next morning, but so far no takers. The piece will have to be re-angled. Should children be allowed to choose their own bedtime? A few more phone calls after lunch, have the copy in by five.

Not that there's anything wrong in snatching a quick hour to have lunch with Guy. He's so rarely available and they do need to keep in touch for Alice's sake, given that he's Alice's father, not that you'd know it, though he does pay her school fees which at £3,000 a term is decent, and he has her up to town for lunch once in a while.

The restaurant is in Charlotte Street, down the road from Guy's office, a typical Guy manoeuvre. She has to cross London, he strolls all of one block. But then as he willingly concedes, he is a supremely selfish man. He concedes it as if it's part of his genetic coding, like his blue eyes. If you want me, say those frank baby blue eyes, you have to take me as I am. And she does. Or did.

The taxi costs £11. At least Guy will pay for lunch. As she slams the taxi door behind her Liz says to herself, I will not fuck after lunch. She repeats it to show she means it. I will not fuck after lunch. So she showered this morning and put on pretty underclothes, that's just thinking ahead, you have to be ready for the unexpected. Guy is not the unexpected. Guy is the shit-souled bastard who broke her heart so badly she vowed never to see him again and has only seen him at roughly six-monthly intervals for the last ten years. Sometimes these meetings have ended in sex, sometimes not. This is a not.

The restaurant is called Passione. Not a promising start. She checks her watch: dead on one. Why am I always on time for Guy? I'm always late for everyone else. Guy of course is always late for everyone, including me.

'Table for two? Guy Caulder?'

She orders a glass of white Verdicchio and has drunk all of it by the time he breezes into the restaurant, ten minutes later. Same old look, meaning old beige cords, green jacket, turtleneck sweater, smoothed down hair: like a Spitfire pilot on home leave, a minor public school boy, the type protective mothers used to tag NST, Not Safe in Taxis. Preposterous in this new century. How does he get away with it?

'Liz. Got caught on the phone.'

A light kiss on the lips. Smell of cigarettes.

'Still smoking?'

'Still giving up.'

He sits and looks at her, his smiling blue eyes taking in every detail, registering approval. She likes the open sexual admiration, feels herself become desirable under his desiring gaze. Of course she dressed this morning for him.

'You look great, Liz.'

'You look exactly the same. Maybe a little fatter.'

He grins, pats his belly. You can't offend Guy, he loves himself too much.

'Too many lunches. I'm thinking of giving up lunch.'

'You're incapable of giving anything up.'

'True, princess, true. But when two pleasures compete, I surrender the lesser one.'

Liz refrains from asking what this means. She's thinking how casually, how proprietorially, he calls her 'princess', which is a private term of endearment from long ago, and how much she wants to hear it again. And this despite the fact that Guy is all take and no give, that he destroys her hard-won equilibrium, that she always cries after seeing him again. I must have no self-respect, she thinks.

'So are you going to ask after your daughter?'

'Of course. How is Alice?'

'I'm worried about her. She's so unmotivated. She doesn't seem to be interested in any of her subjects at school.'

'She fucking better be. I'm paying ten grand a year for her to be at that fucking school.'

'Please, Guy.'

She always did hate his swearing. She likes language, more than likes, she reveres language, and flinches from the sheer numbing laziness of expletives. Which Guy knows.

'Oh, right,' he says. 'The thing is,' he says, 'I like fucking.'

'Yes. We all know that.'

'I like fucking you.'

'Guy. Stop it. We're in public.'

'I'm not speaking loudly. Only you can hear me. I'm simply stating a fact. You're the best fuck I've ever had. Why wouldn't I like it?'

'Look at the menu. If we don't order soon I'll be late back, and I have a deadline.'

Liz fixes her attention on the menu and scans the list of Antipasti but her brain fails to register a single word. She's feeling the heat between her thighs and repeating her protective mantra and hating Guy for talking about sex. I will not fuck after lunch. I will not fuck after—

'So let's not have lunch.'

'What?'

'We can eat when we're alone. We can only fuck when we're together.'

'Guy, what are you talking about?'

'I have the key to a friend's flat. Round the corner.'

'No. Absolutely no. I came here to talk about Alice. Have a civilized lunch. If it wasn't for Alice I would never want to see you again.'

'Okay.' You can't offend Guy. 'The mushroom risotto is good.' Actually his total insensitivity is rather restful.

'I'm not hungry enough for risotto.'

Mistake.

'You're not hungry?'

'Just not hungry enough for risotto.'

'So why don't we go to my friend's flat?'

'Because I don't want to.'

'I don't believe you.'

'How can you say that? You're not interested in me in any way at all apart from sexually, you never ask about Alice till I remind you. You're not a good person, Guy.'

'I'm not following this. You don't want to have sex with me because I'm only interested in you sexually?'

'Yes.'

'What else should I be interested in? Your mind? Your personality?'

'That would make a change.'

'So how about we give half an hour to talking about your personality, and half an hour for a fuck?'

'No.'

'You're a hypocrite, Liz.'

'Oh, it's my fault, is it?'

'You know that if I kept quiet about the sex, and talked all about you, and only got to the sex bit later, you'd be just fine about it. My problem is I'm honest.'

'Your problem is you've never worked out that people don't like being used.'

'Who's using who? I love sex. You love sex. Don't deny it. I know how you fuck. Why do you think I love sex with you so much? Because you're the only woman I know who loves her body and loves the pleasure your body gives you. You're a natural. Christ, just thinking about it makes me hard.'

'That's enough.'

'So I want to use you. Don't you want to use me?'

'No.'

'I don't believe you. Give me your hand.'

'I will do no such thing.'

'Put your hand here and look me in the eyes and tell me you don't want to fuck.'

'No.'

'I dare you.'

He's like a child. She holds out her hand and he puts it in his lap under the table, and she looks into his eyes. He is very hard.

'I do not want to fuck.'

'Liar.'

'Why am I getting all this pressure? You must have some girlfriend you can call.'

'None of them fuck like you.'

Liz begins to feel helpless. The sheer shamelessness of his demands disarms her. That, and the feel of the hard ridge in his lap. Maybe it's all as simple as he pretends.

'How do you know I don't have a boyfriend?'

'Do you?'

'No.'

'So what's the problem? You know you like it.'

This is true. Secretly, humiliatingly true. She's never admitted it to him, and never will, but only with this untrustworthy shit has she ever achieved an orgasm. Her body remembers sex with Guy far too well. She is shivering with longing.

'I hate you, Guy Caulder. I want you out of my life.'

He interprets this correctly.

'I'll leave a big tip.'

The friend's flat is indeed round the corner, above a wine shop in Percy Street. Guy finds the key and fumbles at the lock, while Liz shuts down all mental operations, not wanting to hear the waiting accusatory voice. Instead, she anticipates the look and feel of his body.

The street door open, he goes directly up the narrow stairs without a word, and she follows. The flat is on the second floor. The master bedroom is small, with a big bed and a wardrobe mirror to one side. She stands looking round wondering who lives here, some man, no sign of a woman's things, the duvet cover blue-and-white stripe, cotton-linen mix, very Conran Shop. Then he's pushing her back onto the bed, kneeling over her, still fully dressed, sliding one hand between her legs.

Why so easy with Guy and so difficult with all other men?

Later. The sound of water in the bathroom basin. Guy humming some half-familiar tune. The rush of the cistern. The clunk of a door.

Guy looking down at her, blue eyes smiling, pulling on his pants.

'You love it, don't you?'

'Doesn't everyone?'

'No. Not like you.'

Only with you. Not with the gentle men, the considerate men, the men who ask what I want and listen when I answer. Only with a man who uses my body for his pleasure and breaks my heart.

'Look, I don't want to hurry you.'

'It's okay. I have to get back too.'

She goes to the bathroom, finds a bidet, flinches at the cold ceramic against her hot skin. Pulls on discarded clothing. A quick check in the mirror tells her she looks like a woman who's just been fucked.

'We should do lunch more often,' he says.

'We didn't do lunch.'

'I'm really going to have to run.'

'Let me get my shoes on for Christ's sake.'

Out into the street, where he leaves her. She checks her watch. They've spent barely half an hour together, not enough for lunch. Sex was all he had scheduled, was all he wanted. Knowing Guy he probably had a sandwich earlier.

She walks down Charlotte Street to the corner of Goodge Street and stands waiting for a taxi. There's a sharp wind, it makes her eyes sting. She does not cry.

6

The rain has passed by the time Laura sets off for work. She drives the old Volvo down green lanes, the trees cut close on either side to the height of the highest truck. Overhead the branches are vaulted like the aisles of a cathedral. Through lime-green tunnels to the Newhaven road, through the straggling village of Edenfield, past the church and the shop and the pub, her handbag on the seat beside her, the letter in the handbag. She has made a resolution. She will not reply until she has talked to Henry.

So now as she follows her familiar route to Edenfield Place her mind is busy not thinking about the letter. Instead she thinks about her nine-year-old daughter Carrie, who has got herself into a tangle over her friendships. Carrie's best friend Naomi won't talk to her because Carrie was paired on an art project with Tessa and Carrie and Tessa went on with their art project in break. Now Naomi won't even look at her when Carrie tries to make up and won't answer when she speaks to her and Carrie is frantic with misery. Not that she shows it or talks about it. Only her eyes red from secret crying and her little face white from lack of sleep admit that her soul is desolated. Last night after she was supposed to be tucked up it all came hiccupping out, the dreadful tale of unjust punishment and love denied.

'I'm not Tessa's friend, Tessa's friend, it's only for the project, I had to do it, do it, why does she hate me? I ask her why, her why, she won't talk to me, I try to be nice, but she won't talk, won't talk.'

Is this bullying? Should Laura alert her daughter's class teacher? How do you order one little girl to be friends with another little girl? Laura held Carrie in her arms and told her it wasn't her fault and people just do get jealous sometimes and at least it means Naomi wants to be her friend because it's only when you really love someone that you hurt them this way.

'I know that,' said Carrie, nine years old but wise to the ways of the world. 'I just wish she'd talk to me.'

Laura turns into the park gates and down the long drive to the immense and ugly house. Until recently Edenfield Place was considered absurd, its sprawling mass of turrets and towers assembled with a deliberate asymmetry, a Victorian fantasy of the middle ages created for a pharmacist grown rich on patent medicines. But a century has gone by, the false past has become the real past, and now the Gothic Revival style is admired and preserved. Edenfield Place's listing has been promoted to Grade I. Its third-generation owner, William Holland, Lord Edenfield, finds himself obliged to maintain the acres of carved stone and woodwork, the tiles and the marble inlay, the stained glass, the mosaics, and the Victorian ironwork. The original source of the Holland fortune, no longer generously laced with opiates, no longer enriches its patent holder; and the present Lord Edenfield, known to all as Billy, finds that as the prestige of his estate rises, his ability to support it falls.

Laura Broad, formerly of Bernard Quaritch Antiquarian Books, is one small part of the survival strategy. The library at Edenfield Place houses a famous collection of travel books and maps, established by the family patriarch and enlarged by his son George. No one knows the value of the collection, but it is supposed that its hundreds of shelves bear a treasure that can be exchanged for hard cash. Laura's task is to catalogue and to estimate.

So far she has unearthed one golden nugget: a rare first edition of the *Peregrinaçam* by Mendes Pinto, one of the first Europeans to travel in Japan. She carried it excitedly to Billy Holland, who said, 'How much?' She guessed £30,000. 'Not enough,' he replied. She has raised his expectations too high with her stories of First Folios selling for millions.

She parks by the west wing and goes in by the servants' entrance. Pat Kelly the housekeeper sees her pass by down the passage.

'Cup of tea?'

'Please, Pat. You're an angel.'

Laura works the bank of switches that turn on the library lights, and bay after bay emerges from the gloom. The long hall has only one window, at the far end, but it is enormous: wide and arched and crowded with stone tracery. Above it the intricate scrollwork of the carved wood walls rises to a hammerbeam roof. The floor is a riot of inlaid marble, a flowering meadow that is cold under foot.

She settles down in her work corner, opens the hard-bound lined notebook in which she is listing the results of her search. The first rapid trawl is done: ahead the slow labour, volume by volume, shelf by shelf. She is doing the job for a finder's fee of four per cent. On total sales of, say, a quarter million this would net her £10,000. Surely in a library of this size she can rack up at least that. You need luck, of course. A page annotated by Daniel Defoe. A previously unidentified account of a voyage that turns out to be by a crew member on the *Beagle*. The first Lord Edenfield bought on impulse, in batches, some of which have never been broken up. There is no catalogue, only files of letters from booksellers and intermediaries.

These letters are her initial source of information. Here she tracks dates, titles, prices paid. One by one she is excavating the forty-four big box files, converting the unstable stacks of papers into methodical lists. She has reached File 17.

Pat Kelly comes with tea and biscuits. Pat likes Laura's company, the house can be lonely. She brings chocolate bourbons.

'Pat, you shouldn't. I like them too much.'

'And why not? What harm is there in a little of what you like?'

Pat is Irish, beautiful in a comfortable cushiony way, unassailably good-tempered. Her sympathy is easily roused, most frequently by the stories she reads in the newspaper, where she locates on an almost daily basis tales of the abuse or murder of children. 'The little angel, she'll be in heaven now, her sufferings are over. But what was he thinking when he did it? Does he not have a mother that loves him?'

She also brings Laura reports on her employer, whose solitary life touches her heart.

'The poor man, what does he do all day but watch television? He needs company. Yesterday I heard noises in the chapel. It was him, talking to his mother.'

Billy Holland's mother has been dead for years. A shrine in the chapel created to her memory by her husband George has an inscription that reads: 'You loved so well the Lord took you for his own.'

'Do you mean he was saying prayers?'

'Prayers? Don't I know prayers? He was talking to her, the soft onion.'

Pat proffers the idiosyncratic term with tenderness.

'Well, Mummy, he says. You know I've never been the clever one, he says. I don't know that I can hold it together much longer, he says, with Celia gone.'

'You listened, Pat!'

'So I did. With Celia gone, he says.' Pat's round eyes widen with scorn. 'It's ten years at least since that lady was kind enough to cease tormenting the poor man.'

Laura knows there's concern over money, but not that it has reached crisis point. Celia, the departed Lady Edenfield, was reputed to be a tight manager.

'Do you think he'll sell up, Pat?'

'Not him. Didn't he make a promise to his father? I never knew a man respect his father the way that man does. He says to me one day, Forty years, Pat. My father lived for forty years after my mother died, and never looked at another woman. That's love, Pat, he says.'

'Is it true?'

'It's true enough, there's no denying. As true as it's daft.'

'You don't say that to Billy.'

'Would I say such a thing? But it's a terrible thing to see a good man go to waste.'

By now the tea is drunk and the three chocolate Bourbons eaten, two by Laura. Pat takes up the tray.

'You're the only one comes in here now,' she says.

Laura returns to her file. There, half an hour or so after Pat Kelly has told her George Holland never looked at another woman for forty years, she finds the love letters. They are tied together with string, and there's a covering note dated October 10th 1955.

Doll has returned my letters. I will never see her again. I will not burn what remains of the greatest happiness I have ever known.

She unties the string. The first folded sheet carries a single line written in erratic pencil.

Waiting in lake house 6oc. Doll.

Then another folded sheet, an impulsive line in fluent ink.

Swear to be there if only for a quarter hour. I miss you every minute.
G.

Laura reads no more. These letters have no commercial value. She refolds the papers, re-ties the string.

She walks through empty halls to the chapel. The heavy door swings open without a sound. Inside is a space as big as a city church, illuminated by the melancholy colours of Victorian stained glass. The memorial to the second Lady Edenfield is halfway down the north wall, a marble effusion of urn and drapery presided over by a life-size angel. Laura tracks the carved inscription below for a date of death.

October 2nd 1955.

Eight days later her husband brought his liaison to an end. His forty years of devoted celibacy, it seems, formed the long coda not only to his marriage but to his adultery. Other people's lives always so much more complicated than they seem.

My own life so much more complicated than it seems.

She sits in a mahogany pew and stares unseeingly at the altar furnishings. Only words on paper: but words, paper, these are the constituents of high explosive. Libraries not dry as supposed, not dusty, but coursing with blood, hissing with passion. She has learned in the course of her work to love libraries, to find in long-untouched books the shivery excitement of waking the dead. Now she learns they can destroy the living.

Shall we meet and compare notes on the vagaries of life's journey?

Billy Holland is in the little room he calls his office, though it also contains a single high bed that has an air of being slept in. He is seated at his desk, reading glasses low on his nose, hands clasping greying temples. As Laura enters his big blank eyes rise up to meet hers, and he blinks as if emerging from sleep.

'Oh, Laura. Hello.'

'Sorry to bother you, Billy. I found something I thought you should see.'

'How much is it worth?'

'Nothing of any value, I'm afraid. Even so.'

She holds out the string-tied bundle.

'I'm relying on you, Laura. Rumple— Rumple—'

He waves one hand in the air to grasp the elusive word.

'Rumpelstiltskin?'

'That's the fellow. Weave straw into gold.'

He reads the covering note. Bewilderment spreads slowly over his mottled face.

'What is this? I don't understand.'

'I found them in one of the letter files. I've not looked at them, beyond a first glance.'

He nods, and begins to untie the string. His fingers fumble helplessly. She leans over the desk, and with quick precise movements releases the knots. Easy to do for other people.

She leaves him reading the letters in silence.

7

There was a note waiting for her in her pigeon-hole in the porter's lodge. The handwriting was unfamiliar and there was no name at the end.

4pm. Came to see you but you're not here. If you come to see me I'll be there.

She knew at once the note was from Nick Crocker, without entirely knowing how she knew. She showed it to Katie, who was indignant.

'Why can't he put his name? It's ridiculous.'

Laura wanted to say that it wasn't ridiculous at all, that it was both a test and a declaration. He was saying to her: if you know who I am then I'm right about you. If I'm right about you, we'll meet again. And it was more than that, it was a promise. *I'll be there.*

'He doesn't know when you'll call on him. He doesn't know he'll be there. What's he going to do? Stay in his room for days in case you drop by?'

'No,' said Laura. 'I don't think so.'

He's waiting for me now. He wants me to come. She had that melting feeling she got in her stomach when she was very excited or very afraid.

'So what will you do?'

'I expect I'll look him up. Some time.'

From this moment on she thought about Nick Crocker without ceasing. This certainly was ridiculous. She didn't know him at all. They had talked at Richard's party, but not for long, and she had hardly been able to hear him over the chatter and the music. How was it that on such a slender basis she imagined her life was about to change?

Her first thought was that she would call on him in a day or two. It wouldn't do to seem too keen. On the other hand she had no wish to appear indifferent. Maybe tomorrow evening? Soon, however, she realized she was incapable of waiting until tomorrow. Either this is all about nothing, she reasoned to herself, in which case the sooner I get it out of my system the better. Or it's the real thing at last; in which case, why wait?

She chose mid-evening for her call. Earlier and he might be out at supper; later was too suggestive. His room was at the top of a poorly-lit staircase. The outer door was open.

How to knock? Laura wished to present herself as casual, informal, friendly, confident. Her knock must not be too insistent, nor yet too timid. Her hand hovered, raised before the door panel, and she felt her whole body shaking.

This is stupid.

She took a slow deep breath, and knocked twice.

'Yes?'

The room was in darkness but for a pool of light thrown onto a long desk by an Anglepoise lamp. Nick was sitting at the desk under the window by the far wall, not rising from his studies, turning to look over his shoulder at the door. His face rim-lit by the lamplight.

'Oh. It's you.'

For a fraction of a second she saw that he was surprised: he had not expected her to come. At once she was overwhelmed by the conviction that she should not have come. But now he was up out of his work chair, turning on more lights, acting the gracious host.

'That's wonderful. You found me. Come on in.'

'You look as if you're hard at work.'

'No, it's fine. Glad of the break. What can I get you? Glass of wine?'

'If you have some.'

'I don't have much of anything, but I always have wine.'

He went into the little pantry and she heard the noise of water running into a basin. Cleaning the wine glasses, presumably. She looked round the long room. It wasn't at all like other student rooms. No posters, no discarded beer cans. The pictures on the walls were framed and looked real; engravings, mostly. She recognized one of them from the postcard he had used as a bookmark on the train. It was a monochrome version of the same scene.

At the far end of the room a half-open door led into a small bedroom. A glimpse of crumpled duvet. Nick was in his third year, and enjoyed the luxury of a set of rooms.

She felt her stomach shivering.

Nick rejoined her, holding out a heavy French café glass well-filled with red wine. He smiled as he gave her the glass. She found she couldn't hold his look and turned away, moved over to the deep old sofa, fooled about finding somewhere to stand her glass. She didn't want to do the talking, didn't know what to say, felt the need of clues as to what he expected of her.

'What day is it today?' he said.

'Thursday, I think.'

'Then here's to Thursday.' He raised his glass. 'Happy Thursday.'

She smiled and raised her glass. They both drank.

'I wonder why we haven't met before,' he said. Then, 'No, I don't. I'm such a hermit.'

'Are you a hermit?'

'What with finals looming, and my dissertation to finish.'

A nod towards the papers and books laid out on the desk.

'What's it on?' said Laura.

'Oh, no. Don't ask.'

'Why not?'

He settled down on the only other upholstered chair and stretched out his legs and smiled at her over the top of his wine glass. For a moment he didn't answer. Then in slow deliberate tones he explained himself.

'The fact is, I really do care about the work I'm doing. Quite a lot, actually. But I don't see why anyone else should care. So rather than bore people or embarrass them I've learned not to talk about it.'

Laura felt a small but distinct shock. It was strange to her that these precious first moments could have any other content than their perceptions of each other. Close on the shock came shame. She had assumed that any conversation that took place between them was a cover for another sort of dialogue. Do you like me? Do I like you?

Might you love me? Might I love you? And here he was wanting to talk about his dissertation.

'I'd like to know. Really.'

Anything to avoid having to talk herself. When she was nervous she chattered like a fool. And right now she was extremely nervous. He was so calm and still, his few movements so deliberate, and all she wanted to do was wriggle and scratch. It was like being a child in church.

'I'm writing about landscape art. I'm writing about Arcadia.'

He paused to see how she took this. She nodded as if she understood, which she didn't.

'About Arcadia in art, and Arcadia as a concept. People think of Arcadia as part of the classical furniture, as if it's a myth that we've long outgrown. I don't think so. I think it's as powerful as it's ever been. Partly because it's pre-Christian. It's the anti-Garden of Eden. There's no serpent in Arcadia, there's no forbidden fruit, no original sin. It's the pastoral idyll, the world before towns and cities and, oh, you know, the dark satanic mills and so forth. For centuries artists painted imaginary scenes of Arcadia, using bits and pieces of real countryside, a shady grove of trees, a murmuring spring, a group of contented peasants watching over sheep. Then they started painting real countryside, but it was still really Arcadia. All those Constables everyone loves so much, they're real places, but they're not the only reality of rural England in the early nineteenth century. There was poverty, and disease, and premature death. He could have horrified us. But who wants to be horrified? So he painted England as Arcadia.'

He stopped, afraid that he had talked too much.

'More wine.'

Her glass was empty. She had no recollection of having drunk it. He refilled both their glasses.

'You did ask.'

Apologizing for the lecture.

'No. I'm really interested.'

She was, too. Not in Arcadia, but in his passionate engagement with his subject. All the time listening to him she had been tracking her response, amazed that he could talk to her like this, now, when all that was vivid and immediate to her was his response to her and hers to him. Did he not feel this too? And if not, was it arrogance?

Indifference? Surely she hadn't misread the signals so totally. The unsigned note left in her pigeon-hole most of all. But perhaps he had lost interest in her as soon as he had been sure of her response. There were men like that. Or close up she had proved to be a disappointment.

Laura's fear was that she was pretty but not sexy.

She drank her wine too fast.

'So you see,' he said, 'I'm lost in Arcadia these days, which makes me very poor company. When you spend all day contemplating the earthly paradise you do get a bit spacey.'

He took a cigarette out of a shiny blue packet.

'Smoke?'

She accepted, glad to have something to do with her hands. He struck a match for her. They leant towards each other for him to light her cigarette, the shared action so intimate, so sensual. His flame, her breath.

The harsh smoke hurt her throat. She was unused to French cigarettes. She inhaled and felt light-headed.

'I should stay in your earthly paradise if I were you,' she said. 'I'm surprised you ever come out. It sounds perfect.'

'Almost perfect. But not quite.'

'What's the snag?'

'It's a very famous snag.'

He got up and took one of the framed pictures off the wall. It was the engraving of the group of classical figures round a tomb.

'Et in Arcadia ego.' He handed her the picture. 'It's an engraving of a well-known Poussin painting. You see, the words are carved on the tomb. *Et in Arcadia ego*. "Even in Arcadia am I." The "I", the "ego", is death. Death is the snag.'

Laura gazed at the picture. The tomb was immense, it dominated the scene.

'This is the picture you have as your bookmark.'

He was silent, surprised. Laura realized he was unaware that she had studied him on the train, which could only mean he did not study her. She had blundered. Now he knew she was more interested in him than he was in her.

She lowered her head as if to study the picture in more detail, but really to hide her sudden blush.

'Oh, yes,' he said. 'The train. You're very observant.'

'That's me. Snoopy.'

She looked up and met his eyes through the curls of cigarette smoke. She spoke about the picture to remove attention from herself.

'There seems to be a lot more death than paradise.'

'Yes. All we get is some token trees. It's one of those paintings that presumes knowledge of the whole tradition that comes before it.'

'Is that why it's special for you?'

'Is it special for me?'

'Well, you have it as your bookmark.'

'Yes, I suppose you're right.' He frowned. It seemed not to have struck him before. 'I wonder why. I suppose I must have a morbid streak in me. That doesn't sound like much fun, does it? Unless you take the view that meditation on death makes one all the more inclined to live life to the full. *Carpe diem* and so forth.'

Laura was drunk on red wine and dizzy on French cigarettes. Everything Nick said impressed her. He was so utterly unlike any boy she'd known before. Not a boy, a grown-up. She herself still a girl. She felt her inferiority, but she didn't mind it. She wanted to sit at his feet. She wanted to learn from him.

'Seize the day,' she murmured.

'And the night.'

That was when she knew he desired her. At once a new confidence flowed through her and she was able to meet his smiling gaze. He was older, wiser, more sophisticated in every way, but now she had something he wanted, something she could give him in return. Her gift had very little merit in her eyes, but if he wanted it, there was a deal to be done. He would give her his maturity and his prestige. She would give him herself.

'I've drunk too much. I should go.'

There followed a long silence, in which their eyes remained locked. The silence told as much as the single word that ended it, but it was the word she remembered ever after.

'Stay,' he said.

She stayed. He was in control. She surrendered. Before he had even touched her the surrender was total, and in the act of surrender itself she found an intoxicating freedom. That and the wine.

Ask anything of me. Do what you want. I want to please you more than I want to live. Through you I live. My only beloved lover.

All this without words and before the first true touch. Her whole body shivered with an anxiety that was both delicious and painful.

Will I be good enough for him?

He kissed her. She put her arms round him as she had been longing to do since she had watched him in the train window. She held him and felt his arms hold her, tasted his lips smoky on her lips, and slowly the shivering of her body fell still.

Taking off her clothes in the little bedroom she caught her jeans on her feet and stumbled. The bed was so narrow they had to hold each other close. Light from the main room fell through the open door, but there was no light here. Her naked body a secret except to his touch. No words. She spoke to him with her hands, her mouth, her body, saying: I am yours for ever.

She gave herself to him without reserve, asking nothing in return but his undying love.

This is my room now. This is my bed. This is my lover. Let my real life begin.

Heart of my heart, my meaning and completion.

Laura lay in Nick's arms all that long night, and did not sleep.

8

Barry Eagles joins the production meeting late, clutching a Starbucks cappuccino and a pack of Krispy Kreme donuts, smiling his apologies.

'Caught on the bloody phone as usual. Sorry, people. Look, phone off.'

He sets down his coffee and turns off his phone, a symbolic gesture of commitment that he believes fully compensates for his late arrival.

'Love the final script.'

'Not quite final,' says Henry. 'We're still waiting for Aidan's notes.'

'Oh, Aidan won't give you any grief. He's a real pro.'

Henry frowns. Christina meets his eyes with a quick look of sympathy. Sweet Christina, twenty-three years old and looks sixteen. The quiet clever one who keeps her head down, the hunched stoop of the young not yet proud of their bodies.

'So where is Aidan?' says Barry. 'Isn't he supposed to be here?'

'He's on his way,' says Jo, the production manager. 'He's coming straight from Heathrow.'

'The thing is,' says Henry.

'And your first shooting day is Friday?'

Jo nods confirmation. 'Westminster Abbey.'

'Okay, I'm going to jump right in. We're at least one day over budget, maybe two. I know it's late to be telling you this, but we have to find cuts.'

'Two days!' Henry is shocked. 'I can't do it.'

'Then give me one. Cut the Keats intro, for a start.'

'Cut the Keats intro!'

Henry's best visual idea. The presenter holds up a replica Grecian urn and intones Keats's famous lines: 'Beauty is truth and truth

beauty, that is all you know on earth and all you need to know.' Then
he drops the urn. It smashes in slo-mo close-up. Massey confides to
camera: 'Sheer nonsense, isn't it? Truth is sometimes ugly. Beauty is
often false.'

'I thought you loved it.'

'I do.' Barry Eagles read English at Brasenose. 'It's a gorgeous
shocker. But who reads Keats any more?'

'Jesus, Barry. We're not making the Teletubbies.'

'I need cuts. That's all I'm saying. Get Aidan to come up with a
really contemporary intro, something that doesn't need any special
effects.'

'Aidan's a busy man.'

There's a clue and a half, but Barry misses it. Or chooses not to
hear. Henry likes Barry, and God knows he's saved his bacon with
this gig, eight months on the outside and people think you've retired.
Barry's the master at winning commissions from channel controllers.
Not easy selling a historical documentary on Puritan iconoclasm.
And his trump card in the successful pitch was of course Aidan
Massey and his nationally famous hair.

'Christina.' Barry turns to the researcher. 'Put together some
material for Aidan. Possible leads for an intro.'

'Okay,' says Christina. 'Best if I pass it by Henry first. It's his
script.'

God bless the girl.

'Whatever,' says Barry. Like this is some kind of team logistics.

'I was thinking,' Christina persists. 'Henry could write this up as
a piece for *History Today*. His ideas are really original.'

'Let's get the show out first.'

Oh, beloved Christina. How I would love to write an article, a
book even. But who would publish me? Too late now, my colours
nailed to the television mast, I sail on over the ocean of development.
The voyages grow longer, the sightings of land rarer, and all of it
discovered, inhabited, ruled.

Television, the great image factory. Images the tool of the devil.
Calvin called the human mind 'a perpetual forge of idols'. *Finitum
non est capax infiniti*. Our little minds can't imagine the mystery that
is God, and so we create lesser gods to worship. 'Houses of pictures,'
Henry Clark called churches, and that was not a term of approval.

Pictures induce spiritual fornication.

Henry has his eyes closed in the heart of the meeting.

What am I doing here?

The door springs open and in bounces a small man with a big head, supposedly off an overnight plane. He's pulsating with nervous energy.

'Late, late!' cries the star of the show. 'Mea culpa! BA culpa! On the ground twenty minutes late, no jetway, seven miles of glazed corridors. Coffee! Feed me coffee! Henry, my man! Greetings! The countdown has begun. We're going to have fun.'

'Glad you made it, Aidan,' says Barry, ushering him to one of the black leather and chrome steel chairs. 'Our last gathering before you go over the top.'

Henry watches Aidan Massey gulping black coffee, jerking his upper body back and forth as he pours out the stream of unrelated observations that passes for brilliance. His shock of auburn hair flops over his outsize brow, the hair the authenticator of genius in this image-infantile culture.

Entirely independently of all that is passing in the room, Henry has an idea for the new intro. He makes a note.

Barry is telling Aidan there'll have to be some minor cuts. Aidan takes this in his stride.

'I'll be winging it anyway,' he declares. 'What you have on paper there is no more than a sketch.'

'A fucking good sketch, Aidan. It's going to be knock-out.'

'I'm in Henry's hands.' Oh, you sly shitbag. 'I'm the clay on the spinning wheel. Henry will mould me. Won't you, Henry?'

'Do my best, Aidan.'

Barry throws a copy of the *Spectator* across the table.

'Did you see this? Television's sexiest intellectuals. You're number three.'

Of course he's seen it. The page is already framed and hanging in his downstairs lavatory. But he reads it like it's an amusing surprise.

'Michael Ignatieff at number one. Melvyn Bragg at number two. Who votes on this? *Spectator* readers? Of what sexual orientation? Stock up on Vaseline, Henry. For your lenses, of course.'

And shoot you in close-up so the *Spectator* readers never see that your legs are too short for your body. The trademark Aidan Massey in-your-face presenting style, widely praised for 'immediacy' and 'attack', in fact devised to frame out the star's dwarfish build.

'Maybe you should give me your notes, Aidan. So we can run out a final version of the script.'

'The final version is what comes out of my mouth as the camera rolls, Henry. I know that must drive you crazy. It's not how the book says. But it's what I do, and it has the minor merit of not sounding rehearsed. My kind of television isn't a lecture. It's a conversation with the viewer. I want him, or preferably her, to follow what I'm saying. To get drawn in, to be hungry for more. So I plead guilty.' He taps the *Spectator* on the table. 'I'm a seducer.'

'Images are the tool of the devil,' says Barry, quoting from the script.

Aidan Massey's eyes cloud over. He's momentarily unsure which term is the source of the humour.

'One of your lines,' prompts Barry. 'I love the irony. Today's devil imagery has to be television.'

Henry meets Christina's eyes. They both know Aidan hasn't read the script. He has no idea where the line comes from. Fuck it, enough. Tell it like it is.

'Are you okay with what I've written for you, Aidan? After all, you've had no real input since our first meeting.'

Aidan Massey turns his big handsome head towards Henry and gazes at him in silence: a silence made all the more potent by its contrast with his usual volubility.

'Ever heard of the alien blow-job theory?' he says at last.

'Can't say I have, Aidan.'

'It goes like this. In every survey of sexual habits, around seventy per cent of adults say they've been on the receiving end of oral sex. But only forty per cent say they've given oral sex. That leaves thirty per cent of the adult population getting blow-jobs that no one's giving. Hence the postulation that every night teams of aliens descend on the nation's bedrooms.'

Barry Eagles laughs. Christina smiles. Henry does neither.

'Not following you, Aidan.'

'Things are never the way they seem.'

'About the script—'

'Don't worry about the script, Henry. I'll make it work.'

Later Henry finds himself in the men's room occupying a niche next to Barry Eagles.

'Aidan happy?' says Barry, who left the meeting when the detailed work began.

'Yes, he's happy.'

'That's good.'

'You do realize Aidan hasn't written a word of the script?'

'But he's okay with it, isn't he?'

'Yes, he's okay with it. But it's my script.'

Barry expels a sigh.

'Look, Henry.' He struggles with the buttons of his fly. 'Aidan's a professor of history, not an actor. He brings the project authority.'

'Fake authority.'

'You want to tell the viewers that?'

'No,' says Henry.

'Life's not perfect.'

'What pisses me off is I'm actually proud of what I've done. It's my research, my thesis. It just might be brilliant.'

'But if we don't have Aidan, we don't have a series. Channel Four isn't going to buy you as the presenter.'

'I know.'

'You could try asking Aidan to go with a co-writing credit.'

'Oh, sure. He'd love that.'

He returns to the planning meeting, where they're revising the script to make the necessary cuts. Aidan looks up from the pages with a triumphant smile.

'I can't believe what I'm reading here, Henry. You've caught my phrases, my thought processes, my fucking soul. Fuck you, man! It's like you're inside my head!'

'So you don't have many changes?'

'Why would I want changes? You've channelled me. Listen.'

He reads out a paragraph of script as if performing to camera, striding up and down the room. When he's done the others clap and he leans over Henry, seated at the table, and embraces him.

'Soul brother!' he says.

What's the use? The dead weight of his own anger exhausts him. I'm walking on walls and below only clouds.

9

The noise they make, thinks Alan Strachan. How is it possible that eighty children can make so much noise and still eat their lunch? The throat is not designed for shouting and eating at the same time. They must be shouting between mouthfuls.

'Sir, can I leave the rest, sir?'

'No. You've hardly touched it.'

'But sir, it's horrible. It makes me want to be sick.'

'You don't know till you try.'

'Do you want me to be sick, sir?'

'Well, it would vary the monotony.'

'All right then. Here goes.'

Not a bad kid, Victoria. She'll do anything to get attention. Never sees her parents, of course. They're too busy in their high-powered jobs earning the money to give their children all they could possibly desire except the one thing they want.

'No cheating now. No fingers down the throat.'

A crowd forming. Reassert control.

'Back to your tables, everyone.'

'Is Victoria really going to be sick, sir?'

'Sir sir. Hold up your hand like this sir. Then when I shoot let it flop down like it's dead.'

'What is this, Jamie?'

'Just a joke sir.'

'All right. There you are.'

'Poof!'

Down goes the hand. Howls of laughter.

'You're a poof sir. Just a joke sir.'

Erch-erch-chukka-erch. Oh God she's going to do it.

'If you're sick, Victoria, you clear it up yourself.'

'Sir!' Face red with straining, eyes wide with the injustice of it. 'That's changing the rules!'

'Not at all. Retch and chuck it, fetch the bucket.'

'You just made that up.'

'True.' Look at the time. 'I have to go. Aimee, can I leave them to you? I'm behind on my marking.'

'Yes, yes. Off you go.'

'Bless you.'

Nor is it a lie. Staff room or classroom? Jimmy'll be in the staff room and he'll go on clearing his throat until I talk to him and all he has to talk about these days is the *Sussex County Chronicle*, for God's sake you'd think he was filing copy for the *New York Times*. Ten minutes in the classroom then zip home.

Funny old room. The French windows rattle in the slightest breeze and the desks are never straight. Not that I care. At least there's a view over the playing fields to the Downs. So, Alice Dickinson. My Journey.

> My mother takes me in the car to the station were I catch the train to London were my father lives. he is always bisy so when I go to visit him its only for an hour really and all the rest of the time is my journey. my journey is not very interesting not like when mum comes on the train with me so I dont know what else to write. coming back on the train is just like going out on the train except all the stations happen backwards and sometimes its dark. if my mother is still at work my granma meets me and so my journey is over.

Dear God why don't I shoot myself now? How can I go on living in this vale of unshed tears? No parent would ever send their child to school if they knew what they reveal daily, hourly, about their monotonous egotistical cruelties. Pretend not to notice. Correct the spelling, urge the use of capital letters, instil some sense of punctuation. And all the time before our eyes the hearts harden and the wonder dies.

And what of them, my own composition markers, my anonymous readers, my judges? How can I tell them that for me writing is more than fancy, even more than vocation? My mission is to rekindle the dying fire, to fan it to blazing heat. Just give me half a chance. Give me a leg up. Let me get one foot on the lowest rung of the ladder and you'll see me climb. Twenty-nine years old and I swore I would be on my way by thirty, three months to go, why else the solitude, why else the low pay and even lower esteem? For how can I not see it in their eyes, the surprise and the pity, he seems such a capable young man, what's he doing teaching in a Sussex prep school, you'd think he'd have more ambition than that. Oh yes I have ambition. More even than your little dreams of swimming pools and personalized number plates. Long after I've forgotten you and your children, you'll be telling fibs in pubs about how you knew me once.

Alan Strachan looks up at the clock on the classroom wall. Forty minutes before the next period, every minute of that time needed for marking. Why didn't I do it yesterday evening as I planned? Because I was tired. Always tired in the evening. Not so much tired as out of hope. The reservoir of hope starts full each morning and trickles away in the course of the day. Evenings are dark times. Thank God for television, the light that cheers but does not inebriate.

Go now.

He puts the compositions back in the folder unmarked and leaves at a brisk walk. His car, a fifteen-year-old VW Beetle convertible, starts first time, by no means a courtesy he can presume upon, and he takes this as a good omen. Out onto the lethal main road with its long straight where drivers accelerate and overtake and die. Off again at the defunct petrol station and down the lane into the village of Glynde where he lives. Mrs Temple-Morris coming out of her front door as he emerges from his car.

'You're home early, Alan.'

'Just to check the post.'

'Oh, the post. It's all bills these days. I leave all that to David.' She raises heavily-pencilled eyebrows, delivers a secret smile. 'Not that he ever makes himself useful.'

She sashays off to drive into Lewes to buy the evening meal for the husband who comes home late and leaves early and plays golf all weekend. Fifty if she's a day and still flirting like a teenager.

He pushes open the door to the small terraced house, feels the resistance of the mail heaped on the mat. The hall is dark, as surprised as Mrs Temple-Morris to see him at this unconventional hour. He stoops and gathers, moves on into the kitchen, heart pounding. Turns on the kitchen light, the daylight outside dull with cloud. The latest *TLS*, a phone bill, a brochure for discount sofas. And a white envelope with a typed address. This could be it. Has to be it. He opens the envelope at once, ripping the sealed flap with a decisive stroke of his index finger, and takes out the folded sheet of paper within.

The first glance reveals the red logo on the top right. Now that all doubt is ended and he knows he holds his future in his hands he is overwhelmed by fear.

Let it be over. Whatever the verdict let it slide into the past and its power to hurt me be furred over by time. Assume the worst. Reach beyond rejection. Refuse to be defeated.

He turns the sheet of paper so that its typed face is away from him and holds it up to the light. In this manner the words are filtered by the paper's thickness, and they run backwards, so that the sense will reach him in fragments.

command of language
reluctantly

The puzzle has its value. To crack the code is to win. In this way he draws the sting of the waiting words.

command of language
reluctantly

Faster than conscious thought he constructs the sense of the letter from four words. A little praise as an anaesthetic, then the knife.

reluctantly

Well what did I expect who said it would be easy? I will not let this defeat me. I will persist.

Oh but it would have cost them so little to believe in me and for me it would have been the breath of sweet life itself

reluctantly

The dull clog of disappointment forms round his heart or maybe his lungs. He feels breathless. Everything now takes a little more effort. Tiredness rising up within him. How long must I endure? For I am bound upon a wheel of fire.

Oh give it a rest. It's only a radio play, only a shot at finding a patron and a public. Plenty more fish in the sea. But only one sea. Only one sea.

reluctantly

He turns the paper over, looks first at the signature. Lorraine Jones, Script Editor, Radio Drama. Then he scans the letter with extreme rapidity. My colleagues and I. Considerable ingenuity. Impressive command of language. Lacks the dramatic quality. Reluctantly concluded.

Who are you to reluctantly conclude, Lorraine Jones? Just a pushy little graduate eager to show your editorial skills to your boss so you can get promoted out of the crap job you're in writing fuck-off letters to sad no-hopers and move up into the sweeter air where the real writers live and breathe.

Oh but I had hoped I had hoped I had hoped so much what do I do now what now?

Read the letter. Can't get any worse.

Dear Alan Strachan.

Thank you for sending us your play *Tunnel*. My colleagues and I have now read it, and while we were struck by the considerable ingenuity of the central concept, and by your impressive command of language, we felt that the piece lacks the dramatic quality that makes for compulsive radio listening. Therefore we have reluctantly concluded that it is not for us. If you wish to have your manuscript returned please send a stamped addressed envelope to the above address in the next fourteen days.

Yours sincerely

Lorraine Jones,

Script Editor, Radio Drama.

Right, then, fourteen days and you bin it. Go ahead. What do I care? I've only been getting up at six in the morning to steal two hours before the working day for the last six months to refine my impressive command of language so that I can write something real and strong and true, and to hell with you all it's good, I know it's good, I know it's better than good. How dare you tell me it lacks dramatic quality? Would you tell Harold Pinter his work lacks dramatic quality? Dear Mr Pinter if you wish to have your manuscript returned please send a stamped addressed envelope in the next fourteen days.

I had hoped I had hoped

He pulls the front door shut behind him and drives back to school, the letter folded in his breast pocket. The classroom still empty as he left it, pretending nothing has changed. Only five minutes of break remain. He has not marked the Year Six compositions.

He sits down at his desk and takes out the next one. My Journey, by Jack Broad.

My journey was in a dream in my dream I had to go a long way on a path only the path was thin I had to walk very carfully soon I saw I was walking on the top of a wall there was a drop on both sides I was afraid I must walk on because it was my journey there were walls everywhere I didn't know where to walk the drop frihgtened me it was so far down there were clouds there after a while I didn't mind any more I liked walking on walls and below only clouds I thought if I fell off the wall the clouds would be soft but I didn't fall

The boys and girls drift into the classroom in twos and threes. Alan Strachan looks up and crooks a finger at Jack Broad. The boy approaches.

'Jack. Your composition. It's about a dream.'

'Yes sir.'

'Haven't I told you before that there is nothing in the world more boring than telling other people your dreams?'

'Yes sir.'

'A psychoanalyst will listen to your dreams. But you have to pay him a great deal more than you pay me.'

'Yes sir.'

'How many full stops have you used in this composition, Jack?'

He holds the sheet of paper before the boy. The boy squints at it and seems to be counting in his head.

'None sir.'

'Is it all one sentence?'

'No sir.'

'No sir.' Alan Strachan sighs, takes out his red marking pen, and writes on the bottom of the page, *You can do better than this.* He gives the composition back to the boy. The bell rings for the new period.

'Alice. How do you start a new sentence?'

'Capital letter sir.'

'So why haven't you done it?'

'Don't know sir.'

'Do any of you hear a single thing I say to you? Am I talking to myself here?'

They stare back at him, mute but unthreatened. They have no respect, he knows it well enough. His job is to get them into the expensive schools that will equip them for a life of privilege, that's what their parents are paying for. He's only another kind of servant, like the nanny and the gardener.

Why must it be so hard? Why so lonely and so hard?

Life must go on

Reluctantly

10

The way he looked at me, thinks Marion Temple-Morris, easing her car round the tricky corner by the Trevor Arms. The way his eyes look and then look away, he wants to look but he daren't look, it's so sweet. But what can I do? David would get into one of his rages. He'd say it was all my fault, he'd say I'd led him on. Then it would be, 'You do it to yourself, Marion. I can't help you if you won't help yourself, Marion.' But I've done nothing to encourage him. These things just happen sometimes. No more than a crush, of course, he's still almost a boy, but he's lonely, anyone can see that. Curious the way he was coming in as I was coming out. You'd almost think he'd been waiting for me. Not that he's anything but the perfect gentleman, which if I'm being honest is more than I can say about David.

In the Tesco car park there's a space free in the row nearest the river, and not far at all from the store. Marion takes this as a good omen. Sometimes you have to walk miles bumping your trolley over uneven tarmac, dodging the incoming cars. Everyone lives in the hope of a newly vacated space near the set-down. Of course it's silly to think this way but she does have a belief, call it a feeling, that there are good days and bad days. On the good days it's as if the world is on your side. As for the bad days, well, we all know about them. We've heard quite enough about them, thank you very much, as David used to say.

She picks out one of the shallow trolleys. The deep ones are hard to unload, you have to bend right over to reach the bottom, and whoever needs that amount of shopping? Just an organic chicken breast, some broccoli perhaps, a bottle of Cinzano. A vermouth at the end of the day does no harm, though strictly speaking alcohol is not on the agenda. One must have one's little pleasures or life wouldn't be worth living.

Perhaps, she thinks, I should ask Alan over for supper one day. He lives in that house all on his own, heaven only knows what he eats, it would be a kindness to the boy. But what if he really is sweet on me? Would it be fair to show him what he might take to be encouragement? After all it's not as if I can give him what he wants. The way he can't even look at me, you can tell he's got it bad. He must have been sitting in his car waiting until I came out of the house so he could jump out and pass me on the path. Such a tiny moment, you'd hardly think it was worth it, but of course it's not how long it lasts, it's how intensely you feel. People can fall in love in one second, bang, just like that. They meet and they know it. And what do you do then? Well, it's tragic, really. Some people pine to death. Love is so rare. It's like an endangered species, the nest of a rare bird where the hen-bird is sitting on a clutch of precious eggs. You have to protect it. You have to tread lightly as you go by, or the bird takes fright and then the eggs grow cold.

The woman in front in the checkout queue has a large family, to judge by the load in her trolley. Nobody seems to have told her that Coca Cola and Honeynut Cheerios are a kind of poison for her children. Also eating that sort of diet is far more expensive, which only goes to show that the working classes aren't poor at all any more, just stupid, or perhaps I should say uneducated. But you can't tell them. If I so much as tried to point out the dangers of such a high-fat diet the woman would abuse me, might even use obscene words. David did that once. He shouted an obscene word. I just stared at him, as if to say, So that's how low you've descended. Then he said, 'I can't help you any more, Marion.' This was news, that he'd been helping me. Yes, quite a news flash that was. Hold the front page, David cares about someone other than himself.

Alan is quite another breed. He has a gentleness, a sweetness, that is altogether unusual. If he does have a little crush on me I must be sensitive about it. A clumsy rebuff could dash his confidence for ever. It should be possible to respect his feelings without leading him to expect more than I can give.

No, I don't want any cashback. Yes, I could have taken advantage of the Ten Items or Less checkout, but I'm in no hurry. David won't be coming back until – well, truth to tell, I don't even know. So if he's away so much he could hardly blame me if I showed a little kindness to a lonely neighbour.

Such a sweet funny car Alan has. When you touch it after he comes home at the end of the day it's still warm. Now that the evenings are getting longer he sits at his computer in his front room with the curtains open and the glow of the screen makes his face shine with a pale light. He has a beautiful face, but who is there to tell him so? Such a waste.

He doesn't usually come home at lunchtime. Lucky that I happened to hear his car pull up in the road. Of course it's quite possible that he came back in the hope that he might meet me, if only for the briefest of moments. There was something about him as he came up the path, a nervousness you could call it, as if he wanted something very much but felt he was wrong to want it. Then that quick intent look, and at once the look away. Oh, the poor boy. Not that he's a boy, of course. He must be thirty at least. Younger than me, but you get men like that, they fall for older women. They want to be looked after.

Crossing the car park back to her car Marion recalls her words to Alan about David. *Not that he ever makes himself useful.* The remark, she now sees, has a double meaning. She blushes a deep hot red. He might have understood her to be criticizing David's performance. At the very least he would have understood her to be implying dissatisfaction, and that, surely, is a kind of invitation. A sensitive young man like Alan could not fail to pick up the deeper meaning. And why deny the truth? David does lack the qualities a woman looks for in a man. Once he said to her, 'All I am is your nurse, Marion.' Well, there you have it in a nutshell. A woman doesn't want a man as a nurse. She wants a provider, a protector, a lover.

But suppose Alan did construe her words as an invitation? What should she do? She realizes she must prepare with care and delicacy for their next encounter. To a sensitive young man the slightest nuance of word or look could be critical. It would be quite wrong to ask him to supper, for example. To do so would be to invite an open declaration of his feelings. And what would she say then?

What would she say?

For the first time Marion allows herself to imagine what it would be like if she did not resist. She would make him happy: of that she was sure. She believes she would be happy herself. But what about David? She owes him very little really. He was there when she went through that bad time, but that's the best that can be said of him, that he was there. She came through it all on her own, and with the help of Dr Skilling, of course. If Alan needs me, why shouldn't I make him happy? All we have in this short life is a chance of happiness. Such a chance may never come again.

Back in her own little kitchen she takes out of a drawer in the dresser a small brown button. She spotted this button on her neighbour's path some time ago, and picked it up to give back to him. It must have come from one of his jackets. When you lose a button it's often hard to find a match, so it's worthwhile keeping the old ones.

She holds the button between her two palms, pressing them tight together. Yes, she thinks, it may be that it's time I let change into my life. It may be that he loves me. It may be that I must learn to love him.

With this thought there comes a sensation of deep blessed calm, that she recognizes as the gift of a power greater than herself. She closes her eyes and lowers her head and gives silent thanks.

This will be a good week.

11

Laura crosses the west terrace at Edenfield Place and makes her way slowly down the lime avenue to the lake. There, fringed by rushes, stands the lake house, derelict, long abandoned, considered to be unsafe. A short railed bridge links it to the shore. A cord tied from side to side to indicate that access is not permitted hangs low as a skipping rope. Laura steps over it and passes between tall reeds to the main structure.

It stands on piles encircled by a broad grey deck, its single room timber-walled, hexagonal, many-windowed. The roof is shingled with larch. Some of the shingles have slipped. The doors facing the big house have gone. Inside a mass of dead leaves has been swept by the wind against one wall. Two iron chairs stand looking through blurred windows over the calm surface of the lake.

She steps carefully across the deck, which has rotted away in places to reveal the dark water below. She sits in one of the iron chairs, holds her handbag on her lap as if there's a danger it might be stolen. In her bag is the letter, headed by an address and a phone number. In her bag is her phone.

The burden of memories. So long in storage, impossibly undamaged, as good as new.

A hesitant voice breaks over her reverie.

'Hello? Laura?'

It's Billy Holland on the land side of the bridge.

'Don't want to disturb you.'

'It's all right. I shouldn't be here anyway. It's supposed not to be safe.'

'Oh, it's safe enough.' He crosses the bridge. 'Not that I've been here in years.'

'Watch where you step.'

But he comes to her without caring where his feet fall.

'Do you have a moment?'

They sit on the iron chairs side by side and watch the patterns made by the wind on the water. She holds her letter, he holds his letters. A bundle of fifty-year-old papers no longer tied with string.

'Was I wrong?' she says. 'Maybe I should have left them where I found them.'

'Wrong? No, not at all.'

He's breathing slowly, heavily. With one broad white hand he keeps smoothing the fabric of his trousers over his thigh.

'Haven't been here in years,' he says. 'Funny old world.'

She wonders what age he is. Sixty, perhaps.

'My mother fell ill after I was born,' he says. 'She had to go away. A nursing home. So you see, my father was alone.'

'Please, Billy,' she says. 'You don't have to explain anything to me.'

'There's no one else.'

'Did you know?'

'Oh, no. No, no.'

'So you don't know who she was.'

'A girl from the village, it seems. He calls her Doll. A private name, I suppose. It means nothing to me.'

He stares out over the lake like a man in shock. She says nothing, giving him time and space.

'I never really knew my mother,' he says at last. 'I was so young. She was mostly away. Then she died. I was seven.'

'I'm so sorry, Billy.'

'No,' he says. 'It's not that.'

Again the silence, and the slow rising up to the surface of inadequate words.

'What my father did. What he felt. I suppose it was wrong. But I had no idea that it was possible.'

'People have always had affairs.'

'Was it an affair? There's nothing in the letters to say so. No doubt it was. The main thing is, she made him happy.'

He looks round at Laura and she catches the wistfulness in his eyes.

'That's all we want in the end, isn't it? Someone who makes us happy.'

'Yes,' says Laura. 'That's all we want.'

'Her handwriting. She's not educated, you can tell. And my father, he was very correct. Very proud. But of course all that came afterwards. I only really knew him after it was all over.'

He clears his throat. Then he coughs, covering his mouth with one hand.

'It's possible,' he says, 'that she's still alive. This Doll. I imagine she was quite young. She would be in her seventies or eighties.'

'Yes, it's possible.'

'The thing is.' He coughs again. 'I would like to meet her. If she is still alive. But it's not easy. Not easy.'

'No. I suppose it isn't.'

'I was wondering if you. In the course of your researches. The name discovered, you see. Perhaps one could say the letters belong to this person. This Doll.'

Laura understands.

'You want me to trace her.'

'Ask around, perhaps. Better coming from you.'

'I'll try, certainly.'

'Well, then.' He stands. 'Let me know what you come up with. Much appreciated.'

With that he nods vaguely in her direction and leaves.

Left alone in the lake house, scene of long-ago trysts, Laura finds herself in a strange mood.

That's all we want in the end, isn't it? Someone who makes us happy.

She thinks of Henry. As always when she conjures up a deliberate picture of him he's on a walk, leaning into the wind, somewhere high on the Downs. He's turning towards her, telling her something, his long arm sweeping over the valley below. Henry doesn't just walk, he looks, he sees, he reads the landscape. And as always when she pictures him in this mode, striding along, eager words lost in the wind, she feels a clench of gratitude. He has given himself to her, there's no other way to put it. That simple act of unwithholding is what makes her life possible. She will do nothing to hurt him, nothing to lose him.

But does he make me happy?

There are no gauges, no measures. How happy am I entitled to be?

I have security, loyalty, kindness. Am I allowed excitement? Am I allowed ecstasy?

The words sound ridiculous to her even as she frames them in her mind, as if they belong to a time now gone by, her youth, her twenties. But why should this be so? Sometimes she finds several days have passed and she can't recall how she spent them, other than in the unnoticed round of domestic life, the breakfasts and the school runs, the trips to the supermarket, the suppers and the waiting for Henry to come home. She is living in a world without markers. She is adrift in a coastal mist, all sense of direction lost and all sense of time. Not a condition deserving of sympathy. And yet—

There was a time when I would wait in all day for the phone to ring. I had a lover once whose voice on the phone made me tremble.

I will not burn what remains of the greatest happiness I have ever known.

She takes out Nick's letter and passing the information from her eyes to her fingers without any conscious process of decision-making she taps out the numbers on her phone. Then she pauses, her finger on the send button.

If I press send, it will begin again.

What! Such vanity. Such melodrama. Nothing more than a phone call. The satisfying of curiosity. The chances are he won't be there anyway.

'Hello?'

She recognizes the voice of an old friend from university days.

'Richard? It's Laura.'

'Laura! Oh my God! It's been too long. How are you?'

'Not so bad. And you?'

'We were just talking about you. That is so weird. How long is it? Has to be five years. How old are your children?'

'Jack's eleven now. Carrie's nine.'

'I don't believe it. Hey, you'll never guess who's showed up here.'

'Who?'

Why am I pretending I don't know?

'Nick Crocker! Blown in from California. Hold on.'

She hears his voice speaking to someone else. 'It's Laura Kinross. Do you want to say hi?' So Nick has been keeping secrets too.

'Laura? Nick's right here. He'd like a word.'

And there he is. The long-forgotten voice, entirely unchanged.

'Laura? Is that you?'

'Yes. It's me.'

Her heart bumps even as she keeps her voice neutral.

'When do I see you?' he says.

No preliminaries as ever.

'So what happened to you?' she says.

She doesn't see him for twenty years and already she's into the accusations. But he doesn't even hear her.

'Say where and when. I'll be there.'

She runs her diary through her head to scramble all other thoughts.

'How about today week? Next Wednesday.'

'How about tomorrow?'

She has no idea what's happening tomorrow except that it's too soon.

'Friday. We'll give you supper. You can meet Henry and the children.'

'Fine. Friday.'

She gives him her address and phone number.

'Right,' he says. 'Friday.' And he's gone.

He never was good on the phone. Laura presses the end-call button and realizes she's given him her mobile number, not the house line. She's become two people. The other one, the secret one, is doing things behind her back.

And yet what is there to be ashamed of? An old friend, a former boyfriend, is coming to supper with her family. Henry won't mind. He'll be curious to meet him.

She goes on sitting in the derelict lake house absorbing the brief phone conversation. She begins to find contradictions. He implied he had only a few days in the country. So why send a letter? He could easily get her parents' number from Richard. Why not phone them? If he's staying with Richard, he must know her married name. Richard was at the wedding. So why write to her under her maiden name?

I always knew you'd come back one day.

This unbidden thought appals her. She thinks of Carrie and her crisis at school. Of Jack's strange composition that Henry likes so much. Of Henry deep in the seventeenth century, explaining to her over dinner the sin of idolatry. The Puritans called the defacing of statues the sacrament of forgetfulness. Henry loves that.

That's all we want in the end. Someone who makes us happy.

12

At the end of term they parted to spend Christmas with their families. Saying goodbye at the station Laura told him, 'Phone every day.' Nick said, 'Or write.' He didn't fully understand that he had become part of her. They had spent every night together since that first sleepless night, she was only fully alive when she was with him. The rest of the time she was waiting.

They kissed and stood close, not speaking, their arms folded round each other. It was cold and they both wore heavy coats. She pressed her cheek against his cheek.

On the train she experienced a wave of panic. She wanted to leave her seat, throw herself from the moving train, run back to him. He was fading, becoming insubstantial, only she could make him real with her warm touch. Then the terror passed, to be replaced by a sensation of listlessness. What did it matter where the train was carrying her? It carried her away from him. After Christmas there would be another train, which would take her back to him. The days between had no colour or distinction. Her life was in suspension.

At home the change in Laura did not go unnoticed.

'You're pale as a ghost, darling. Are you ill?'

'No, Mummy. I'm fine.'

'I'm going to feed you up. Diana, we must feed her up.'

'She might be anorexic,' said Diana, a hopeful glint in her eye.

'Of course she isn't,' said their mother, fearing that she was. 'That's a horrible thing to say.'

'Is it?' said Diana. 'Sorry.'

Diana found her later sitting on her bed in a dressing gown staring into space. She demanded to be told what was going on.

'I met this man,' said Laura.

'And he's messed you about.'

'No. I just miss him.'

'Christ, is that all? I thought at the very least you'd got pregnant and he'd dumped you.'

'No.'

'So what's the problem?'

'I said. I miss him.'

'Well, I miss Hamish too. But nobody wants their life totally taken over. What's this boy's name?'

'Nick. He's not a boy.'

'Are you sleeping with him?'

'Of course I'm sleeping with him.'

'All right, all right. Just checking. I hope you're keeping up with the pills.'

'Yes.'

'You could always go onto the rhythm method. That way you get a week off every month.'

Diana thought this funny and a little shocking, but Laura didn't react. The phone rang in the hall. Laura jumped, and the blood drained from her face. She waited, trembling, for her mother's voice to call up the stairs, but no call came.

'Do you have a photograph of him?' said Diana.

'No.'

'No picture to kiss at night?'

'I have him.'

Diana was silenced. She was also piqued. Laura's malady was beginning to look like true love, and Diana did not allow Laura to be happier than she was herself.

'So where is he now?'

'With his family. In Highgate.'

'Highgate? He'll be out on the town, then. Still, what you don't see can't hurt you.'

By the end of the second day no call had come and Laura was frantic. She called Nick's home. He came to the phone.

'What's the problem?'

'Why didn't you phone?'

'I said I'd write. I have written.'

'Oh, Nick. Letters take far too long. Tell me what you said in your letter.'

'It's different on the phone.'

'Please.'

'You'll get it tomorrow.'

She realized with a sinking heart that he was not going to give her the consolation she craved. He had told her before that he was not good on the phone, but she had paid little attention. What was there to be good at? Now, with their first ever phone call, she was finding out. Without his smile, without his touch, his voice felt thin and far away. All she wanted him to say was *I love you, I miss you*. These few words would keep her alive until the post came tomorrow. But she dared not ask.

There had grown up between them over the last two ecstatic months an understanding that their love was unlike other people's love. There was a rightness in their coming together that was close to perfection. Therefore they never flaunted their happiness, and they never hoarded it. Something so special did not need to be put into words, nor could it be threatened by the attentions of others. They were united, they told each other, but they were free. No promises made or required. They had only to catch sight of themselves reflected in a shop window walking arm in arm, beautiful as angels, and they knew they were made for each other.

How then could Laura say on the phone, 'Tell me you love me'? Particularly when anyone passing the hall could hear every word.

'So what are you up to?' she said.

'Nothing much. Putting up Christmas decorations.'

'I just want it all to be over. I'm supposed to go to this party tomorrow. I think I'll say I'm ill.'

'No, you should go. Have fun.'

How can I have fun without you? There is no fun without you. There is no life without you.

'You wouldn't say that if you could see the people round here.'

'Oh, well. You know best.'

'Honestly, Nick.'

'What?'

'Nothing. Just me being silly.'

'I told you I'm no good on the phone.'

She relied on the closing phase of the conversation to extract something to sustain her. She lowered and softened her voice accordingly.

'Better go. Good to hear your voice.'

'And you.'

'You know I love you.'

'Me you.'

And there it was.

His letter came the next morning. She was waiting for the postman, and took it before anyone else saw it.

Sweet you. My window looks over rooftops, distant trees, cold blank sky. In my mind I'm sitting with you before the hissing gas fire. Avocados and Beaujolais and bare feet. I should be working on the great work. Dark comes so early. London does darkness well, glitter more glamorous than daylight. How goes the daylight in Sussex? I picture stern lead-coloured waves rolling in to a deserted promenade. Chalk cliffs, seagulls, you in your long blue jersey, hair streaming in the wind. Because we're apart I learn how close we are. More than close. I carry you in me like a part of myself. Does that make sense? Of course you're not me, you're you. My beautiful other. That sounds too possessive. We are each other's other. Christ I don't know. Drink to me only with your eyes and I will pledge with mine.

She cried a little as she read the letter, without quite knowing why. She wanted so much to be with him again, it was an ache in her arms.

After Christmas they were reunited in a remote farmhouse in Radnorshire. The house was entirely unsuitable for winter habitation. It had no electricity and no hot water, and its only source of heat was the fireplace in the kitchen. Here, wrapped in duvets, they warmed tomato soup on a kerosene camping stove and drank cheap red wine. They read *Middlemarch* aloud to each other by candlelight. For five days they had no visitors and went nowhere, except to the village shop in Painscastle for bread and matches.

Nick found Dorothea's decision to marry Casaubon incomprehensible.

'She's being a chump. Unless she's after his money.'

'She wants her life to have a greater purpose. I buy that. She admires him. She believes in his great work. I believe in your great work.'

She was mocking him. She had discovered he liked it when she laughed at him.

'I wonder what your great work will be. A thing of wonder, I'm sure. So you see, I believe in you.'

Unspoken, ahead, the day in June when he would graduate, and she, two years younger, would be left behind. Sometimes he talked of Paris, or Florence, but to her such plans were meaningless. How could he go so far away from her?

'This is my great work,' he said, putting down the book. 'You and me.'

This was all she had ever wanted to hear.

'I do love you, Nick.'

He kissed her. Then beneath the duvet his hand felt for her body, ran down her flank to her thigh. His signal of desire at once awoke in her a thrill of response. She wanted him to want her, wanted him to crave her and be addicted to her. When they made love the sensations that flooded her body were overwhelmingly intense, but at the heart of the intensity was a fierce cry of possession.

Enter me, push deep into me, find all you need in me, never leave. My darling, my only one, I have you now, you're mine now.

13

On Wednesday afternoons all the main school who aren't in matches or rehearsing the play are supposed to watch and cheer those that are but Toby Clore says who cares and it's only old Jimmy on duty. He says he's going down to the wood and you can come if you want. Angus is going and Richard Adderley so Jack says maybe he'll go along too and they don't seem to mind. The wood is out of bounds even on a non-match afternoon but Toby Clore doesn't have much to say to Jack usually so Jack is excited to be included as well as nervous.

Getting away is easy. Underhill is batting and has scored thirteen. Old Jimmy stands on the terrace watching the match and telling Mr Kilmartin how he's become a part-time reporter, so Toby and the others just sort of mooch off down by the tennis courts as if they're going nowhere in particular. Then once they're past the big laurels Toby says 'Go!' and they dive through the trees and run. They run all the way down the track to the wood, and don't stop till they reach the Drowning Pond, which is one of the reasons the wood is out of bounds. There's a thick greenish scum on the surface of the water. If you poke a stick into the pond you never reach the bottom, which either means it has no bottom or that there's soft sludgy stuff down there, which is just as creepy.

There's a dead branch lying half over the green water, quite a big branch, big enough to stand on. Angus stands on its end where it rests on the bank and Richard Adderley dares him to walk out over the water, if you can call it water. He takes one step, but the branch starts to sink and he jumps off quickly.

'Loser,' Richard Adderley says.

So Richard Adderley has to show he can go further down the branch, which he does, but then as he jumps off his shoes go right into the slime because the branch dips under the kick of his jump.

'Your turn, Jacko.'

Jack does not want to step onto that bobbing branch but he understands that he has no choice. Some token attempt must be made for the simple reason that the others have allowed him to come with them. If he does not walk the branch he must leave them and return to not watching the cricket match. None of this is spoken of course, or even barely framed as a thought. Just the way of things.

He steps onto the end of the branch where it's safe, and finds his balance. Even here the branch rocks a little. He wonders what the green slime feels like to touch, or far worse, to swallow. He takes one very small step, propelled forward even as he is held back, locked in fatalistic dread, doing what he does not want to do but must. Toby Clore isn't even watching. Why hasn't Toby walked the branch? But Jack knows the answer. Toby doesn't need to prove that he's a total banghead. This would be nothing for Toby. He would jump right into the green slime if he felt like it. Toby only ever does what he feels like. This is why Jack admires him so much, even though Toby is neither bigger nor cleverer than he is. He is just more free. There's a crazy carelessness about him that is pure glamour. Toby Clore's wildness speaks to Jack of possibilities beyond pleasing those in authority.

Then Toby looks round and declares, 'Let's make the cows shit!'

Off they run to the far side of the wood, leaving Jack on his branch, but he doesn't mind because now he doesn't have to walk the branch after all. He chases after them, panting some way behind them, heart singing with gratitude. They crawl through a barbed-wire fence, up a bank of nettles, into the springy hoof-pocked turf of the big tree-fringed meadow beyond. A herd of black and white cows grazes quietly on the far side, near a farm road.

Jack has heard reports of this game but has never done it before. The other three, veterans all, form up abreast like the leading rank of an army column, and set off at a grand march across the meadow towards the cows. Jack catches up and falls into place on Angus's left. They march in exaggerated style, making big slow steps, and swinging their arms high and stiff by their sides. Jack likes the march, because the four of them swing their arms in time, and this makes him one of them. The cows look up in mild surprise.

When they're close Toby calls out a command in an army-style voice.

'Squad! Prepare to charge!'

He starts to windmill his arms. The others do likewise.

'Charge!' yells Toby. 'Shit or die!'

The four boys whoop and holler over the tummocks of grass, thrashing the air with their arms, and the cows scatter, cantering away, braying in fear. As they go they hoist their tails high, and cow shit comes plopping from their bottoms, plop-plop-plop.

A great roaring and down the farm road comes a mud-coloured Landrover at tremendous speed, its wheels spitting dirt and stones. Before the boys realize what is happening the vehicle has juddered to a stop and a small mud-coloured man has hurled himself upon them and seized the nearest boy. This happens to be Jack. He holds Jack by his shoulder with one iron and hurting hand and in his other hand he brandishes a steely gleaming double-barrelled shotgun.

'You little bastards!' he says. 'You bloody little bastards!'

He stabs his gun up into the air. The other three have gone still. They stare back at him in utter silence. He's so angry and dirty, his eyes so mad and shining, his hair so wild, he paralyses them with fear. They have never met him before but he is familiar to all of them. He is the Dogman. His dogs are in the Landrover even now. Jack can hear them whining.

'I should shoot you,' he says. His voice makes a scary bubbling sound in his throat like he can't swallow. 'The law's on my side. Maybe I will.'

He moves a finger and they hear a clicky noise come from his immense gun. Richard Adderley has gone chalk white.

'Please,' he says. His voice is very small, just a whimper.

'Please,' echoes the Dogman. 'Please what? Please spare your nasty little life so you can grow up to be a *stockbroker*? We don't need any more *bloody stockbrokers*! Why don't I put you out of your misery *now*!'

He points the muzzle of the shotgun at the sky and pulls the trigger. The explosion is cataclysmic, terrifying. It echoes round the trees, round the meadow. Jack feels his heart hammering.

'Now *get off my land*!'

They turn and run. Run and run. Stung by nettles, scraped by barbed-wire, back through the wood to the Drowning Pond, on up the track, to stop at last, white-faced and gasping, by the laurels. Here they stand, bent with hands on thighs, getting back their breath, exchanging looks, already starting to turn the experience into an anecdote.

'What a saddo! Did you see his hair?'

'He would have killed us.'

'No way.'

'He's a wacko. I'm telling you. Everyone says so.'

'Hey, Richard. Did you think he was going to shoot you?'

'No. Maybe for a moment. No.'

'I loved him.' This is Toby Clore. 'We don't need any more *bloody stockbrokers*!'

Jack looks at Toby Clore with admiration untinged by comprehension. You can never tell which line Toby's going to take.

'Dogman rules!' says Toby. 'Why don't I put you out of your misery now!' He mimes firing a shotgun at the clouds. 'Boom! So did Jack wet his pants?'

'No,' says Jack.

'Good for you, Jacko.'

They hear the bop of a bat on a cricket ball, followed by a thin cheer. Underhill's score goes up to seventeen. A lifetime has gone by, Jack has been through fire and water, almost to the gates of hell itself, and the First Eleven has scored four more runs.

14

Old Mrs Dickinson is taking her rest when her daughter rings the first time. Not that she's old, the seventies are young these days, but she lives alone and can please herself. The rest lasts no more than an hour, but somehow it's always in this hour that things go wrong. Not even a proper siesta, not in bed, only sitting in her usual armchair by the fire, but she does go to sleep. This afternoon on waking she sees the answerphone light winking, but in the same moment she hears the sound of the lawnmower outside and knows with a terrible certainty that Victor is mowing the daffodils. Every year they have this same battle, and every year he forgets or ignores her instructions.

She clasps the ends of the chair's arms, braces her frail frame, and pulls. Two pulls and she's rising. The trick is to get the momentum going, that way you can lock the lower limbs in place before gravity strikes back. Arthritis is so time-consuming. So many little stratagems to do what used to be instinctive. Some parts of the body give up sooner than others, and in her case it's the joints. The mind still untouched, praise God.

Perry jumps off his chair where he too has been having his rest, and detecting her intention to go outside, begins to yap. This is a mistake.

'Be quiet, Perry! Stop that! Shut up! I can't stand it!'

The little dog, hearing what sounds to him like an answering series of excited barks, works himself up into a frenzy of yapping. The old lady becomes maddened by the noise. She reaches for her stick and strikes the dog on one flank.

'I said SHUT UP!'

The dog cowers and bleats. The old lady is overcome with remorse. But now she's up from her chair she can't bend down again to fondle the miserable beast, so she heads on towards the back door. She experiences a resurgence of anger at Perry for inducing in her this spasm of guilt.

'Well, what do you expect when you make a racket like that? What do you expect? It's more than flesh and blood can bear. I've told you time and again, but you just don't listen. You know you don't, Perry. You're a very bad dog.'

As soon as she steps out into the back garden she can see that most of the daffodil leaves are gone.

'Victor!'

She shouts as loud as she can, but it's no use. When the mower engine is running the great booby hears nothing.

'Victor! VICTOR!'

She struggles slowly across the cut lawn to the apple trees, and plants herself in the path of the machine. As the mower lumbers round and heads towards her, he sees her at last. He registers surprise, but it takes several seconds for the discovery of her presence to translate into the decision to stop the mower. As the old lady knows all too well, for Victor the act of mowing has an irresistible fascination. He regards the mower as a species of wild animal, a bull perhaps, that is powerful and only partly under control.

'Mrs Dickson!' His voice heavy with disapproval. The mower must never be stopped in mid-mow. 'Mrs Dickson!' In all the eleven years he has worked for her he has never got her name right.

The old lady points. She speaks with what she intends to be calm authority, but it comes out as a peevish shriek.

'You have mowed the daffodils!'

He turns to look, and turns slowly back. Victor is in his seventies also.

'No,' he says, respectful but unyielding. 'The daffs have been over since April.'

'The leaves, Victor! The leaves! They must be left until they wither!'

Victor looks at her with watery but unrepentant eyes.

'If I leave the grass another week, it's too long for the machine. All this rain we've been having.'

'If you cut the daffodil leaves too soon, the bulbs won't grow, and we'll have no daffodils next spring.'

'Plenty of daffs. No shortage of daffs.'

It's enough to make a saint scream. Mrs Dickinson is no saint.

'Victor, I asked you not to cut the orchard till July. Now, I did. I want you to admit it.'

'By July the grass is too long for the machine.'

'Did I or did I not ask you to leave the orchard till July?'

'You asked me to keep your garden tidy, Mrs Dickson. I'm doing my best.'

This is Victor's sanction, the veiled threat he dangles over her head. If she nags him further he will deliver the next level of warning, which goes, 'If you don't like the way I do things maybe you should find someone else who is more to your liking.' Mrs Dickinson is helpless in the face of this quiet intransigence. Gardeners are impossible to find these days. Victor knows the garden well and he keeps it looking neat. But why must he destroy the daffodils?

'I know you're doing your best, Victor. But you see, daffodil bulbs are fed through their leaves. If you cut the leaves too early, the bulbs starve, and we get no flowers in the spring. That is why we don't mow the grass where the daffodils grow until July. Not May. July.'

'Right you are.'

Is that assent or dismissal?

'So you do understand, don't you, Victor?'

'I better get on. The rain'll be back soon enough.'

Unreassured, powerless, thwarted, Mrs Dickinson makes her careful way back to the house, planning each footfall lest the ground prove treacherous. The important thing is not to fall over. If you fall over, you can't always get up.

As she enters the house she becomes aware that the phone is ringing. She knows at once, by that sympathetic magic that is common in the lives of lonely people, that it is her daughter Elizabeth calling to ask her to pick up her granddaughter Alice from school.

'Hallo, Mum. Look, I'm tied up here for a couple more hours. Would you mind?'

'Alice. School. Yes.'

'I should be home by seven at the latest.'

'Yes. All right. Goodbye.'

Mrs Dickinson replaces the phone, aware that she has been short with her daughter, but what else can she say? She believes it's wrong of Elizabeth to be up in London working when her child needs her at home. It's not as if Alice is unaffected. You have only to look at the child to know that she's deprived. It may be a good school she goes to, but what a child needs most is a mother. And a father, if it can be managed, but Elizabeth never even took the trouble to get married. It's all very well saying Guy's a bad lot and wouldn't have married her anyway, but what's she doing getting pregnant in the first place? And who else is going to marry a woman over thirty with a great hulk of a child? It's not as if I didn't warn her. But she paid no attention to me, I might as well not have spoken.

She looks at the clock, thinking with annoyance that now she won't have time for the farm walk that Perry so loves. She looks down at Perry. He is sitting at her feet gazing up at her with wistful longing. Now that her anger has shifted its focus onto her daughter, she has kinder feelings towards her dog.

'You're a good boy, Perry. Why shouldn't you have your walk? But you're not to chase the sheep.'

Stick in hand once more, she leaves the garden by the rear gate. A well-maintained path runs along the back walls of the row of cottage gardens, and comes out onto the busy road just opposite the farm. She keeps Perry on a lead until they have crossed the road. Once on the farm track she lets him run free.

As the poodle bounds joyously away from her, leaping from puddle to puddle in the rutted track, Aster Dickinson experiences an associate freedom; as if Perry carries with him her own questing spirit. She has done her best, but life has not been easy since Rex left her. She has raised a child all on her own, and well into her forties, and there's a price to be paid for that. Not that she hasn't paid the price gladly, Elizabeth being the miracle child so long hoped for, though also one must presume the reason why Rex left. So, a costly child. Elizabeth understands nothing of this, of course. The young are selfish; that is their privilege.

On the far side of the belt of trees there is a fence, a gate, a cattle grid. Perry flattens himself to crawl under the gate, not waiting for her to open it. There are sheep in the field beyond.

'Perry! Perry! Come back here!'

He turns to look at her, his expression sorrowful. He does not want to be put on the lead. Of course he doesn't. We would all rather be free to do whatever we like all the time. But life isn't like that.

'Come here, Perry!'

Slowly, reluctantly, dragging his hind legs, he comes to her. She clicks the lead onto his collar ring. They walk on.

He tugs on the lead all the way. For Mrs Dickinson the sensation seems to come from within herself, the yearning to be free as much her own impulse as the holding back. Ahead the field opens out into a great natural bowl, one of the many hollows scooped out of the lower slopes of the chalkland hills. It's the kind of space that calls to you to reach out your arms and run and play at flying, to swoop over those rippling contours of grass. But the old lady and the dog, tethered to each other by the lead, do not run.

By the concrete pillbox they turn back and retrace their steps.

As she enters her own garden once more, Mrs Dickinson hears the sound of the mower and sees Victor mowing the remainder of the daffodil leaves in the orchard. A red haze of fury forms before her eyes. Perry runs on ahead to the back door of the house. She draws a long breath, preparing to confront Victor with the full force of her righteous anger, when she hears the tinny chimes of the grandfather clock in the passage strike the hour. She is already late for school. She hurries into the kitchen and picks up her outdoors bag. Perry starts to yap.

'One more yap out of you,' she says, waving her stick, 'and I knock your brains out!'

She reverses out of the garage at thirty miles an hour, clipping the left gate pillar with her right mudguard. This is a common occurrence. The gate pillars are awkwardly placed.

She hurtles down the street to the main road, recovering her equilibrium as she goes. Driving soothes her. The slow clumsy motion of her unaided body is replaced by a smooth and thrilling power, and her natural impatience can at last be assuaged. As a result her car, a Peugeot 305 Automatic, is dented and scraped all over, one headlight is cracked, the rear bumper is buckled, and she has long given up the unequal struggle to retain her wing mirrors. Wing mirrors are a piece of poor design. They stick out too far, even the simplest manoeuvres snap them off. She feels the car is more drivable without them.

She bounds out onto the main road, and accelerating away from the Edenfield roundabout she reaches seventy on the straight before being forced to slow down for a farm tractor. The tractor makes a great noise but goes no faster than twenty miles an hour. Mrs Dickinson bears it for a few minutes and then can bear it no more. She swings out to overtake, sees to her surprise a silver car approaching at speed, accelerates fiercely to get past the tractor, hears the blast of the silver car's horn, feels the slam of air as they pass within inches of each other, the silver car banging on the verge, and pulls back into her lane entirely unharmed, indeed, exhilarated. She rams down the accelerator once more, and briefly touches seventy-five miles an hour before she's braking hard ahead of the right turn to Underhill School.

I'll give Alice the rest of the leg of lamb for supper, she thinks. She never gets real food at home.

15

Jack's late getting out of class after last bell because old Jimmy picks him out for a little chat. You'd think he could see Jack is busting to go but Jimmy Hall lives in a universe all of his own. Carrie's class does gym last lesson on Wednesdays which means they get let out early to change, and Jack suspects her of meaning to bag the front car seat. By law and tradition the front seat is his this afternoon. Carrie sat in the front last time so now it's his turn. Legally there's no argument. But Carrie is a cheat and a liar and not to be trusted.

'Do you ever read the *Sussex County Chronicle*, Jack?'

'No, sir.'

'You should. Tell your parents. Good for local democracy, you know. We all need to keep informed.'

'Yes, sir.'

'More to writing newspapers than meets the eye, Jack. No good just saying this happened, and this, and this. You have to tell a story.'

'Yes sir.'

Old Jimmy has no one to go home to so he hangs around after school for as long as he can and comes in at weekends, which is sad, but Jack feels no pity. He can hear the clatter of running feet in the hall and the rumble of cars in the drive.

'Got to go, sir. My mother'll be waiting.'

'Off you go, Jack. Off you go.'

Out into the crowded hall and push through the scrum of blue blazers to the porch where Mrs Kilmartin stands, big as a church. Jack lets himself be carried on the wave of home-going bodies into the open air. So far no sign of Carrie. Jason Ferris's mother is there with a new Labrador puppy on a lead, drawing a crowd. Jack hesitates by the coned-off section where they're supposed to wait for their pick-up, checking to see if anyone else from Carrie's class is out yet. Peter Mackie passes by and idly and for no reason at all hits him on the shoulder, hard enough to hurt.

'Hey! What was that for?'

'Only a joke. Can't you take a joke? Jacko can't take a joke.'

Naomi Truscott comes out with her blazer on, which means Carrie's class has been out for at least five minutes, and Carrie's always one of the first. With a lurch of insight Jack realizes she must have gone on ahead, she'll already be on the far side of the rhododendrons, waiting to intercept their mother's car before he even sees it.

He sets off down the drive at a run, and there she is, a solitary figure with a drooping head, and there's his mother's car drawing to a stop. Even at this distance Jack can tell Carrie is starting to cry. He is outraged. He runs as fast as he can, fuelled by his sense of the unfolding injustice. As he approaches, Carrie has the car door open and is climbing into the front seat, when she knows beyond a shadow of a doubt that it is his turn in the front seat this afternoon.

'Carrie! Get out! It's not your turn!'

His mother fixes him with reproachful eyes.

'Please, Jack. Carrie's upset.'

'But it's not her turn in the front!'

'Oh, really. What does it matter where you sit? Now jump in the back. We're holding up the other cars.'

Jack is speechless with shock. How can she say it doesn't matter where they sit? She knows as well as he does how carefully the turns have been negotiated.

'Come on, Jack. Get in.'

Jack gets in and shuts the door. Carrie looks round and for a second he glimpses her triumphant face and he can't bear it.

'It's my turn! It is!'

His mother weaves the Volvo past the other cars, exchanging friendly waves with fellow parents, looping round the school porch and out towards the main road again.

'Carrie's upset, Jack. Be more sympathetic.'

'No she isn't. What's she got to be upset about?'

'She's been having problems with Naomi. You know that.'

'No she hasn't. I saw them playing together in break. They were just fine.'

He had, too. That is, he had seen them talking together, heads bent and close, and no one walking away.

'Well, I think that's Carrie's business, don't you?'

'But she's lying!'

'I am not!' Carrie bursts into tears.

'All right, darling. Jack, please leave her alone.'

Jack feels helpless in the face of his sister's outrageous manipulation. How can his mother not see it?

'It's still my turn,' he says, clinging fiercely to the one undeniable truth.

'Jack. I don't want to hear another word. Now tell me how your day has been.'

He says nothing. She doesn't want to hear another word. She just said so. He was going to tell her about the Dogman, but not now.

'Did Mr Strachan hand you back your composition?'

Silence.

'So did he?'

'Yes.'

Jack hasn't given one single thought to his composition since getting it back. Life has been too full.

'Did he like it?'

'Not really.'

'Oh.'

Jack catches a small note of dismay in his mother's voice. All at once it strikes him there is ammunition here. There is the opportunity for a counterstroke. He makes his voice small.

'He wrote on it, *You can do better than this.*'

'Oh, darling. I was so sure he'd like it.'

'Me too.'

His voice is so small now his mother can hardly hear him. The strategy is working.

'Sweetheart! What a beast that man is. He's wrong. It was a wonderful composition. Daddy was terribly impressed.'

'Was he?'

Now his sad little voice is breaking her heart. She pulls the car into the side of the road. She turns round, reaches out a hand.

'Were you terribly disappointed?'

'Sort of.' He feels his eyes fill with tears. His mother's sympathy is so delicious that the required emotions rise up in him without effort on his part. He finds he has been hurt by Mr Strachan's dismissal of his dream. He had hoped for praise. Instead he has been rejected. A tear rolls down his cheek.

'Oh, darling.' His mother dabs his cheek. 'Carrie, why don't you climb in the back and let Jack come by me?'

'But Mummy—'

'We're halfway home already, darling.'

So Carrie goes in the back and Jack goes in the front and for the next ten minutes his victory is doubly sweet, because it has been won after an initial reversal. He knows Carrie's submission is only temporary, but it is his turn in the front, not hers, she deliberately set out to violate the treaty, and now order is restored.

'I'm going to tell Daddy about this,' says his mother. 'It's just not good enough. It makes me angry. It really does.'

She turns the car off the road and down the short drive to home.

16

Martin Linton manoeuvres the ancient mud-encrusted Landrover down the farm road, weaving round the deeper pot-holes, banging into the shallower ones, his dogs yipping softly in the back as they smell home. The road has not been resurfaced by the Edenfield Estate for twenty years now. He receives the repeated hammer-blows to the suspension with a bitter satisfaction. His life has been so punishing for so long that he has come to source his pride in his ability to endure hardship. The jolting ride sings a song to which he has words: 'Do your worst you'll never—, do your worst you'll never—, do your worst you'll never—, knock me down.' He recalls the sight of the Underhill boys pelting away across the field in terror.

Should have shot the little shits.

To the end of the track and into the yard. Nettles grow in the cracks where the concrete paving has buckled. The old flint walls of the great barn are beginning to crumble. Wind and rain have scratched at the lime mortar and etched it away so that now the flints stand out like teeth. Here and there the roof tiles have slipped, letting in the weather to rust the farm machinery stored within. Only the barn's timber frame is sound. Posts, beams, rafters, purlins all oak, the original timbers cut and slotted over three hundred years ago, and still too hard to knock a nail into without bending it. From a practical point of view the steel and aluminium Atcost barns in the storage yard do a better job, being virtually maintenance-free and entirely weather-proof. However those modern structures draw no envious glances from passing walkers; whereas the handsome old barn beside Home Farm causes them to stand and stare, consumed with covetousness.

The dogs jump out as soon as the Landrover stops, and bound up to the back door of the house. Martin always comes and goes by the back door. The front door looks onto the village street, and has an eighteenth-century portico, and a brick path leading to a pretty iron gate. It's so little used that the hinges have rusted, and ground elder covers the front step.

'Down Bess! Down Sal!'

The dogs stand back to let him through. The door opens into a dark back kitchen, where he eases off his boots and his damp coat and washes his hands in water from the cold tap, the only tap above the big chipped white sink. A trug of new potatoes stands on the table, the black earth still fresh on the egg-white skin. He relishes the chill of the cold water on his hands. From the kitchen next door come familiar sounds: the shrill squeal of his daughters' voices, the racket of the dogs running round and round the table as they always do on arrival, the soft admonitory tones of his wife.

Jenny is sitting at the table, a newspaper spread open before her. The girls see their father in the doorway and come running. He picks them both up, one in each arm, and they rub their noses against his stubble, and wriggle and squeal at the delicious prickliness. Jenny looks up and manages a smile for him.

'You shouldn't be digging potatoes,' he says.

'Oh, well.' She's over nine months gone now, and permanently exhausted.

'Daddy Daddy Daddy,' sing the girls.

He lowers them carefully to the ground. They're both in nightdresses, barefoot, ready for bed. He opens his hands and receives one small hand in each big hand. This is the ritual.

'Kiss Mummy.'

Poppy goes first, three years old, round face and blue eyes. People exclaim when they see her, 'A cherub! An angel!' She has a fierce and stubborn will, which her father traces back to himself, but her beauty, her sweet manipulative charm, is all Jenny's.

'There, darling. Don't squash Bobby.'

The baby is to be a boy called Bobby.

Lily follows her sister in her mother's arms: Lily the silent, Lily the grave. At five years old she has a reading age of eight. She reads *My Naughty Little Sister* stories over and over. Her father knows she is unusual, and will grow up to be a remarkable person, and will do great things.

Then up the stairs they go, hand in hand, step by step, all silently counting the steps as they go. Fifteen to the half landing, fourteen more to the top. Pad-pad-pad go the bare feet along the carpetless boards of the landing to the girls' bedroom, the pink-walled heart of the house.

'Into bed, now. Cuddle up.'

He sits in the rocking chair between their two beds and reads them their story. He dearly wants his cup of tea, and then his bath, but this nightly self-denial is one of the ways he is able to feel, as a bodily sensation, his intense love for his daughters. The book must be held on his lap just so, so that each of them, squirming under bedclothes, can hang out of the beds' sides and follow the pictures. The stories are baby stories, for the benefit of Poppy, but Lily doesn't mind. They remind her of when she was young.

He reads *Goodnight Moon*. Their lips move as they follow the familiar words with him.

'Goodnight comb. And goodnight brush. Goodnight nobody. Goodnight mush. And goodnight to the old lady whispering hush.'

Poppy's finger touches each item as it's named. Martin reads slowly, because this is bedtime, and soon they'll be asleep.

'Goodnight stars. Goodnight air. Goodnight noises everywhere.'

He kisses them, kneeling on the floor so that he can rest his head beside theirs on the pillow. Out goes the reading lamp, to leave only the soft pink glow of the night light.

'Sleep tight, my darling ones.'

'Daddy Daddy, what shall I dream about?'

'Dream about—'

He scours unvisited corners of his mind, all the more available notions long ago exhausted. His eyes fall on a rarely-worn pair of fluffy slippers.

'Dream about slippers. A family of slippers. And they have a birthday party.'

There's usually a birthday party, or a wedding.

So he leaves, pausing for a moment in the doorway to look back on the two heads, already snuffling into sleep. This is his treasure.

Downstairs, Jenny has made his cup of tea, aware to the second how long it will take him to tuck up the girls. She is back studying the newspaper, the property pages of last Friday's *Sussex County*

Chronicle.

'Listed historic *farmhouse*,' she reads out to him, letting the emphasis fall gently but devastatingly on the last word. 'Five bedrooms, outbuildings, mature garden, tennis court, swimming pool, nine acres. One million three hundred thousand.'

He drinks his tea and savours her soft-spoken contempt in silence.

'Rare opportunity to buy a substantial family home in sought-after Downland village. Period *farmhouse* modernized to a high standard. Nine hundred and fifty thousand.'

She closes the newspaper. Again, she looks up and smiles for him, because she's almost too weary to smile.

'How's it been today?' he says.

'You don't want to know.'

'Can't be much longer.'

'Lily was two weeks late. If I have another week of this I'll, I don't know what I'll do. I'm peeing every five minutes.'

Martin feeds on the sight of his pretty wife, so pink-cheeked and bonny, the very picture of a wholesome country lass.

'I saw lordy about the rent today,' he says, using the name by which Billy Holland is known across the Edenfield Estate. 'He said there's nothing he can do. I'm to talk to Shit and Fucker.'

'What a surprise! Why didn't we think of that? He's as helpless as we are. He can only sit there with his mouth open while his agents stuff him with cash.'

Martin listens, his good temper restored by his wife's soft stream of venom. Theirs is a good marriage, cemented, as so many good marriages are, by a shared hatred of their enemies. Over the years of their union, which has coincided with a decline in farm revenues, they have armed themselves for what has become a state of siege in an unending war. The enemies are the townies who have relocated to the country, and now form the majority. The townies are frightened of cows, and object to the mud left by tractors in country lanes, and think rabbits are cuddly pets, and seek to preserve the habitat of wild flowers. They have children who are shocked by the sight of animal carcasses and call themselves vegetarians but eat burgers and sausages. They have a townie religion according to which nature is holy, and man, the perverter of nature, is the source of evil. They think of the English countryside as an unspoiled natural environment now under threat, unaware that it is the most intensely farmed landscape in the world, and that everything they see and love has been fashioned by the hard labour of men. Born and bred in regions of tarmac and paving stones, they have no inkling of the raw power of the land, with which civilized man has been doing battle since the dawn of time. Let the despised farmers withdraw from their ceaseless vigilance and within a few short years the wilderness would return, in all its monstrous abundance. Not stately groves of beech trees, not waist-high meadows of flowering grasses, but bramble and nettle and thorn, thistle and ragwort and bindweed. In this desolate wasteland toxic chemicals will be dumped, drug addicts will ply their needles, and rapists will lie in wait for children playing truant from school.

'Put on some water for the potatoes, will you?'

Martin does as he is asked, and more. He will gladly wash and scrub the potatoes, halve the bigger ones, nick out the eyes, put them in a pan, and check them as they cook. New potatoes spoil if over-cooked, they go soft and disintegrate. Fifteen minutes in boiling water, and they should come out sweet as nuts.

'Caught those bloody boys chasing the cows again.'

'Shoot them,' says Jenny.

'God knows I'd like to.'

'Really they should all be culled when young. The population of bankers is out of control.'

Martin bends down and kisses her, lingering to feel her swollen belly.

'How is he?'

'He's a damn wriggler.'

Martin can feel the baby moving. The sensation of touching his wife and his unknown child all in the same moment overwhelms him. The water in the potato pan starts to bubble, rattling the lid.

The front door bell rings.

Nobody uses the front door. Frowning, Martin goes out by the back door, to the side of the house, and calls, 'Who is it?'

Shortly two middle-aged ladies appear, making their way with uncertain steps into the farmyard. They both wear cord britches, thick socks, serious boots. They both clutch extendable ski-poles. They both have very small rucksacks on their backs. They are ramblers. This is bad enough in itself; but they are in his yard, and that is unforgivable.

'I do hope we're not disturbing you.' The one who speaks is tall and has grey hair. 'We've been following the South Downs way. We're putting up in the village pub for the night. Such a pretty village! We were wondering if we could take a peep inside your lovely barn. It is eighteenth century, isn't it?'

Martin stares unblinkingly back at her. He speaks with no inflection of any kind.

'Perhaps you'd like a guided tour.'

'Oh, well! If you could spare the time.'

They give each other quick excited looks that say, Aren't we lucky! Martin contemplates their rainproof jackets, the straps on their ski-poles, the maps in clear plastic pockets dangling on strings round their necks.

'Follow me.' He crosses the yard towards the barn doors. 'This entire complex of historic buildings is what used to be called a *farm*. Using entirely traditional methods, the farm workers used to manage the land *in order to produce food*. Of course, today the raw material for food is shipped in from cheaper countries, processed in factories, flavour-enhanced and packaged for the convenience of the modern consumer.'

They have reached the barn doors. The ramblers are exchanging nervous glances.

'Why! Here's a surprise! The barn is still being used to store animal feeds! Can this farm be caught in a time warp? Are we seeing ghosts of the past?'

'I do hope we're not a nuisance—'

'As I expect you've already guessed, what we have here is a working model, staffed by trained historians who take on the roles of farm workers in order to bring the past to life.'

'I think we should be going, Louise.'

Puzzled by Martin's absence, Jenny appears at the open back door.

'There! The farmer's wife, looking out into the authentically-recreated farmyard. If we're lucky, we'll see her feed the happy hens who peck and scratch the organic soil, ranging freely where they will—'

'You've been most kind. Come on, Louise.'

Martin's voice rises, becomes a little more shrill.

'You will note that the farmer's wife is in calf. Traditionally all farm animals are mated in the early autumn and calve in the spring, in time for the new grass.'

'Oh, dear. Oh, dear.'

He pursues the now thoroughly alarmed lady ramblers up the track towards the lane, his voice rising once more, to a helpful shout.

'And here we have another traditional figure, going about the Lord's affairs. Yes, it's the village parson, the friend of the poor.'

The rector is passing, on his way to the church. He is accompanied by Mrs Huxtable, another impossibly tall older woman, who leans sideways and wags over the little rector as they go, no doubt telling him his business, as is her habit. Martin is now in full flood.

'I can only apologize that the authentic game of cricket on the village green has been cancelled, following accusations of match-fixing, and pending the results of the drug tests.'

The grey-haired lady rambler throws a frightened glance back at Martin.

'I'm so sorry,' she says.

Martin too now stops. Those timid eyes chasten him. He draws a long breath.

'I'm sorry too,' he says. 'We're all sorry. We live in a sorry world.'

He bows his head, and turns back down the rutted lane to his farmhouse. The potatoes will be ready, and must be taken off the stove and drained. He must run his bath. He must update his accounts. He must feed his dogs. He must stand in the bedroom doorway and look on his girls, asleep in the rosy light.

17

The Reverend Miles Salmon agrees with Mrs Huxtable on the matter of Trick or Treat. Although this seems to be what she wants, which is his assent, his endorsement of her views, his actual answer does not satisfy her.

'That's all very well, Miles. But for evil to triumph, it's only necessary for the good to remain silent.'

'Oh, yes. Absolutely.'

'I know it's all supposed to be fun for the little ones. But what lesson is it teaching them? That witches, and devils, and bad spirits of all kinds, are a joke. Are they a joke, Miles?'

'Yes. Quite.'

'No, I'm asking you as a minister of the Christian church. Are the powers of evil a suitable subject for children's games?'

'No, no.'

'Then surely you must say so.'

'Yes. Indeed.'

'When will you say so?'

'Well, you see, in a way I'm saying so now.'

Mrs Huxtable smiles. She has extracted from the rector an implied disagreement. She knows from her long experience of committees how important it is to provoke the opposition into revealing its true colours. The reason so little ever gets done is that the English middle classes are crippled by politeness. Face to face, they will not confront each other, and so their conflicts are rarely resolved. Of course once a disagreement is flushed like a frightened pheasant into open view, a less aggressive strategy becomes appropriate. Careful handling is called for. The pheasant must be chivvied into the path of the guns.

'Miles, I do understand your position. You don't want to appear a killjoy. You don't want Christians to be seen as killjoys.'

'Just so. There you are, you see.'

'But you must say something.'

She smiles again. It's her duty to give him some of the superabundance of her own strength, so that he can do the right thing. Duty and strength. And love, of course.

'From the pulpit, Miles.'

'Ah, yes. You think so?'

'This Sunday. Halloween is six months away. I doubt if anyone will be thinking much about it, one way or the other. But once stated, clearly and unequivocally, the ruling, as it were, will be on the statute book. Then Oliver and I and Margaret and the others can spread the word.'

This is Mrs Huxtable's plan. She is fully aware of the rector's shortcomings. All she requires is his statement from the pulpit, to which she can then refer. It wouldn't do for people to say that the ban on Trick or Treat originated from her herself. She is to be no more than the agent of enforcement.

'Good,' says the rector, seeing her turn to leave. 'That's settled, then.'

'Thank you, Miles. I'm sorry to bother you over this.'

In the church door, just before passing from view, and following another of her precepts learned in the committee room, she pauses to summarize the meeting's conclusion.

'Just so there's no confusion. You have agreed to speak against Trick or Treat from the pulpit this Sunday.'

'That's the thing,' says the rector.

With this, Joan Huxtable decides to be satisfied.

Miles Salmon, left alone in the chilly church, moves slowly down the aisle making sure that all is as it should be. The church is not beautiful. It was over-restored in the late nineteenth century, and the dark oak with which it was then lined and decorated is ornate without being delicate, lending to the long shadowy tunnel of the nave the saddened air of a guildhall built for some long-declined trade. A colourful banner, stitched by the members of the Mothers Union for the millennium, proclaims JOY TO THE WORLD in irregular scarlet letters on a yellow ground. The joy makes little headway against the gloom. The church is not listed in the guidebooks, and is of no special interest to anyone, except perhaps to the local families whose many generations are remembered on wall plaques and brasses, and in the undistinguished nineteenth-century stained glass windows.

Nevertheless, St Mary's Edenfield does receive occasional visitors, and these visitors do not always respect its dignity. The rector has found sweet wrappers, empty cider bottles, even used condoms between the pews. For himself, he takes no offence at this. If people come to his empty church to eat sweets, drink cider, and make love, he's happy that the building is proving useful. But there is a view in the parish that the church should be locked except when in use, and he doesn't want to supply evidence for this case. All four church wardens, whose job it is to clean the church, and who therefore resent any activity that disturbs the dark and polished silence, are stalwart door-lockers. So every evening the Reverend Salmon cleans the pews himself.

He is a small slight man with prominent eyes and ears that stick out like mug handles; now entering his sixty-eighth year; mild of manner, and without an enemy in the village. There are those who complain that he is spineless, but even they criticize him without animus. Those that speak highly of him use terms more commonly associated with pets. He is 'a dear sweet man', he 'understands every word you say', he is 'a comfort'.

The rector switches off the lights, and emerging into the small porch, draws the door shut after him. In the dusk of the churchyard he sees one of his parishioners, old Dick Waller, tending his son's grave. Dick's boy was killed in a head-on collision on the notorious straight stretch of the A27 that runs from Edenfield roundabout to Middle Farm. He was seventeen.

'Best kept grave in the churchyard, Dick.'

'So it should be, vicar.' Dick Waller is the head gardener at Edenfield Place.

He straightens up, brushes the soil from his knees, and eyes the orderly display of pelargoniums.

'I like to think he knows I've not forgotten.'

'Oh, he does, he does. He watches you as you plant the flowers for him, and he smiles, I'm sure he smiles. He knows that where he is now the flowers never fade. He's waiting for the day when you can join him, and he can show you his garden, and say to you, Nothing for you to do here, Dad.'

'Oh, I shouldn't like that. I like to be busy.'

'He smiles when he hears you say that, too.'

'I wish I could believe it, vicar.'

'You don't have to believe it, Dick. Just tell yourself it might be so. And when your time comes, well, start thinking what you might say to him, if he were to be there, waiting for you.'

'I should tell him he was a damn fool on that road.'

'So he was, Dick.'

'But I should like to see him again. I don't deny that.'

So they part, the rector and the gardener, both much of an age. It's over twenty years since Dick Waller's boy was killed, but as he leaves the churchyard and climbs into his pick-up, his eyes are blurring. Unable to see to drive, he sits in the cab without turning on the engine and thinks of nothing much, and is comforted.

The rector continues on his way, passing just beyond the yew trees the handsome Georgian house that would once have been his home. The old rectory was sold long ago. These days Judge Huxtable lives there, second in social standing only to Lord Edenfield himself. The rector is housed in a terraced Victorian cottage on the village high street, built originally for the estate carpenter. Miles Salmon has enjoyed the use of this cottage for thirty-seven years, all by himself, and he has made it fit his habits and needs so precisely that he couldn't conceive of living anywhere else.

In the street near his gate he meets old Mrs Willis, hunched in her electric buggy, also on her way home. Because she is deaf, and her head is bent down so that she sees only the road before her, he touches her on the shoulder as she goes by and speaks to her in a loud clear voice.

'Almost home, Gwen.'

She brings her buggy to a stop with a jerk that causes her to rock forward.

'That you, vicar?'

'Of course it is. How are you today, my dear?'

The rector shouts. The old lady whispers.

'I've had another one, vicar.'

'Another one, eh? And what is it this time?'

Mrs Willis has visitations from the spirit world. Her most frequent contact is a Native American chief's daughter called Standing Holy.

'There's to be a surprise visitor, vicar. I must be true to my heart.'

'True to your heart, Gwen? Do you have a secret lover?'

'No, vicar, no.' She laughs a small tinkling laugh.

'You take care, Gwen. Don't go letting strange men into the house.'

'No need to worry about me, vicar. All is to be destroyed in the coming whirlwind.'

Gwen Willis's spirit contact has told her that a great whirlwind is to sweep over the face of the earth, causing lamentation and destroying property.

'The whirlwind, yes,' says the rector. 'I remember.'

'You must tell people, vicar. They don't listen to me.'

'I'll do my best, Gwen.'

The electric buggy jerks into motion once more. Miles Salmon heads on through the gate into his own house, walking with the unhurried step and slightly bowed head he adopted long ago, as the demeanour proper to a parish priest. But as soon as his front door closes behind him, unaware that he is doing this, he unfolds like a music stand and becomes a different man. He unbuttons his clerical collar and shrugs off his black jacket. He exchanges his black lace-up shoes for a pair of rope-soled slippers. He mixes himself a small but potent vodka martini. Then he sits down with his untouched copy of the *Times*, and opens the paper to the Court and Social page. This is the only page he ever reads. He gave up all other forms of the news long ago.

The High Sheriff has given a breakfast at the Ritz Hotel, London W1. The 346th Annual Festival Service of the Corporation of the Sons of the Clergy has been held in St Paul's Cathedral, the sermon preached by the Bishop of London with twelve other bishops in attendance. On this day, Mafeking was relieved and the Daylight Saving Act passed, though in different years. As he reads there steals over him a state of mind and body to which he looks forward all day, a gentle floating sensation, an elevated perspective on the world, not unlike, he imagines, that of God the Creator himself. From this furry cloud he gazes down on the doings of men with keen amusement. Their grandeurs and follies, and ultimately their futility, of which they are so childishly unaware, parade themselves before his unjudging eyes as a kind of pre-prandial cabaret. In all this, Miles Salmon makes no presumption of superiority himself. He may see as the Creator sees, but he too is a creature. He too, with his failed ambitions and lost dreams, is a joke.

Only now, fortified by alcohol and irony, does he turn to his phone messages. Dutifully he writes down the calls to be returned in the morning. One requires immediate action. Peter Ansell, the Diocesan Secretary, would like an urgent word. This charming young man with the lowly title is in fact the most powerful official in the diocese, the aging bishop not excepted.

'Oh, Miles. What have you been saying now?'

Ansell's voice contains no accusation. He runs the diocese through a complex process of collusion.

'What am I said to be saying?' responds Miles.

'Apparently you've been alleging that the Church of England deals in drugs.'

'Have I? When?'

'A charity event. St James's Hospice.'

Of course, the silent auction to raise money for the local hospice.

'Yes, yes. I was asked to say a few words. I think I was making a point about the comforts of faith, you know. Faith versus morphine. Faith allied with morphine. I'm sorry, I'm not making myself clear.'

'I think I get the picture. I'm afraid the stoats and the weasels are everywhere these days. Do be more careful.'

'Yes. I will.'

'The bishop has had a phone call. I'll respond on his behalf. Confusion caused by use of imagery. Bang this one on the head.'

'Thank you, Peter.'

Miles sighs as he hangs up, and sets about cooking his evening meal. There's rarely any trouble within the parish. It's the outer world, the non-churchgoing spectators, who insist upon high moral standards and doctrinal orthodoxy. Fortunately the only sins that attract attention are sexual, whereas Miles's failure is entirely theological. To be specific, some years ago he stopped believing in the divinity of Jesus. After that more and more of the tenets of Christianity dropped away; until the day came when he stopped believing in God altogether. For a time he had supposed this was a crisis, and that he would be obliged to resign his living; but before he could summon up the courage to leave his beloved house, and rather to his surprise, he found that having no faith made him a much better parish priest. Lacking any certainty of his own, he took to responding, humbly and lovingly, to the needs of those who came to him in trouble. His job, it was plain, was to give comfort; so he told each sufferer whatever it was he or she wanted to hear.

His loss of faith has not turned to anger or bitterness against Christianity, he has simply come to read the Gospels as he reads Bunyan or Milton or Blake. There are profound values there, and wisdom, and poetry. But if one of his parishioners becomes convinced she's in contact with Sitting Bull's daughter, a spirit who reveals to her that a whirlwind is coming to destroy the world, well, who is he to tell her it's nonsense?

Miles Salmon has concluded that God does not exist, but that religion is both real and necessary. He does sometimes worry that he must contradict himself daily, but his experience over the years has taught him that people are less interested in consistency, or even in truth, than one might suppose. What they care about is being right. And when viewed from the privileged vantage point of his vodka-induced cloud, they can all be said to be right, in their own terms.

For his supper this evening he has a tinned steak-and-kidney pudding from Marks & Spencer. Its instructions call for half-an-hour in a pan of boiling water. He puts the water on to boil, pours himself a second drink, and takes it out through the back door into his small back garden. It's not much more than a patch of lawn, a flower bed beneath a south-facing wall, but he's been tending it for so long now that it feels like an extension of himself.

A single wicker chair stands on the raised paving to the left of the door, too small an area to call a terrace, but here each evening when the weather permits he sits and sips his second drink. He has no newspaper, no book. His eyes read the ever-changing story of his miniature realm.

The prunus in the far corner is shedding the last of its blossom, the litter of white petals now curling on the grass, discolouring to the tones of the earth. The daffodils and the tulips are long over. A few purple irises are still in bloom, standing proudly apart from each other. The roses are coming into bud, another month at least before they flower, the Empereur du Maroc first, its clustered fists swelling to such an impossible size before they unleash the great maroon flowers. He has trained a climber up the wall, a Zéphirine Drouhin, and nearer the house spreads his beloved Cristata with its bearded buds. June is not far off now, the time of glory, when his garden will glow with crimsons and pinks, and the water meadows beyond the wall will be sweet with the scent of summer all the way to the river.

The phone rings, summoning him back into the house.

'I hope I'm not getting you at a bad time.' The voice of Laura Broad. He calls her image to mind. Not a churchgoer, but Miles Salmon prides himself on knowing everyone in the village, by name at least.

'Not at all. How can I help?'

'I've been working in the library at Edenfield Place, and come on a reference to someone who would have lived in the village in the fifties. The only name I have is Doll. I'm trying to trace her.'

'Doll? No, I don't know of any Doll. But I only go back to 1963, I'm afraid.'

Later, eating his supper, reading *Mansfield Park*, he is nagged by the ghost of a memory. He knows he has heard or seen this name before.

Who do I know called Doll?

18

The headmaster finds Alan Strachan alone in his classroom.

'Oh, Alan. Thought you were long gone. What's this about Alice Dickinson?'

Long gone certainly. Only my outer form remains, taking refuge in routine work from the heart-sucker, the vacuum-cleaner of joy, the waiting void.

'No idea.'

'Crying in the changing rooms for no reason.'

Holy smoke, the man's a philosopher! The authentic wail of humanity: *crying in the changing rooms for no reason*. Dear Alastair however seems all unaware of the depths he plumbs.

'I wasn't told.'

'She's one of yours. Look into it, will you?'

'Yes, of course.'

'Single parent, you know.'

'I'll have a word tomorrow.'

Why am I colluding with this meeting of the eyes, this imperceptible lift of the shoulders? Is the pain of existence reserved for the children of single parents? Enter the Two Hypocrites. First Hypocrite: I believe what I say because I am stupid. Second Hypocrite: I say what I don't believe because I am afraid.

'If you're likely to be around for the next half hour, I wonder—'

'Just off, actually.'

I'm not supervising boarders' prep, no sirree. I swear they think round here that a man without a wife is a man without a life. How laughably far from the mark that is. So it's home to my full and frank existence to unpack the cargo of my loaded hours.

Just get up and go.

Five minutes from door to door if the lidless Beetle does the only thing it was created to do. What does a car feel when it fails to start? Failure. Go with that feeling, brother, use it, find its force, turn it to positive energy. Depression is displaced anger, anger is displaced love. There's a through-line from what you're feeling now to the greatest power in creation, which is love. So just fucking ignite your mixture, okay?

Frum-frum-frumble-frumble. Five minutes. Time enough to make a plan. There's a room waiting where old friends have turned traitor and are in league to hurt me. I refer to item, one desk, upon whose surface lie Post-It notes bearing brief creative exudations; item, one keyboard, much caressed by my own heated fingertips; item, one swivel chair upon which I have swivelled with the masters. All now have joined the conspiracy. A great betrayal has taken place. From a faraway command post the sinister unseen leader of the coup, Lorraine Jones, Script Editor, has suborned my former allies and equipped them with knives with which to stab me.

Lorraine, you underestimate me. You think because my play lacks the dramatic quality necessary for compulsive radio listening that I am made of milk and water. But I will not be tipped over and left to drain into the long grass. You think I am crushable. See me unfold. Am I downhearted? See me celebrate. This evening not an end but a beginning. This evening I please myself.

In this way Alan Strachan tempers the molten stuff of self-indulgence into the keen blade of defiance. He has a plan. He will not sink into the sweet seductive arms of melancholy. He will celebrate.

The celebration is shaped by its component parts. In the cupboard under the stairs there rests a bottle of Meursault, given him at the end of last summer term by a child he has now forgotten, no doubt pulled from daddy's cellar by mummy, who didn't know quite how good it was, and saved since then for an appropriate occasion. It should however be given time to chill. To eat he has eggs, he has bread, he has olive oil. An omelette and a glass of wine. Who said that? And while the white burgundy achieves its perfect drinking temperature, let the self-pleasing begin with the simplest and the best life has to offer: the premeditated wank.

Now that's what I call a plan.

He leaves the car as always in the street outside his house, and unlocks his front door for the second time this day, humming the melody of 'Stranger on the Shore', which a child practised on a saxophone in his hearing in afternoon break, and has lodged in his brain. He hums when he's nervous. Lorraine Jones is waiting for him.

Moving rapidly, looking only at what he needs to see, he extracts the bottle of wine from the under-stair cupboard and lays it horizontal in the fridge in the kitchen. He passes through into the front room, in which he has been accustomed to pursue the activity about which he is not thinking, and opens the bottom right-hand drawer of an item of furniture that has no known function. In the drawer, beneath crammed paper files, his fingers feel for the shiny surface of a magazine. Passing back through the kitchen, magazine in his right hand, he scoops the cordless phone with his left hand from its cradle on the wall, and so makes good his escape up the narrow stairs.

Do your worst, Lorraine Jones. I have faced your crack troops and come through unscathed. Watch and weep.

In the bedroom he tosses magazine and phone onto the bed and draws the curtains closed against the afternoon daylight. He switches on the reading lamp by the bed and switches off the harsher more God-like centre light. He stacks the two pillows, one on the other, against the bed head. He feels inside the box of Kleenex that sits on the bedside table, and eases out three tissues to form a graspable bulge for future use. He takes off shoes, trousers, underpants. He settles himself on top of the duvet and bedcover, his back supported by the pillows, and taking up the magazine, begins to turn the pages from the back towards the front.

Yes, the look is inherently ludicrous: clothed to the waist, naked below as far as the socks. But who is there to see? Unobserved by all, he creates his own reality. He is about to enter another world, a world where everything is as he wants it to be.

In no hurry, he lets his eyes roam over the advertisements for phone sex services. 'Fuck my tight hole.' 'Stick your cock in me from behind.' 'Just wank as I finger my wet cunt.' The crude words are balm to his troubled soul. Here is an unequivocal promise that will be delivered. That for which he longs will come to pass. Lorraine Jones has no power here. Lorraine Jones is helpless.

Lorraine Jones is waiting for me, naked, legs spread in invitation.

He laughs aloud. Is this just a touch obvious? Too much of a give-away? What the fuck. It's all a game.

Will you do this for me, Lorraine? Not reluctantly. Anything but reluctantly. You have to get into the spirit of the thing. You have to give it all you've got. And in return, I will make you beautiful. I will illumine you with the flattering glow of my desire.

'Thirty second wank-off action. No long intros, no boring rubbish. Dirty hard fuck talk which will make you cum over your hand and phone GUARANTEED!'

Tell me about it. Like at one pound a minute you're going to let me get away with a 50p orgasm? Hope springs eternal. Once, dialling a number he was never able subsequently to rediscover, he stumbled *in medias res*, with no preamble of any kind, and experienced the essential wonder of a joy granted before it was looked for, without struggle; a sweet grace. But never since.

He only uses the pre-recorded services. Many, perhaps most of the services cry LIVE! ONE-2-ONE!, but the presence of a living woman on the other end of the line would contaminate the dream. What could he say to her, or she to him? Better by far the scripted recorded voice, with all its mock eagerness and its mock cries of ecstasy, because what is this but the performance of a play, a one-woman show for an audience of one?

He dials the number. A cheery female voice, English attempting American, begins thus:

'Cock, cunt, fuck, spunk are some of the words used on this line.'

Alan Strachan is impressed. As an English teacher and sometime stylist he appreciates the unusual construction: lead with your aces, seize the attention, turn the object into the subject. Rules exist to be broken. Moreover, now reverting to his role as consumer of this service at one pound a minute, he understands that a contract has been made. Correct terms will be applied throughout. No nonsense about proud manhood, melting hunger, sweet jets of passion. There's a time for imagery and a time to tell it like it is.

'You must be over eighteen to use this service,' continues the cheery voice, 'because our girls are kinky, horny, dirty tarts who love to fuck.'

So that will have weeded out the seventeen-year-olds. But mock not, this is excellent material, and entirely beyond the reach of irony.

As a matter of fact irony can fuck off. No such thing as an ironic erection.

Tenderly, like a fond parent waking a sleeping child, he tickles his curled cock in his lap. An answering tingle runs down his bare legs as far as his socks.

'We have no stuck-up bitches on this line, only girls who when they see cock, take cock! In their mouths, in their arses, up their cunts! Your climax is guaranteed! The girls on this line will leave you with spunk dripping all over your phone! You have been warned!'

This is beginning to sound like the boring intro which the mendacious advert promised to omit. He could hang up and try another number, but the likelihood is that he'll come in at the start of another intro, and so be at least two pounds behind. He might as well stay where he is. In due course, another two pounds or so later, the promissory future tense will give way to the present tense, and the party can begin.

'Are you ready for some seriously hot sex action? Get your cock out and get ready, because in just a minute we've got a gorgeous girl coming on line. She's got her knickers round her ankles and her fingers in her pussy and she just loves to wank herself off.'

Pussy? This is breach of contract. We English wankers do not thrill to the feline. Give us back our unlovely but erotically charged *cunt*.

'You've dialled the UK's number one porno wank line. All our fuck-hungry tarts guarantee to give you the wank of your life. All our girls have tight hard asses, and juicy moist pussies. So, stiff boy, I hope you've got your cock in hand . . .'

We've been here before. Lose marks for padding. Even so, past experience suggests that the most brazen smut-peddler starts the show in the end. When that happens the intro tape gives way to a second tape, with a different voice. Please God I don't get a script about her first fuck or some such past-tense shit. I don't want another man in the room. Don't tell me about his giant dick. I want her talking to me, alone. I want her saying she wants to have sex with me. That's the game, that's the show, that's what I'm paying for: no memories, no promises, in the present, now.

Here it comes, the new voice. Is this you, Lorraine?

'Hi, there. In a moment I'm going to bend over the sofa and let you fuck me from behind. But what's the hurry, big boy? First, why don't I give you a sexy view of my wet pussy from below?'

Bingo! This is the real thing. Direct speech, real time. Do it for me, Lorraine!

Alan can feel his cock responding with an equal enthusiasm. He runs his fingers up the insides of his thighs: this such a precious moment, the moment before, the time of awakening, when he feels his entire body tense and become alert, as his cock fills and grows.

'Now I'm standing over you. There. Look up. I've still got my panties on, but you can see how wet my pussy is, can't you? Look, I'm pulling my panties tighter, so you can see the shape of my cunt lips.'

Aah. Pussy has become cunt. The more powerful for the delayed use. A real writer at work here. This piece has the dramatic quality necessary for compulsive radio listening.

'Reach up. Feel my arse. Feel my pussy through my panties. You like that? My, that's a fine hard cock you've got there!'

And so it is. In so short a time his cock has reared up into full erection. His fingers stroke it, up and down, up and down, not yet applying pressure. His body shivers with fuck longing. Ah, Lorraine! Who would have thought you would know what I want, to the word, to the acted act? See – I'm reaching up.

'Pull my panties down. Take it slowly. Down they come. Now look up. You see how I'm parting my thighs, bending my knees, all to give you a good view right up my naked cunt?'

Christ! I'll come if I'm not careful.

'Keep rubbing that gorgeous cock as you look. But don't come yet. Remember, I want you fucking me from behind!'

Mind reader. Reader of the minds of men. Pure interactive radio drama. And yes, there's going to be a satisfying climax.

The voice on the phone is still talking, but now from far off. At some point as his orgasm began he must have dropped the phone from his ear, he has no memory of doing so. With one trembling hand he recovers the phone and switches it off. Then he closes his eyes and lies perfectly still, allowing the sweet flood of orgasm to withdraw, sucking back down the million pathways of his body. He feels his cock shrinking, leaving behind a cooling trail of sperm. He pulls out the bulge of Kleenex and mops his belly, moving carefully over his cock-head, which is still sensitive even in retreat. Only then does he become aware of an alien sound.

Bang bang bang!

The front door. A voice calling.

'Mr Strachan! Please come quickly!'

Talk about timing. Reality intrudes, in the form of Mrs Temple-Morris. Alan Strachan jumps off the bed, pulls on trousers, fumbles for shoes.

She's standing on his doorstep, trembling.

'Please. Upstairs. Noises.'

She can hardly form the words. Her teeth are chattering.

'Yes. Of course.'

Why am I doing this? I have no weapon, no means of self-defence. I'm not even wearing underpants.

He goes into the next door house and stands at the bottom of the stairs, stamping his feet. He shouts, 'Who's there?'

No answer. He listens. No sound. He goes up the stairs, his heart hammering, and opens doors, and looks without entering, and then enters. An unused spare room, empty. A main bedroom, also empty. He forces himself to look in a wardrobe, makes a token sweep behind hanging coats and dresses. Nothing.

'It's all right. No one here.'

'I'm so sorry to trouble you. Are you sure? When my husband's away overnight I get so nervous. I am so sorry.'

'No problem. I understand.'

'I heard banging noises. I thought it might be an intruder upstairs.'

'Not this time, I'm glad to say.'

'I'm most grateful. Most grateful.'

He returns to his house next door, which is divided from Mrs Temple-Morris's by the thickness of a party wall. Up in the bedroom Alan Strachan sees the copy of *Men Only* lying on the floor, on top of his unretrieved underpants. He sees the phone and the crumpled Kleenex still on the bed. He sees the pillows crushed against the bed head. He sees how the bed head tilts on the uneven floorboards, leaning against the party wall. The memory of orgasm has gone, obliterated by the three minutes of fear he felt in Mrs Temple-Morris's house, before he learned that the man she had heard making banging noises upstairs was himself.

As he clears the bed, pulls the bedclothes straight, replaces the pillows, he is struck by how little remains. The pleasure so intense, now so entirely gone. Our revels now are ended. Though there's still the bottle of white Burgundy chilling in the fridge. Meursault against the void.

An omelette and a glass of wine. Yes, it comes back to him now. The cookery writer Elizabeth David.

He goes down to the kitchen and turns on the television for company while he cooks. Some football game. He lets it run. The commentator's voice fills the room, together with the baying of the crowd. He glances at the screen from time to time, but makes no attempt to follow the action. He cracks eggs and drinks wine and discovers he is forming a new idea about his play. He lets the idea grow without making any further demands on it, while he cooks and then eats his omelette, and drinks his wine.

His idea makes him laugh. Not for the BBC of course. Some small London theatre, the Bush or the Gate. Give it a shot. Nothing to lose.

He switches off the television and carries his glass through to the front room. He turns on his computer and opens the file that contains the latest version of his play. His idea requires him to change one character. Give her a new occupation. Change her name, too. To what?

He summons up the Find/Replace box and commands that the name SHANA FINN be replaced throughout with the name ELIZABETH DAVID. Then he starts to work on her dialogue. Elizabeth is a foul-mouthed young woman. In her defence, she is a single mother who needs the money. She charges a pound a minute. Her objective is to keep the audience on the hook for the duration of the play.

ELIZABETH   Hi there. In a moment, I'm going to bend over the sofa and let you fuck me from behind.

19

Alice Dickinson sits in her grandmother's house staring out of the window.

What I don't understand is why does Granny have to go on? Other people's grannies give them treats and keep chocolate biscuits in a drawer and don't go on at them with every single thing they do. I'm supposed to be perfect just because I'm her grandchild or something. So how come she's not perfect? Which she is not. She's cruel to her little dog in my opinion, hitting him when he yaps, and in general she's always angry and she says things. But I don't care. It's all totally random.

'Alice dear, don't just sit there staring into space. Why don't you read that book I found for you?'

Because that book you found for me is super dull and I don't understand a word and Mum told me it's sad in the end and I don't like books with sad endings. Also as it happens I'm not staring into space I'm looking out of the window to see when Mum is coming.

'Alice. I spoke to you.'

'Did you, Granny?'

'You know you heard me. You're not deaf.'

'Sorry, Granny.'

Sorry I'm not deaf. I wouldn't mind being deaf. There's not so much people say that's worth hearing and there's lots you're better off not hearing.

'You know, Alice, it's not easy for me having you after school like this. I do think the very least you could do is speak when you're spoken to.'

'Yes, Granny.'

Now she's going to do that noise she does, that's like she has a problem breathing and may die soon. I wish she would. Pip, pip, pip, here is the news. Grannies are not the only ones having a hard life. You try being in 6B with Chloe Redknapp and Emma Biggs staring at you and not saying anything when you speak and saying to each other, 'Did you hear a sound, Emma? I thought I heard a faraway squeaking.' Actually I don't care because Chloe and Emma don't have friends they have slaves and I'm not the slave type.

'If you're not going to go on with *Black Beauty* then I think you can make yourself useful.'

Oh God she's going to make me pick flowers or something. Hurry up, Mum. I know you said to be helpful to Granny because she's helping us but you don't know how awful it is. What I'd really like is for you to have a taxi take me home like Victoria Clemmer does and I'd wait there till you get back from work. I could make you your supper and have it waiting for you when you come in, when you're always so tired and hungry. I can do pasta I'm pretty sure and I could certainly lay the table. You could ring me on your mobile when you're nearly home and I'd have everything ready.

'You could help me sort out the photographs. I've been meaning to do that for a long time. I think it would interest you. I have photographs of your mother when she was a little girl of your age.'

'Actually, Granny, I'm feeling quite tired.'

'Tired? Too tired to look at photographs?'

'Well yes, really.'

Now she's going to get all stressy, she's making that shape with her mouth. I don't care, it's true, I am tired. And anyway I don't want to see photographs of Mum when she was a girl because Granny will start telling me how Granddad left and that is so ultra boring.

'I simply don't know what to do about you, Alice. You have no interest in anything. Are you like this at school?'

'Oh, yes.'

'Doesn't it make your teachers very cross?'

'Sometimes.'

'So why do you do it? I can't believe you're just a lazy, selfish, badly-brought-up little girl.'

'I expect I am really.'

Just stop going on at me. I don't care. Think what you like about me. Mum'll come soon now. It's Mum and me and all the rest of the world can blow itself up we don't care. If Mum died I'd die too at once, I'd kill myself. Maybe if I ask her she'll let me not go to school. Only who'd look after me when she's away at work? She works for both of us, she's brave and clever and I'll do anything she asks me, even sit here for hours with Granny going on at me.

A car in the road outside. Yesss! Slowing down. Heaven heaven heaven soon.

'I think that might be Elizabeth now.'

Everyone else calls her Liz. She's her own daughter, why does she have to talk about her as if she's a stranger?

'Don't be in such a rush, Alice. I need to have a word with your mother before you go.'

Car stopping. Car door opening, shutting. Quick footsteps on gravel. Mum always walks fast. Her hand on the front door handle—

'Mum!'

'Hallo, darling. There's a welcome.'

Oh Mum I've missed you and I love you, I love the feel of your arms and the smell of your perfume and the way you go on holding me long after you've kissed me. If only it could be for ever.

'Thanks for having her, Mummy. Has she had her supper?'

'She's been given supper, Elizabeth. But she's not a good eater, you know.'

'Oh, well. Never mind. Have you got your things, darling?'

Dear intelligent Mum knows not to ask questions even though Granny is absolutely bulging with all this random stuff she wants to say about me. That's the dearest thing of all about Mum, you don't need to say things to her, she just gets it.

'Alice, go out into the garden for a moment, will you? I need to talk to your mother.'

No! Tell her no, Mum! She can't! You're tired. We can go home now.

'Just very very quickly, Mummy. I've had a long day.'

Well if Granny thinks I'm not going to listen she can cha-cha-cha because this is about me and I'm entitled to defend myself. Just because I can't see you doesn't mean I can't hear you. People are always making that mistake. All you have to do is stay very still and no one knows you're there. That's how I heard Chloe Redknapp saying Alice Dickinson's a weirdo, let's just pretend she isn't there.

'It's Alice. What is the matter with her?'

'Nothing, as far as I know.'

'She's surly. Uncooperative. Dull. Elizabeth, she does nothing! You must have noticed.'

'She's fine with me.'

You tell her, Mum. Granny's the problem. I'm fine with you.

'I do think you may be missing something here, Elizabeth. After all, I probably spend more hours in your daughter's company than you do, because you choose to do a job—'

'I don't *choose*, Mummy. I have no *choice*. I must do a job or starve. There's no one else to pay the bills.'

'Yes, well, that was a choice you made, I seem to remember.'

'Oh? What choice was that?'

Don't shout, Mum. Don't get angry. Let's just go.

'Was that the *choice* not to marry a man who had no wish to marry me and never even suggested it? Was it the *choice* to have a baby when I could have had an abortion?'

'You know perfectly well what I'm talking about. Once these things start wrong they go on wrong and they end up wrong.'

'They end up wrong?'

No Mum don't be so hurt it doesn't matter let's just go home and be us and all the world be somewhere else.

'You mean Alice is ending up wrong? Because if that's what you mean then go on and say it.'

'Don't raise your voice to me, Elizabeth. That doesn't get anywhere.'

'SAY IT!'

I can't bear you to be so upset Mum, let me hold you, let me kiss you, it's all going to be all right, you see, I'm coming, I'm here—

'Alice! Darling! There, darling, there. It's nothing, nothing at all. We'll go home now.'

See, Mum, see. I saved you. Go on holding me for ever. I'll always save you.

'What can I say, Elizabeth? If you raise your voice, certain people hear.'

'Yes, all right, Mummy. I'm wrong as usual. I expect I started wrong. Now I'm tired and Alice has to get to bed so I think we'll just go now. Say thank you to Granny, Alice.'

'Thank you, Granny.'

She's making that shape with her mouth but I don't care I've got
Mum and I'll never let her go again.

The car is safety. I love our car.

'Were you listening?'

'Sort of. I couldn't help it.'

'I'd have listened.'

'I'm glad you came, Mum.'

'Darling. I'll always come. You know that.'

'Yes. I know that.'

Mum hates to be away from me and to have to work so hard, but
she does it for me, because she loves me, and that means she's so
clever and brave that just thinking about it makes me want to cry.
But I don't cry just like Chloe and Emma can't make me cry because
that's my way of helping Mum. I know how hard it is for her, and I
won't make it harder for her whatever they do to me. I only cried
a bit today because I twisted my ankle in games and it hurt, that's
all, it was nothing to do with those others, they don't bother me.

'So are you hungry?'

'A bit. Do you mind?'

'What did she give you?'

'Some meat. Some beans.'

'Some meat? You funny old thing.'

'I did try.'

'You'd better have some pasta with me.'

Darling Mum. She simply understands. She's bliss.

So we have this quiet supper together and she doesn't go on at me
in any way at all and I go to bed and everything's just fine so why I
start crying I don't know. I'm not even feeling sad, I'm feeling happy.
Mum's sitting on my bed stroking my hair and telling me how she
saw Dad today and how he wanted to know all about me which I bet
is lies but it's lies for love and I love her even more as I listen and
she strokes my hair, and all at once I'm crying and crying and can't
stop myself.

'Darling darling darling my own one my little one.'

'It's all right Mum, it's nothing, I'm fine.'

But there are all these tears.

'Tell me. Tell Mummy. I'll make it better.'

'No, really. Really.'

Crying and crying. Just hold me close, Mum. Hold me close for ever. I do love you so terribly much.

'Is it school? Are you having problems at school?'

'Not really. Nothing really.'

'Tell me, my darling. Let me help you.'

'Just some of the other girls, that's all. They're so stupid. I don't care. I'm only crying because I love you.'

'Tell me, my darling. What do they do?'

'Sometimes they pretend I'm not there. That's all. It's nothing.'

'They pretend you're not there?'

'Only some of the time.'

'How many of the girls do this?'

'Not all of them. Some of them.'

Not crying so much now. I mustn't cry, it upsets darling Mum. I can bear anything in the world except hurting her.

'See. I'm not crying any more. I'm fine.'

Don't look so worried, Mum. You're my beautiful mother. Everyone says so. Don't look so serious.

'They shouldn't do that to you, Alice. That's bullying.'

'Oh, no. No one hurts me. I just hurt myself.'

'You hurt yourself?'

'I twisted my ankle in games. That's what made me cry in the changing room. But it doesn't hurt now. Look, I've stopped. Everything's all right again.'

Oh those beautiful, sad eyes.

'Who are you supposed to talk to, at school? Who's your form teacher?'

'Mr Strachan.'

'Does he know this is going on?'

'Mr Strachan? No, of course not.'

How would he know? He's a teacher. Teachers have no idea of anything at all. They think Chloe Redknapp is just too darling with her little smiles and her perfect manners.

'You should have told me.'

'No, honest, I'm fine, Mum. I don't care. I don't even like them.'

'Oh, sweetheart.'

I'm going to start crying again and I won't, because Mum looks so sad and I know *exactly* what she's thinking because we always know what each other is thinking. She's thinking it's her fault because she doesn't spend enough time with me and it just isn't her fault, not remotely, and anyway I'm fine and I don't care.

'I'll try and call in at the school tomorrow. See if I can have a word with Mr Strachan.'

'What for, Mum? He can't do anything.'

'Don't worry. I won't embarrass you. Just a little chat about how you're getting on.'

'But you have to work.'

'I'll make some time. Now you must go to sleep.'

When Mum kisses me at night she's sitting on the bed and she leans down and I put my arms round her and give this little pull. At first she always resists but then she sort of folds down onto me and that's the moment I love the best, when I feel her weight on me. It's like then I know she'll always come to me, whatever stands between us, all I have to do is pull.

'Love you so much, Addle.'

That's my baby name. No one else in the whole world knows it, not even my dad. Only Mum and me. Only us two.

'Love you, Mum. Love you the most and the longest.'

'The most and the longest.'

When she leaves my room she always stops for a moment in the doorway and looks back at me, like she doesn't really want to leave me, and I love that moment too. Then she leaves and shuts the door because I've learned to sleep in the dark and now it's dark and I've still got the heaviness of her on me and the silhouette she makes in the doorway against the landing light and it's enough. It's all I want. Everything else is just random.

20

Marion sits in front of the television but she sees and hears nothing. The chattering screen is her chaperone. It wouldn't do to be sitting alone with her thoughts. Not after the extraordinary developments of this very evening. Also it's important that she doesn't over-excite herself. Dr Skilling has explained to her that her gift, which is her acute degree of sensitivity, is also a danger to her. Not that she needed Dr Skilling to tell her this. She has known since she was a little girl that she feels things more intensely than most people. Quite literally so: she has pale skin which burns easily, even in weak sunlight. Her eyes ache after too much reading. She feels the cold. But far more significant than mere physical symptoms, she suffers from, or is gifted with, a heightened sensitivity to emotions. She can tell what other people are feeling, even from the tiniest clues. With David, of course, the clues were anything but tiny. He had one response to all difficulties. 'Take your bloody pills, Marion.' She's told him more times than she can remember how important it is for her to remain calm, but he pays no attention. Well, he's not here now, so she can be as calm as she likes.

What a drama this evening! She goes over it in her mind once more, allowing the excitement to settle into memory. There was fear to start with, real fear. She heard banging noises upstairs. There was no doubt about it in her mind, she had an intruder. As soon as she grasped this fact she was flooded with terror. In her own house! Where could she go? The intruder could descend the stairs at any minute and assault her in her own living room. Her own house had become a trap. At once she left the house, and stood outside on the brick path, shivering in the cool air.

Was it then that I thought of Alan? No, earlier. From the very first wave of panic my mind reached out to him. Yes, even then, in the heart of the fear, there was a still small voice saying, This will change your life. Sometimes that's what it takes to bring people together, a crisis, a tragedy. You could say that's what brought David and I together. I would not have been in that place were it not for my crisis. You think if someone has witnessed the kind of pain that I went through that he'd understand you, but it's not true. I became more sensitive. David became more selfish.

What did I do? Did I shout? No, I knocked on the door. On his door. Well, he is my nearest neighbour. We share the same house, really. I've often been struck by that fact. You could even say that we're living together. My little joke.

He came very quickly. He saw with one glance how frightened I was. But as soon as he was there before me, I stopped being frightened. I think that tells you something. Young as he is, he has the power to make me feel safe. I know Dr Skilling would be very pleased to hear me talking this way. 'You need to be with people who calm you down, Marion,' he says. Guess who that does not include. With Alan all it took was one look and I knew he understood, and was in control. He's gentle, Alan, but he's not weak. You might think to look at him that he's frail because he's so thin, but it's the spirit that counts. Alan has the spirit of a tiger.

He went into my house. He went upstairs.

Alan went into my bedroom. Alan stood beside my bed. Alan was there, in my most private place, in the place where I sleep, in the place where I am utterly vulnerable. Even now, an hour or more after he's gone, I can feel his presence in my bedroom, as if he has altered the composition of the air in there. Which of course he has. He has breathed there. He has exhaled. There is a trace of Alan in the air of my bedroom. There now, there's a perfect example of my gift of sensitivity. Very few people would pick up so subtle a change as that.

I'll go to bed myself soon. Not quite yet, I'm not quite calm enough yet. But when I go upstairs I will in a sense be going up to Alan.

The intruder had gone, it seems. I don't trouble myself to puzzle out how. These incidents have multiple causes, and multiple effects. There may have been no intruder at all. It's perfectly possible. What there was, beyond question, was an incident that drew Alan and I together. I choose to understand my life in this way. Both

Alan and I are shy, in our different ways, and we need a little help to bridge the natural distance that exists between strangers. Strangers! The very word seems absurd when applied to Alan. I feel I know him so well. I know when he gets up in the morning, and when he leaves to go to school. I know when he comes back home, and when he turns out his lights at night. Many times I've driven past the school where he teaches, and pictured him in his classroom with all those little faces gazing up at him. I'm sure he's an excellent teacher.

What did he think when he found himself in my bedroom? What did he feel? There's no point in being prudish about it, a bed is a bed. I like pretty things about me, he'll have noticed the lacework on the pillows, and – dear Lord! – my nightie lying on the bedspread! How could I have forgotten that? What can Alan have thought when he saw my nightie? He's not a complete fool. Blush as much as you want, Marion, there's no one to see. He thought the only thing he could have thought, of course. He thought of me wearing the nightie. And then?

Customs have changed so much since Mummy's day. I realize now that Mummy was afraid of sex. She saw it as something to be controlled, or better still, avoided. Nowadays there's a healthy openness about sex, though of course it goes too far, and look at the results, abortions, single mothers, rapes, AIDS and so forth. But there is a balance. We can allow the sexual side of our nature to stake its claim, in the right place and at the right time, and not feel ashamed. Actually there's not much shame any more. A little more shame wouldn't come amiss. But there has to be a balance. I too have my share of sexual feelings. It would be a lie to deny it.

And Alan? He's a man. He stood in my bedroom, he looked at my nightie. Of course there was an element of sexual feeling there for him. It's entirely natural. And then when he came downstairs I felt it so strongly, the current of feeling in him, one might almost call it arousal. He could barely look at me. I'm sure he felt appalled at the thoughts he was having, he's such a gentle boy, but he shouldn't blame himself. Such thoughts are natural. He's a man, I'm a woman. It's the way nature has made us.

I have such a powerful premonition about Alan. There's a wordless channel of understanding between us that's drawing us closer to each other with every passing day. I feel certain now the time will come when I'll lie in his arms and we'll make love – yes, make love! – and it will be strong and gentle, and afterwards there'll come the deep calm my spirit craves.

I am the older of the two of us. It falls to me to make the first move. I must find a way to show him that I understand his feelings, and that I return them.

Dear Alan. Darling Alan. I'll go to bed now. I'll go to breathe the air that you have breathed. I'll go to sleep with you, all through the night.

21

It's just before nine o'clock when the car's headlights sweep the front of the house, sending a sabre of light across Jack's bedroom ceiling. Jack is not asleep. He hears his father's tread crossing the gravel to the front door, and then the familiar rattling of keys. His mother always drops the latch in the evening, just in case.

There follows an interval, in which he supposes his father comes in and gives his mother a kiss, and then he hears the strong thump of feet climbing the stairs. His father will look in on Carrie first, but she's been in bed for over an hour and will be asleep. The coming goodnight kiss belongs to Jack alone, the privilege of his two extra years.

The bedroom door opens, bringing with it a swish of light. The landing light is off, but light comes climbing up the stairs, bouncing round corners from the bathroom, from his parents' bedroom, spilling into his room, where he is supposed to be asleep. Comically, his father enters like a blind man, as if the room is a cave of darkness. Jack watches from his bed as his father feels his way past runaway trainers and unexpected chairs.

'You awake?'

He whispers, always. Jack is awake, always.

'Yes.'

He sits on the side of the bed, where Jack has made a space for him, ever since the car's lights swept across the ceiling, by wriggling up closer to the wall.

'Had a good day, darling?'

Jack has prepared for this moment.

'Got my composition back,' he says.

'Did your teacher like it?'

'He said I could do better.'

'Do better? How?'

'I forgot to put in full stops and stuff.'

'That's all he said?'

'He didn't like it being a dream.'

His father is briefly silent. Jack can feel him filling with anger. This excites him.

'Your teacher is a dickhead.'

A dickhead! Such a totally brilliant concept! A head like a dick! A stiff dick, naturally. Like in the chalk outline drawn on the up platform of Glynde station, above the legend JW IS A WANKER.

'He's one hundred per cent wrong. And I shall tell him so.'

'No. You can't.'

His father strokes his hair.

'My dinner's waiting.'

His warm snuffly kiss.

'Night, Daddy.'

Henry is tired and drinks more wine than usual. It's a good wine, a Rhone red. He reserves the best bottles for these ordinary evenings when it's just the two of them. Guests talk too much to notice what they're drinking.

'This teacher of Jack's. The one who thinks creative writing is all about punctuation. I can't believe it. It makes me so cross I want to hit him.'

'Poor Jack. He was disappointed.'

'I'm appalled, Laura. I really am. Jack wrote something magical. And this little shit of a teacher tells him he forgot to put in full stops. That's like a murder.'

'Maybe I should have a word with him in the morning. Though I'm afraid it won't make any difference.'

'He shouldn't be teaching. He should be sacked.'

'I'm not sure we can manage that.'

'He should be working in a local council office. He should be checking application forms for senior citizen bus passes.'

Laura looks on as he refills his glass yet again. She understands the source of his anger.

'How did it go with Aidan?'

'Hell. He's shameless. The man's vanity is impregnable.'

'Did you talk to Barry about the credit?'

'Briefly.'

'And?'

'And nothing, of course.'

'But that's so unfair. Really, Henry, you shouldn't let them do this to you.'

'Well, they're doing it.'

'It's your work. You deserve the credit. You have to put your foot down.'

'What am I supposed to do?' His voice peevish now, his irritation directed at Laura. 'Walk out?'

'I'm not saying that.' Laura is hurt. She was only trying to be supportive. 'They couldn't do it without you.'

'Of course they could. There's dozens like me out there.'

'That's not true, Henry. And you know it.'

'I can't walk out.'

Because he needs the work. Because he needs to earn money. Because however much he earns it isn't enough.

Maybe I should walk out. What am I trying to prove? Only that my existence is necessary. Scratch that little itch of the ego. A fantasy, of course. All of us are replaceable. All of us are in the process of being replaced.

'I know you can't walk out now. But I hate to see you so—' She hesitates. So helpless? 'So unhappy.'

Henry shrugs.

'I'll get over it. It's only a television programme.'

He knows she's only trying to help, but her sympathy inflames the bruise. Now he has guilt on his plate too. Some dinner.

Not meeting her eyes, conscious of having behaved badly, he makes an attempt to escape his own ill humour.

'So how's your day been?'

'Actually, I've had a little drama.' She speaks in a manner that is almost off-hand, not wanting to imply that her day has been in competition with his. He's so prickly these days. 'I found some letters from Billy's father. You're not to tell anyone. He had an affair.'

'Billy had an affair?'

'No. Billy's father, George. Billy was knocked sideways by it.'

'Poor bastard,' says Henry. 'Oliver Handy was telling me the other day the estate is virtually bankrupt.'

'And I called Nick Crocker. He wrote me that letter.'

'Oh, yes. What's up with him?'

'I don't know. He never says much on the phone. Anyway, I've asked him to supper on Friday.'

'I'm shooting on Friday.'

'Damn. So you are. I forgot.'

'Christ knows when I'll be home.'

'I'll change it.'

'No, don't bother. It's you he wants to see, not me. I expect I'll catch a sight of him before he goes.'

'Well, if you don't mind.'

After they've eaten Henry loads the dishwasher and reaches a decision.

'You know what I'm going to do? I'm going to take the children into school tomorrow and have a word with that teacher of Jack's.'

'Can you spare the time?'

'It'll only add half an hour.'

'Well, if you're sure, that would really help me. You know we've got Glyndebourne on Saturday?'

'Oh, Christ. I'd forgotten all about that.'

'I was thinking of buying myself something to wear. If you don't mind.'

'Why should I mind?'

'Oh, you know. Money.'

'No, I don't mind.'

'If you take the children in, I could get an early train. Be back in time to pick them up.'

Henry's scanning the television listings in the paper.

'There's a big match on. Do you mind if I catch the end? It's the kind of thing film crews talk about. I should at least know the score. Can you bear it?'

He turns on the television. A wall of howling spectators banked up behind a goal. Patrick Vieira is preparing to take a penalty kick for Arsenal. The commentator is shrieking with excitement, the Turkish fans are baying and drumming, the game has gone through extra time, the score is nil-nil, but Arsenal are losing on penalties.

If Vieira misses this kick the match is lost. By pure chance Henry has joined the game at its decisive moment.

On this May night in Copenhagen, in the heart of the Parken Stadium, a man in a yellow shirt pauses for an instant of concentrated stillness. Then he starts to run. No one else moves. He runs, and kicks, and the ball sails through the air, and slams against a goalpost, and bounds away to one side. The Turkish supporters go wild. The man in the yellow shirt bows his head. The Arsenal coach looks aside. Galatasaray has won.

'So much for Arsenal.'

Henry switches off the television and begins the process of shutting down the house. Outside lights. Back door lock. Front door lock. Downstairs lights, room by room. Preparation for sleep so like preparation for death: one by one the lights go out, and then the darkness.

As always, he's in bed first. He hears the bathroom lavatory flush. The click of the bathroom light switch. Then Laura joins him, turning out the bedroom light as she gets into bed, letting in cold air as she lifts up the duvet.

For a few moments they lie there, side by side, motionless. Then her hand feels for his, and holds it lightly.

'So you'll take the children in the morning.'

Her voice soft in the night, meditative.

'Yes.'

'I'll go right after breakfast. Catch the 8.20. That would be perfect.'

She's talking to herself. Telling herself the story of the next day. He's waiting for her silence.

Her fingers stroke his fingers. He squeezes her hand in response, very lightly. He yawns, and changes position, stretching his body. His foot brushes her foot. She makes her toes wiggle against his foot, a friendly greeting. He turns on his side, letting his arm reach further as he turns, so that his hand falls against her side. He makes a small patting movement with his fingers against the cotton of her nightdress, feeling her warm body beneath.

'Mmmm,' she says.

If she now lets her right hand slide across the space between them to touch his flank, as he is touching hers, then he will roll nearer and his arm will reach across her. If she makes no answering move, his hand will pat her one more time, as if to settle them both down for the night, and he will murmur, 'Sleep well, darling', and will withdraw. In this way, by deploying a certain ambiguity, overtures may be made and not accepted without loss of pride.

'Mmmm,' murmurs Laura, her right hand heavy by her side.

She feels a little guilty, particularly after their testy exchange at dinner, but she is truly tired, and the one small move would be the prelude to much more effort. It's not that she dislikes sex with Henry. There are certain times of the month when she actively solicits it. But as a rule she doesn't feel the urge in the abstract. Her sexual appetite, like a clockwork motor, runs on a relaxed spring, and must be well wound up before it will go. She knows men work differently. Men can be switched on like electric lights, and on the whole, it's the woman who has control of the switch. Hence her mild guilt on the nights when she does not respond. However she also knows that if Henry is in great need he will persist, and in persisting will wake her body even as it prepares to sleep. So you could say the decision is his after all.

How complex it all is. She likes it that he still desires her. She likes it when he lets her feel the urgency of his desire. The truth is she needs that pressure, that imperious sense of demand, to activate her own excitement. And once begun she needs time, and patience, and careful touching. Then, little by little, her defended body will melt, and she will feel as power what before was vulnerability. Then she will reach out to him of her own accord, hungry for the passionate embrace.

But on this May night in Sussex, Laura's hand makes no answering move. Henry's hand returns to his side. He rolls into his sleep posture, on his right side, his forearms crossed against his chest, his knees slightly bent.

'Good night, darling. Sleep well.'

He hears the sound of her breathing slide quickly and easily into the rhythms of sleep. He himself will not sleep for a long time. He knows the signs. There's too much unfinished business waiting for his attention.

Finitum non est capax infiniti. And yet we try, we try. We make pictures all the time, our imagination in overdrive. The sin of idolatry a betrayal of God, a kind of adultery, spiritual fornication, they called it. Lusting after what is false but visible, near and desirable. Nowadays every city street a house of pictures, walled with images of desire. We torment our gaze, condemn ourselves to permanent dissatisfaction, the consumer as the modern idolater. This was his new idea, the basis of a new intro to his film. Piccadilly Circus, perhaps, with its electric hoardings. What do they sell these days? Coca-Cola? McDonald's? There's a candidate for defacement, the leering painted paedophile Ronald McDonald.

And all this will gush from the motormouth of Aidan Massey. *Ad maiorem Massey gloriam.* Who am I but the anonymous craftsman at work high on the cathedral scaffold? Thine be the glory.

What was it Laura said she wanted to do? Buy a dress for Glyndebourne.

If you don't mind. Why should I mind? Oh, you know. Money.

She hides it from me, her only deception, the extent to which her parents subsidise our lives. Hides it out of love, to give me pride, knowing I work for money to save my pride. A man must work. Must provide for his children. If not, what am I? A kept man. A walker. A eunuch.

Ah, sex. The right to demand sexual pleasure has to be earned. You have to put your foot down.

Some thoughts once expressed in words can't be unthought. Some frontiers once passed admit no return. My life that has seemed so substantial is in fact an act of faith. No, not faith, magic. An illusion that convinces from a distance. The quickness of the hand deceives the eye. Never ask to know how the trick is done. The magic, once lost, will not return.

My life is slipping out of my control. Tell me what lies to tell myself, to feel again as I felt yesterday. Tell me what hopes to bury, what dreams to dash. I'm well-trained in the habits of compromise. I know how to accept the inevitable. I know how to live with reality.

But what if I should cease to believe?

Let's go somewhere together, Laura and Jack and Carrie and me. Down into the secret valley, to the monument to the lost traveller.

I thought if I fell off the wall the clouds would be soft but I didn't fall

Have I done enough?

Not enough never enough no never enough

22

As Laura's twentieth birthday approached, her friends wanted to know how she planned to celebrate it. She told them she had not yet made up her mind. The truth was she had not been able to get Nick to focus on the question, and so did not know what sort of celebration he would like. Of course it was her birthday and she should be able to do whatever she wanted, but without Nick there, without Nick enjoying himself, there would be no pleasure in it for her. She was learning that he had moods. One minute they would be happy together doing nothing in particular; the next minute he would fall silent, or even disappear. He never went anywhere far, just into the next room, or out into the street. The place that he went to he called On My Own. She called it Away From Me. At such times, when she discovered his absence, she stopped breathing.

'So what shall we do for my birthday?' she asked him one lunch time, spreading out food on the table in her room.

'I don't know,' he said. 'What do you want to do?'

'Whatever it is, I want to do it with you.'

'Of course.'

Bread, pâté, tomatoes, proper plates, not paper. This was one of Nick's rules, like wine must be drunk out of proper glasses.

'What would be nicest? A big party with all our friends, or just you and me somewhere special alone together?'

He laughed to see her earnest face.

'Laura darling, it's your birthday.'

'Yes, but if you don't like it then I won't like it.'

'But if you like it I'm bound to like it. You being happy makes me happy.'

'Really?'

It was the right answer but she didn't believe it. Nick had such definite ideas about things. For example he didn't really like her friend Katie O'Keefe. He never said so, but Laura could tell. Not that it mattered, because Laura saw much less of her old friends since getting together with Nick. There seemed to be so much less time.

'I've got your present already,' he told her.

'What is it?'

'Wait and see. It's a surprise.'

This was wonderful. He had anticipated her birthday. He had thought about what she might like. He had gone out to a shop somewhere and picked it out. He had it hidden away even now. At every stage he had been thinking about her and she had not known it. This, more than the waiting package, was his gift to her.

But Katie, of course, expected a party.

'You have to see your friends some time, Laura. You can't spend the rest of your life just with Nick.'

'It's just that he's working so hard right now. After his finals are over we'll be more sociable.'

'He's got finals. You haven't.'

'Anyway, I've not decided about my birthday. May's a terrible month. Everyone's revising.'

'So we need a break. We'll all pitch in with the booze. Paulie can play his old rock'n'roll records.'

'Nick's not a great dancer.'

'So what? Nick's not everything.'

But Nick was everything. Without Nick in her arms Laura had no wish to dance. Katie wouldn't understand. By her own admission she had never been in love. It was impossible to explain to her what it felt like, how it was as if she was half a person and only became whole when she was with him.

In the end they decided on a picnic lunch. They invited half a dozen friends, they were all to contribute food and wine, and they were to go up river by punt. This was Laura's plan. Nick had spent part of the summer before he met her punting tourists for tips and had become very skilled.

The day turned out sunny. Nick wore his shirt unbuttoned. He stood tall and at ease on the rear platform plying the long heavy pole with grace, while the punts that followed lurched from bank to bank of the river and became entangled with low-hanging branches.

The drinking began as they set out, and soon the zigzag convoy was loud with ironic cheers and laughter.

'Oh fuck, fuck, fuck!' cried Richard Clements as he drove his punt into the bank.

'Richard you arsehole! You made me spill my wine!'

Lesley Draycott laughed so much she got hiccups, and every time she hiccupped she jumped, and every time she jumped her short skirt rode higher up her legs. Hal Ashburnham kept hold of his pole too long and fell into the river. Franco Souza sang 'Old Man River' in a high piping voice. The day grew warm.

They laid out their picnic on a random spread of tartan rugs and discarded jackets, and more bottles of wine were opened. Felix's contribution was a loaf of sliced white sandwich bread, for which he was universally mocked.

'*Mein Gott!*' cried Hal. 'What would Manet say?'

'Where was I supposed to find a baguette?' complained Felix.

'Not a baguette.' Nick with his eyes closed mentally reconstructed the Manet painting. 'A round loaf, I think.'

'And the woman's naked!' Richard turned to Laura. 'Laura! We need a naked woman!'

'In your dreams, Richard.'

'I didn't know you knew.'

'Anyway,' said Katie, 'it's all sexist bullshit. Why don't the men strip off too?'

'I'm stripping off!'

Hal Ashburnham, soaking from his tumble in the river, peeled off his shirt and jeans to reveal a lissom white body. Not quite naked, he struck a pose, one arm akimbo, head looking down.

'Culture quiz. Who am I?'

'A prat in pants!'

'The Mona Lisa!'

'Michelangelo's David.'

'Thank you, Nick.'

Laura watched Nick and saw that he was happy and so she was happy. When at last the wine ran out four of her friends knelt before her and serenaded her with a song that was topping the charts when she was two years old.

> 'Tell Laura I love her
> Tell Laura I need her
> Tell Laura not to cry
> My love for her will never die . . .'

Laura clapped and clapped and saw Nick smiling and thought how strange it was to be twenty years old.

'Nick's a great singer,' said Franco.

This was a surprise to Laura.

'Are you, Nick? I didn't know.'

'Haven't you ever heard Nick sing Elvis?'

Nick was grinning and shaking his head, but now all the party set up a clamour.

'Elvis! Elvis! Elvis!'

Laura thought he didn't like it and was about to stop the chant when she caught an apologetic smile flashed at her and realized he was going to do it.

'I'll get you later for this, Franco, you traitor.'

He rose to his feet and adopted a mock opera-singer pose, holding out his hands towards Laura. Then he started to sing. To Laura's utter amazement his voice was deep and true, not quite Elvis, but not at all comical. She realized she was not going to be able to stop herself crying.

> 'Love me tender, love me sweet,
> Never let me go.
> You have made my life complete
> And I love you so.
> Love me tender, love me true,
> All my dreams fulfil.
> For my darling I love you
> And I always will.'

She took him in her arms and kissed him, pressing her wet cheeks to his, and all their friends cheered. He had said to her in song words he had never said before, words she had longed for him to say.

He gave her his birthday present. It was a walnut tied up with a slender red ribbon. Inside the hollowed-out nut was a pair of silver and agate earrings.

'Oh, Nick. They're so beautiful.'

And he had chosen them. He had searched the shelves of jewellers' shops with her in his mind, looking for the adornment that would become her.

She put the earrings on then and there, attaching to herself as she did so his publicly-declared love. She was still crying tears of happiness.

Later that day Nick and Laura went to the photo-booth on the station concourse and took pictures of each other. In Nick's strip of four pictures he looked smiling, then solemn, then he turned his head in profile and looked sideways at the camera, then he had his eyes shut. In Laura's four pictures she wore her new earrings and looked this way and that, and smiled, and wanted to be as lovely as possible. His pictures were for her, and her pictures were for him. But then, everything was for him. Her radiant beauty, her happiness, her body, her soul.

That night he told her he might go to New York. There was a possible job in a small art gallery there from September. Laura wondered to herself how they would manage things but trusted they would find a way. September seemed very far off.

23

In the small hours of Thursday morning the last of the moonlight finds Alan Strachan at his desk, lit by the lesser moon of his computer screen, in the very moment of completion; which is also the very moment at which euphoria turns to despair. All night long, buoyed up by a raging flaming conviction that he has found the answer, that he has only to keep pace with the demon of invention and chase the words from keyboard to screen, he has breathed fierce new life into his failed play. Now, the task done, the night almost over, the adrenalin that has flooded his nervous system is draining away, and his sleep-deprived body is turning on him to take its revenge.

Don't listen don't believe only because I'm tired. Sleep now.

He runs from the room, not stopping to close down the computer, and throws himself fully dressed onto his bed, pleading for oblivion to save him. Tormented by tiredness but wide awake, he lies on the bed, thrashing from side to side, helpless to resist the sucking away of his precious store of conviction.

Why did I think how could I believe why can't I see but I see too much and too clearly. My poor man's wisdom made infantile by my sad man's comedy. Cruel to let me hope so much for so long. And what now? What other life to live? What other dream to dream? No, no more dreams. Only dull plodding reality. Build on the ugly concrete foundation of truth. The play is a failure, always will be. The years of struggle the product of vanity and self-delusion. But cruel to let it last so long. Cruel to leave me with so little, and so tired. Cruel to deny me sleep.

So he sleeps.

When he wakes, it's full daylight, and checking his watch he finds he's missed most of morning assembly. Fortunately he's already dressed, though neither having slept properly nor breakfasted at all he feels like shit and looks the same way. There'll be coffee in the staff room.

As he shambles blinking through the school's front hall to the sanctuary he seeks, a parent looms up before him.

'I'm told you're Mr Strachan,' he says.

'The rumour is correct.'

But the parent does not smile.

'Is there somewhere we can talk for a moment?'

They go into the school office, currently empty, and there stupid as a doll he stands nodding and grinning when all he wants is a mug of coffee and an armchair.

'It's about my son Jack. He wrote a composition for you, about a dream.'

Alan Strachan struggles to remember. Nothing whatsoever comes to mind.

'Oh. Right.'

'You criticized his punctuation. I'm not saying you were wrong to do that. But punctuation! I mean, it's not such a big deal, surely?'

The man seems to be angry.

'I'm sorry. I don't quite follow you.'

'A child brings you his dream. There's more there than punctuation. He's offering you, well, his soul, really. Doesn't that deserve more from you than "Could do better"? Look, I'm trying not to sound like a pushy parent. Forget he's my son. He could be anyone's child. He could be Shakespeare. He could be Milton. You have the power to make him feel that. And what do you tell him? "Could do better". He's eleven years old! He's not some tired old hack slogging along for a pay cheque like the rest of us. He's a child. Let him have his dreams.'

The words *pay cheque* hold Alan Strachan's attention.

'If I've let your son down,' he says, 'I'm sorry. I'm sure you expect and deserve better service for your money.'

'I don't want service. Jesus, money! It rots everything it touches. Listen, all I'm saying is believe in him. Don't let his dreams perish.'

Alan Strachan becomes aware that the children are streaming into the hall. Assembly is over, and the noise is indescribable as always. For once the babel of unbroken voices is welcome. Too much reality too early in the day.

'Yes,' he says. 'Yes, of course you're right.'

'Well, that's all I wanted to say. Who was it who wrote, "Tread softly, you tread on my dreams"?'

He holds out his hand.

'Yeats.'

Alan Strachan allows his hand to be shaken. Passing children stare and giggle. The parent strides out through the swinging doors, scattering blue-blazered infants as he goes. Alan Strachan is about to continue on his interrupted way to the staff room when the Headmaster's voice snags him.

'Oh, Alan. Did I see you in assembly?'

'Sorry, Alastair. Running a little late this morning.'

'There's a parent looking for you.'

'Yes. I know.'

The staff room already a jostle of colleagues. He moves in a trance towards the trolley. Jimmy Hall is pouring from the coffee jug, holding it at a dismayingly acute angle.

'Morning Alan.'

The last of the coffee trickles from the spout. Jimmy Hall beams over his brimming mug.

'Have you seen the local rag?'

'No.'

'I've started doing the odd bit for them. Local items, uncredited, nothing to set the Thames on fire. Thought it might interest my Year Threes.'

'Right.'

'How daily life turns into news. What's newsworthy and what's not. I'm learning a lot myself, to tell you the truth.'

Alan Strachan leaves the staff room, feeling giddy and a little nauseous. Barely ten minutes to go before his first class. He heads across the lawn towards the tennis courts, wanting only to be alone.

I could have been Shakespeare. I could have been Milton. Don't let my dreams perish.

It seems to him now that the parent was a product of his imagination, an accusing voice conjured up by himself from his own nightmares. No sleep, no toast, no coffee, and he's hallucinating in the school hall. The angry father is himself, and the child whose dreams he seeks to protect, that child too is himself.

I bring myself my dream. I offer my soul. I could do better.
As if I didn't know.

'Alan!'

Fucking Alastair. Is there nowhere I can be alone?

'Alan! That parent who wants a word with you is still waiting.'

'I've seen him.'

'Her. She's in the library.'

'Oh.'

I am bound upon a wheel of fire. What are the chances that this new female rebuker has a Thermos of hot black coffee? Not great, pal. Not great.

He pushes his unruly hair into token order, and tries but fails to lift his shoulders out of their defeated slouch. He feels as he makes his way to the library as if his skeleton no longer has enough rigidity to support him. His eyes sting.

She's standing in the bay window, looking out at the Downs. He remembers her, she's the single parent. He retrieves the name. Dickinson.

'Mr Strachan.'

'Yes.'

'I know it's not a good time. But I really would like a word about Alice.'

'Right. Right.'

'How do you find her this term? Do you think she's coping all right?'

'Well, I don't see – yes, as far as that goes – I mean, you know, everyone has their ups and downs.'

He sits down on one of the child-sized chairs, a little more suddenly than he intended. Alice's mother seems surprised. She does not sit, even though there are plenty of other child-sized chairs. She looks down at him, frowning.

'How do you think she's getting on with the other girls in her class?'

'The other girls? Oh, not too badly, I think. They're not a bad crowd.'

'So she has friends?'

'Oh, yes. Yes.'

'Who?'

'Who?'

'I mean, which of the girls in the class would you describe as Alice's friends?'

He closes his eyes. They sting when he looks at her, because behind her is the bright glare of the bay window.

'You know how girls are. They change friends daily. God only knows who it is today. Ask Alice.'

'I have asked Alice.'

Her voice sounds odd. He knows he should open his eyes but he can't. He wants to lay his head on the table.

'You don't have the first idea, do you?'

Oh, please. Take me away. Bury me.

'You've been her form teacher for almost three terms and you don't even know how unhappy she is.'

So much unhappiness. The blind leading the blind. Bury my heart at Portland Place.

'She's unhappy?'

'Yes.'

'We're all unhappy.'

Did I say that aloud?

'*What did you say?*'

He opens his eyes. His eyes sting so much. He can't stop them watering. What might look to an outsider like tears start rolling down his cheeks.

I could have been Shakespeare. I could have been Milton.

'I'm sorry,' he says. 'I'm sorry.'

She's sitting down on a child-sized chair. No longer silhouetted by bright distance.

'What's the matter?'

'I'm so sorry. I'll stop in a minute.'

'Would you rather talk about this later?'

Her voice is changed. She's become hesitant, gentle. Unfortunately this has a loosening effect on the remains of his self-control. He bows his head and weeps freely.

'This isn't about Alice.'

He gives a small shake of his bowed head.

'You're unhappy.'

A small nod.

'I'm sorry. I've chosen the wrong moment.'

She gives him a cotton handkerchief. He wipes away his tears. Humiliating, to cry in front of a parent. Pull yourself together.

He looks up, tries a smile. Now that she's on his level he can see her face. A friendly face.

'I'll keep an eye on her today,' he says. 'I'll let you know.'

'Right.'

She stands.

'My number's on the school list. I'm usually out, but there's an answering machine that has my mobile number.'

Now she's leaving, and he hasn't even stood up.

'You're right, Mr Strachan. We're all unhappy.'

24

The satisfaction of driving a car on the public roads is that you know where you are. There's the geography of it, to start with; you can say, without any ambiguity, that you're proceeding west on the long straight of the A27, and therefore that you will arrive in a few short minutes at the Edenfield roundabout. This is a prediction that will come true. Roads are reliable, they behave as advertised. Important not to overlook the solace of this simple fact. After all, how many ventures in life promise one outcome and deliver another?

Then there's the social justice of it. Those who drive on public roads submit themselves to the absolute authority of a set of laws. These laws admit no exception. They control the actions of rich and poor alike. They establish, in any situation of conflict, who is right and who is wrong. The driver who finds his road crossed by a broken white line as he approaches a junction must give way to the driver who has clear tarmac before him. The lesser road gives way to the greater. This means that even a mighty Range Rover, if on a minor road, must wait humbly for the passing of a puttering three-wheeler or groaning cyclist. On a roundabout, each line of traffic waits its turn to enter the system in an order understood by all. Where there are traffic lights, the red light has a power that approaches the divine. It has only to glare from beneath its beetling brow and everything that moves towards it ceases to move. No barrier descends. No policeman raises a white-cuffed arm. Simply a red light, and a body of collective knowledge. In our envious strife-torn world, this is a source of wonder; or would be, if we ever stopped to consider.

So thinks Henry Broad, who has put his foot down with Jack's teacher, touching sixty as he passes the Glynde turning. The tension generated in him by the encounter is fading, soothed by the orderly

justice of the highway. Not that it was much of an encounter. The
fellow looked totally out of his depth. Though God knows, teaching
English to well-spoken eleven-year-olds has to be classed as the shallow
end if anything is. Laura would have handled it all differently. She
would have asked his opinion, discussed Jack's progress, slipped in a
gentle criticism at the right moment. He had meant to do something
of the sort himself. It was the waiting that screwed it. He hates to
be kept waiting. Can't help, childish though it is, feeling that the one
keeping him waiting is exerting power over him. Saying in effect, my
time is more valuable than yours. And then this pale-faced youth
appeared, clearly just out of bed.

Oh, well. At least it did me some good.

The car in front is going slowly, for no obvious reason. A small
red Honda, driven by a small man with big ears. Why do slow drivers
always have big ears? He has a stretch of open road before him, and
he's idling along at forty.

Henry checks his mirror: the line of cars is bunching up behind
him. He looks ahead. Just enough room to get past if he goes now,
and goes fast.

Tick-tick-tick goes the indicator. Growl of the engine as he drops
two gears. Kick down on the accelerator for the gratifying surge of
power. Exactly as he pulls out he sees a white van hurtling towards
him, out of nowhere. Too late to get back in. Strain the Golf to eighty,
ninety, hug the white line, force the wheel at the first opportunity,
cut back into his own lane. The white van flashes past. The red Honda
brakes hard. Henry doesn't look in his rear-view mirror, choosing
not to witness the anger of Big Ears. Instead, to justify his rash
overtaking, to escape that accusing glare, he accelerates again, and
speeds away down the open road.

Heart hammering, aware he's driving badly, Henry slows right
down at the approach to the Edenfield roundabout, under the brow
of Mount Caburn. A long line of container lorries is winding its way
round the island, across his road, down through Edenfield village to
the ferry port at Newhaven. They drive nose to tail, no doubt all
hurrying to catch the same sailing. He sits tense, almost crouching,
riding the clutch, hopping forward in little surges, probing for a gap.
The truck drivers high above him pay no attention, heaving their great
sixteen-axled rigs round the curves.

He glances in his mirror and sees, as he knew he would, the red Honda pulling up behind him. He avoids eye contact with the driver, or any other details that will give him human form. He feels the skin on the back of his neck prickle under the scrutiny of the small man with the big ears. Naturally Big Ears hates him. He will pursue him with the relentless tenacity of the wronged, and will attempt to corner him and shame him in a public place. Henry imagines but does not meet those baleful eyes. Then at last he sees a gap open up between the lorries, a small gap, but enough. He thrusts the Golf onto the roundabout, earning a loud blast from an offended truck horn, but what does he care? The truck is going to France. Let him carry his disapprobation across the sea to a foreign land.

Ahead, of course, how predictable, the red lights of the railway crossing are flicking from side to side, and the striped barriers are starting their descent. Enraged by the unfairness of it, Henry causes the Golf to give one savage leap forward, and judders the car over the railway lines at seventy miles an hour, bare seconds ahead of the dropping barriers.

As he hurtles up onto the dual carriageway he hears the train go by, and knows that his nemesis is barred from following him by the beeping barrier and the noisy train. He imagines the small angry man spitting his rage onto the plastic fascia of his Japanese dashboard. Let him spit. He has no name, no face, and now he's dwindling in the rear-view mirror, and now he's gone from sight.

Henry joins the steadily moving stream of cars coming off the Lewes roundabout, and so dives into the orange twilight of the tunnel. The morning rush hour is tailing off. The traffic moves smoothly through the town. Over the river, past Safeway, past the bottom of School Hill, and the Friends Meeting House, and the Chinese restaurant, to the sharp left turn down to the station car park.

A woman in an Audi is pulled up by the barrier, fumbling in her handbag for the necessary coins. Henry draws up behind her and watches with growing astonishment as she searches the inner recesses of her purse. How much looking does it take to identify and select a few coins? Then to his greater astonishment he sees her get out, point her key fob at the car to lock it, leaving it blocking the entrance to the car park, and without so much as a backward look, head off into the station. Henry can't believe she's doing it. He pulls out his own handful of coins to see if he can supply the £2.30 needed to raise the barrier, and sees at once that he only has the coins for his own needs. Two pounds thirty! Who dreamed up such an eccentric figure? No change given, declares the notice on the yellow pillar. *No change given.* God help us all.

The Audi lady will be on her way to the newspaper kiosk for change. Had she not locked her car, he would release the hand brake and roll it out of the way himself. The nerve of the woman! No word to him, not even so much as a guilty apologetic glance. And now she's gone, disappeared into the station building. He has no option but to sit and wait.

By now the brief moment of calm he experienced on the long straight is no more than a memory. He feels like a prisoner, hemmed in by walls of anger, tension and guilt. Without any words having passed between them, without even eye contact, he has entered into brief but intense relationships with three other people: Big Ears, a truck driver, and the Audi lady. All three have generated frustration and conflict. Just when he could have done with a quiet journey up to town he is subjected to this sequence of aggravations. Anyone could be forgiven for seeing something deliberate in it all. It has the look of a plot. After all, what are the odds on meeting, in one morning journey to the station, a big-eared driver in a trance, an unending convoy of container lorries, a train, and a woman with no coins in her purse? Who is the mastermind behind this complex operation, designed to destroy his sanity? God? Aidan Massey?

The Audi lady is returning. She avoids his outraged eyes. How many other drivers' mornings has she wrecked? He glances in his mirror.

No, no surprise. A twisted smile at the sadism of fate forms on Henry's lips as he sees the red Honda roll to a gentle stop behind him. He watches as the driver's door opens and the man with the big ears gets out. He fixes his attention on the man's feet, as if by such a childish stratagem he can render himself invisible, or at the very least insignificant. Then he takes his eyes off the mirror altogether and stares ahead at nothing.

He hears the footsteps of nemesis approaching his car door. He doesn't turn, or move in any way. Nemesis walks on past him without stopping. He is making for the Audi lady, who has just reached her car. Big Ears will vent his anger on her, and so the storm will pass him by.

But no, it seems nemesis wants only to be helpful. He is offering the Audi lady some coins. The Audi lady smiles, grateful and apologetic. She shows her own handful of change, obtained along with today's *Daily Mail*. Nemesis turns back to his car. Only now does Henry Broad, looking up with a rapid and evasive glance, see that he is the rector of Edenfield, Miles Salmon.

Henry and the rector sit together on the train to Victoria. Henry is not a churchgoer, and knows Mr Salmon by sight only. The rector knows him as the owner of the fine property called River Farm. He says nothing about the incident on the A27. Henry, feeling the need to clear the air, gives him an opening.

'I've just dropped the children off at school. You must have been driving from Edenfield to Lewes at about the same time.'

'I suppose I must.'

'Dangerous stretch of road.'

'Yes. I always take it slowly.'

Is it possible he noticed nothing? Of course he is a man of God, maybe he's already forgiven and forgotten.

'Your wife phoned me yesterday evening,' says the rector. 'Hoping to trace a villager from the past.'

This means nothing to Henry.

'Something she found in the library at Edenfield Place.'

'Oh, yes.'

Henry remembers what Laura told him. Some letters. An affair.

'Poor old Billy,' he says.

'Yes. We hear there are financial problems. There are rumours that the estate's to be sold. I do hope not. We should hate to have some Arab prince living there.'

How about that? The old boy's a racist.

'You don't like Arabs?'

'Oh, no. It's not that. It's the wealth that's the difficulty. Some member of the Saudi royal family bought the Calthorpe estate, I'm told, and they never go there. Stands empty, year in, year out. I would hate to see Edenfield Place empty. We villagers are rather proud of it.'

We villagers. We churchgoers. We real inhabitants.

'Laura and I still feel like newcomers. Eight years now. But that doesn't make us real villagers.'

'Not at all,' says the rector courteously. 'Your beautiful young family brings us joy. You're certainly real villagers.'

Henry is touched. My beautiful young family. He thinks of Laura, already in London, on her way to wherever one goes to buy expensive frocks. Harvey Nichols?

It's the wealth that's the difficulty.

He returns the rector's courtesy.

'I suppose I'm making an excuse for not going to church.'

'Please!' The rector raises both hands, palms outwards, smiling. 'No excuses are required. If the church offers you nothing you need, why should you go there? We don't go to the doctor until we get ill.'

'But I suppose everyone gets ill at one time or another.'

'And so does everyone feel the need of – well, not of my services, I confess, nor of my church – let's say, the need of a greater context in which to set our life. One grows weary of narrow horizons. One longs for a view.'

'Yes. Maybe that's so.'

Henry falls silent, thinking over the rector's words. The rector does not speak. Henry watches the greening woods roll by beyond the train window. He glances at the rector, and sees at once that his travelling companion is silent not for want of something to say, but to allow him, Henry, the space to think. This is not a common experience in Henry's world. Conversations with friends or colleagues take the form of alternating acts of self-assertion. Most statements are opinions, and most opinions are designed to raise the speaker's status. Out of politeness one waits for the other person to stop before starting to speak oneself; but this waiting one's turn does not involve listening. The other person's speech serves rather as a useful interlude within which to find the right words to present one's own next opinion.

'I'm working in your neck of the woods right now,' he says. 'Making a television film about Puritan iconoclasm. Trying to get inside the minds of the men who smashed the stained glass and defaced the statues.'

'Do you know,' says the rector, 'I've always had a secret urge to break things. Sacred things most of all.'

Henry laughs.

'Me too. My inner vandal.'

'I think it's a sign of respect, don't you? One only wants to break things that have power over one.'

'Yes, I suppose so.'

Henry is surprised. The rector is more interesting than he had expected.

'What brings you up to town?' he asks.

'This is my monthly outing. I have a sister in Ealing. She has what she calls a maisonette but what I call a flat. She gives me lunch. She lives very quietly. Sometimes I think that but for my monthly visit she never speaks to a soul. Though she does pray aloud.'

'By herself?'

'Yes, it is unusual. Vocalized prayer tends to be reserved for group worship. Quite why, I don't know. After all, if the entire congregation prayed in silence throughout one assumes the Almighty would be able to hear them.'

The more the rector says, the better Henry likes him.

'You're quite right,' he says. 'One does grow weary of narrow horizons.'

'But you. A television director! I speak from my pulpit to thirty people, you to millions. I envy you that.'

'Oh, it has its down side. Believe me.'

'Of course. This is the human condition. We're designed for unhappiness. Hence our constant hurrying about.'

'We're designed for unhappiness? Isn't that rather a doctrine of despair?'

'You could call it despair. But a doctrine, no. Just a hunch.'

'Why would God design us for unhappiness?'

'Well now, there's a question. Why indeed? Why create us in the first place? And why, having made man, forbid him the fruit of the tree of knowledge? Why force him to choose between being either ignorant or wicked?'

'Why indeed?'

'The answer, of course, is original sin. It has to come from something. I'm very attached to original sin. It explains so much, without being in any way personal.'

'And lets us off so much,' says Henry. 'I'd rather believe we're all responsible for our own sins.'

'You may very well be right,' the rector concedes. 'But yours is the harder path to follow. You believe in original happiness.'

'Do I?' Henry is amused by this picture of himself.

'Which means, of course, that any deviation from perfect happiness is a failure on our own part.'

'I was claiming responsibility for my sins, not for my unhappiness.'

'My dear sir.' The rector wrinkles his brow. 'Sin is unhappiness. They are the same thing.'

'Sin is unhappiness! Nonsense! Sorry, but I can't let you get away with that. What if I fall ill, or lose my job, or my wife leaves me? Is my unhappiness sinful?'

'Yes, it does seem rather hard. I can't say I've thought the matter through. And yet – are all sick people unhappy? Must losing your job make you unhappy? You see, I have a glimpse of a way of living – perhaps I should say, a way of being – in which these external accidents make no difference, no difference at all. But I think that to get to that place, if it is a place, one must be without sin.'

'Which is impossible.'

'Perhaps.'

'So God help us all.'

'Yes, yes. Or we can help each other.'

The refreshment trolley comes rattling towards their seats.

'Would you like a cup of tea?' says Henry.

'No, thank you. But if they have a KitKat?'

They do. Henry pays for the chocolate and for his own tea. The trolley lady gives him an extra plastic cup for his teabag. Miles Salmon notices this.

'They don't always do that,' he says. 'It shows imagination on that young lady's part.'

He eats his KitKat with care, one stick at a time.

'Tell me,' Henry asks him, 'in the light of this conversation, would you say you are happy?'

The rector thinks about that.

'There are times. This may be one of them.'

'You don't wish for things you haven't got? Or feel you could have done more with your life than you have?'

'I don't think so, no. But then, I was very timid when I was young. Not at all ambitious. I could never be a television director. I would be quite incapable of ordering people about. You make far greater demands on yourself than I do, Mr Broad.'

'Maybe I do.'

Henry gazes out of the train window at the countryside dressed in the new green of high springtime. That singing green. There should be a word for it.

'Then again, maybe I'm an idiot.'

Tread softly. You tread on my dreams.

25

At Victoria, Laura Broad directs the cab driver to South Molton Street.

From the moment of waking this morning she has permitted herself the rare luxury of thinking only about one thing. Let Henry chivvy the children over their breakfast and into their blazers and school shoes. She is preparing herself for the mission ahead. Not a grand mission of any value to mankind, but nonetheless one that demands planning, focus, and drive. She has decided far too late in the day that she needs a new frock for Saturday. The summer ranges will be in. And this chilly spring, she needs something warm.

She has dressed tactically: comfortable shoes for all the walking, no laces or buckles because she'll be taking them off many times. An elasticated skirt, easy to slip out of. A loose top, that she can pull over her head without messing her hair too much. Pretty underwear, because the saleswomen see everything.

She has made herself up with care. She'll be examining herself in mirrors again and again, and must be able to withstand the scrutiny. She has chosen her lightest handbag. She means to have more to carry on her return journey. She will travel alone. This is her day. She wants no companion whose needs she must consider, whose face she must check for signs of boredom. She has a mission to accomplish, and wants no civilians to slow her down.

The dress or outfit that she seeks has as yet no form. She does not set out with a clipping from a magazine, or a preference for a style or colour. It could be anything. At the same time, it could be only one thing, which is *itself*, because it already exists. When she sees it she will know it. Somewhere it's waiting for her, hanging on a rail, partly hidden by other uglier garments, and not at first available in her size. She will track it down, and by a combination of persistence and extravagance, she will possess it. Like Howard Carter, who looked on the desert rubble of the over-worked Valley of the Kings and knew that somewhere before him lay the tomb of the boy-pharaoh, so Laura Broad, stepping out of a taxi on Oxford Street and looking down South Molton Street, knows her object of beauty is already present, and requires only the patient clearing away of all that obscures it.

She begins slowly. Later, as the hours slip by, she will feel the pressure, she will move rapidly, she will accelerate towards the moment of commitment. Now, at ten in the morning, the shops are beginning to open, and she can permit herself to drift.

She works the windows of Browns. South Molton Street is already busy with pedestrians, walking briskly down towards Bond Street, talking on mobile phones. Outside Vidal Sassoon a cluster of trainee hairdressers smoke and chatter. Laura sees none of this. She has already begun to screen out all non-essential sensory information, including hunger and thirst, to concentrate her powers of attention on clothes.

She moves from window to window, down the neighbourly terrace of cream-painted houses that is Browns; each house modest in size, the whole yielding floor after floor of possibility. She comes to a stop before a mannequin wearing Dries van Noten. A fine silk jacket over a heavy slub-silk waistcoat, offered in the display with a pair of slinky trousers that she is no longer thin enough to wear. But the jacket has promise. It's a gleaming tobacco-brown, cut short at the waist, matador-style, its narrow sleeves embroidered with stars and spirals of tiny coloured beads. The waistcoat beneath is honey-coloured, undecorated but heavily textured by the knit of the fabric. It gives the mannequin a touch of the old Annie Hall look. Laura studies the effect carefully, transferring both garments in her mind to herself. The problem, of course, is what to wear with them. A skirt would look too Annie Oakley; but those pencil-slim trousers? She checks the price card that stands on the window floor like the artist's name check at an exhibition: jacket £765, waistcoat £251. A thousand pounds and the lower half of her body still unclothed. How much is too much? The answer, as always, is relative. It depends on how much wear she'll get out of an item, and on the price of the alternatives. Henry need not know the figure. He never asks.

Oh. Money.

Laura's family was not rich when she was a girl. They were what is called comfortable, which meant that paying the children's school fees left little over for anything else. Laura still feels to this day that the natural season for buying smart clothes is the sales, where a large part of the sense of fulfilment comes from the price reduction displayed on the tag. For so many years she has gazed on these small biro figures, one impossible number with a diagonal line through it, one just-possible number beneath, and thought with amused contempt of the gullible and profligate women who paid the higher price. Then one day her mother rang up and said, 'Guess what? Daddy's got a buyer for his company. We're going to be rolling in money.' The windfall, coming late in her father's career, has been generously shared with Diana and Laura. The share has dwindled, of course, since buying the house, and this and that, but still seven figures. Funny how shy everyone is about money. The numbers always modestly draped so their intimate lineaments remain obscure.

It's a strange sensation, knowing she can have what she wants: one that teeters dangerously close to its opposite, which is discovering that you want nothing. To defend herself against the void, Laura sets herself several conditions that must be met before she commits. The outfit must not be the most expensive among those she likes. It must be classic enough in style to be wearable for at least three seasons. It must be the sort of look that Henry likes. And she herself must be convinced beyond reasonable doubt that it is *right*.

She goes into Browns. At once, as she begins her long patrol of the racks, she feels the outer world fall away. A good clothes shop is designed like a church, to concentrate the mind on the one object of contemplation. No one stands and gossips here. No lesser concerns register themselves. No one eats, no one drinks. No one sings, no one laughs. The sales assistants watch in attentive silence, speaking only to say, 'Do you need any help?' The entire energy of this white-walled space is directed towards Laura and her sacred quest. The staff of Browns, like spectators at a race of champions, silently will her on to glory. But all know, Laura knows, the South American-looking assistant with the sweep of dark hair knows, that this race is no sprint to be won by a burst of showy speed. This is a marathon.

Laura's eyes rake the racks, eliminating whole rooms of possibility in less than a minute. Plaited fabrics, floral prints, denim, leather, all fly past, never to be seen again. She lingers briefly over a pretty summer dress by Etro, light and sexy and elegant at £505. But the forecast for Saturday is not good, she would have to wear a warm outer layer, and the charm of the garment would be lost.

'Are you looking for anything in particular?'

'I'm fine, thanks.'

She wants no help, no interference. The assistant does not take offence. Laura is a serious shopper, the kind they are here for. Her short unsmiling response commands respect.

Up stairs to higher floors and more racks. Astonishing how much information the eye can glean from an item seen only edge-on between dozens of others. Colour and fabric, of course, the basis for ninety per cent of her rejection. But she can also intuit how it will hang, whether it's her kind of dress, from the far side of the room, simply from the glimpse of it on the hanger.

She catches a flash of orange, a muslin top, entirely transparent. The colour draws her first, a deep burnt orange. She lifts it off the hanger. A long veil-like broad-sleeved jacket, offered here to be worn over a shot-silk dress in aubergine. The muslin top is designed to be worn open, and hangs almost to the knee. It's utterly impractical, and very beautiful.

Her roving eye then falls on a cluster of silver and grey garments. After the noon heat of the orange, the silver-grey speaks of twilight. She is interested in grey, the right grey makes her look younger. She feels her heart beat faster, sensing treasure. She crosses to the rack. Jacket, tee shirt, trousers, all made to be worn together, all in the same tones, but all different. She's puzzled by the fabrics. She feels the jacket sleeve between thumb and forefinger. What is it made of? Some shot material, a shiny silver woven with a dove grey. She searches out the label. 'Linen 80%, polyamide 20%.' The jacket is wide, loose, collarless, buttonless. Zoran, a designer she doesn't know. The trousers too are wide and loose, and they have a look she has never met before. She takes them out, and at once sees why. They are cut in two fabrics, one on top of the other: a silk chiffon lying on a silk satin. Because the two materials cling together, the effect is of a single but subtle fabric, which shimmers with the slightest movement. Laura is captivated.

An assistant approaches, sensing her interest.

'Do you have this in a twelve?'

'One size only, madam. Zoran doesn't do sizes.'

Doesn't do sizes! How can that be possible?

'Of course, if you're very big you can't wear them. But you'll have no problem. Try it on.'

Laura knows she's no fashion model. But nor is she unusually big. Evidently these miraculous garments are made to flatter a variety of shapes.

She goes into the changing cubicle and strips with rapid efficiency. The cloudy garments slide onto her with seductive ease. She looks at herself in the cubicle mirror, and then, coming out into the wider room, watches herself walk towards a mirror on the far side. Never before have clothes hung so well on her. Astonishingly, the iridescent folds make her body beneath seem slender, almost coltish. She slips off the jacket and tries the effect of the tee shirt and trousers alone. The tee shirt is silver silk, seamed on the outside, which gives it the look of gleaming armour: a breastplate worn above the fluid lines of the straight wide trousers. She feels like an heiress from the 1920s.

She draws the jacket back on. Warm enough for a spring evening. Could this be it?

'How much for the three?'

'Around eleven hundred.'

Too much. Also she has come upon them too early in the day. Even more glorious clothes may be waiting elsewhere. She has not yet earned the right, in hours spent and energy exhausted, to take her reward.

She returns to the cubicle and gets back into her own clothes.

'It's the last one we have. I could put it aside for you.'

'No thank you.'

Laura is mildly offended by the crude sales gambit. Does the assistant think she's so new to the game?

She moves on. But now there is a subtle shift in her attitude. She has located a possible outfit. Whatever she considers next will be measured against it. This gives her a new confidence, which in turn decides her to head down Bond Street and try the Donna Karan store. Donna Karan is not usually her style, though she did once buy a very expensive, very impractical and very beautiful pair of Donna Karan shoes. It's the store itself that attracts her.

She walks briskly, preparing herself for the coming experience. I am beautiful, she tells herself. I am rich. I am entitled to the best. I am beautiful. I am rich. I am entitled to the best. All only a game, of course. But for the short time that you play, you get more out of it if you're serious.

You are beautiful. You are rich. You are entitled to the best.

For the opening night of the Glyndebourne season on Saturday. Not for Nick, who comes tomorrow evening, Friday. Nick whose only image of her is now twenty years old. How can she compete with her own youth? She blushes in the middle of South Molton Street to learn how much she wants Nick to find her attractive still. Not because she wants him back. That time is past, she's living a different life now. No: she just wants him to regret what he threw away. She wants him to be sorry not for her, but for himself.

She pauses outside the Donna Karan store, preparing herself for the transition from street to temple. The huge windows are backed in black drapes, and hold a very few headless mannequins, all clothed in slender black. In the best shops the dummies have no heads. This delivers a number of messages, the most powerful of which is, only the clothes matter. Not beauty of face, not mental ability, not personality. With dress alone you can be whatever you want.

The glass doors are high. Within, a cavernous space floored in Portland stone, with walls of black French-polished plaster, broken by white shelves bearing a few, a very few, very elegant objects. A wide basin made of crazed clear glass. A bulbous black two-handled water jug fashioned from car tyres and canvas webbing. A single mottled-blue candle the size of a barrel. Further away, beside the wide sweep of stone stairs, rise floor-to-ceiling mirrors, and high panels of gold leaf, and low black leather couches. Higher still, lost in the black ceiling, pinpricks of light beam secret and selective illumination into the expensive air.

Where are the clothes?

Two headless mannequins stand at the foot of the stairs, wearing severe black jackets barely big enough to fit Carrie. Over on the left side, where three sales assistants stand murmuring to each other, pointedly not intruding on Laura's privacy, a single rail of all-black garments hangs suspended by some unseen power in space. Nowhere is there anything so vulgar as a price tag to be seen. As they say, if you need to ask the price, you can't afford it.

Laura sweeps slowly up the staircase, watching her posture in the mirror wall. All this is for me. I am the priestess of this temple. I am beautiful. I am rich. I am entitled to the best.

Of course it's all a nonsense, this reverential hush, this ostentatious display of discreet good taste, these assistants who never look up, yet who register her every move. Intimidating, yes. But also thrilling. Laura feels it intensely, and revels in the feeling: this is a stage, and I am the centre of attention. It's this more than anything that the extravagant use of space delivers. The few who enter these doors become special. Think by contrast of shopping in Marks & Spencers, or even Harvey Nichols. Among the crowds and the bustle, in the literal vulgarity of it all, the sense of a unique self drains away. Here, entering retail space that costs over £4,000 a square metre, in much of which nothing at all is on display, a lovely woman can feel she has value.

Upstairs, where the store reluctantly admits that there are actual clothes for sale, she scans the all-black rails. A smart very simple very long black wool skirt at £710. A leather jacket of kidskin so fine you'd think twice about wearing it out of doors, at £1,995. After a while the figures cease to carry weight. Is £2,000 too much for a short-waisted leather jacket? Is £10,000 a year too much for a prep school? Is a million pounds too much for a house? None of these purchases, the jacket, the schooling, the home, has become any more glorious over the last twenty years; but the zeros have kept growing on the numbers' ends, like empty carriages being added to a slow-moving goods train. When she is old, no doubt a leather jacket will cost £10,000 and the school fees will be a million. What difference does any of it make? At what point should one be shocked, and say, no, too much? The Clemmows have a wide-screen plasma display television, one of the flat ones, and Stephanie Clemmow told Laura it had cost £7,000. For a television! Then she said, to put the price in context, 'It's no more than a First Class airfare to Hong Kong, and Richard does that every other week.' And there were those City boys in the paper recently who spent, what was it, £40,000 on a restaurant dinner? Two bottles of Petrus at £15,000 a bottle, or some such laughable figure. Did any of it matter? What did they get for their money but a few glasses of wine?

No, it's not that easy. Their money buys them more than wine. It buys the worshipful attention of the staff. It buys the conviction of privilege. It buys the envy, even the awe, of others, when the tale is told. Money buys confidence. Admit it. Without Daddy's money sweeping her along like a warm wind, Laura could never have sailed into the Donna Karan store, where she knows she will buy nothing. This is a place for the thin and young and rich, but if the only one of the three you can manage is rich, well, that will do nicely.

Will Carrie come here one day? Laura has only to think the thought to feel her heart clench with a fierce protective love. Nervous gawky Carrie, who has inherited her father's sandy hair and poorly coordinated body, would be miserable here. No amount of money could buy her ease in such a place. Better for it to be out of reach. Better to be poor.

The thought has occurred to her before. Not a serious thought. Only a little Marie-Antoinetterie, a nostalgia for a remembered simpler life. Money removes anxieties. Money oils wheels. Money eases pain. And yet. And yet.

Oh. Money.

Laura leaves the Donna Karan store as slowly and as regally as she entered it. The interlude has, on the whole, proved calming. Now she crosses the street and enters the white-wood mock-colonial villa that is the Nicole Farhi store. Here serious shopping resumes. The blonde parquet floors hold rack upon rack of casual clothes, of the kind you can fling over chairs. The boy behind the till calls out a cheery hello as she passes, in a manner that would get him sacked across the street. There is music playing, some soft indie rock that is unfamiliar to Laura, but that she knows is designed to make her feel she is now among the style-setters, the urban elite, the affluent young.

She checks her watch. Time is passing. A quick cruise down one wall and she pulls out only a silk sleeveless top with beaded bands, not the sort of thing she's here to buy at all. A slight chic garment priced at £170. After the £2,000 jacket this seems modesty itself. She tries it on, standing between the two giant pivoting mirrors that show you the back of your head, and more disturbingly, your bottom. The garment is sweet but not quite right. The momentary glimpse of her own rear view comes as an unpleasant shock. What has happened? Why does everything seem to droop? She has the disagreeable sensation that her flesh is slowly dripping down her body, and will one day form a blubbery puddle round her ankles.

How much was the silver-grey outfit that comes in only one size? Eleven hundred? You'd barely get an arm and a tit from Donna Karan for that. The woman in Browns said it was the last one. Not a wink, not a blush, as she trotted out the tired old lie. I suppose it works on some people. Oh, the last one, they think. What if someone else were to walk in ten minutes after I leave and buy it?

Frowning, beginning to feel pressured by time, Laura completes the circuit of the racks, and finds nothing. Nicole Farhi's not quite smart enough, if I'm honest. Better bite the bullet and do Fenwicks on the way back.

On the way back to where?

There it has been, nestled at the back of her mind, knowing its time will come, feeding on the darkness, putting down roots, growing in size and assurance: back to Browns. Back to Zoran.

How much time left? Lewes by three means the 1.46 at Victoria, which means looking for a cab soon after one, and it's quarter to twelve now. An *Evening Standard* placard reads: 'Anna Ford to marry Moon Man.' How very odd. How old would Anna Ford be now? Somewhere in her fifties, surely. And still very lovely. What is a Moon Man?

She's about to enter Fenwicks, has in fact just hit the wall of scent samples that in her poorer days represented the portals of glamour, when with a clang like the closing of an iron door she thinks, What if it wasn't a lie? What if the assistant at Browns was telling the simple truth? Laura re-runs her excellent visual memory of the rail of clothes, looking for reassurance that there are many more of the ones she picked out. But the others are different. Small differences, certainly, but different. She can't be sure that the exact three garments she tried on, which hung so flatteringly on her, which moved with such seductive grace, are replicated elsewhere on the rail. Why on earth didn't she take the trouble to look at the time? The answer isn't hard to find. At the time the silver-grey outfit was no more than an early lucky hit, a promissory glow on the horizon. In the two hours that have since gone by it has been silently transformed into the one and only answer to her prayers. And maybe, just maybe, it's the last one. After all, it must be left over from the spring season, and everywhere now the summer stock has taken over. What if someone walked in ten minutes after I left and bought it? What if they're walking in now, right now, climbing the stairs to the upper back, glancing along the rack, homing in on that intriguing glint of silver?

Laura panics. She turns round in Fenwicks doorway, colliding with two women entering behind her, and walks fast back up Bond Street. Please God let it still be there. Too proud to run, she pounds the pavements with the big cat prowl of the professional walker. The silver-grey outfit dances before her mind's eye, now shining like the moon, dazzling and taunting her with its desirability.

Anna Ford to marry Moon Man, she says in her head, in time to her hurrying footsteps. Anna Ford to marry Moon Man.

South Molton Street is entirely filled by elegant women carrying Browns bags. Any one of them could contain her outfit, leaving the rack bare, the morning a failure, and the coming Saturday an evening of self-punishment and regret. She wants to snatch the bags from their hands as they pass, demand the right of search, seize back what is rightfully hers, saying like a child in the playground, I saw it first.

Sweating slightly for all the chill of the day she reaches the door to Browns and storms the stairs. The same assistant is there. From the look on her face Laura knows the assistant understands the entire psycho-neurotic scenario playing in her head.

'Not gone yet,' she says.

A wave of blissful relief bathes Laura's trembling frame.

'Though one woman said she might be back for it.'

Not necessary. No sales pressure needed now. The deed is done. The moment of commitment took place in the doorway of Fenwicks. These processes are mysterious.

'I'll have it.'

The assistant takes the outfit off the rail. Laura examines it carefully, lovingly. Yes, it will do. It will be perfect. It will be hers. Thank you God.

As the assistant swaddles the delicate garments in layer upon layer of tissue paper, Laura sits on the padded window bench and experiences the final stages of this emotion-packed morning. She feels a sense of relief, of course, but this is now fading. Beneath the relief, a warm layer of satisfaction. Beneath the satisfaction, some eddies of unease. The price is £1,035, less than the eleven hundred quoted, almost half the cost of the little leather Donna Karan jacket. Not therefore too much of an extravagance. And the classic styling will never be out of fashion. Suppose she's still wearing it in thirty years time, that comes to, oh, not much more than thirty pounds a year. Really rich women have designer dresses costing tens of thousands. You couldn't call this really rich shopping. Well-off, maybe. Not rich.

Oh. Money.

At Victoria Station, where Laura is in good time for her train, she gets herself a cup of carrot-and-coriander soup and an *Evening Standard*. Anna Ford is to marry Colonel David Scott, who commanded the Apollo 15 mission in 1971, and walked on the moon. Colonel Scott is sixty-seven. He is, says Anna Ford, lovely, extraordinary, and very learned. Ms Ford is fifty-six. Her two teenage daughters have given their blessing. We are very happy and hope to spend our future together.

On the train, Laura holds her Browns bag close, feeling the soft fat bundle inside, and reads about the lives of strangers. As the train enters Sussex, so her special day comes to an end. The jealously guarded space she has created and within which she has moved is opened to the waiting throng of her everyday concerns. Has Carrie had a good day at school? Did Henry speak to that teacher? What will she give the children for supper? Has Annie remembered to remake the beds in the spare bedrooms? Does the Volvo need filling with petrol? When does half term start? There are haircuts to book for the children, and friends to play, and oh God there's dinner to make for Nick, just a simple supper but let it be delicious, let it haunt the rest of his life. Cold roast fillet of beef, new potatoes, pick up the beef at Middle Farm on the way to school. It's all getting very tight.

Her shopping trip slips into the past, and becomes a memory of a simpler age. Only the crisp cream carrier bag remains as proof that it really happened. In it, her hard-won treasure.

We are very happy and hope to spend our future together.

26

Jack watches till the cars have passed and then makes a run for it, across the open track to the cover of the derelict barn. Here he waits, his heart beating violently, for the Dogman to pay his daily visit to the sheep.

Your dad's mental.

'You tread on my dreams!' Toby Clore imitates Jack's father, pointing his finger at Jack and not smiling, which makes it not a joke. 'You tread on my dreams!'

I don't care, Jack says. Not my problem. Oh no, says Toby, not your problem having a dad who's mental. Not your problem until they take him away to the funny farm.

All through the first two periods of the day Jack tormented himself in silence, paralysed by humiliation. Why did he do it? Why make a scene in public over something nobody cares about? Why say things like 'You tread on my dreams' so that Angus Critchell can hear and say it back to him in a funny voice?

Dimly Jack is aware that if he were Toby Clore and it was Toby Clore's father who had said 'You tread on my dreams' to Mr Strachan in the hall, he would find a way to turn it to his advantage. He would say, See, my dad's mental, and everyone would envy him and want their dads to be mental too. But this trick is beyond Jack's reach. All he can do is lie low for the morning and hope that the memory of the shaming incident will fade.

After lunch he risks tagging along with Angus, who when asked he names as his best friend. Angus doesn't actually tell him to get lost. When Toby Clore and Richard Adderley show up, Toby says, We don't want mental people in our club, and Jack doesn't say, I'm not mental, or even, What club?, he says, Why not? Richard Adderley says, Because you're mental. Jack thanks him silently for his copy-cat scorn, knowing that now Toby will respond differently, just to be different. And Toby does look at him with his head on one side, the way he does. So you're mental, Jacko? Probably. Jack is beyond resistance. Richard and Angus laugh. Jacko's mental. But Toby isn't laughing so they stop. People who are mental, says Toby slowly, can do things normal people can't do, because they just don't care. Perhaps Jacko's like that. Are you like that, Jacko? Probably, says Jack softly. So if we have him in the club, says Toby, he'll do the things we can't do. He'll do anything. He just won't care. Not his problem.

In this way Jack is let into the club, which is the Dogman Fan Club. The Dogman Fan Club has come into being to record, publish and glorify the sayings of the Dogman.

'He's like Jesus,' explains Toby Clore. 'We're like Matthew, Mark, Luke and John. It's the Gospel according to Dogman.'

The way Toby Clore says this, without smiling, as if he really means it, makes the parody even more sophisticated in Jack's eyes. However, as Toby points out, they are only at the very beginning of their enterprise. They have one sentence recorded, one authentic utterance of the prophet: 'We don't need any more bloody stockbrokers.' They must record more, much more. However, the prophet is quick to anger, and carries a gun.

'Jacko can go. He'll do anything. He's mental.'

In this way, by a process he did not intend but finds himself unable to stop, Jack is on his way to intercept the Dogman, and to cause him to shout out some more holy words. Of course, he thinks, as he crouches in the derelict barn, I could always just make something up. I could pretend I saw the Dogman and he chased me and shouted something, and they'd never know. Except he can't think of anything to make up, and Toby would know. Somehow he just would. So Jack understands that he must wait for a decent interval and hope that the Dogman doesn't show up.

He peeps over the pile of tumbled flints that was once a wall. The sheep are grazing quietly in the steep-sided Downland hollow. Jack looks at his watch. 3.09pm THU 18.5.00. In fifteen minutes the bell will go for prep after games. He'll stay ten minutes at the most.

The watch is too big for his wrist, and has ten functions. It tells the time in two time zones, and the day, date and year. It's a calculator, a calendar, a phone number store, and it has three games. There's a button that turns on a little light at night. He begged for it and was bought it not even on his birthday or for Christmas, on the grounds that it was a necessity and more or less educational. It cost £25. He gloried in it for one day. Then Richard Adderley came to school with a watch that did everything Jack's did *and was a radio*. After that it wasn't the same any more. He goes on wearing it even though it hurts his wrist a little because he feels guilty about making his mother buy it. But he only uses it to tell the time.

Toby Clore doesn't even have a watch. 'If I want to know the time, you'll tell me, won't you, Adders? But actually I don't want to know the time.'

Jack ponders the mystery of Toby Clore. Toby's not exactly Jack's friend, and he doesn't exactly make Jack happy. So why do I hang around him? Why do I want more than anything to hear Toby say, Come with us, Jacko. Why am I here, cold and frightened, breaking the rules, risking being shot, just so that Toby Clore will look at me and say, Good for you, Jacko? It's not as if there aren't others I could go round with. He pictures them in his mind. There's fat Daniel Chamberlain. There's barmy Will Guest. There's always someone no one else wants to be with who'd be glad, more than glad, honoured, by Jack's friendship. But the thought alone makes Jack shudder with dread. If he had to go round with Dan Chamberlain or Will Guest he'd be finished. His life would be as good as over. Better to brave the terrors of the Dogman, if by doing so he retains his precarious foothold on the higher terraces where Toby Clore's slightest word is law.

He hears the distant barking of a dog. Looking out between tall nettles, he sees the sheep begin to move, slowly at first, then in a gathering panicky stampede. They lumber towards the track, where a barbed-wire fence hems them in, and here, caught between the dog and the wire, they surge and cry, while the barking bounces round them.

Jack stands up. Still unable to see, he clambers onto one of the remaining sections of wall. The dog is a small white poodle. It isn't doing anything to the sheep, it's just running round and round and yapping at them, as if calling them out to play.

Then Jack hears a vehicle coming down the track, and sees the

Dogman's mud-streaked Landrover. The vehicle stops by the fence and the Dogman is out, a stick in his hand, shouting at the white poodle.

'Scram! Shoo!' he shouts.

The poodle becomes even more excited, and yapping shrilly, bounds at the terrified sheep.

'Down! Get out! Get lost!'

The Dogman pushes through the mass of sheep towards the poodle, his shouts rising in fury. The poodle responds with an ecstasy of yapping. To Jack, it's all clear. The poodle thinks it's a game. The more the sheep cry and the Dogman shouts, the more he responds in kind.

The Dogman gets through the sheep and swipes his stick at the poodle.

'Get away! Get away!'

The poodle jumps up at the stick, yapping, trying to seize it in his jaws. The Dogman kicks and misses, swipes with his stick and misses.

'You little shit! Get away!'

Yap-yap-yap-yap-yap! The poodle has limitless powers of noise creation. Just when you think the note can go no higher it jumps in pitch and becomes even more maddening. The Dogman is maddened. Even at this distance Jack can see that. Jack is happy enough: he has something to report to the club, and he hasn't had to show himself.

Then it gets much better.

'You dirty little brute!' shrieks the Dogman, and swiping his stick in a ferocious downward swipe, he makes full contact with the poodle's upward-leaping head. The barking stops. Too far away to see what has become of the dog. The Dogman bends down to check. His mobile phone starts to ring. Jack hears him answer it.

'Yes. Yes. I'm on my way.'

He returns to the Landrover at a run. He jumps in and drives away, very fast.

The sheep, no longer harried, drift apart and resume their quiet grazing. The poodle lies hidden by the meadow grass. Jack checks his Casio watch. 3.14pm THU 18.5.00. He makes his way back towards the school playing fields, filled with the import of what he has witnessed, and the status it will give him in Toby's eyes.

The Dogman killed a dog.

The poodle is dead, he's sure of it. Well, almost sure. The way the barking stopped. The way the Dogman just left it there after his phone rang. If the dog had been just stunned he would have picked it up so he could take it to a vet. Or hit it again, to finish it off.

The Dogman is a kind of god. The poodle is a living sacrifice to his power. Toby will like that. Jack hurries faster across the park.

From somewhere behind him he hears a thin high distant voice, like a bird. *Pee-wee. Pee-wee.* He looks back and sees an old lady, walking slowly, far away by the lake's side. Her bird-like call follows a cycle, first plaintive, then imperious, then angry.

'Pee-wee! *Pee-wee!* PEE-WEE!'

27

Keep looking down only one more shoe-lace to tie then out of here. Such a special smell the changing room, not stinky like the boys but still sick-making. Should have had a shower but the others always get in there first and it's not as if I get sweaty, not at rounders, not the way I play. *Just run, Alice.* Never hit the ball, just wave the bat in the air and run. What's the point? They call it games but it's not a game it's a test, everyone's watching, and you miss and they all groan and shout, *Just run, Alice.*

'What's this? Something in my way.'

Sit still, head down. Chloe thinks she's funny. Go somewhere else. On a train with Mum going to Fishguard.

'It's a pile of old clothes.'

'It's Alice.'

Victoria isn't part of the game, she doesn't get it. I get it, I'm part of the game. Couldn't play it without me.

'Oh, Victoria, you utter retard.' Chloe never shouts. She just makes her voice sound like she's laughing. She'll be doing her big blue eyes thing where she stares like she can't believe what you just said. 'Everyone knows Alice ran away to join a circus.'

No, please, not the circus one. Now they're all giggling which makes her worse. Lie down on Mum's lap. Maybe we'll see the baby seals this year.

'Is this a circus, Victoria? Are there elephants here?'

'You're nuts, Chloe.' Victoria doesn't get it. But Chloe doesn't do it to Victoria, I wish she would, that's mean to Victoria, but why does it always have to be me?

'Anyway it can't be Alice. It doesn't speak.'

If I had a knife I'd stick it in her face. In her mouth. I'd stab a knife in her mouth, right in deep.

'Say something, Alice.'

'There's nothing there, Victoria.'

Ready to go. Chloe wants me to bump into her so she can go on with her game. I should bang her down and stamp on her head except I won't. *Just run, Alice.*

'Can you feel something, Emma? A sort of pushy something?'

'Must be a puff of wind.'

'A poof of wind. A gay fart.'

Go round the other way while they're laughing. Chloe with that did-I-say-anything? look she puts on when she gets a result. Out of here any second now, home soon or is Granny coming to get me? Don't look don't listen just run.

Outside is safe there's everyone standing about and cars rolling up with mothers calling out of car windows and even if Chloe and Emma go on with their game I can't hear them. Outside I can move away always a little further away. Outside is okay even if it's cold, even if it's raining. Inside is where you have to not look and not hear and go somewhere else in your head.

I'm on a train with Mum. We like trains. We sit side by side not facing and sometimes I lie down on her if I'm sleepy my head on her lap and she strokes my hair. She says maybe we'll see the baby seals this year if we go very quietly along the cliff path. But the train is the best because you don't have to do anything at all but something is happening. It's just you and Mum being together and nothing else to think about and no one gets bored or says God look at the time. The time just rolls along in this beautiful empty way so that you'd almost think it could go on for ever.

'No one come for you yet, Alice.'

'No, Mrs Kilmartin, but I don't mind.'

That's what I'm good at, not minding, because if I started minding I'd die or maybe kill someone. Nothing matters really things just happen and the trick is not to mind. That way they lose because they want you to be unhappy but if you don't mind you're never unhappy you're just nothing. Which is fine.

Everyone mostly gone now. Granny not usually so late. Even Will Guest has gone and his mother's always the last because she's always on the phone, even when she opens the car door for Will to get in she's on the phone. Chloe and Emma long gone. But tomorrow it all starts again.

'Alice? What are you doing here still?'

Oh God not Mr Strachan.

'My granny's picking me up, sir. She must have got late.'

'Do you have a phone number for her? I think I should make sure everything's all right.'

He has such funny hair Mr Strachan like it's trying to get away from him. He presses the keys on his phone slowly like he's not sure which is which. He's wearing a red tie. That's supposed to mean something isn't it?

'No answer. We'd better call your mother, don't you think?'

'Oh no sir. You don't have to do that. I'm fine waiting.'

Don't call Mum it'll make her think she's done something wrong and she hasn't.

'Just in case there's a problem with your granny.'

He makes the call but when it's ringing he hands over the phone which is really unusual so no one else has said anything before her.

'Hello Mum it's me and I'm fine, sorry to bother you. Mr Strachan said I should call you as Granny's late.'

'Isn't she there yet, darling? My God, she is late! Have you tried calling her?'

'Mr Strachan did and there's no answer. But I don't mind waiting at all.'

'Oh God, oh God. I'll come as quick as I can. Let me have a word with Mr Strachan, darling.'

Now Mr Strachan's saying no problem, not to worry, no trouble at all, I've got a heap of essays to mark, and he's talking in an ordinary voice just like it's no big deal and I could kiss him. All I want is Mum not to be worried not to feel she's done anything wrong which she hasn't ever.

Mum on the phone.

'Darling, stay at school till I get there. Mr Strachan says he'll look after you. I'm so sorry, I can't think what's happened to Granny. You'd better read a book or something.'

'I'll be fine, Mum. I'll do my French vocab, that way I don't have to do it later. Honest, no problem. Don't rush. I'm fine.'

So now we're in the empty English classroom which is spookily quiet but okay really and Mr Strachan's doing his marking and I'm doing French vocab. The clock over the white board actually has a tick which I never heard before. Mr Strachan nods his head while he's reading as if he's having this silent conversation with the handwriting, but instead of saying something he jumps out his pen and goes scribble scribble. Just like he did on my composition. Funny to think he was doing it to all those other compositions too. You kind of have the feeling yours is the only one the teacher has ever thought about. Maybe he writes the same stuff on everyone's paper.

'You okay?'

'What? Yes.'

'I bet you're hungry.'

I look at the clock. It's almost six. I am hungry. He's got this secret drawer and out comes can you believe it a packet of custard creams.

'Don't tell anyone,' he says.

Not chocolate but almost better because of the hard dry outside and then suddenly the soft sweet centre all mixed up with it. But Mr Strachan is breaking his biscuits apart, he gets it so one half has no cream and the other half has all the cream.

'Usually they crumble when you do that,' he says. 'It's harder than it looks.'

It is too. It just crumbles into bits.

'Now,' he says, 'I can lick the raw cream.'

He does it. This is totally amazing. A teacher with a best way of eating biscuits.

'Go on. Have as many as you want.'

It's an orgy. This is so amazing. Not just having biscuits, the whole thing. Mr Strachan's careful fingers pushing in, then a quick snap and he's got it apart without losing a crumb. That's an art.

'You're having a bad time, aren't you?'

'What?'

'I mean in school.'

Now he's looking at me and his wavy hair is waving at me.

'No sir. I'm fine.'

'You said that four times when you were calling your mum.'

'Did I?'

'It's Chloe Redknapp, isn't it? She's a disturbed child. There'll be problems at home, you can bet your life. Don't say I said so.'

I do bet my life. Every day I bet my life. Look down, say nothing. Dangerous talk. Chloe Redknapp is a disturbed child. There is a God.

'Father likes the ladies. Mother likes a drink or two. Something along those lines.'

Heaven. Sing choirs of angels, sing in exultation. I love his red tie.

'So little miss blue-eyes has to take it out on somebody. Which is no excuse, of course. She should be ritually disembowelled.'

What's that when it's at home? Like being made to sit on the lavatory till you're dead? Don't laugh. Mustn't laugh. Oh God he's nodding at me and all that funny hair and Chloe pooing herself to death and who cares anyway?

He's laughing too but not out loud, sort of shaking.

'So what are we going to do?' he says.

'Oh no, nothing, please, you mustn't!'

'Fear of reprisals. Very understandable. But think about it, Alice. If we kill Chloe Redknapp she can't cause any more trouble ever.'

Unbelievable. I'm in a dream. This is not happening.

'Sir!'

'Going too far? Maybe you're right. But she must be stopped. She's a menace.'

'She doesn't realize. She thinks it's just a joke.'

'Oh, Alice. You rotten liar. She wants to make you miserable. You know she does. It's what turns her on.'

Maybe it's a dream but let it go on. He can see. He sees. Like magic. Like he's a wizard. My very own lovely wild-haired wizard. I can say it to him, he knows already. I can say anything to my wizard.

'I hate her.' Say it louder. 'I hate her! She says I've run away to a circus. She makes them all pretend I'm not there. I hate her!'

'Obviously. But we've agreed we can't kill her. So what can we do?'

'Put a curse on her.'

God knows I've tried but it never works.

'What curse?'

'So she gets covered with spots all over her face.'

Chloe has perfect skin.

'Big swollen red spots,' says Mr Strachan. 'With fat yellow tops.'

'And her hair could all fall out.'

'And her eyebrows.'

Brilliant! No eyebrows would be so freaky.

'And she could poo in her knickers!'

'In assembly,' he says. 'Runny poo.'

'Running down her legs!'

Laughing hurts, oh God now hiccups, any time soon I'll be crying, I love Mr Strachan, he's my darling wizard who knows everything especially how to be so silly you just laugh till you cry. Stupid to cry it's not like I'm unhappy or anything but something's opened up inside and everything's just falling out.

Mum!

Darling Mum in the classroom doorway looking surprised but she's got a smile on her face because she can see us laughing. Into her arms and feel her warm and soft and beautiful.

'Here now, darling. Here now.'

Mr Strachan's voice all normal and grown-up again.

'We've been talking,' he says. 'We've not done as much work as we should.'

'So I see.' Stroking my hair. Hugging me close. 'You okay, darling?'

'I'm fine.' Now I'm giggling. Did I really say that four times? 'Let's go home.'

'Come on, then. Say thank you to Mr Strachan for looking after you.'

'Thank you.'

Walking across the empty car park to our car holding Mum's hand and skipping, hopping, light as a bird. Honestly I could fly, it's like I've been let out of prison, and all that's happened is a total stranger has turned out to know how it feels to be me. *Just run, Alice.* Oh, I'll run. I'll run so fast and so far no one will ever catch me again.

'You seem to have had fun.'

'He's awesome, Mum. I love him.'

28

Laura clears away the children's supper, half listening to Carrie as she sits on the stairs talking to her best friend Naomi on the phone.

'I don't know what I want to do,' Carrie is saying. 'You say first. Why does it always have to be me who decides? I said first last time.'

When they got home from school Laura took Carrie upstairs to show her what she had bought. Carrie rubbed at the fabric, twisting her mouth about, unable to lie. 'You don't like it.' 'It's a bit, well, grey.'

Handel on the radio. Time for a glass of wine before Henry comes home. Leftover lasagne for supper, sometimes it's even better reheated the next day, or am I just being lazy? *Buffy the Vampire Slayer* in the living room, steal a few moments in the kitchen armchair, sink into ancient cushions, take the weight off aching feet, drink wine, let the music flow like an unending stream—

The front door bell rings.

'Jack! Someone at the door!'

Jack likes opening the door to people. It makes him feel he's the owner of the house. Also Laura's fingers are covered in food residue.

She sluices her hands under the cold tap and ponders whether or not to run the dishwasher. There isn't really room for her and Henry's supper but if she runs it now Henry will have to empty it later when he's tired, which he hates. On the other hand if she leaves it to run after dinner she'll have to empty it before breakfast, which she hates.

Jack appears.

'It's a man,' he says.

'What man?'

'Don't know.'

'Oh, honestly, Jack. Can't you do better than that?'

She dries her hands on the roller-towel behind the door and goes into the hall. There standing on the doorstep before the open front door is Nick Crocker. Behind him a taxi reversing out of the drive.

'Nick?' she says.

'Hi. I found you.'

Same voice. Soft, relaxed, barely requiring a response. She feels the heat in her cheeks. He found me. Ridiculously, staring at him as mindlessly as Jack, she speaks the words that rise unfiltered to her lips.

'You're not meant to be here.'

He looks exactly the same. This is some kind of time warp. The same mass of curly hair, the same broad high cheekbones, the same wide mouth.

'I said Friday.'

'Oh, well,' he says.

He gives an easy shrug. No apology. No explanation.

'I'm not ready for you. You were supposed to come tomorrow.'

What must I look like to him? Hair all over the place, wearing an apron for God's sake. All those wrinkles round the eyes.

'Come on in, at least.'

He shuffles his feet on the doormat, hunches his shoulders. Did he used to do that? Yes, the same don't-notice-me stoop. Part of his arrogance.

'This is Jack. Henry's not home yet. Carrie!' Yell up the stairs. 'Come and say hello! This is Nick. He's an old friend.'

He gives each child a proper look, a smile, a nod of his head. She takes him into the kitchen and offers him a drink. All she wants to do is run upstairs and fix her face before he sees how old she's got. Why isn't he old?

'Just a beer if you have one.'

He's looking round at everything like he sees everything. Stainless steel extractor hood. Fridge magnets holding paper notes. The big house suddenly grown unbearably bourgeois in the bright light of his attention.

Carrie goes back to her phone conversation. Jack goes back to the television.

'Where are you staying?'

'Some hotel up the road. The Riverside.'

'That's no distance at all. I could have picked you up. You should have phoned.'

'I did phone.'

'Yes, but . . .'

He seems puzzled that she should be so agitated.

'I can go away again if you'd rather.'

'No, no.'

She gives him a cold can of beer from the fridge and a glass.

'You deal with that. I have to run upstairs for a moment.'

In her bedroom she dabs at her nose, then assaults her hair with brisk ferocity until it's cowed into submission. Two quick spritzes of Diorissimo. A swoosh of Plax round her mouth. All the time her mind racing, absorbing the astonishing reality that is Nick.

The first shock of recognition has passed. Of course he's changed. He's heavier, slower, quieter. But still handsome, if anything even more so. Time unfairly kind to men.

Why show up a day early? It's like a surprise inspection. Catch me on the hop. What for? His little display of power. Nick always liked to be the one with the power. Used silence as power. Not that I worked that one out until much later.

She finds him mooching about the kitchen, glass of beer in hand, peering through the back window at the garden. She pours herself another glass of wine.

'You have a view,' he says.

'Yes. Nothing between us and the river. There's a gate at the bottom of the garden. Through there and you're into open country.'

Plenty of scope for solitary walks.

He's looking at her in that way he used to look, half smiling, waiting for her to speak, to blunder, to reveal.

'So,' he says. Meaning, here we are again. Meaning, you start. Christ, it's as bad as Carrie and Naomi.

'Henry should be home soon.'

He nods. His smiling silence propels her helplessly into further speech.

'He's making a history documentary for Channel Four. They start shooting tomorrow. It's about iconoclasm.'

This is completely stupid. But Nick is interested.

'What period? Bonfire of the vanities? Savonarola?'

'No. English Puritans.'

Of course Nick knows all about it. Probably written a book on it. So he and Henry will get on like a house on fire. Except he's not staying.

'So what are your plans?'

'We could go for a walk,' he says. 'Through the gate at the bottom of the garden.'

'I meant in England. In Sussex.'

'Oh. To see you.'

She looks away, shocked by the simplicity of his words. He speaks as if they're alone together, which they are, but not like that. Not yet. Not here, in the kitchen, where Henry will join them at any moment.

So what do I want? To go somewhere alone with him? Nick's reappearance in her life has swept her back to an earlier self, a pre-Henry self. This is between her and Nick.

Is that a betrayal?

She resolves to abide by the courtesies. A friend arrives unexpectedly. There are conventions.

'Stay and have supper with us if you like. It won't be much. I was just going to warm up some leftover lasagne.'

'Thanks,' he says. 'I'm not really hungry.'

'You have turned up at supper time, you know.'

'Have I?'

He must be jet-lagged or something. He goes on looking at her and says no more. He's challenging her, she can feel it. Come on, he's saying. When do we begin the real conversation?

'So do you want to sit and watch us while we have supper?'

'No,' he says. 'No. I'll go back to the hotel.'

When Henry comes home. That's what he means. When they're no longer alone. She can't stop herself.

'So you don't show up for twenty years, then you call for five minutes.'

'I thought we could fix up when's a good time.'

That's what he always used to do, talk in that soft reasonable voice, so that it was her who was in the wrong, her who was putting an unwarranted load of emotion onto simple arrangements. His eyes say, What's the problem?

So when's a good time? A good time for what? She's already invited him to family dinner tomorrow evening. So he means a good time to be alone together.

'I have to work tomorrow,' she says. 'Then it's the weekend and we're going to Glyndebourne and the children are around. Maybe Monday.'

'Monday, then. We could go for that walk.'

'You'd better give me a number in case I have to cancel.'

'I'll be at the hotel.'

He looks round as if the hotel is just outside the door. It's not far, no more than five minutes in the car.

'Do you want me to run you back? I'll have to wait till Henry comes home so there's someone here with the children.'

'If that wouldn't be too much hassle.'

She realizes she wants him to go. She needs to be on her own to discover what she feels about his reappearance. She wants him to go but to return.

'So what's this work?' he says.

His first sign of curiosity.

'It's at the local big house. Edenfield Place. I'm archiving the library.'

He nods, satisfied with this information.

'What about you?' she says.

'What about me?'

'Well, I don't know anything about you, remember? What you do. If you're married. If you have children.'

'Not married. No children. I'm in the art trade.'

'What does that mean?'

Now that she looks she sees that he's wearing expensive shoes. And the Riverside is a pricey hotel.

'I buy and sell works of art. Mostly English watercolours. Towne. Cotman. Turner.'

'So where do you live?'

'Santa Monica.' He pushes his hair back from his face and it shocks her how well she knows that gesture. 'You look good, Laura.'

'Oh, sure.' But she blushes.

'You remember the strip of pictures we took of you?'

'Just about.'

Just about perfectly. One straight, one smiling, one where she looks quite mad. Nick used to say that was the one he loved best.

'I keep them in my bathroom. In the mirror.'

'Why?'

'Old times' sake.'

He gives her one of his smiles, accompanied by a look of such penetrating intensity that she almost gasps. Does he know he's doing it?

Don't say anything. Don't collude.

He turns away from her, looks out through the window into the twilight. His reflection soft as a ghost on the glass panes, like the first time she saw him on the train.

'I knew as soon as I heard your voice on the phone,' he says. 'Nothing's changed.'

'That's not true, Nick.'

'I didn't know it at the time. But what we had was a once-in-a-lifetime thing.'

Laura finds she can't speak. Nick doesn't turn round. Her silence gives him hope, but all she feels is confusion. A rushing sound in her ears.

The crunch of a car on the drive.

'That's Henry,' she says.

Henry's footsteps on the gravel. His key in the door. She hastens into the hall to meet him as he enters, which she never does.

'Nick's shown up,' she says. 'He got the wrong day.'

A frown of exhaustion crosses Henry's face.

'Don't worry. He's not staying.'

Nick himself appears. Henry is well-behaved.

'Heard all about you,' he says, shaking Nick's hand. 'You're quite a family legend.'

'How's iconoclasm?' says Nick.

'Smashing,' says Henry. 'Are you sure you can't stay?'

'Another time.'

'Nick's at the Riverside,' says Laura.

'Very nice,' says Henry.

'I'm going to run him back.'

In the car, navigating the narrow lanes in the twilight, she resists the nervous impulse to chatter. She no longer knows what's happening, she's excited and afraid. She has done nothing wrong, she has said nothing she need be ashamed of. But when he said 'What we had was a once-in-a-lifetime thing' she didn't deny it. She didn't laugh and say, 'Oh Nick, how can you be so silly? We were practically children.'

All through that long-ago July they'd spent hours in a car together, in Nick's burgundy-coloured Vauxhall Viva, as un-cool a car as you could get, and so poorly maintained that it smoked in cold weather. Only Nick Crocker could get away with a car like that. Laura had loved it, was proud to occupy its sagging passenger seat and inhale its reek of petrol fumes and Gitanes. Long drives had been their best times, Nick's characteristic silence masked by the car's rattle and hum, the passing scene filling in the blank between them. Sometimes even then Laura had realized that this was not the way it should be. She was happiest with Nick in cars or when he was asleep, at those times when she seemed to possess him wholly, when his eyes were on the road ahead or closed, and not on her, withholding love.

'Henry seems like a good guy,' he says.

'He is.'

'Must be doing all right. That's quite a house you've got.'

'Yes. We're very lucky.'

'An old farmhouse, right?'

'Yes.'

At the end of the lane, as they approach the main road, they pass the Critchells' barn. The huge floor-to-ceiling windows that have replaced the old barn doors glow with light.

'Who lives there?' says Nick.

'They're called Critchell. He's a lawyer.'

'A lawyer. And he lives in a barn.'

'What is this, Nick?'

'Nothing, really. Just one of those slow but irreversible changes.'

'What changes?'

'The thing about England used to be that it still had countryside. But it's gone now.'

'Don't be silly, Nick. Of course it's not gone.'

Quite a relief to talk about nothing. But also strange. For a moment back there by the kitchen window he'd been on the point of making a confession.

She turns down the short drive to the hotel. Its historic walls washed by hidden lights.

'Used to be an abbey,' says Nick. 'Now it's a Relais and Chateaux.'

Laura pulls the Volvo up by the stone porch.

'So we'll see you for dinner tomorrow evening,' she says, sounding all bright and easy. 'About seven thirty?'

'Sounds good.'

He touches her arm lightly with one hand, gives her a smile, and goes into the hotel.

Laura drives home slowly, cocooned in the car's headlights, the bright bubble of space never expanding before her. She feels like an astronaut, a moon man, travelling through the outer reaches of the cosmos. Her everyday life has retreated to some infinite distance.

She's young again and her heart is breaking.

29

In high summer they returned to the abandoned farmhouse. The grassy bank outside the kitchen window was bursting with wild garlic and lush green clover. The house's water supply, no more than a stream redirected through a pipe into the deep white sink, played trickling music to accompany their daily life. Where in winter they had huddled before the only fire, now their playground was the wide Welsh hills. They walked for hours, sending the curious sheep flurrying away in sudden flight, descending the hoof-pocked paths through deep grass to lunch in half-empty pubs. Returning down valley lanes they hitched lifts on passing farm vehicles, their bona fides established with the name of their borrowed home.

'Bailey Bedw, is it? There's been nobody there since Thomas Evans died. So have they put in electricity, then?'

'No, not yet. We use candles.'

'Candles, is it? And no television? It's a long old day without television.'

Laura played house, cleaning shelves to lay out their modest belongings, re-hanging sagged curtains, filling china mugs with bunches of wildflowers to stand in sunlit windows. Nick sat at a wooden table in the farmhouse parlour with art books spread round him, at work on a treatise with which he planned to make his name in the art world.

'You see,' said Laura, 'it was a good idea of mine.'

She had such fond memories of the farmhouse from their few cold days in January. How could it not be heaven in July? Here was the peace and solitude Nick needed to complete his work; and for her, there was the mass of reading to get through before the start of her second year. If there was to be a second year. Nick still talked of New York in the autumn.

'Let's see what happens with your blot book,' said Laura.

Anything could happen, she reasoned. His treatise could lead to a job offer in England; or if need be she could go to New York with him.

Nick's new subject was an eighteenth-century watercolour painter called Alexander Cozens, who had come up with a method for drawing what he called 'automatic landscapes'. Cozens's approach was ahead of its time, and broke away from all contemporary systems of perception.

'We all see what we're predisposed to see,' Nick explained to Laura. 'We see according to conventions. There's no such thing as an innocent gaze. So how can we ever see anything new?'

This love of change secretly disturbed Laura. She did not long to see the world in a new way. In the letters she wrote to her friends she declared herself to be perfectly happy, because being with Nick was all she wanted in life. Still after nine months together her love for him possessed her almost to the exclusion of all other thought. She could not imagine any way in which their love could be more perfect. And yet she was often tortured with baseless anxiety.

When Nick went out to walk alone, as he did sometimes, saying that he needed solitude to form his ideas, she became immobile until he returned. She felt his physical absence like an ache. She took care not to tell him of her weakness, being sure in herself that it was a weakness. But since any change could only be for the worse, she could not share his excitement over new modes of perception.

Alexander Cozens's innovation involved ink blots. The idea was to force the eye into creating original work by splashing ink at random on paper. You then stared at the blots until you began to see rocks, trees, houses. Out of this scatter of elements you then created an entirely new imagined scene – an 'automatic landscape'.

'Every time you're starting again from nothing.' Nick found in the new method a prescription for life. 'Wipe the slate clean. Know nothing. Start afresh.'

'But what if you're happy with what you've got already?'

'That's stasis. That's stupor. You might as well die.'

Laura knew that Nick was right because he was cleverer than her, but it felt wrong. It felt like an idea you might propose in an argument, not a principle by which to live your life.

'They all tried it,' Nick told her. 'Gainsborough, Constable, Joseph Wright of Derby. It was quite a craze for a while.'

In his treatise he was linking the blot method with twentieth-century abstract painting, in particular Jackson Pollock and his drip method. Some art was closed and some was open. Open art had no single meaning, and imposed no single response. Perhaps it even stilled the gazing mind's lust for meaning altogether, and so opened a window onto what truly is. So ran Nick's multiplying thoughts.

Every other day Laura drove Nick's Vauxhall Viva to the Co-op in Hereford to stock up on supplies. When she made these trips, Nick roamed the hills alone. On her return she called out to see if he was in the house ahead of her. If he was not she turned on the radio and played music to fill the void.

The early evenings were the best time, better even than the nights. The farmhouse was set in a hollow, with only limited views from its deep windows, so they had dragged two armchairs out of the back parlour and up the grassy slope to the edge of a small wood. Here beneath the shade of an oak they sat and watched the sun descend over the hummocky hills and drank vermouth and talked in a drifting inconsequential sort of way. The chairs were side by side, close enough to reach out and touch each other. The evenings were warm. No one else ever passed down the long unmade track that led to their hidden valley.

Sometimes Nick sang, as he had done at the riverside picnic. He knew all the songs from the popular musicals, which seemed so unlike him, and made Laura love him even more. There he sat, his long legs stretched out before him, crooning 'Shall We Dance?' from *The King and I* while the sheep drifted over the far hillside.

One day they went to the cinema in Hereford and saw *Close Encounters of the Third Kind*. On the way back Laura told Nick that her parents had rented a house in Provence for the whole of August, and they were invited too.

'After all,' she said, 'it's not as if we've got any other plans for the summer.'

Nick didn't say much either way in response, but she had learned that was how he worked. Often he would come up with a rejoinder to something she'd said days later, as if there'd been no interval at all.

'Diana will be there, with this new boyfriend of hers. And a couple of old friends of my parents. It's near a village called Aups.'

Then one evening they didn't sit under the oak tree. Nick said he needed to think, and he went out for a walk alone. He was gone for half an hour or so, not long, but for Laura it was an eternity. This was not his usual time for a walk.

When he came back she was in the kitchen at the sink, scrubbing potatoes. The spring water had chilled her hands.

'I'm sorry,' he said.

'Sorry? What for?'

There was a pause. Then he said,

'This isn't working.'

She took her hands slowly out of the sink and dried them on the tea towel.

'What do you mean? What's not working?'

'Us.'

'What are you talking about, Nick?'

'I need some time on my own.'

'You have time on your own. As much as you want.'

'I mean, just me.'

'I don't know what you mean, Nick. Just me? You've always been just me.'

'Well, except there's you.'

'How am I a problem?'

'Not a problem. I just need my own space.'

'What about me? What am I supposed to do?'

'That's up to you.'

They stood there in the kitchen, unable to move, as evening turned to night. She couldn't even bear to light a candle. She wanted to hide in the gathering darkness. Dread was rolling over her, wave upon wave, like an ocean. What he was telling her was unthinkable, impossible, and so long expected.

'It's not that I've stopped loving you,' he said. 'I still love you. But I need to be on my own now.'

'You still love me?'

'Yes.'

'So why don't you want to be with me?'

'I don't know. I can't explain. I've been feeling cramped. I can't go on like this.'

'Cramped? I've cramped you? How? When have I ever stopped you doing whatever you want?'

'You haven't.'

'I don't understand what you're saying. You say you love me, but you don't want to be with me. It doesn't make any sense.'

'No, I suppose it doesn't.'

He spoke in a low voice, his eyes cast down. Laura felt utterly helpless. A madness was overwhelming her, and she didn't know where it had come from or why.

'If you love someone you want to be with them. That's what loving is.'

'I do love you,' he said. 'But I want to be free.'

'So what am I supposed to do?'

'I don't know. That's for you to decide.'

'Do you want me to go?'

'Laura, I can only tell you what's happening to me. I can't tell you what to do.'

'But you want to live on your own. That's what you're saying.'

'Yes.'

'So one of us has to go.'

'I'll do whatever you want.'

'I want to stay with you. I want to go where you go. You know that.'

She was crying. She must have been crying for some time.

'Even so,' he said.

There was no appeal. He was quietly implacable.

'It's my fault, isn't it?'

'No, it's not your fault. You've done nothing wrong.'

'So why have you stopped loving me?'

'I haven't stopped loving you. I just need to be on my own now.'

'Because I'm cramping you.'

How could she tell him he couldn't leave her? How could she say to him, Without you I have no life? This cramping of which he complained was her love itself. He had stopped loving her because she loved him too much. This was the only sense she could make of it all.

'If I promise to love you less will you stay?'

He almost smiled at that. But it made no difference. The decision had been made on that solitary walk. The more she demanded reasons the quieter he grew, and none of it made any difference.

'So what do you want me to do?'

'I haven't really thought.'

'Do you want to go?'

'Maybe.'

'And leave me here alone?'

'No, not that, obviously.'

'So what? Am I supposed to go?'

'That's up to you.'

She felt she was going mad. He kept saying he wasn't telling her what to do, but this silent decision of his had boxed her in. He was telling her what to do, but not in words.

'If you don't want me here then I have to go, don't I?'

'I still love you, Laura. This isn't because of anything to do with you. It's just how I am.'

'So I'll go, then. I'll go first thing in the morning.'

She hoped by turning the parting into a reality that he would come to his senses and ask her to stay.

'You'd better drive me into Hereford. Then you can clear up the house before you leave.'

'If that's what you want,' he said.

She hit him.

'It's not what I want! It's what you want!'

She hit him and hit him, there in the darkening kitchen, as the stream trickled ceaselessly down the sink. Of course the blows led to embraces. She clung to him, weeping, unable to believe the horror into which they were falling, falling even as he held her in his arms.

They went to bed at last. She clung to him in bed, refusing to believe that anything had changed. They made love as they had done almost every single night since they had been together, and she felt as close to him as ever. Then they slept.

On waking she saw the bright daylight glowing in the flimsy curtains, and rose to go quietly to the bathroom. He slept on, as he always did. In the bathroom she remembered. A wave of giddiness made her reach out for the bathroom wall.

She dressed, went down to the kitchen, put the coffee pot on the flame of the little kerosene stove. When he came down, wearing pyjama bottoms and no top, she gave him his coffee. He drank it and then said,

'When do you want to go?'

30

Friday, last day of the school week. Alice trotting off so bravely to her classroom, smiling for me to show I don't have to worry, but I do. I've not forgotten what it's like, God knows school can be torture, I want to tell her it's not the whole world, only one tiny corner of the world, but it's not true. It's the whole world all right. And these laughing running children in their bright blue blazers designed to convey an image of order and privilege are wild animals just as we were, forming packs, asserting dominance, demanding submission. Why must it be like that?

Oh my baby how have I failed you? No one in all of history has ever loved their child as much as I love you. I love your funny long face and your skinny legs. I love to feel you close to me, holding on to me, not because you can't bear to be parted from me, you run off smiling, but because we just belong together, you and me. I never want to let you go, want to be with you always, I'd come to all your lessons with you if I could, sit by your side and pass notes when the teacher's not looking, but I know I have to let you go. Only why must there be so much unhappiness?

'Ah. Hello there.'

There he is, the one I have to talk to, and blushing because he wept in front of me. He's not sure what to call me, he knows I'm an unmarried mother, *the* unmarried mother. In the upper economic zone there are many single mothers but all comfortably divorced.

'Mr Strachan. I was hoping to catch you.'

'Is everything all right with your mother?'

'Yes, she's fine, thanks. No, actually, she isn't. Her dog was killed. It's all a bit of a tragedy, in fact.'

All Mummy can think about is that bloody little dog, you'd think she could have picked up a phone, but I knew nothing till the teacher called. A child surely has a higher claim on the attention than a dog, especially a dead dog.

'How did it happen?'

'We don't really know. She found him dead in a field.'

Poor old Mummy, I mustn't be too hard on her, that little dog was her child, more than me really. At least he didn't go off and produce a bastard, though he might have done, no I think he'd been neutered.

'But you were wonderful with Alice. I haven't had a chance to thank you properly.'

'It was good to get to know her a little.'

'Well, whatever you said to her she's totally in love with you now.'

I wonder what his name is, I can't go on calling him Mr Strachan, he has to be younger than me, only a boy really. He has a sweet face, hard to think of him as a teacher. The truth is even we parents can't help relating to teachers as power figures, we become children again, stand up tall, don't shuffle your feet, Elizabeth, what's that you've got in your mouth.

'When you have time maybe we could have a talk about how she's getting on.' He's using that bad-news voice that doctors put on. 'I'm a little better informed than I was a day ago.'

That's because I made him cry. At any rate he cried. Who knew that teachers cried?

We're all unhappy.

But this I need to know.

'Now. Let's talk now.'

Ding-ding-ding! The bell for assembly.

'I can't now. But if you're picking Alice up at the end of the day.'

'Yes, I am. My mother's not up to it yet, I'm afraid.'

You can say that again. Like a bloody zombie. Poor Mummy. Oh God here comes the swarm. Alice could show up again any minute, lost and faceless in the stream of clones. Every one of whom carries a mother's heart in her heartless hands.

'I'll look out for you, then. It's Alan, by the way.'

That's perceptive. In the midst of the mounting chaos to notice that I'm finding the naming awkward. But then so is he.

'I'm Liz.'

Funny little smile as he goes. What's he doing being a teacher in a nancy little Sussex prep school? What am I doing sending my daughter here? Same thing we're all doing, trying to buy a little safety, a little advantage. No reason to suppose she'd be any happier anywhere else, she's the quiet kind, too tall for her age, not yet started her periods, oh my sweetheart you have all that to come, the bother and the anxiety and the shame, still so much shame. 'Nothing shocks us any more,' they said to Lenny Bruce, 'you can tell jokes about anything, there are no more taboos.' And he said, 'Sanitary towels.'

There she is with her class, hasn't seen me, slip away, she won't want to see me. Once you tear yourself away from your mum you harden like a scar over a wound, you scar every single morning, you have to. Sometimes I wonder how it would have been different if Daddy hadn't left us but he did and to tell the truth Mummy never smiled again. Is it worse for me or for Alice who's never really had a daddy to start with?

Some of them holding hands not all and not Alice. Into the day's battle she goes head high and dread in her heart, a gallant soldier who doesn't know why there has to be a war, and Jesus nor do I. It gets better darling as you grow older, better but not that fucking good.

31

Jack passes Toby Clore a note in history saying 'Dogman latest!' and when it's break he just strolls off down to the tennis courts and knows Toby is following. He feels sure and strong because he has a secret and for a very short time remaining he is the one with something to give and Toby the one who wants it. This is so unaccustomed a feeling that Jack almost decides to keep his secret, except that knowing Toby he could go cold in one second and disband the Dogman Fan Club. So Jack will tell him, but in telling him he seeks to win a privileged position in Toby's circle. He wants it to be a secret for the two of them. Not Richard Adderley, not Angus Critchell. It's to be his special bond with Toby.

So Toby comes after him, not fast, not as if he really cares, like it's something to do in a boring break, and he's got Richard and Angus with him.

'Just Toby,' says Jack. 'It's about the Dogman.'

'Why?' says Angus. 'We're all in the club.'

'This is serious, Angus. I shouldn't really tell anybody.'

'So? Why tell Toby?'

Oh how sweet their hunger. And it's all true. It's serious.

'Trickle away, people,' says Toby in his lazy voice. How does he come up with these words? They're simply perfect, like he's being polite to small children. Angus and Richard hate it so Jack tries his hardest not to smile.

They don't go far away. They hang about between the trees scuffing pine cones and looking round every two seconds to see if they can come back.

'So what's the news, Jacko?' says Toby, leaning against the wire netting of the tennis court, reaching out his hands wide on either side and holding the wire mesh as if he's practising to be crucified.

'I was watching out for the Dogman,' says Jack, whispering. He's thought a lot about how to tell his secret. He doesn't want it to be over too soon.

'Can't hear you.'

'I saw the Dogman,' he hisses. 'In the field with the sheep. There was a dog.'

'There's always dogs.'

'Not his dog. A little white dog.'

'Okay. So there was a dog.'

'It was chasing the sheep. He shouted at it to stop. He shouted, You little shit.'

'That's not bad. We'll have that.'

Not too impressed so far. But Jack knows there's more. This is the beautiful moment.

'The dog wouldn't stop barking, so he hit it. Then he ran off. He hit it with his stick. *He killed it.*'

The climax. Toby says nothing, but Jack knows he's got him all right. Even Toby can't be cool about that.

'And no one knows but me. No one saw but me.'

'Well, Jacko,' says Toby at last. 'You know what this is?'

'What?'

'It's a sign. Woe to the world.'

Jack laughs aloud in sheer delight. Now Toby is going to make it into one of his cracky games and he'll be by his side right at the heart of it. All mental together.

'Woe to the world!' he echoes.

'None shall escape the wrath of the Dogman,' says Toby, the gravity of his manner reproving Jack's laughter. 'First the dog. Then all mankind. But!' One hand raised. One finger pointing skyward. 'His true disciples will be spared.'

'You and me, Tobe.'

'We are his true disciples, Jacko. But does he know it?'

This is Toby in full flow. Jack marvels as he listens. Where does he find these ideas?

'The Dogman doesn't know you saw him, Jacko. He doesn't know you're keeping his secret. He doesn't know you've told me. We could have him put in prison. But we won't, will we?'

'No.'

'Because we're his true disciples.'

'You and me, Tobe.'

Jack knows he shouldn't push it, but it excites him so. Richard and Angus are just burning to ashes with curiosity, they can see even from over by the trees that Toby's off on one of his joyrides.

'But he has to know, Jacko. He has to give us a sign that we're among the chosen ones.'

He pushes his hands deep into his pockets and scowls at the ground. Jack remains respectfully silent. Toby is making a plan.

Angus shouts out, 'Can we come back now?'

Toby shakes his head. Jack, Toby's new closest associate who alone knows what's going on, shouts back to them. 'Not yet.'

Oh how sweet to be on the inside.

'If the Dogman knows we're not telling on him he'll be grateful. And if he's grateful, he'll show it.' Thus Toby reasons aloud. 'And grateful people give things to the people they're grateful to. That's all true, isn't it?'

'Yes,' says Jack.

'So the Dogman has to give us a gift. That'll be the sign.'

'A gift?'

'He has to give us money, Jacko.' He says this gravely, as if it's more a burden than a present. 'Money will be the sign.'

'I don't think he'll want to give us money, Tobe.'

Jack is beginning to feel uneasy about the way things are going.

'Not money to spend, Jacko. Money as a sign. Twenty pounds each.'

'Twenty pounds!'

'Here's what you do. You write the Dogman a letter saying you saw him kill the dog, but you'll keep his secret if he gives us the sign. Which is twenty pounds each.'

'That's like — isn't that blackmail?'

'Only if we want the money to spend. This money's for a sign.'

'He'll tell our parents.'

'We don't put our names, duh.'

'So how does he give us the money?'

'The sign.'

'The sign, then.'

'We say in the letter where to put it.'

'Where?'

'You don't have to be in the club if you don't want, Jacko. Me and Angus and Richard can write the letter.'

Toby stares past him. Jack can see how close he is to shutting him out. It's like a door closes in his eyes and he doesn't see you any more. You play Toby's way or you don't play.

'No, I want to do it. I'm the one who saw him.'

'That's why you have to write the letter.'

'All right.'

'You tell him to put the signs in a jar and tie a long piece of string to the jar and sink it in the Drowning Pool and tie the end of the string to a tree.'

Jack is dumb with admiration. Toby summons the others.

'So what's going on?' says Richard.

'Jacko's going to sort it,' says Toby. 'Don't ask because you won't be told.'

Jack hears this with a fierce thrill. Their frustration is his feast. Their ignorance is his power.

'No one will ever know,' says Toby, 'except me, Jacko, and the Dogman.'

He raises his arm and bends it at right angles over his head. This is the salute he's invented for the club.

'Dogman rules!'

The other three make the salute.

'Dogman rules!'

Jack writes the letter in Religious Studies while old Jimmy Hall is going on about the Garden of Eden. He writes it with his left hand to disguise his writing.

Dear Dogman. We saw you kill the dog. We will never tell if you give us a sign. The sign is £40. Put it in a jar in the Drowning Pool tied by a string to a tree. Dogman rules!

Toby approves the letter.

'Now put it in his door.'

'But he'll see me!'

'No, he won't. You think he stands there all day looking at people who come to his door?'

'I don't go into the village. Not for no reason.'

'So think of a reason, duh.'

32

Who can she call? In her time of greatest need Aster Dickinson calls Victor Peak, her gardener. He comes and picks up the little white furry body and carries it back to her house. His silence is what she needs, she accepts it as his own tribute to her grief. He lays Perry in the low chair by the fire and sits with her for a while. Then once again understanding her needs, he goes.

She slips into a half-sleep, and waking thinks it was all a dream.

'Perry? Where are you?'

He lies in his chair, unbearably still.

It's so like when Rex left and that was her fault too, thirty years ago but it might have been yesterday. He slipped out of her life with his face averted as if he thought she would hit him, which she now regrets she didn't. And yet she was to blame then as she is now. She is hollowed out by the inescapability of it all, the way she kills the things she loves. She loved Rex, well you do, you make your choice, not that there was much choice back then. You make your bed and you lie in it and he's there beside you. Then one day when you thought it could never happen you're pregnant and from then on you're tied together, you and this man and this baby, or that's what you think. You've got his name and the baby's got his name and how can he wriggle his way out of that? That's love, isn't it? Not the being cosy and comfortable and whatever it is he wanted and claimed he never got. It's the iron bond of new life, our child, our Elizabeth, whose life has naturally turned out bad, her man left even before the child was born, so what hope is there for Alice? At this rate when her time comes she'll be impregnated by some boy whose name she never quite catches and who she never sees again.

She knew Perry was dead as soon as she found him, after a long hour tramping the valley where he had run on ahead of her. The way his head lay in the lush grass, the angle very slightly wrong, forever wrong. Not an accident, how could it be an accident, but who would do such a thing?

My fault, she thinks, helplessly hounded by guilt. She recalls the countless occasions on which she hit him with her stick and every blow now falls on her own unprotected flanks. She tortures herself with the memories. I said I'd kill him and now I have.

You're the best friend I ever had, Perry.

The day passes. So long as she doesn't leave her chair she still has him. She wants to die too, go with Perry wherever he's going, walk after him as he runs through eternal valleys.

Elizabeth comes and says what she can but it makes no difference.

'He can't stay here, Mummy. Victor can dig him a grave in the garden.'

Later the rector comes. Someone has told him. He kneels down by Perry's chair and for a moment she thinks he's going to say a prayer over Perry but he's only looking. She avoids meeting his eyes, not wanting to bring upon herself his clumsy attempts at consolation.

'I'm so sorry, Mrs Dickinson,' he says. 'But you will see him again, you know.'

She frowns, caught by surprise. No other statement could have held her attention as this does.

'There is a theory that animals don't have souls.' The rector speaks in a ruminative way, as if to himself. 'But of course, we can't know that. They live and die, as we do. I don't see why they wouldn't have souls, if we have souls. And if they do, then their souls must live on after death, just as ours do.'

She listens in some perplexity. No one has ever said such a thing to her before. People think because she's an old lady that she must be a believer, but all she believes in is loss and loneliness and knowing you've done it to yourself. If there was a God in heaven Rex would have suffered in punishment for the pain he caused. Instead he's living his comforted life in Maidenhead.

'I don't think so,' she says.

'Who's to say? It's a matter of humility, I tend to think. A matter of accepting how very little we truly know. Once you take that step, you open up a universe of possibility.'

'I'm sorry,' she says. 'I don't understand what you're talking about.'

'No, I'm not good at making myself clear. I think the thing is we have a way of not allowing ourselves to believe what we would so dearly like to believe, because it seems somehow too easy. Too convenient. But the truth is what it is, quite independently of our wishes. Just because you want so much to see Perry again, that does not in itself mean you won't.'

But I don't deserve to see him again. One more loss in a life of loss.

'He may live on somewhere. He may be watching you now, hearing your voice, feeling your grief.'

Oh, too sweet, too easy. If only it were so.

'If you close your eyes and think of him as he was when he was alive, maybe you'll feel his spirit.'

Oh, Perry. My only friend.

Mrs Dickinson closes her eyes and remembers. She hears Perry's snuffling yelps from behind the front door when she comes home. She feels his paws on her legs, bouncing up at her, making those little squeals that were his way of talking. She puts her hand to his face, his cold nose, his licking tongue.

Oh, Perry. Don't leave me.

'Talk to him,' says the rector.

To her own surprise she hears herself begin to speak, her eyes still tight shut.

'Dear Perry. I'm sorry I shouted at you. You're the best friend I have. I miss you terribly. The house is too quiet without you. Please come home. Don't leave me here on my own.'

Silly old fool, what am I saying? But it's good to cry at last. Warmth of tears.

'Does he seem closer now?'

'Yes.'

'You can talk to him any time you want.'

'But he doesn't hear me. He can't hear me.'

'We don't know. We know so very little. It might be so.'

Let it be so. The need too great. Rather an old fool than the silence of for ever. She bows her head. A kind of acquiescence.

'Do you think you can let him go now?'

He means the body. Yes, let him go. This isn't Perry. Perry was always in motion, always under her feet, always running in circles, bounding, twitching, alert even when seeming to be asleep, a passing cat would have him springing from his chair, yipping at the closed window.

My defender, my guardian, my companion.

'I don't know what to do,' she says.

She looks to the rector with a new humility, newly respectful of his wisdom.

'A burial, I think. A headstone, if you wish it.'

Because he says 'a headstone' she thinks he must mean in the churchyard. The notion pleases her.

'I'd like that,' she says. 'A simple service first.'

'A service?'

'Before he's buried in the churchyard.'

'Ah.' He hesitates. 'I'm not sure that's possible.'

'But if he has a soul, like us?'

She can't quite say why, but this idea is taking hold of her. If Perry is buried in the churchyard, with a church service and a headstone, then he must have a soul. And if he has a soul, she will see him again.

'You don't think a grave here in your garden, near to you?'

'People aren't buried in gardens.'

'No, no.'

She can see his reluctance. People aren't buried in gardens. Pets aren't buried in churchyards.

'It doesn't matter,' she says. 'What difference does it make?'

But he's looking at her thoughtfully, and she knows he understands. It makes all the difference in the world.

'After all,' he says, 'why not? We don't need to make a fuss about it. Why don't you come to the churchyard tomorrow morning, quite early, perhaps eight o'clock? We can say some prayers, and find a quiet corner of the churchyard, and lay Perry to rest.'

After this he departs. Mrs Dickinson sits in her chair by the fire as before, but something has changed. It's a matter of humility.

'We don't know, do we, Perry? We don't know anything, really.'

33

The cameraman is called Ray. His assistant is called Mo. The sound man is Oliver. The sparks is Pete. The make-up girl is Rowan. Then there's Milly, Henry's PA, and Christina, his researcher, and Decca, their abbey minder. So throw in the director and the star, currently pacing the flagstones under the abbey walls, and there's eleven of them gathered in central London, ringed by the traffic forever roaring round Parliament Square, tracing the footsteps of the iconoclasts of 350 years ago.

It should be a time of excitement, or at least satisfaction, for Henry. His project is finally under way. But he is too anxiously aware of all that can go wrong to enjoy the moment. Oliver is not happy with the spikes of sound from the passing buses. Ray tells him the light is too flat. The crew vehicles are parked by Church House and Milly isn't completely sure they have permission. Rowan wants to spray Aidan Massey's hair with fixative to stop it blowing in the wind, but Aidan says hairspray makes him look like Margaret Thatcher. A crowd is gathering on the pavement to stare at their activities, and Christina is talking to them, keeping them from calling out, but all it takes is one idiot. Once these exteriors are done it'll be much easier shooting inside the abbey, though then there'll be ten times the hassle with lights.

Big Ben strikes the hour. The bing-bong-bing-bong goes on for ever.

'We don't like that,' says Oliver.

'Losing light,' says Ray. 'I'm down a stop since we set up.'

A woman in the crowd of onlookers has spotted the star.

'It's Aidan Massey! Look! Over there!'

Clouds rolling in from over the park. If it starts to rain we're fucked. Ray's telling Pete to walk a light-fill during the track and now Pete has to run a new cable. A road digger starts up somewhere in Victoria Street.

'We don't like that,' says Oliver.

This is the moment Aidan Massey chooses to make some changes to the script. Henry beckons Christina to join him for moral support, and the three of them huddle by a buttress and look at Aidan's changes. He's added two words. Or rather, he's added one word twice.

'The spoken word thrives on repetition,' he says.

The added word is 'sexy'. He's only had this script for three weeks. He's only let them set up and lay tracks and rehearse and do his make-up and agree the camera moves, and now that at last they're ready for the take he's actually giving some attention to the words he's going to say.

'That's fine, Aidan. You do that. No problem.'

One fucking word. Jesus! He catches Christina's eye.

'And on the subject of sexy,' Aidan says, 'those are very tight jeans you're wearing, Christina.'

The poison dwarf thinks he's a ladies' man. He truly does.

'Losing light,' says Ray.

Henry looks up at the gathering clouds. Not that there's anything he can do about it except worry. He can't lose today's shoot, the budget's too tight.

'Let's go everybody. You good for a take, Aidan?'

'Ready when you are, maestro.'

The machinery of filming grinds into action at last. Preparation is everything. When it's time to roll there's nothing to do but watch and listen.

My lines coming from his mouth. My ideas projected by his handsome head, filling the camera frame, making it bulge at the edges with Thatcherite hair. A little knot of highly focused professionals trotting slowly along one wall of Westminster Abbey on a dull day in May.

'Back in the seventeenth century people took idols seriously,' Aidan confides to the camera. 'We're not talking golden calves. We're talking our innate human desire to see what we worship. An image. A picture. A beautiful face. A beautiful body. Yes, this is all about sex.

Idols are the sexiest of sexy images. Back then they called idolatry "spiritual fornication".'

Cut. Thank you, Aidan. You were great. Fabulous. How was it for you, Ray? Oliver? But we can live with that, can't we? Well done everybody. Once more for luck.

Christina whispering.

'You'd almost believe he understands what he's saying.'

Share a quick smile. At least one other person knows the truth. Aidan's right about the jeans. Run the track again. Traffic wardens peering at the minibus. Big Ben groaning towards a bong. Crowd getting boisterous.

'Hey, Aidan! I'm your number one fan!'

Who was it thought he was sexy? Oh yes, Belinda Redknapp. Christ! Takes all sorts.

Re-set by the north wall. Get the exterior sequence done by lunch. Knock off the piece to camera, send Aidan back to his hotel or is it club? Buckle down to the cutaways. The fun starts when the presenter leaves. A bit of real directing.

'So I've got my added word, Henry. Still okay?'

Jesus, one word. Why's he so excited over one fucking word? Who am I fooling? He knows and I know that this one word is symbolic, it stands for authorship. Aidan Massey has spoken. In the beginning was the word, and the word was sexy.

Rowan retouches the star's nose and brow, and he walks the talk.

'Here on the north side of Westminster Abbey you see an empty niche. There used to be a statue here, of the Virgin Mary. In May 1645 a mason called Stevens was paid by a committee of MPs to hack it out and smash it to fragments. Images, the iconoclasts believed, do the work of the devil. Give us too many sexy images to incite our lust, and we're on the fast track to hell.'

Henry circles the cropped grass with Ray to locate a camera position for the mute wide cover shot. Aidan crouches over the monitor as Mo runs him a playback of the take. The abbey towers over them all, living history as they say, even though it's made of stone. The earth beneath my feet is living history, thinks Henry. Who else has stood where I'm standing, through the long centuries?

Raised voices round the camera. The star is throwing a hissy fit. He's calling for Ray.

'I want the camera moved! I want another angle!'

He's telling Pete to give him more light, he's snapping at the make-up girl to fix his hair all over again. The crew look to Henry, hesitating, unsure who to obey.

Henry joins Aidan.

'What's the problem, Aidan? It's looking great.'

'It's looking like shit, Henry. Wake the fuck up and do your job! You're supposed to be the director. Let's see some fucking directing.'

Henry turns red. All this in front of the crew.

'Maybe we should have a quiet word.'

'Losing light,' says Ray.

'It's not rocket science,' says Aidan. 'Camera here, me here, a simple track, then lose me on the tilt up. End on abbey towers against the sky.'

'One big beast of a stop pull,' says Ray.

'Okay, Aidan,' says Henry. 'This is my job.'

'So why aren't you doing it?'

'I am doing it.'

'Then you don't know your job.'

Henry struggles to control himself.

'You think you could do it better, Aidan?'

'Damn fucking right I do!'

Christina steps in.

'We've not got much time,' she says, touching Aidan's arm. 'Why doesn't Aidan go back to the bus, have a coffee, Rowan can take a look at his hair, while Henry sets up the shot?'

'Thank you,' says Aidan. 'At least there's someone here who gets it. That's all I ask.'

He stomps off to the bus. Henry draws a deep breath.

'Set up to do the last take again, Ray.' He avoids Christina's eyes, ashamed to have lost authority before her. 'Thanks, Christina.'

She whispers to him.

'You know what it was? The camera angle made him look short.'

'Oh, for God's sake.'

She lowers her voice still further to add, 'You could do his job better than him, too.'

He smiles at that. He glances up and catches her sweet mischievous look and feels his burden grow lighter.

So is this what we do it all for? A woman's smile. A woman's admiration. Ugly little Picasso painting his models into his bed. All the arts a form of seduction. We shine, we shine, cheating the flowers to open their petals to our little suns. Even the married men. Most of all the married men.

How much is enough? When are we supposed to be satisfied? Monogamy just a social arrangement, introduced to protect property rights, subsequently elevated into a secular religion. As a result of which I feel guilty at taking comfort from Christina's smile.

The digger starts up again, clawing through tarmac to the soil beneath, which is living history.

'We don't like that,' says Oliver.

Milly hurries across to the building site to negotiate another pause.

'We've lost light,' says Ray, tapping his light-meter. 'We can't do it.'

'We're doing it,' says Henry.

'It'll look like shit.'

'Just shoot it, Ray. I don't have to use it. We've got the other takes in the can.'

Most likely I'll run the sound over rostrum shots, seventeenth-century engravings of the abbey, whatever I can scrape together. The cutting room the arena of second chances. Mistakes excised, poor decisions corrected, new order imposed.

If I could re-edit my life, what would I do? Not this.

34

On her return from Wales Laura retreated to her childhood room at home and refused to come out for three days. Her mother left trays of food outside her door which she picked at in the small hours of the night. Also at night she locked herself in the bathroom and ran the shower endlessly, washing and washing her rejected body.

She came out at last, pale, ashamed and angry, not wanting her family's clumsy concern.

'Darling,' her mother said, 'we've been so worried about you. Promise me you won't do anything stupid.'

'Of course I won't.'

'What can I get for you, darling? What would make you happy?'

'Nothing.'

Laura felt the unfairness of her sullen and brutish manner but she couldn't help herself. She hated to see the pity in her mother's eyes. Her father, utterly out of his depth, hurt her with every well-meaning word.

'The man's a shit. That's all there is to it. Just as well you found out in time.'

The only one of them she found bearable was her sister Diana. Laura's undisguised misery returned Diana to the days when she had to pick her little sister up out of the dirt of the playground, and with the same brisk practicality she set about brushing her down after this new tumble.

'Honestly, Laura, trust you to get yourself into such a mess. It's all your own fault, you know.'

'Yes, I do know.'

'I told Roddy all about it.' Roddy was Diana's fiancé. 'Roddy has a cousin who actually got left at the altar, can you believe. She was so ashamed she went off to Tanzania to work in a school for the blind.'

'Maybe I should go to Tanzania.'

Diana helped in another way. She called everyone they knew and told them of Laura's humiliation. This had the great merit that Laura didn't have to tell anyone herself, and need not fear any innocent but out-of-date enquiries after the late Nick.

His name was studiously avoided in her presence. For the first few days, when she was still expecting him to phone, she used the formula: 'Has anyone called for me?' Then when she realized there would be no call she began to look out for the post. 'Any post for me?' But there was none.

How was it possible for him not to want to be in touch with her? She couldn't understand it at all. For all her silence, for all her avoidance of his name, he was in her mind and in her heart every minute of every day. The first wave of grief had passed. She no longer lay on her bed sobbing and wanting to die. But the smallest reminder of him still had the power to render her motionless with pain.

He lay in wait for her everywhere. He besieged her. He booby-trapped her. On Thursdays there he was, raising his glass, saying 'Happy Thursday'. She couldn't hear the sound of running water without flinching. The smell of French cigarettes, songs from old musicals, her dog-eared copy of *Middlemarch* – again and again her fragile equilibrium was rocked by some chance encounter with her lost happiness. She did her best to avoid her memories, but they were legion. His reach encompassed so much of her world: parties, pubs, darkened rooms; rivers, railways, empty roads; green hills and blue sky; Cambridge, London, New York. Words too were treacherous, words she could hardly escape like *there* and *stay*. Sometimes she caught herself uttering low groaning sounds like an animal in pain, and she would search back to find the trigger: a station concourse, a glass of wine, even her own face. She no longer looked in mirrors. She wanted to be faceless.

The songs were the worst of all. Any love song hurt her, because she had identified with all of them when she had been in love. When? She was still in love. Nothing had changed for her. He was the one who had changed.

For my darling I love you
And I always will.

Only he hadn't. Why not? What had she done wrong?

Her college friend Katie came down to Sussex for a few days, but it wasn't a success.

'He's just a bastard, Laura. You're not the first one he's treated like this. He's just an arrogant selfish bastard, and you're a million times better off without him.'

This wasn't what Laura wanted to hear.

'You're totally wrong. You don't know him at all. That just shows you don't have one single clue about him.'

'Well, I know how he's treated you.'

'He's done nothing wrong to me.'

'Laura! How can you say that! He dumped you.'

'So? Has it ever occurred to you that he might have had his reasons?'

'What reasons? Why would any normal guy want to dump someone like you?'

'Nick is entirely normal, Katie. And perceptive, and considerate, and thoughtful, and as a matter of fact he's probably the person I'd go to first if I wanted advice on anything important. I respect him. So if he thinks it's best for us to be apart I'm willing to accept he has his reasons.'

'Oh, sure! Like he wants to fuck around.'

'Oh, for God's sake.'

'I just can't bear to see you so unhappy, okay? I want you to forget him and move on.'

'I will. I just need time.'

'He's not worth it, Laura.'

'Stop saying that! If he's not worth it, what kind of a fool does that make me?'

A big fool. A jumbo-sized fool. The kind of fool who deserved to be dumped. So Laura's thoughts went round in circles, and contained tight within every circle was the conviction that it had all been her fault.

She brooded on this endlessly. She was convinced that if she could locate what she'd done wrong then there was a chance of putting it right. Then he would come back to her.

She was not pretty enough. People called her pretty, but all you had to do was look more closely and all the defects jumped out at you. Her lips were too thin. She had a gap between two of her top teeth. Her breasts were too small. She had freckles on her back.

She was not sexy enough. She wasn't quite sure what it was some women did in bed that made them sexy, but she suspected it was nothing to do with positions or techniques. It was all about taking the lead sexually, making moves unasked. Laura was no prude, she was willing to try anything. The hard part was taking the lead. Her shyness lay in her fear that she would get it wrong; that her advance would be unwanted, or worse still, ridiculous. So she always waited to be told what to do. Maybe just being available for sex was not in itself sexy.

She was not clever enough. She had failed to hold his interest. Nick was so much cleverer than her, she had known it from the start, it had been one of his great attractions for her. Laura was not indulging in false modesty here. She knew she was clever in her own way. She was a good learner, she could fulfil a brief, she was efficient at passing exams. But she was not original. Left to herself she had no ideas other than those she had been taught. Nick was full of ideas. It would never have occurred to her to contrast the classical myth of Arcadia with the Christian myth of the Garden of Eden. She was clever enough to appreciate the originality of Nick's mind, but not clever enough to match it. So he had become bored with her.

She was not independent enough. She had invested herself so completely in her love affair that she had hardly existed apart from Nick. This had made him feel cramped. She had been a weight round his neck, a drag, her very presence in his life had made demands on him, so of course he had had to cut free of her. She had become a pathetic needy person who no one could love.

So Laura went round and round in her circles of self-blame, suffering intensely with regret at her past self. But through all the obsessional punishment she kept one part of her past unblemished. Nick remained in her memory the only perfect man she had ever met, or would ever meet. They had not parted through any fault in him. By assigning all the fault to herself she left open a door to a future in which they could be reunited. All she had to do was grow older and wiser, until at last she was worthy of him.

When after several weeks of suffering Laura reached this conclusion, she did something she had never done before. She wrote a letter to the future. The letter was to Nick, and it was to be put aside until they met again, and became lovers again. This would be many years in the future, two or three or even four. Over these years she would change a great deal. When she had fallen in love with Nick she had been a girl. In that future time when she would give him the letter to read, she would be a woman.

Dear Nick. I'm writing this not long after you asked me to leave you. I'll give it to you when you ask me to come back. I know this day will come because there'll never be anyone for me as wonderful as you. As for you, I wouldn't be giving you this letter if you hadn't ended up thinking something similar about me. If you don't then I'll never give you this letter, and you won't be reading it now, so it doesn't matter.

I've never stopped loving you. I thought for a time that you had stopped loving me. But then I realized that it was impossible for you to just switch off the love I had felt in you. So I decided that somehow you still loved me, even though we had to be apart. That was when I stopped sorrowing and started living, confident that in your own time and in your own way you would come back to me.

Now you have come back. I want you to know that not one day has gone by in which I haven't thought of you. The truth is we have never parted. Whatever road I've travelled I've always known it leads back to you.

You remember how you said to me that first night, 'Stay.' I stayed then. I have stayed ever since. I have never left you, just as I now know you have never left me.

Here's the first note you ever wrote me. It says what I feel – until we meet again.

I love you. Laura.

September 1978.

She put the letter in an envelope, along with the strip of photo-booth pictures of Nick, and the red ribbon that had tied up his birthday present to her, and the note he had left in her pigeon-hole that read: 'Came to see you but you're not here. If you come to see me I'll be there.'

She sealed the envelope and wrote on it: *'For N.C., one day.'*

35

In the vaulted library at Edenfield Place, wearing an unflattering cardigan against the chilly air, Laura abandons the attempt to focus her attention on the file box before her. She turns her thoughts to the mystery that is Nick Crocker.

Why has he come back? To pick up where he left off twenty years ago? To become her lover again? Absurd though it seems, she finds herself thinking this can be his only motive. The monstrous egotism of it makes her gasp. Why should she – married, with children – why should she – except of course that people do it all the time.

Laura finds she's angry at him. This pleases her. She prefers anger, an honourable emotion, to the other feelings, feelings she can hardly name, dread and triumph and vindication, and a secret hunger of the heart. Hunger for what?

Then she recalls the touch of his hand on her arm, in the car by the hotel, and all at once she catches the timidity of the overture, the helplessness, and her anger disperses like mist on the wind.

What we had was a once-in-a-lifetime thing.

Is that true? They were together for ten months, and then it was over. At the age of twenty her life ended. Half a lifetime ago. The memory still has the power to hurt. She still wants to understand. It was cruel, wasn't it?

And now, this unwarranted return, this too is cruel. What's done is done. The lost years can never be given back.

So if he hadn't left me, would I still be with him now? Would we have children together? She flinches from the thought as if it stings her, it does sting her, because it erases her babies, Jack, Carrie, and she wants to hold them tight, never let them go.

And Henry?

If her love for Nick was unique, never to be repeated, what love has she for Henry? She tries to remember their first meeting and fails. It's as if she always knew Henry, he was always there, she has only to turn round and smile. Yes, she does remember now, it was in Quaritch's, where she was working as a lowly assistant. Henry sat across the table from her, walled by cases of antiquarian books, and took notes in a hardback notebook. So like Henry: a man who doesn't throw away his notes. Greville said to her, 'Be nice to him, Laura.' The pretty young assistant assigned to look after the young television researcher. And she was nice to him. She could see that he found her attractive, and she liked that. It was a kind of game. She the secret agent, her mission to charm. The joke was that Henry, duly charmed, never had the power to fulfil Greville's dream. There never was a television programme featuring – what was it? – Oriel College's sale of their Shakespeare First Folio, Quaritch's greatest ever coup. What remained was Henry in love. No, too strong a word for that phase of their relationship. In hope.

Did I fall in love with Henry?

Not like the first time. But Nick was long gone. For a year or so there had been Felix, though neither of them really believed they were doing more than marking time. Then there was the Mad Russian, who made her laugh and behaved impossibly badly and proposed to her daily. Some other shorter-lived liaisons, now forgotten. Then Henry.

Never any anxiety with Henry. He invited her to his election night party, quite a modest affair in his flat in Hammersmith. She liked his friends, and she liked him for not laughing at Michael Foot. A week or so later they saw a film together, one of the Star Wars films, and ate in an Italian restaurant afterwards. He tried to construct a Jedi philosophy from the meagre clues in the film, and she knew as she watched him across the stripped-pine table that she would marry him.

'I think I've got it. Yoda is Welsh.'

'Welsh?'

'Listen to his speech patterns.' He put on a Welsh accent. 'Clear, your mind must be. Not believing is why you fail.'

Laura laughed.

'The Force is Welsh, which means the Dark Side can only be

English. The British Empire, you see. It all adds up. George Lucas has created a galactic version of the American War of Independence.'

'What are you on about, Henry?'

'Nothing much,' he said. 'Just burbling.'

He was happy in her company, and that made her happy.

Seven weeks later he asked her to marry him. It should have been a big decision but it just felt natural, as if it was the next thing to do.

Pat Kelly comes in with tea and biscuits and the chance of a little chat.

'Something's up with lordy,' she says. 'Something's tickling his toes.'

Laura knows but can't say.

'More talking in the chapel, Pat?'

'It's the shifting about of the man. You must have seen him. You know how he has a way of looking at you like he's asleep with his eyes open? Well, something's woken the man up.'

'Money troubles, maybe.'

'Could be money, true enough. But if you ask me I'd say the man needs his comforts. No one can go year after year without his comforts.'

'Do you mean love, Pat?'

'Love, for sure, and cuddles and kisses and all the rest. Men need their comforts.'

'And women too.'

'I don't deny it. Women too, for sure. Don't we all?'

'Are you married, Pat?'

'In a manner of speaking.' Pat brushes back her thick black hair and straightens her skirt round her plump waist, as if the mention of marriage recalls to her that she has a body. 'The old bastard's not dead yet, but he's long gone from me. That man is a waste of God's breath and always will be. But as they say, good men are hard to find. I'm thinking I might get myself a cripple in a wheelchair.'

'A cripple? Why?'

'So he can't leave me. If he tries, I wheel him back.'

She laughs, and Laura laughs too, their laughter echoing round the high hammerbeam roof.

Pat leaves her to her work, but returns almost at once to say Laura has a visitor.

'What visitor?' Laura never has visitors here.

'Says he's an old friend.'

'Oh.'

'Shall I send him in?'

'No. I'll come out.'

Nick Crocker is standing in the galleried main hall staring round him in wry appreciation. The hall is three storeys high, the entire upper storey a canopy of carved wood and glass.

'What a place!'

'What is it, Nick? Why are you here?'

His gaze descends to meet hers. A shrug: isn't it obvious?

'To see you.'

'But you're coming to dinner this evening.'

'No. I don't think so. I'd rather see you on your own.'

'Nick, I'm working.'

'It won't take long. Is there somewhere we can go?'

He looks through the open door to the chapel.

'This house really is something else. When was it built?'

'1870, 1880, something like that.'

'It's insane. I love it. Like the castle in Disneyland, pure pastiche. Walt's fantasy version of Neuschwanstein, which was mad Ludwig's fantasy version of a medieval castle. Dreams built on dreams. It must have cost a fortune. Where did the money come from?'

'Patent medicines. Laced with morphine.'

'Opium dreams. Perfect.'

This is how she remembers him: maddeningly distractable, impossibly well-read, knowledgeable on every subject, ironically amused by the details of the world around him. But ask him what he feels himself, what he cares for, what he's hurt by, and he's silent. Knowledge, irony, silence: the Nick Crocker method.

But here he is. If this isn't pursuit, what is? Whatever he's come to say, she doesn't want to hear it in the house. Better to seek the privacy of the open air.

'I'll show you the lake.'

They go out onto the west terrace and so down the lime avenue to the lake. Laura has resolved not to be the first to speak. This is Nick's party. He can dance.

In the long grass on either side a few surviving pink-and-mauve fritillaries hide among the withered daffodil leaves. Nick stops and crouches down to examine the delicately drooping heads.

'Aren't they exquisite? The colouring! Each speckle has its own shadow. And look inside! There's a dome Brunelleschi would have been proud of.'

He's right, of course. Laura feels ashamed that she's not looked more closely before.

'And you see how each one stands alone? No vulgar crowding together like daffodils. These would be snake's heads, do you think?'

'I really don't know.'

Then as they turn into the lake walk, without preamble, 'I don't forget, Laura.'

'Don't forget what?'

'All of it.'

Laura says nothing. Nor does he seem to expect her to speak.

'Most of all the last day.'

A cold wind is blowing off the lake. Laura shivers. Nick seems oblivious. He's wearing a cotton jacket, a tee shirt, jeans. He looks at the overgrown path ahead, never at her. He says, 'That was the worst day of my life.'

'The worst day of *your* life?'

'I know I made a mess of it. I know I hurt you.'

'Do you?'

'Laura, I was twenty-two years old. I wasn't in control. I wasn't in charge.'

'Nor was I, Nick.'

'No. We were both young. That's all. We were young.'

Twenty and prickly-proud and arrogant-ignorant and timid in bed. Not a time to remember without shame.

'We were young all right.'

'I had this thing about freedom. How I wanted no possessions. No baggage, no clutter, no demands, nothing.'

'I remember.'

'I needed all that empty space to become whatever I had it in me to become. To grow edges – to make a shape – it's not easy to put into words.'

'And I was the baggage and the clutter and the demands.'

'You were everything I wanted. But who was I? That's why I was so scared.'

'I don't blame you, Nick. I'm sure I was far too clinging. Too needy. Too adoring.'

'No. Don't say that. I don't think either of us are to blame. I loved you in my way, and you loved me in your way.'

'And it didn't work out.'

He's silent for a moment. Then, 'Back then, did you ever think about our future?'

'Of course.'

'What was it? What sort of future did you see?'

'What you'd expect. We'd stay together. We'd get a little flat in London, or New York. Do our jobs. Support each other, encourage each other. Maybe get married one day. Have children. See them grow up.' She smiles, shakes her head, suddenly afraid she'll cry. 'All the usual stuff.'

'That's what I thought about too.'

'So you did a bunk.'

'I wasn't ready.'

'It's okay, Nick. It's called fear of commitment. It's not at all original. But just for the record, I never asked for anything. Not one single thing.'

'Yes, but the thing is, I loved you. That's what made everything different. I knew this was either it for ever – or I had to get out of your life.'

Laura remembers the pain of that time and feels a rush of pity for her past self.

'Why, Nick? Why all the melodrama? Why all the this-forever or that-forever? You could have just given it a go, seen how things worked out, taken it day by day.'

'Is that how you were back then? Giving it a go? Seeing how things worked out?'

Of course he's right. It was all or nothing, because it was all, always all. She never believed in nothing, not till it happened.

'I went over it for days. For weeks. It seemed to me the longer I left it the worse it would be for both of us. So it had to be now. Today. Then today went by, and I said, tomorrow. Day after day went by, and I couldn't do it.'

'And then you could.'

'I did it badly, I know. I was in a terrible state. It was like cutting off part of my own body.'

'It was like a killing, Nick. Like an execution. I wished I had died. I really did.'

'All right. I won't compete. It hurt you more than it hurt me.'

'You were the one who was doing what you wanted.'

'Yes. I'm not denying it. I'm not denying anything.'

'And then you didn't call, or write, or anything. Just silence. Like you died or something.'

'Yes. I know.'

'For over twenty years.'

'Yes.'

'You don't think that's overdoing it?'

He smiles at that.

'Probably.'

'And now here you are.'

'Here I am.'

A silence follows. He's trying to find the right words.

'I didn't call or write,' he says at last. 'But I've thought about you every day from that day to this.'

'Oh, come on, Nick. That's ridiculous.'

'I've tried to forget you. God knows I've tried. My last girlfriend, we were together for six years, I told myself this is it, settle down, get married. But I couldn't do it. It's very simple, really. You're the one I gave my heart to all those years ago, and I don't have it to give to anyone else.'

Laura is silent. She hears the rushing sound in her ears and she feels the trembling melting sensation in her stomach, but whether she's gratified or angry or fearful she can't tell. She's a little stunned.

Nick understands this.

'That's what I wanted to say. I'll leave you to think about it. Pick me up from the hotel on Monday. We'll go for our walk.'

He strides away across the park to the house. As he goes he takes out a phone and calls for a taxi to get him back to the hotel.

Laura returns more slowly, waiting for her understanding to catch up with her feelings. She finds herself in a state of bewilderment. The uncertainty is not over what to do, there's nothing to do, Nick has proposed no course of action and none is possible. But what does it all mean? Does she believe him? And if she does, what has changed?

She looks at her watch. Just past twelve.

I have a husband. I have children. I have things to do. Phone Diana to find out when she's coming down, confirm the baby-sitter for Glyndebourne, make something for the children to eat tomorrow, is Carrie friends with Naomi again? Are my babies happy? Am I doing enough? I'll do anything for them, there are no limits, I'll sacrifice anything, just ask me.

Billy appears as she crosses the hall back to the library.

'Anything on that matter we spoke about?'

'Nothing so far, Billy. Sorry. I have been asking around.'

'Good. Good. Seven years, you know.'

'What's seven years?'

'My father knew this Doll for seven years. I can't find it in myself to blame him. After all, seven years of happiness. That's something, isn't it?'

He shuffles back into his room, waving one hand in the air as he goes.

Laura packs up her boxes in the library, switches out the lights, closes the door after her. As she turns to face the high galleried hall she is caught unawares by a shiver of sensation that begins in her legs and floods her stomach and chest and makes her face burn. Before she has time to qualify or judge it she knows it for what it is: a rush of joy.

36

The hush of the classroom as twenty eleven-year-olds scratch away at their desks. Alan Strachan finds himself thinking about Liz Dickinson and wondering if she has a boyfriend. Just because she's a single mother doesn't mean there isn't some other man about the house. Though if there was surely he'd share the duties of the school run and ease the burden on the granny. But then again she's attractive, no denying it. Not pretty, too real for such a girly word, but there's something there in her face that makes you want to, oh, get closer, nuzzle up. Must be her eyes, or the lines round her eyes. What is that look in her eyes? There's a word for it, or several words. Resigned. Acceptant. Unjudging. Yes, that's part of it. You look at her and you feel she'd understand.

Who am I kidding? Understand, sure, we all know what that means. Not hard to tell where that one's going. But who else am I to turn to in my dreams? The erotic current does not flow strong in the staff room. Not unless you include the Australian gap-year students, all of eighteen years old, and if you include them then why not the girls in Year Eight, one or two of whom are so achingly gorgeous it doesn't do to let the eyes linger too long or you wake up turned into a paedophile. Thirteen years old! Jesus! Why has nature played this trick on us? The physical peak of perfection and not to be touched. Ring them round with the electric fence of our longing and our shame, then plaster every billboard on every street with images of women made to look younger, longer-legged, thinner. The corporate logo of Planet Desire a pubescent thirteen-year-old girl, the perfect icon of the hunger that can never be satisfied, so stuff yourself with beer and chocolate and anaesthetize all lusts.

But I'd rather have Liz Dickinson any day.

Thank God, the bell for break.

'Chloe, stay behind a moment. About your composition.'

'But sir! It's break time.'

'Won't take a second.'

Now she hates me. Can't be helped. She'll have to forego the pleasure of torturing Alice Dickinson for a few minutes.

'Actually it isn't about your composition. I just said that so no one would know.'

It seems I have her attention. Big blue eyes, wavy blonde hair, perfect skin, evil heart.

'It's about Alice.'

The eyes close inside. The shutter is down. She's going to give nothing away for free. That's fine with me, babe. I have the jump on you in this little encounter. I've had time to make a plan.

'I thought you might be able to help me. But I have to ask you to keep this between ourselves. For Alice's sake. Will you promise?'

A slow cagey nod. She's getting it now, this isn't a court of law and she isn't the defendant. So who is she?

'Someone's bullying Alice. I don't know who, she won't tell me. But it's making her very unhappy. You've probably noticed how quiet she is these days.'

Another slow nod.

'I'm not asking you to tell me who it is. That would be telling tales. But I've noticed you're the one the others look up to in class. I thought maybe you could have a word with whoever's responsible. I expect they're just doing it for a joke. You could make them see it's not a joke. You could even tell them it could get them expelled.'

'Expelled!'

'Oh, yes. We take bullying very seriously. That's why I was hoping you could help me sort it out quietly. Do you think you can?'

She twists her lips, chews her lower lip. Wrinkles that perfectly smooth brow.

'I suppose I could try.'

'I shouldn't really admit this, but I think they'll pay more attention to you than to me.'

She likes that. The presumption of power, always an acceptable compliment.

'I don't know,' she says.

'Our secret.' Hand out for her to shake. Physical contact, almost as binding these days as a blood oath. There, her slender hand in mine. 'If anyone asks, say I've been banging on about full stops and commas. Really boring, and not fair in break time.'

That gets an actual smile. Conspiracy in place. Off she goes, pink as an assassin, charged up with secret explosives. Poisonous little tart. Let's hope it works. It would be good to have an actual improvement to report to Liz after school.

So it's Liz now, is it?

37

Alone that early evening in the production office on the Goldhawk Road Henry pours himself an industrial-strength gin and tonic and runs through the tapes of the day's work. Nothing that can't wait but the trains will be crowded and he feels the need to be alone. Also Nick Crocker will be at home having dinner with Laura and it takes more reserves of energy than he's got to be sociable with a stranger, particularly one who is no stranger to his wife. So do some work, see what's there, mark up some takes for Dylan, revise the schedule for the next day's shoot, which is Monday.

The offending piece to camera returns to life on the office screen. He sees at once that the camera is too high and the angle too wide, at least at the start of the take. He tries to remember if that was his doing or Ray's, and if it was his, why? Aidan Massey enters frame in the middle distance looking strikingly like a monkey. Henry runs the take three times for the sheer pleasure of it while he downs his gin, and begins to feel the tensions of the day melt away.

Why did I do it? Why didn't I even notice I was doing it?

He's both amused and alarmed to find his secret self is sabotaging his public actions. He could never use a take like this. Aidan Massey in monkey mode makes the enterprise ridiculous. But anger will find an outlet somewhere. Aidan Massey has come to embody everything that is unjust and futile about Henry's life. He is the lie, and the lie corrupts everything.

A tap on the door and Christina comes in.

'I knew you'd still be here.'

She looks uncertain of her welcome. He offers her a smile. She's welcome.

'Just taking a look at what we've got.'

He spins the tape back.

'Look at this.'

Still standing, Christina watches the take.

'See. I told you that's why he lost it.'

'I feel like accidentally making a hundred copies and spreading them round the business.'

Christina giggles.

'He looks like a dwarf.'

'He is a dwarf.'

'You were very good with him today, Henry. He behaved outrageously. You kept your cool.'

'Not really. Thank God he fancies you.'

'What do you mean?'

'It's you who calmed him down. You got him off my back. Do you want a drink?'

'Why not?'

So Christina has a gin and tonic too. There's more than enough gin and not enough tonic. Henry shares out the proportions as fairly as he can.

'So do you fancy him?'

'God, no.' Christina pulls a face. 'I think he's repulsive.'

'A lot of women do fancy him.'

'Not me. He gives me the creeps. Plus he's a total fake.'

'Tell me about it.'

Henry stretches out on the sofa, feet up on the coffee table, and allows himself to be warmed by Christina's sympathetic understanding. She's still too shy to meet his eyes for more than a second, but she's on the stool in front of him and they're ripping into Aidan Massey together and that's enough.

'You know how he said today he could direct better than you?'

Henry groans.

'You should have said to him, Fine, you direct. I'll be the star of the show. Which I happen to have written.'

'If only.'

'Actually I'm serious. You'd be great on camera.'

'I don't think so.'

This is not Henry's particular ambition or vanity but he appreciates the vote of support.

'I don't know what I'm doing in this job,' he says after a moment. 'I love the reading and I love the writing. All the rest, the filming and screening and publicizing and ratings and reviews, I hate all that.'

'You should be an academic.'

'I was a teacher for a while.'

'I bet you were good.'

'Not really. I couldn't keep order. No, that's wrong. I could keep order. I just didn't want to. I wanted them to want to learn. There were some. It wasn't all bad.'

'I wanted to learn,' says Christina. 'I still do.'

'What turned you on to history? Can you remember?'

'Oh, yes. It was reading *The Diary of Anne Frank*. She was so like me, except that she was history, you know? Daddy took me to Amsterdam to visit the Anne Frank house when I was twelve. After that I started reading everything about the war.'

She calls her father Daddy without even thinking. Henry tries to remember how old she is. Twenty-three?

'How about you?' she says.

'I don't remember. It was so long ago. I've always loved history.'

But he does remember. There was a picture book he had when he was seven or eight, each picture covered two side-by-side pages, each of the same valley. There was a river curving down the valley in the shape of an S, and a little hill and a big hill. In the first picture there was an Iron Age fort on the big hill. In the second picture a Roman town. By the final picture there were trains and gasworks and streets of red-brick houses, but it was still the same valley underneath.

'Yes, I do. It was a book called *A Valley Grows Up*. Do you know it?'

'No.'

'It must have been out of print for years. I loved that book. The valley goes from the Iron Age to the twentieth century, picture after picture.'

He's sitting once more in the old green chair by the bay window, his legs curled beneath him, the book open in his lap, experiencing all over again the shock of the past.

'It hit me one day, reading that book, that history didn't happen somewhere else. It happened right here. I mean, in the same actual physical space. Like this room we're in now in Shepherd's Bush. A real shepherd might have sat under a tree exactly where we're sitting, only five hundred years ago. He's here with us now in some form, a ghost or an echo or something. Imagine all the people who've occupied this room, this space we're in now, over thousands of years. Imagine them all existing at once, like a crush at a party. They were here. It's not make-believe. They were real people, and they were as close to us as I am to you. Closer. People act like history is the study of other worlds, like it's some dark undiscovered continent, but it's not. It's here. Right here.'

He stops, realizing he's been going on too long. Christina is gazing at him with a little furrow of concentration between her eyes.

'Anyway, that's how it started for me.'

'And it's still like that for you. Or you couldn't talk like this.'

'Like what?'

'Like you care.'

'Like I care. Do I care? I don't know. It doesn't seem as much fun as it used to.'

'That's terrible, Henry. Don't say that. Don't let a creep like Aidan Massey spoil it for you.'

'Oh, it's not just Aidan Massey.'

'So what is it?'

He smiles at her and thinks how pretty she is and wonders that he never noticed it before. She wants so much to understand what he's feeling. Nothing so seductive as unwavering attention.

'I hardly know myself, to tell you the truth.'

But I do know. It's the choice I made when I took my first job in television. My beloved history sold into captivity. A performing bear waddling through its ungainly dance to distract a bored multitude.

'It's something to do with growing up,' he says.

'Like the valley.'

'Like the valley.' As she says it he sees the link for the first time. 'It's all there in the title, isn't it? A valley grows up. That's the message. History is a journey towards maturity. It's structurally optimistic. Today is older than yesterday. The present knows more than the past. We travel faster, we have more money, things are getting better, turn to the next picture, the world's for ever improving. Except one day you wake up and you know it's not. Then it hits you, maybe we've had the best of it. Maybe from now on things get worse. And suddenly history, the glorious glow on the horizon, becomes everything you've loved and lost.'

Maudlin lyricism. A sure sign of too much gin. But Christina's buying it.

'You should be a writer, Henry.'

An author. A star. Then would you fuck me, sweet Christina? Would you unzip your snug jeans and peel down your knickers and let me put the palms of my hands on your sweet bum and pull you close and fuck you?

'Shouldn't you be going home?' he says.

'You too.'

'What I mean is, isn't there someone waiting for you?'

'My flatmate? She'll be out on the town.'

She's not stupid. She understands the exchange of information. Between them there is a region of space, three or four feet across, a valley where a river runs, a gulf of almost twenty years, which can be bridged by the reaching out of a hand. But it must be his hand.

'I've drunk too much,' he says. 'I've talked too much. I blame Aidan Massey.'

'Henry,' she says. 'Do you have any idea how special you are?'

Her limpid eyes on him, hopelessly unable to disguise her feelings. The mournful luminosity of unrequited love. Christ, how long has this been going on?

'I used to,' he says. 'Not any more.'

He can't stop himself from playing the part she assigns to him, the misunderstood genius, the warrior weary of war. He wants to be in her arms, to feel her kisses on his face, it's not even the sex any more, it's the consolation.

Console me, Christina.

'Well, you're wrong. I'm only doing this job because of you. All the rest are a bunch of tossers, Aidan Massey included. But you, Henry, you're the real thing.'

'I try,' he says, smiling into her unsmiling eyes. 'I try.'

On the train back to Sussex, eating a sandwich from the Whistlestop food mall on Victoria station, drinking a small bottle of Hardy's red, Henry examines his conduct in the evening office, drawing up a balance sheet of pride and shame. He never touched her, not so much as laid a finger on her, and it would have been easy. A goodnight peck on the cheek wouldn't have been out of place, and might have, would have led to more. He's glad now that he didn't. But why didn't he?

The habit of honesty. At least to myself.

Was it because of Laura? Not really. Laura doesn't come into it. Work is a separate universe. One of his colleagues even has two families, his home family with a wife and children for the weekend, and a work family with his assistant and child during the week. Everyone who knows finds the arrangement disturbing because they sense how easily they could do the same. It doesn't go against nature. Historically more men have been polygamous than monogamous. Love is not a finite commodity. And yet, and yet. Henry's infidelities never stray beyond his imagination. Not for Laura's sake, for his own sake. He's protecting something, without quite knowing what it is.

Or maybe I'm just a coward.

John Betjeman, when asked in extreme old age what he most regretted in his life answered, 'Not enough sex.'

38

Friday evening already and from time to time Marion wonders where David is but to tell the truth she doesn't really care. His last appearance was at a particularly bad time. To help her through it Dr Skilling prescribed a rather wonderful little pill, it was so small that when you popped it out of its blister pack if it went on the floor it was impossible to find again. But it was quite a little miracle worker for a while. Then when there came another bad time Dr Skilling wouldn't give her any more in case she became addicted, but what he didn't know was that she had some left. Just in case. That was the time David was with her. How long ago was that? Hard to say. The years all look the same after a while.

Alan came back from school late but he's there now, in the house next door, the other half of *their house*. Marion has been preparing for this all day. She has prepared in the outward sense by bathing and washing her hair. She has dressed with care, nothing too unusual, but one might as well look one's best. She has made up her face with perhaps just a touch more eyeshadow than usual, a touch more eye-liner, after all it will be evening light when he sees her. But more than all this, she has prepared herself mentally and spiritually.

There was a time in her life when the prospect of a social event, for example a party or a dance, would bring on one of her panic attacks. Fortunately Mummy was always very understanding, and allowed her to be excused unless she felt entirely easy about the event. This period in her life was a long one, it covered her girlhood and teenage years. Much of her grown-up years too, really. And yet here she is, preparing for a social event – for that is what it is – and she's feeling no panic at all. This is because she and Alan have had time to get to know each other. It was the same with David, there they were in the same place, there was no pressure. Though of course in the end David was a disappointment. Alan is quite different. No heavy-handed attempts to 'help'. His attentions to her are subtle and discreet. Just look at the place he chooses to park his car, where he can peep into her windows as he gets out. Well, that tells you everything. Hardly a word has passed between them, and yet they have a connection, an understanding. All that is to happen this evening will unfold easily, naturally.

She has chosen Friday after careful thought. Saturday evening is the more usual choice for entertaining, but it carries a slight air of formality about it, or worse still, of what is now called a 'date'. Also it's the one night of the week when he might have made other plans. Friday is supper, not dinner. Friday is friendly, not dress-up. And should the evening run late, well, Saturday is not a work day. It's important to think about these things. You have to get the details right. Really, when you think about it, all of life is details. Everything that has happened between her and Alan over the last ten months – is it only ten months! – has been an accumulation of tiny details.

A simple dinner, pre-cooked, waits in the kitchen. A ragout of lamb that needs only to be heated on the hob; a salad that needs only to be dressed. A bottle of Chianti, not the vulgar sort that comes bundled in straw, waits on the sideboard. Some ripe Brie and a packet of Duchy Original oatmeal biscuits. Each item chosen with care to reflect taste but not ostentation. The dinner is to be casual, spontaneous, an unexpected treat. Ever afterwards he'll say, 'Do you remember that first evening we had together? It was perfect.'

What pleases her more than anything is that no words are necessary. Perhaps their entire dinner will pass in silence. They'll be quietly content simply to be together. That's how it is when you have their kind of understanding. It will be revealing to see how he reacts when he sees the coat button. She's placed it on the dining table in a saucer between their two places. He'll recognize it at once, of course. He'll see that she has found it and kept it, and he'll understand all that this means. Will he speak? Most likely not. Just a glance at the button, and their eyes will meet, and no words will be necessary.

However, for it all to begin, some words must be spoken. She must proffer the invitation. 'Oh, Alan, I've made such a delicious stew, I thought you might like to share it with me.' The phrasing is unimportant. But when should she speak? She looks up at the gold carriage clock on the mantelpiece: just past seven. Better not leave it too late or he'll be making something for himself to eat. He hasn't done so yet, he's still upstairs in his bedroom, she can tell from the creaking sound his stairs make when he goes up or down. But he'll be in the kitchen soon, and that's when she must go out of her gate and in at his gate and knock on his door.

It's really quite exciting. She feels proud of herself. This will be something to tell Dr Skilling on her next visit. 'What, no rapid breathing?' he'll say. 'No dizzy spells? Well, we are getting on famously.' No point in explaining to Dr Skilling that the improvement in her general well-being owes nothing to his battery of drugs; not this time at least. He doesn't deal in the deeper emotions. And what could he do if he did? You can't prescribe love. It comes or it doesn't. It's a free gift of the spirit.

Creak-creak go the stairs. Her breathing accelerates, her vision dims. No, she tells herself. No, no, no. I am in control. This is a good day.

She goes out of the house, leaving her front door a little open. She goes down her path. It's all happening as if in a dream, because she has imagined it so many times. The click of her gate, the rasp of his gate. The scrape beneath her shoes of the weeds that grow in his path. The dark green of his door, the tarnish on his letter box, the scent of his honeysuckle.

The door opens before she can knock.

He stands before her, changed, shaved, smelling of cologne. In one hand he has his keys, in the other a bottle of red wine. For a moment she is too astonished to take in what's happening. Then her astonishment gives way to a rush of joyous comprehension. Of course! He has been waiting for her. With the telepathic insight of a lover he has divined her plan and anticipated her – no, not anticipated – he, like her, has been waiting for the sound of her footsteps on his path. That's so like him.

'Oh, Alan!' she says. 'You knew!'

'Knew what?' he says.

She feels her breaths come faster. His face is melting before her.

'I'm just going out,' he says. 'Is there anything you need?'

'No, no. It's quite all right. It can wait.'

She reaches for the picket fence that divides their two gardens. She must not fall over.

'I'd better go, then. I'm a bit late.'

He pulls his front door shut after him and locks it.

'Have a good evening.'

Away he goes down the path, out of his gate, into his waiting car. Marion remains motionless by his closed front door. He never looks back once. The engine starts. He drives away, with his clean-shaven cheeks and his cologne and his bottle of red wine, to have dinner with somebody else.

She makes her way back to her own house, moving slowly, as if through water. It was like this the day she went a little too far out when sea-bathing, and unable to swim began to walk back, with the waves rising behind her. It was like this the day David left, only it was another house in another town, and many long years ago. Losing David was hard, that had been her longest stay in the hospital, most of which has left no traces on her memory. But losing Alan—

Oh yes, he's gone. No question about that. The look on his face. The tone of his voice. 'Knew what?' he said. Now, no escape. Marion's gift of sensitivity has become her curse. Whatever love Alan felt for her is dead. So quickly! But the heart has its own time zone. Love can flare up and be consummated and die in the space between words. Some other person has entered his life, and she, Marion, is forgotten, and the waves are rising.

Why should I be surprised? Hasn't this always been the way? Everything I've ever loved has been taken from me, and always will be.

She sits down in her kitchen but she does not eat. How can she eat? In the hurting silence of her solitude the room changes round her. Little by little it becomes cold and strange. This is more than a blurring of her vision. After a few minutes she finds she no longer recognizes her surroundings.

This has happened to her before. There was a pill that stopped it then. Are there any left? She takes seven different pills each day, and can no longer remember which pill serves which function. The sensation is unbearable, far worse than before. It's as if the world has turned against her.

I am being cast out. Nothing belongs to me. I have no home. I have no country. I am naked and I am alone. Soon I will start to drown.

Up the alien stairs to the alien bedroom. There on a bedside table stands a small basket lined with strawberry-print cotton. She takes the basket into an alien bathroom. From an alien tap bright water gushes into an alien glass. As she drinks she sees in a mirror an alien creature with white face and hollow eyes. The waves are rising.

Oh, Alan. You are everything to me. Am I nothing to you?

Resist no more. The waves come rolling in and Marion drowns. She is drowning now. The drowning never ends.

Please understand, I don't like to make a fuss. This is no longer life. This is death in life. Don't take me back to that place. I'm so afraid of that place. Just take me away, oh, I don't know where.

Take me away.

39

Liz Dickinson has a thing about having guests for dinner that she can't control. When the guests arrive she's never ready, the table is heaped with plates and cutlery, the food is either under-cooked or burned, she's wearing jeans and an old jersey like a student, and her hair is still damp from a rushed shower. The message is this is not a fancy dinner party. The message is I've done nothing special here so don't expect too much. It's all very childish and to do with fear of failure but there's nothing she can do about it. However many times she swears to herself that this time she'll be better organized, she always contrives to be burning the sausages when the doorbell rings.

'Oh God! Come on in to the kitchen. There's a bottle of something somewhere.'

It's all Alice's doing. At pick-up time she asked if Mr Strachan could have supper with them. 'Then you can talk about me as much as you want.' Liz couldn't meet his eyes. 'I'm sure Mr Strachan has other plans,' she said, 'and my cooking isn't anything special.' But he turned out not to have other plans.

He has brought a bottle of his own.

'I've only just put the potatoes in,' she says.

'It's called evil potato,' says Alice. 'They're smashed up with butter and grated cheese and put back in their skins and sort of toasted.'

'What's evil about that?'

'The butter and cheese. Obviously.'

Alan Strachan finds the corkscrew and opens her bottle, and even finds some clean glasses. They make conversation as Liz maintains her customary slow-motion panic.

'Someone said you're a journalist.'

'Yes. The *Telegraph*. Sorry.'

'Why sorry?'

'Mum's put me in the paper loads of times.'

'Can you see a cheese grater anywhere?'

'She wrote a huge article on being a single parent and I helped a lot, didn't I, Mum?'

'The beast must be fed.'

'I'm not a beast!'

'Not you, darling. The feature pages.'

'Well anyway,' says Alan Strachan, 'the good news is Alice and I think we have her problem sorted. Right, Alice?'

'You said not to kill Chloe,' says Alice.

'Upon reflection.' He raises his glass. 'To Chloe Redknapp, who will never know how close she came to an early death.'

Alice giggles. Liz finds the cheese grater under a food-stained copy of *Vogue*.

'What I don't understand, darling, is why you never told me about this before.'

'I'm fine, Mum. Honest.' She meets Alan Strachan's eye and blushes. 'Now, anyway.'

'Chloe Redknapp! The pretty girl with blue eyes.'

'She's a monster,' says Alan Strachan. 'Not her fault, needless to say. Blame the monster parents.'

'Father likes the ladies, mother likes a drink or two,' says Alice.

'Hey, hey!' says Alan Strachan hastily. 'I made that up.'

'Quite a talk you two had,' says Liz.

'Can I watch *Friends*, Mum?'

The school teacher checks his watch. It's almost six-thirty.

'Re-run of Series One,' he says. 'Which one is it?'

He turns pages in today's *Telegraph*. Finds the television listings.

'The one with the lasagnes. Okay.'

Alice is goggle-eyed.

'Have you seen it, sir?'

'I have.'

'Is it a good one?'

'Not bad.'

'Watch it with me, sir! Please, please!'

'Not tonight.'

'Then can I have some kettle chips to eat while I watch, Mum?'

Off she goes to the TV in her bedroom clutching a crinkly bag. This is deeply strange, this secret passion of an English teacher. Shouldn't he be telling Alice the plots of Shakespeare plays?

'You seem to know a lot about *Friends*.'

'Yes. I've become a bit of an addict, I'm afraid.'

'God, this kitchen is a mess. Let's get out of here. The potatoes'll take another forty-five minutes at least.'

Into the living room. Always fun to watch the faces of strangers entering this room. The walls are deep red, almost blood red, everything else is white. White curtains, white shelves, white sofa and armchairs, white painted floorboards. The great thing about striking décor is no one ever notices the chaos the room's in.

'Wow!'

'It's a bit much, I know.'

'No, it's great.'

'People think just because I'm a writer I have no visual sense. But I do. What I don't have is a cleaning lady. Other than me.'

She throws miscellaneous items off chairs, gym kit, flip-flops, pencil cases, used mugs of tea. She settles herself into the deep sofa, her guest into an armchair.

'That episode of *Friends* she's watching,' Alan Strachan says. 'It has some quite frank moments.'

'Oh, it all goes over Alice's head.' Not that she's ever asked her, she reflects as she speaks. 'What sort of frank?'

'Well Rachel has this Italian boyfriend called Paolo, and he shows up at Phoebe's massage parlour—'

'Massage parlour!'

'Herbal massage. Shiatsu.'

'Oh, okay.'

'And he's naked on the couch, and he finds Phoebe sexy, and she's looking down at him – we only see her face, of course – and her line is something like, "Boy scouts could camp under there."'

'Under where?' Then she gets it. She laughs because she's embarrassed that she didn't get it. 'That won't mean a thing to Alice.'

'That's fine, then.'

She stops laughing, realizing she sounds like a moron.

'Have you memorized every episode?'

'Not deliberately. But I have an odd sort of memory. Nothing ever seems to go away.'

'So what is it about *Friends*?'

'Well, it's fun. It relaxes me.' He's pushing his hair about with his hands. 'Okay, if I'm being honest I think *Friends* is a work of genius. I mean, I really do. The best dialogue on television today.'

'Wow.'

'I know that makes me what the children call a saddo.'

'A saddo? No, not at all. It makes me want to know what you see that I don't see.'

'Okay.' He rises to the challenge. 'That episode Alice is watching, the lasagne one. Rachel breaks up with her Italian boyfriend—'

'The one with the tent-pole.'

'Right. She dumps him because Phoebe tells her he's come on to her.'

'In the massage parlour.'

'Right. And Phoebe feels bad. And Rachel comes out with this classic *Friends* line. She says, "It's better that I know, but I liked it better before it was better." Isn't that perfect?'

It's slowly creeping over Liz that this teacher of Alice's is unusual. All slight and slender, with an innocent untouched face and hair you want to stroke. And the things he says.

'I think you're a writer, Alan.'

He blushes. Bullseye. He's so sweet she wants to lick him.

'Not really. Not yet at least.'

'But you want to be.'

'Look, I'm a school teacher. We're here to talk about Alice. Who's great, by the way. I mean, if I was a writer would I be stuck in a little Sussex prep school? Not that it's a bad school in its way. No. I've done nothing. Nothing at all.'

So that touched a nerve.

'More wine, please,' she says. 'For me too.'

'I haven't apologized properly for taking my eye off the ball,' he says as he fills their glasses. 'I should have caught this Chloe Redknapp business much earlier. I'm really sorry.'

'So should I.'

'I think things will improve now. Anyway, I'll be watching.'

'So what sort of writing do you do?'

'Oh, you know. The kind that gets rejected.'

A quick look to catch her reaction. A lop-sided grin. But there's anger there too. Why wouldn't there be?

'Television?'

'More stage stuff recently.'

He doesn't want to say more. She doesn't press him.

They eat supper together in the kitchen, the three of them. The evil potato is a big success.

Alice begs and begs to be allowed to stay up to watch yet another *Friends*, which is showing at nine o'clock. It turns out to be a new one, and the hundredth episode. Phoebe is going to give birth to triplets. Both Alice and Alan get so excited that Liz gives way, and they all watch together in the living room, with Alice in her pyjamas ready for instant bed when the credits roll.

Liz finds the experience surreal.

'I don't get it. Who's the father?'

'Oh Mum! She's being a surrogate for her brother.'

'Why?'

'Shhh!'

The doctor in the delivery room keeps talking about Fonzie. Who's Fonzie? Joey seems to be going into labour too. Then Chandler does a dance and Monica says, 'Don't do the dance!'

Alan punches the air.

'I love it! You saw that? She never even turned round. She just knew he'd do the dance. These people just know each other so well.'

Then at the end Phoebe is allowed to hold her new-born triplets for a few private moments before handing them over. This isn't comedy at all. This is heartbreak.

'Jesus!' says Liz. 'I thought all they did was sit in a café and make jokes.'

'That last line of Phoebe's,' says Alan. 'She's being strong, then one of the babies starts crying, and she says, "Well, if you're going to cry", and she cries too. Have you any idea how brilliant that is?'

'I'm totally lost here,' says Liz. 'Did you like it, Alice?'

'Of *course*.'

'Giving away her babies?'

'Phoebe's like that.'

Alice goes up to bed. Liz tucks her up.

'Mum, can he stay for ever?'

'I don't think so, sweetheart.'

'Don't you just love him?'

'I think he's a bit odd.'

'Yes, but *lovely odd*.'

Downstairs again Alan Strachan is ready to leave.

'I've a friend who works at the Royal Court,' Liz tells him. 'Why don't you let me see one of your plays? Maybe I could show it to her.'

'I've only got one ready to show. It's a bit more, well, frank than *Friends*.'

'Too frank to be staged?'

'Oh, no. Anything goes these days.'

'Are you afraid I'll be shocked?'

'I suppose I'm afraid you'll think it's no good.'

'I expect I won't even understand it. I seem to be much stupider than I thought.'

He doesn't say he'll show her his play but he doesn't say he won't, and then off he goes and she stays up for a while thinking about it all. Liz is the kind of person who doesn't know what she thinks about anything right away. She needs time for her feelings to settle.

By the time she goes to bed she finds she agrees with Alice's summary. Alan Strachan is lovely odd.

40

There's no school thank you Jesus this Saturday but Jack wakes at the usual time and can't go back to sleep so he goes down to the kitchen and has breakfast all on his own. He reads *Red Rackham's Treasure* while he eats his Weetabix, the cereal only he likes, plying the spoon with practised rapidity to catch the most of the lingering crunch before the milk penetrates to the biscuits' core. The Tintin book, read a hundred times before, is as much part of the ritual of Jack's breakfast as the deep striped bowl, the caster sugar, the full cream milk, the pyramidal arrangement of the three biscuits. In this way he prepares himself each morning for the stress of the school day.

'It's a home weekend, Jack.' His mother is surprised to see him down so early.

He nods. He knows.

Laura fills a kettle for her tea and a coffee percolator for Henry's coffee. She stands over a list she's written on a big lined pad.

'You know we're going to Glyndebourne this afternoon? The Clemmers' au pair is coming to babysit.'

'Okay.'

Jack finishes his breakfast and gets up, leaving the Tintin book and the bowl on the table.

'Thought I'd go for a ride on my bike.'

He tries to say it as idly as he can, not wanting his mother to ask questions.

'What? It's half-past seven in the morning.'

'I know.'

'You can't go out on your bike at half-past seven in the morning.'

'Why not?'

'Honestly, Jack! Where would you go at this hour?'

'Into the village.'

'No. It's ridiculous.'

Jack raises his voice a little, instinctively steering the issue away from its particulars onto the principle at stake.

'That's not fair. You never let me do what I want. You say I should take more exercise. You've let me ride my bike into the village before.'

'Yes, Jack, but not early in the morning.'

'What's so different about early in the morning?'

'I don't know. There's nobody about.'

This is precisely Jack's motive for wanting to go now. He has a letter to deliver and he does not want to be seen delivering it.

'Well, I'm going anyway,' he says.

'Jack!'

The phone rings. He could walk away while she's on the phone but that would be outright disobedience. Also he believes that he has right on his side; so he uses the interruption to marshal his arguments.

'Oh, Diana,' says Laura to the phone. 'No, I'm up. What time are you getting here? Yes, that's fine. Not wonderful, cloudy and grey right now. No, Henry won't mind. He doesn't claim to be a wine expert. I'm not saying Roddy's an expert. I really don't care, Diana. Something new, I bought it on Thursday. No, not madly expensive. Brown's. How about you? Yes, I will. I will. Bye.'

'There'll be less cars on the road,' says Jack.

'Fewer cars.'

'It'll be safer.'

'That's simply not true, Jack. This is the time people go to work.'

'It's Saturday.'

'Jack, there's always traffic on the Newhaven road, you know that. Big lorries too. Just leave it for a while, will you? I've got too many other things to do.'

'But why? Traffic's not a reason. Just give me one reason why. You're always saying I should take more exercise. Well, riding my bike's exercise.'

Henry appears in his pyjamas.

'Who on earth was that?'

'Diana of course. Wanting to know what the weather's like before deciding what to wear. You know we've got Glyndebourne today.'

Henry nods mutely, pours himself a mug of coffee. Jack pads softly to his father's side.

'Dad, can I go for a ride on my bike?'

'Don't see why not.'

'Jack!' His mother can't hear, but she knows his methods. 'You know perfectly well I said no. You shouldn't go asking Daddy when I've already said no.'

'Yes, but you didn't have a reason. I've been allowed to go for a ride on my bike before, haven't I?'

Henry says, 'Let him go.'

'Oh, Henry.'

'He's eleven years old. He's not stupid. I'd rather he was out on his bike than playing those damn computer games.'

Jack knows he's won. He doesn't want his parents to argue.

'I'll be really careful, Mum. I'll look out at every crossing. I'll stay right by the side of the road, and if a big lorry comes I'll get off and walk.'

Laura shrugs, annoyed.

'If Daddy says you can.'

Jack runs out to the garage and pushes his bike across the gravel to the road. It's colder outside than he expected and he wishes he had gloves, but there's no way he's going back into the house. The air makes his eyes water as he rides down the lane, and the verges have this sharp sweetish smell that you never smell in the car. Every time he brushes against the verge in his zeal for road safety his left thigh gets drenched with moisture. The letter is in the pocket of his jeans, folded over to fit in, he can feel the ridge it makes with every turn of the pedals.

He forks left at the three poplars, past the electric gates to the Critchells' drive, and at the T-junction onto the Newhaven road he gets off and pushes his bike. Nothing on the road, despite his mother's fears, so he gets back on and bikes into the village. All quiet in front of the Fleece Inn, where later there'll be crowds of hikers gathering to walk on the Downs. The gate in the church porch is open. In the shadow of the church tower there's a man digging, but he doesn't look up. Past the shuttered shop, and the row of terraced houses with blue doors, all the same blue. And there's the flint wall and the narrow iron gate that says Home Farm.

Funny how things join up. The way to school is the other direction entirely, you turn left onto the Newhaven road, not right into the village. And yet by some mystery to do with turns in the road, the fields beyond the school playing fields join up with the fields at the back of the village, and this house that's right in the middle of the village is where the Dogman lives.

Toby found it out.

'You can't miss it,' he said. 'It's the only house that's all mucky and has weeds in front.'

Jack cycles past the Dogman's house and slows to a stop by the village hall. He turns round and rides back again, more slowly this time, his heart beating loudly. He doesn't want to be seen. If anyone appears, on the street or at a window, he's not going to do it. But there's no one.

He brakes, jumps off, leaves the bike lying on the narrow pavement. Pushes through the iron gate and up the weed-clogged path to the front door. Breathing fast, he pulls at the folded letter and can't get it out of his jeans pocket. He has to bend over and pull, then it's out, but the iron flap on the letter box won't give, it seems to be rusted shut. He forces it with his fingers, willing it to give, and at last it shudders ajar. He pushes the letter in, pokes his fingers after it, hears it fall free on the other side. Then he turns and runs. Back down the path, scrape the gate closed, yank his bike upright, swing it round to face the road home—

An old lady is rolling silently along the pavement on an electric buggy. Her body is bent, her face turned down and sideways. She sees where she's going by this witchy sideways peeping.

Did she see me post the letter?

Impossible to say. He's dimly aware that he's noticed her in the village before, but he's never paid her any attention, and has no notion of her name. So with luck she has no notion of his.

He pedals past her with his face averted, and then looks back, imagining the view from her buggy. Of course she saw him post the letter. There's no way she could not have seen him, the one moving object in the whole scene. Jack wants to go back and find the letter and take it away before the Dogman reads it, but the door will be locked. It's too late now.

A sense of dread grips him as he cycles home. The letter is blackmail, and blackmail is a crime. People go to prison for it.

Most likely the old lady's too gaga to know what she saw. Most likely her eyesight's so bad she can't tell one boy from another. Most likely the Dogman will just laugh when he reads the letter and throw it in the bin. Most likely nothing will happen ever.

But there is just a very small possibility that the Dogman has already found the letter. That he's about to go all round the village, red with anger, asking if anyone saw who pushed the letter through his letter-box at quarter to eight in the morning. Then the old lady will remember the boy on the orange and purple bike. No one else has a bike in those colours. If her eyes are good enough to drive her buggy down the road, they're good enough to see an orange and purple bike.

Best if I hide it.

Duh! What good is that? The police come to the door and say, 'Does anyone in this family own an orange and purple bike?' Mum says right out, 'Jack does.'

He turns off the road into the lane to home.

I must have been mad to think no one would see me. I'm a total jackass.

But they can't prove it.

This thought brings sudden relief.

So I was in the village at the time. So it's my bike. I never sent the letter. Prove it. You got to have proof in a court, you can't just say, Well, what were you doing in the village street if you weren't delivering the letter? If you can't prove it, I'm innocent. That's the law.

He pushes his bike into the garage and enters the house by the back door. Mum and Dad still in the kitchen. They're arguing.

'You know you'll love it, Henry. And anyway, Mummy's got the tickets, which is very generous of her, and I can't say, Oh, Henry's changed his mind at the last minute.'

'I don't see why not.'

'It's far too late to get someone else now.'

'So leave the seat empty. Put your coats on it.'

'Do you know how much those seats cost?'

'You want me to pay your mother back?'

'Please, Henry! You know you'll like it when you're there.'

'I'm back,' says Jack.

'Jack, your jeans are soaking.'

'They'll dry.'

He goes up to his room and strips off all his clothes. He's decided to have a shower and put on clean clothes. This won't stop him being identified by the police, they're allowed to search the dirty clothes basket, but he still wants the feeling of being a different person.

While he's in the shower working the bar of soap between both hands to make foam he has a new thought.

Can you leave fingerprints on paper?

He becomes aware of a banging on the door. For a split second he feels a stab of sheer terror. Then he hears Carrie's voice.

'Hurry up! I need the loo!'

'I'm having a shower!'

'Hurry up, Jack! I'm bursting!'

'Go away!'

And there's something else too. There's some way they have of finding tiny traces you've left on things and proving they come from you. They catch people years and years later that way.

Jack rubs the lather all over his body, more thoroughly than he's ever done before, wanting to erase all traces of his day so far and be again the boy eating Weetabix and reading *Tintin*. But there's no going back. What's done is done.

41

Jimmy Hall stands silent and unseen at the back of the church as the service proceeds. There before the altar rails, resting on a small table, stands a wooden coffin that is about the size of a wine box. He thinks it may well be a wine box. He makes a note in his notebook. On the box is a home-made floral wreath. There are five people in the church apart from himself, and none of them has noticed him. Jimmy Hall is accustomed to this, and is learning to find a peculiar distinction in his invisibility. He is the spectator. No one knows just how much he sees, and therein lies his secret power. Everything that makes him insignificant – his middle age, his small stature, his balding head, his forgettable features, his unwanted area of expertise, and his bachelor status – conspire to render him uniquely equipped for his new role. He is a reporter. He is a newspaper man.

The image fits his sense of himself so perfectly that he wonders he never thought of it before. Reporters, like private detectives, live alone and dress shabbily. They have no money, and commonly no family. Their job is their life, their vocation and their obsession. They believe in the good story, the well-turned phrase, and nothing and nobody else. They are loners with attitude.

At the age of fifty-six Jimmy Hall finds himself standing on the lowest rung of what could become an entirely new career. He is present in the church of St Mary's Edenfield today in his capacity as roving reporter for the *Sussex County Chronicle*. While driving through Edenfield from Denton, where he lives, to the school, where he goes even on non-school days to help out with the boarders, he observed the strange little entourage entering the church. He recognized among them one of his pupils, Alice Dickinson. Alert as every newspaper man always is to the chance of a story, he pulled his car in to the side and entered the church after them. Alice came when beckoned, and told him that the service was for a dog.

Jimmy Hall saw at once that a dog funeral would make a quirky but touching human interest item. He has hopes of being rewarded with his first-ever byline. Snippets of news supplied by him have been printed before, but always within longer pieces credited to 'our Correspondent' or 'the *Chronicle* news team' or sometimes 'Arthur Joby'. Arthur Joby, a veteran of old Fleet Street, is the editor and mainstay of the *Sussex County Chronicle*, and he is Jimmy Hall's mentor. He has promised that Jimmy Hall will get his own byline when he submits an item of sufficient interest to warrant a hundred words or more.

The vicar is now saying a prayer over the wine-box coffin. The elderly couple in black are presumably the dead dog's owners. The girl from school, Alice, is present with her mother.

'I am the resurrection and the life, saith the Lord. He that believeth in me though he were dead yet he shall live, and whosoever liveth and believeth in me shall never die.'

Odd to say such prayers over the body of a dog. Are there dogs in heaven? Jimmy Hall suspects that there are not. But he is a journalist, not a theologian. He's here for the human touch. He must find a moment to talk to the mourners. Arthur Joby has taught him the technique. Never say, 'What are you feeling?' Few people can articulate their feelings. Give them options, as in a multiple choice test. All they have to do is tick the box, and bingo! you've got a quote. Talk to the vicar too. Add the usual descriptive colouring and he should have no trouble reaching the hundred word mark.

By James Hall. By James M. Hall. By Jim Hall. By J.M.Hall. Anything but Jimmy. Jimmy's a little boy's name, but he's never been able to shed it. Now he's known as 'poor old Jimmy', which is simultaneously infantile and senile. He accepts the name as he accepts the world's indifference, knowing that appearances deceive.

How did the dog die? Does it matter? Get the names. Spell them correctly. Look for the shorthand phrase that places social class: luxury home, golf club member, pub regular, single mum.

The prayers by the altar seem to be finished. The old husband is picking up the wooden box. The vicar is leading the mourners up the aisle.

Jimmy Hall shrinks into the shadows. They do not see him but he sees them. After they have left the church he follows. At such times the press is discreet. Discreet but ever-present.

A quiet Saturday morning in the churchyard of St Mary's Edenfield. The grave has been dug round the far side of the church, close to the oil tank, where a patch of nettles has been strimmed for the purpose. The wooden box is lowered into the hole as the vicar prays.

'We therefore commit his body to the ground, earth to earth, ashes to ashes, dust to dust, in the sure and certain hope of the resurrection to eternal life.'

The old lady scatters a handful of earth on the box.

'Goodbye, Perry,' she says. 'Goodbye.'

The old man starts to shovel the heap of earth back into the hole. It seems the service is over.

Jimmy Hall steps forward.

'Sorry to intrude,' he says. 'I'm here for the *County Chronicle*. Do you have a moment?'

The old lady stares at him blankly.

'Come on, Mummy,' says the young woman he understands to be Alice's mother. 'Let's get you home.'

They depart without another word. Alice has her head down as she follows behind. Jimmy Hall tries the old man wielding the spade. He uses another of Joby's tricks.

'Excuse me, sir. Could you confirm the correct spelling of your name?'

People sometimes don't like to give their name, but they hate having it spelled wrong.

'P-E-A-K, Peak,' says the old man, neither looking up nor ceasing in his labour.

Jimmy Hall has more luck with the vicar.

'A very moving service, vicar,' he says.

'Bereavement is bereavement,' says the vicar. 'In whatever form it comes.'

'I didn't catch the name of the deceased.'

'Perry. Like the drink, you know.'

'A dog, I understand.'

'A dearly loved poodle.'

'And Mrs Peak is heartbroken, I suppose?'

'I'm sorry?'

'She finds it hard to believe her little friend is gone for ever.'

'Yes, yes. No doubt about that. But for ever is a long time, don't you think? You can say for ever, or you can say eternity. Eternity feels to me like a place, you know. Which is more comforting somehow.'

Jimmy Hall makes notes, but he is conscious that he is missing the personal note. The reader wants to know how it feels.

'How does Mrs Peak speak about her loss?'

'I'm sorry?'

'For example, does she call his name and wait in vain for an answer?'

'An answer?'

'Well, a bark, or some such.'

'I wouldn't know.'

Jimmy Hall is pre-armed for just such a response. 'If they're not sure it happened,' says Arthur Joby, 'then they can't be sure it didn't happen.'

'So it's possible?'

'The poor lady has certainly taken the loss very much to heart.'

PERRY THE POODLE LAID TO REST
By our Reporter JAMES HALL

On Saturday morning in the historic graveyard of St Mary's Edenfield Mr and Mrs Peak paid their final tribute to their dearly loved poodle Perry. Mrs Peak wept as the flower-decked coffin was lowered into the grave by her husband. Speaking after the simple but moving service she said, 'It's hard to believe my little friend is gone for ever. I call his name and wait for an answering bark, but it doesn't come.' The Rev Miles Salmon, who conducted the service, comforted her with the words, 'Eternity is a place you know.' As the devoted group of mourners made their way out of the churchyard there was one onlooker at least who thought he heard a ghostly parting sound. Could it have been 'Woof-woof'?

One hundred and twenty-eight words. If you count headline and by-line, one hundred and thirty-nine. Jimmy Hall re-reads his copy with considerable satisfaction. The final line strikes him as combining humour and pathos in a particularly happy image. This is the touch of personal style that elevates the mere reporter into a writer.

He phones his copy through to Editorial, which turns out to be Arthur Joby himself.

'Well done, old chap,' says Joby. 'You know what? I think I can do us both some good with this.'

'Excellent. What do you think of my final touch?'

'I'm talking about the story. The pet funeral. I think you've dug up something that could go places if we move fast.'

'Do you think it warrants a byline?'

'We'll see, old chap. We'll see. I'll make a call or two.'

42

Alice is making molasses cookies from a recipe brought home from school and playing her Abba Gold CD on her Walkman. She has set it up complete with its auxiliary speakers on the top of the fridge. Out of consideration for her mother, who is supposedly working at her laptop on the kitchen table, the volume is low. The juddering hum of the Kenwood blending flour, sugar, butter and black treacle easily overpowers the thin throb of 'Dancing Queen'.

Liz drinks coffee and lets her eyes roam over the word-dense screen, but her thoughts are elsewhere. She's recalling how Alan Strachan wept in the school library and said, 'We're all unhappy.' Overlaid on this is the line of dialogue he so admired from *Friends*: 'I liked it better before it was better.'

There's a place we want to be but it's not here. A way we want to live but it's not the way we live now. So where? What?

She looks up at Alice, happy with her music and her sweet dark goo. But she too endures terrors daily. Why must this be so? The question, asked in silence, remains unanswered. Liz feels a shudder of loneliness. This is why we bond and mate, not for sex but for conversation. There are thoughts that need to be spoken aloud, endorsed, amplified, contradicted. Worse than financial anxiety, worse than the endless complications of childcare, the single parent has no one to tell her daily, hourly, minute-by-minute story.

The phone rings.

'Liz? It's Kieran. Birmingham, remember? The glamour years.'

Kieran Walsh. She trained with him on the *Birmingham Echo*.

'Kieran? My God! Long time.'

'Aren't you impressed I found your number? I even know your

address. You live in Lewes, and Lewes isn't far from a village called Edenfield.'

'What exactly is this all about?'

'I'm with this press agency these days and I just took a call from the old boy who runs the local rag. I think it could be a real runner for one of the Sundays, which means we have to move fast. How would you like to pick up a quick couple of hundred?'

She sees Alice about to pour her cooking mixture into a baking tray.

'Grease it first, Alice.'

Kieran chuckles down the line. 'You tell her, girl.'

'My daughter. She's eleven.'

'Fucking Ada! Eleven! Now I'm depressed. So what do you say?'

'What's the story?'

'You a churchgoer, Liz? Stupid question. Never mind. The vicar of St Mary's Edenfield conducted a funeral service this morning, the whole banana, coffin, grave, prayers. Wait for it. For a dog.'

'I know. I was there.'

'You were there!'

'It was my mother's dog.'

'This is fantastic! Can you do me five hundred words by noon?'

'No, I can't. This is private, Kieran.'

'Not any more it isn't. There was a local reporter there. I told Alfie I'll take the story but if I don't he'll sell it somewhere else. You can't spike it, Liz. So you might as well write it.'

'Oh, God.'

'What's the problem? Dear old lady, beloved pet, tender-hearted vicar. Solid gold human interest.'

'Can I use a pseudonym?'

'Call yourself King Kong, I don't care. I'll bike you a photographer, vicar by doggy grave etcetera. You know the form.'

Alice doesn't take the news well.

'What about my cookies? I can't leave them, they'll burn. It's Saturday. I thought you didn't work on Saturdays. What am I supposed to do?'

'It'll only take half an hour, darling. An hour at the most.'

'We've already been in that church for hours. I hate it. It's creepy. It smells.'

As always Liz compromises.

'Well, I suppose if the Horners are in. I expect Sarah would agree to look out for you.'

'I'm fine, Mum. Just don't be too long.'

Liz finds the rector in his little terraced house on Edenfield's main road. He ushers her in to a neat sitting room which is so clearly arranged for single occupation that it's almost comical. The one armchair has a reading lamp on its left and a side table on its right, the kind that swivels across the chair to form a meal tray. There are newspapers and books in stacks on the floor and a pair of soft beige slippers before the unlit fire.

'Not very grand,' he says, 'but ample for my needs.'

He points her to the armchair, but she doesn't sit.

'About your mother, is it?' he prompts.

'In a way. She's so grateful to you, Rector. You really have made an immense difference.'

'Well, that's something, isn't it? We could sit in the kitchen if you like. There are two chairs there.'

So they sit facing each other across a small table covered in white oilcloth. The kitchen, like the sitting room, has been tailored round the little bird-like vicar.

'You've been here a long time.'

'Thirty-seven years, would you believe? I know every inch. When we have power cuts, when there's a high wind and the lights go out, I get around much as I do with the lights on.'

He shuts his eyes and reaches for the shelf on the wall by the table.

'Tall mug. Short mug. Egg cup. Mug with pens in.'

He touches them as he names them. Opens his eyes and smiles.

'So you see, I shall be quite able to look after myself when I'm senile. But happily that day has not yet arrived. Now what can I do for you, my dear?'

She explains. He bows his head and wrinkles his brow and tugs at one ear.

'Not really my sort of thing,' he says.

'I'd just as soon not make anything of it,' Liz agrees. 'But there was a local reporter there, apparently, so there's going to be something in the papers whether we like it or not. So I thought, better I do it myself.'

'Yes. I see.'

He traces patterns on the oilcloth with the tip of one finger. A spiral maze from which he would like to escape.

'It's what they call a human interest story. Old lady's beloved pet dies. A church burial gives her comfort.'

'Well, that was the point, of course.'

'So many people will identify with the story. People grieve as much when their pets die as if they were members of their family.'

'Which they are, of course.'

'I can tell my mother's side of it. With a few quotes from you.'

He closes his eyes in thought, tipping his head a little to one side.

'Would there be a theological aspect to this?'

'Theological? God, no. This is for the Sunday papers.'

She hears the irony in her words and smiles. The rector also gives a wry smile.

'Theology on a Sunday. How silly of me to suggest it.'

'So will you help me?'

'It seems I must. But you will keep it as short as you can, won't you?'

Liz takes out her notebook and leaning forward on the table, her eyes fixed on the rector's face, her head gently nodding understanding and agreement, she causes him to open up his heart. This is what she does. This is her skill. Create a bond of trust, listen and repeat, make him feel nobody has ever understood him so well before. And the sad part is that this is true. A good journalist will discover more of her subject than his most intimate family or friends have ever known.

Miles Salmon, himself a professional listener, has no defences against such soft-spoken interrogation. He yields up his secrets without a struggle. The dog funeral becomes the prelude to far deeper revelations.

'It's such a peculiar function, you see. In a sense the parish priest has no role any more. We're like the farmers, I sometimes think. There was a time when the farmers were the heart of the community, because everyone worked on the land. Now as you know farm workers are a very small minority. But the fields are still there, and the barns, and the livestock. It's the same with the church. The building remains, and carols at Christmas, and weddings and funerals. But very few people are churchgoers. Twenty or thirty on a Sunday, if we're lucky.

The farmers are converting their outbuildings for holiday lets, or selling up altogether. But what are we priests to do?'

'My mother turned to you when she needed help.'

'No, no. She didn't. Victor Peak told me what had happened. I called on her unasked.'

'So that's what you priests are to do.'

'It's one answer, yes. When one can. One doesn't like to intrude.'

'Like with non-believers, you mean.'

'Oh, there are no non-believers. There are non-Christians, of course. But everyone believes in something. Take your mother. I'm not aware that she is in any strict sense a Christian. But we were able to find common ground.'

Liz is struck by this. It begins to dawn on her that there is more to this modest vicar than she supposes.

'My mother's a very angry person, below the surface. Not that far below, either. But you got through to her. How did you do that?'

'I didn't really do anything. There was a time when I supposed my job was to pass on the teachings of the Church. I don't do that any more. Most people already know what it is they need to find peace. My place is to listen, and to affirm what they believe. It seems to help. People feel so isolated, you know.'

'And it doesn't really matter what they believe?'

'No, I don't think so. Do you think it matters? What we believe is little more than an accident, really. The accident of where we were born, and when. But times change, and circumstances, and so beliefs change too. No point in telling anyone they're wrong to believe what they believe. It's like telling them they're wrong to have had the life they've had.'

'And what about you? What do you believe?'

'I believe I know very little. Very little indeed. Probably much like you.'

He's looking at her with such a sweet amused expression on his face that Liz feels he understands her better than she understands him.

'But I'm not a parish priest.'

'What you're doing now, my dear, coming into my house, listening to what I have to say, granting me the dignity and the respect of taking me seriously — and the time, most of all the time — this is what I do for my parishioners. It may not seem much, but they say each person who takes on a job gradually adjusts the job to suit their abilities.'

'Would you call yourself a therapist?'

'No, no. Nothing so expert. Nothing so purposeful. Therapists try to cure people. I don't cure anyone.' He chuckles to himself. 'I'm not sure that most people want to be cured. They'd rather tell you about their diseases. No, that sounds too medical.' He looks across the table at her, pressing the fingertips of both hands together, seeking the truest expression of what he's thinking. 'People want to tell their stories, but they're afraid they're too trivial to deserve the attention of others. They are trivial, perhaps, compared to the great dramas we read about in the newspapers. But if you could enter the minds and hearts of each person you meet in the course of a day I think you would be surprised by the intensity of their feelings. I may think I'm the only one whose voyage is through wild seas, but we're all sailors in the storm.'

Suddenly he blushes, catching the sound of his own eloquence; ashamed she might think him pompous.

'But you know all this. You haven't come here for sermons from me.'

'No, I'm really interested.' Liz is scribbling notes. 'You've thought about these things a lot.'

'Ah, well. I live alone, you see.'

'Do you mind me asking how old you are?'

'I shall be sixty-nine on my next birthday.'

A knock on the door.

'That could be the photographer,' says Liz.

'What photographer?'

The photographer is wearing biker leathers. He's called Steve.

'Vicar by dog's grave, it says here. S.A.F.P.'

'I really don't want a picture,' says Miles.

'I'm so sorry,' says Liz. 'I forgot to tell you. There has to be a picture or they won't run the piece.'

'Then by all means don't run the piece.'

'Then someone else picks up the story and they send their photographer.'

'But if I don't want to be photographed . . .' He looks from Liz to Steve and sighs. 'They'd do it anyway, wouldn't they?'

'And you'd look as if you had something to hide.'

'Yes, I suppose I would. What an odd business it is.'

They go with Steve to the churchyard and the rector shows the photographer the grave.

'That's just a pile of earth. That won't look like anything.'

Steve roams the churchyard.

'Tell you what,' he says. 'You stand here with the angel behind you. That'll look like something.'

'Like what, do you think?' says the rector.

'Angel. Heaven. Get the picture?'

'Angel. Heaven.'

He shakes his head. Liz feels guilty.

'Do you mind?'

'It makes very little difference, my dear. If it must be, it must be.'

He endures Steve's demands with patience, looking at the camera when asked; only demurring when Steve proposes that he gazes at the stone angel.

'I think it might look as if I was worshipping the angel, don't you? And that would be misleading.'

As Steve is packing up his gear he finds he has dropped a lens cap somewhere among the graves.

'Fucking typical,' he says. 'Sorry vicar. Saturday's not my favourite day.'

'Oh,' says the rector. 'Why's that?'

'If something's going to go bad on me, Saturday's when it happens. Broke my wrist on a Saturday. Girlfriend left me on a Saturday.'

'I suppose at least that means you get six good days a week.'

'Six good days? Right.' A big grin spreads slowly across Steve's face. 'That's good, vicar. That's very good.'

It's Miles Salmon who finds the lens cap in the deep grass at the foot of a headstone. Steve completes his packing and carries his gear to his motorbike, calling out by way of a farewell, 'Six good days! That's good!'

'Another satisfied customer,' says Liz.

Miles is on his knees by the headstone where he found the lens cap, pushing back the long grass.

'I never noticed this before,' he says.

The headstone is very simple, grey stone blotched with orange lichen. The inscription reads:

Sacred to the memory of Edward Willis,
died January 21 1947,
beloved husband of Gwendolen.
At rest in the Lord.

Lower down, carved in sloping letters as if to indicate direct speech, are the words:

Ted. Always in my heart. Doll.

43

Diana and Roddy arrive, and within minutes Diana has cornered Laura, her unblinking eyes holding her captive.

'So tell me about Nick.'

Laura's Sussex life has no bearing on Diana's metropolitan concerns, and when her bored gaze passes regally over Laura's house and husband and children it's only to confirm that there's nothing here to merit her attention. Her habitual expression when spoken to is one of mild surprise, as if to say, 'How curious to think that this person imagines I want to hear this.' Often, having been spoken to, Diana says nothing at all in reply, and her sleepy eyes swivel to find a new focus. The speaker is left with the sensation that perhaps no conversation has taken place after all. And in truth this is the case. Somewhere inside Diana's mind a door has closed, and she has heard nothing.

There is, however, a key to this door. Diana is genuinely interested in all forms of bad news. Her senses are finely tuned to the small scurries and squeaks of panic in her friends' lives, which like the bird of prey she slightly resembles she picks up even when passing at a distance. Like a sparrowhawk she drops down on her victims with deadly precision; and having extorted the bad news, having killed and eaten, as it were, she is content to sit still, one leg elegantly crossed over the other, smiling in a generalized fashion, absorbed by the pleasures of digestion.

'So tell me about Nick.'

'He's living in California,' Laura says, keeping a studiously neutral tone to her voice. 'Apparently he's some sort of art dealer now.'

'Yes, but why?'

Roddy appears with a cool-bag of champagne.

'Should I put this in the fridge?'

As always Roddy looks lost. He stands gazing round the kitchen with a helpless air.

'Go away, Roddy. We're talking.'

'Oh. All right.'

He wanders back out to the car. Laura busies herself with lunch, not wanting to have Diana's conversation.

'I've just got some soup and bread and cheese,' she says. 'We're having such a grand meal this evening.'

'Is he married?'

'Apparently not.'

'Does he still look the same?'

'Pretty much. Older, of course.'

'So what does he want?'

'Oh, I think he's just curious. See what's happened to me.'

Diana gazes at her in hungry silence, not believing her, willing her to reveal the true story. Henry appears at just the right moment.

'Hello, Diana. Good drive down?'

Diana tilts her head one way and then the other to be kissed, but doesn't trouble herself to speak. Laura knows Henry's in a strange tense mood, but there's been so much to do she's had no chance to acknowledge it, and in Diana's presence both of them are careful to offer no hostages.

'We'll go in Roddy's car, darling. Why don't you load the chairs?'

Henry nods and goes out to the garage. Jack appears.

'Mum, you know the old lady in the village?'

'Which old lady in the village? Say hello to Diana.'

'Hello Diana.'

'Hello Jack. You look smaller. Have you shrunk?'

'I don't think so.'

'Maybe it's just that Max has shot up recently.' Max, Diana's son, much the same age as Jack but always ahead. 'Not that I see much of him these days, he's always off somewhere with his friends. I expect you're the same.'

Jack, who is never off anywhere with any friends, makes no response to this. He turns to his mother.

'The old lady on the little electric buggy thing.'

'Oh, yes. I know the one you mean.'

'What's her name?'

'I've no idea, darling.'

Diana takes advantage of the interlude in their conversation to scan the kitchen.

'That's the new Magimix, isn't it? They're madly expensive.'

'My old one gave up. After fifteen years.'

'You always were clever with money.'

As usual within five minutes of entering the house Diana makes Laura want to scream.

Outside the kitchen window she sees Roddy and Henry standing scuffing gravel, eyes on the ground, talking. So odd the way men talk, never meeting each other's eyes. Henry rather likes Roddy, he says he's a deep thinker in his way, only you have to wait a long time to find it out. Like running the hot tap in the back kitchen, Henry says. It runs cold for minutes, but in the end it runs hot.

What we had was a once-in-a-lifetime thing.

He never leaves her thoughts. He's been present from the moment she saw him standing on the doorstep, shrugging his shoulders.

Carrie's dangling about, picking at the cheese.

'Carrie, do something useful. Lay the table.'

'I did it last time. It's Jack's turn.'

'Then go and tell Jack to do it.'

'He won't. He never does.'

'Oh, for heaven's sake.'

She starts laying the table herself. Diana is helping herself to a glass of wine.

'Do you do any cooking yet, Carrie?' And without pausing for an answer, 'Isla cooked us all dinner the other day. She called it a Moroccan tajine. I'd have called it a casserole. But it was quite, quite delicious.'

Isla is thirteen and has a boyfriend and causes Diana endless anxiety because she's too intelligent for her school. All these details communicated to Laura entirely without shame, as if Diana is unaware that they are transparent moves in the lifelong competition between the sisters.

Laura had hoped to shame Carrie into laying the table, but Diana has scared her away.

'There's only one reason why old boyfriends come back,' says Diana now they're alone again. 'For more.'

'Don't be silly, Diana. It's been twenty years.'

'So what does he want, then?'

Roddy and Henry come shambling in from the drive. They seem to be talking about stoicism.

'It's interesting, though,' Henry is saying. 'There's a lot of stoicism in Christianity.'

'Zeno committed suicide,' says Roddy.

'You could call that detachment.'

'Overdoing it, surely.'

'Roddy,' says Diana, pouring him but not Henry a glass of Henry's wine, 'why don't you and Henry go and have great thoughts in the other room?'

'Lunch is pretty much ready,' says Laura. 'Call the children, will you, darling?'

After lunch Laura showers and washes her hair and promises herself she'll tell Henry as soon as they have a moment together. But tell Henry what? Nick and I talked over old times. Nick turns out to have been as messed up by it all as I was. Nick told me he still loves me.

Can I say that to Henry? Why upset him when it means nothing at all?

If it means nothing at all, why not tell him?

Once more Laura experiences a fierce surge of possessiveness. This is my secret. This is my past. This is me before Henry.

I will not burn what remains of the greatest happiness I have ever known.

The tremor in his voice as they walked by the lake. He's both nervous in her presence and outrageously sure of her. Their love transcends all other love. He asserts this ludicrous proposition, presumes her agreement – isn't her heartbreak endorsement enough? – and now he's returned for Act Three, the resolution. Boy meets girl, boy loses girl, boy gets girl back. And yet he's terrified. Somehow, Laura senses it, this is Nick's last throw of the dice. He needs her. And this unexpected fragility touches her more than she dare admit.

You're the one I gave my heart to all those years ago, and I don't have it to give to anyone else.

The things he says.

She's drying and brushing her hair, drying and brushing, when Henry touches her arm, making her jump. She hadn't heard him over the noise of the dryer. He wants her to tie his bow tie.

'I hate these fucking things,' he says.

Laura ties his tie and pats his shoulders but she can't give him what he wants, not here, not now. She knows that sullen and pugnacious look, that lowering of the head. He has decided that he's going to have a bad time, and his only satisfaction will be in finding himself proved right. She could talk him out of it if she really made the effort, could laugh with him at Diana's transparent boasting or at Roddy's monk-like unworldliness, sustained as it is by the enormous sums of money he earns at his bank. But she has too much to do, she hasn't even begun to dress yet. A man puts on his dinner jacket, no thought processes are involved, no decisions necessary, and he's ready in five minutes. Laura needs an hour minimum.

'Don't look so miserable, Henry. It's no fun for the rest of us.'

'You know I hate Glyndebourne.'

'No, you don't. You hate the audience. You love the music.'

'I feel like I'm in Jack's dream. Walking on walls, high above the clouds.'

'Go away, Henry. Let me get dressed.'

White sky outside. No sign of rain at least.

Laura takes the grey silk and linen garments out of her wardrobe and hooks the hanger over the mirror. She catches sight of herself in her underwear easing on her tights, and looks away. Bad angle, the sag of her stomach seen from one side, bending down. Not that she's fat, just no longer flat, not for a long time. But she was once. The girl who lay in Nick's arms was beautiful. She knows it now, never believed it then.

Was I happy then? Before he left me?

She tries to remember, but what comes back is mostly the intensity of her longing, the waiting for the sound of his tread on the stairs, the sweet release from anxiety when he came. There must have been ordinary days, days when they were together and in love, complete in themselves, but they have been outshone by the dazzle of the moments of intense feeling, every one of which is associated in her memory with meeting or parting.

If we were so much in love, why were we always parting?

She lifts the silk trousers from the hanger and draws them carefully over her legs. Then the linen top. Then the shoes, cream leather with a single strap and a discreet wedge heel. She stands before the mirror giving little tugs to the garments to allow the fabric to sit comfortably on her body and to fall freely. She's looking at herself but not yet committing to the true appraisal. This is still work in progress. There's still the necklace to choose, earrings, bracelets, clutch bag. A scarf, perhaps. But on the whole she's pleased. The material responds beautifully to movement. In the evening light, walking in the gardens, she'll look her best.

If only Nick could see me like this.

Henry is irritable, aware that he's poor company. He keeps thinking of Jack's school composition. Was it a nightmare, or was it a dream of escape? It seems important to find out. Jack himself is nowhere to be seen, and Laura has told him to go away, so he goes into Laura's study to look for the composition in the place where she keeps all the children's creations.

The first thing he sees when he opens the desk drawer is a scrap of paper with a scribbled note. The second thing he sees is a letter in Laura's handwriting that begins: 'Dear Nick.' Without thinking, he takes the letter out and starts to read it. The phone rings. He pays it no attention.

I'm writing this, not long after you asked me to leave you. I'll give it to you when you ask me to come back. I know this day will come because there'll never be anyone for me as wonderful as you.

Upstairs in her bedroom, Laura realizes that no one is going to answer the phone, so she goes to the bedside extension and picks it up. As she does so she's aware of a staring face outside the open bedroom door. Jack.

'Hello?'

It's Miles Salmon, the rector. He thinks he's traced Billy Holland's missing lady. He's sure it's old Mrs Willis.

Laura says, 'Oh, yes. The old lady in the electric buggy.'

Suddenly Jack's by her side, tugging at her sleeve.

'Stop that, Jack.' The boy will stretch the material, it's delicate fabric. 'Sorry, Rector. Go on.'

The rector tells her about the inscription on the grave. He says he'll leave Laura to pass it on to Lord Edenfield.

'Yes, I'll tell him. He'll be most grateful.'

She hangs up and there's Jack looking up at her, white-faced.

'What's the matter with you, Jack? You shouldn't interrupt when I'm talking on the phone.'

'What did he say?'

'It was the Rector. It was nothing to do with you.'

'He said about the old lady.'

'Please, Jack. It's nothing to do with you. Has Lenka come yet?'

'I think so.'

Laura returns to her dressing table. Billy Holland will be at the first night of Glyndebourne. She'll tell him there.

By the time she comes down all the others are ready.

'Heavens!' says Diana. 'How much did that cost?'

Diana is startling in black and scarlet but on her petite form, inherited from their mother, the look works. Her lipstick is exactly the same red.

'Very nice yourself,' says Laura, touching her own lips to show she's noticed.

Diana is pleased. 'Took me hours to find the right one.'

'The right what?' says Roddy.

'Lipstick, Roddy.'

'Why?'

'Don't worry. Your tie's crooked.'

'Of course it's crooked,' says Roddy. 'It's real.'

Laura shows Lenka what to cook for the children's supper and gives her a sequence of phone numbers to call in an emergency. Henry joins them. Diana says to Henry, 'I hear you're working for Aidan Massey now.'

'In a manner of speaking,' Henry says.

'What fun. It must be like being back at school.'

Laura kisses Jack and Carrie.

'Don't just sit and watch television for the next six hours.'

'What else are we supposed to do?' says Carrie.

'I don't know. Play a card game.'

'You want to play cards, Jack?'

Jack shakes his head.

'See,' says Carrie.

The sound of car doors opening and shutting. Laura follows, conscious as she goes of the slip and swish of the layers of silk against her legs.

'So what is it we're seeing?' says Roddy.

'Oh, Roddy,' says Diana. 'I've told you. It's *Figaro*. A new production.'

'Oh God,' exclaims Roddy as the engine of his enormous BMW purrs into life. 'That means they'll be in camouflage jackets and it'll be set in an abattoir.'

Laura waves for the children. She feels Henry sulking beside her. She wonders if it will rain. The car sets off.

'Are we going to risk the gardens?'

'Careful, Roddy!'

The car swerves to avoid a walker making her way down the lane.

'What the hell's the dozy cow doing in the middle of the road?'

Laura catches a glimpse of the walker as they sweep by. She's an elderly woman with severe grey hair, wearing a quilted nylon jacket and Wellington boots. She walks with a stick. From the look on her face it seems she never heard the car coming and doesn't see it now as it speeds away from her down the lane.

Diana turns back to speak to Henry.

'So have you seen the famous Nick, Henry?'

'Briefly, yes.'

'You know who he looks like? Your man. Aidan Massey.'

'Oh, Diana!' exclaims Laura. 'Nick doesn't look anything like Aidan Massey.'

She glances at Henry. He's looking out of the window.

'I don't think we should risk the gardens,' she says. 'The forecast is for rain.'

44

This is the way they came on his last walk, all that time ago, an unimaginably vast chasm of time that was only Thursday and today is Saturday. But the intervening hours have closed on the past like an iron door. It is beyond her reach.

He ran on ahead down this track, released from his lead because this is not a road for cars. Here he could be allowed a little precious liberty. Costly liberty.

He runs from side to side of the track pulled by smells, never lingering, a quick snuffle and off again, always another more enticing smell tugging for his attention. What must it be like to be him? She reaches into her past for a comparable experience, perhaps going as a child to the fair after dark, running from one brightly-lit stall to another, unable to choose between the candy floss and the toffee apples and the doughnuts that are fried before your very eyes. But Perry isn't greedy. He doesn't smell in order to eat, he smells to know. What is it he knows? What impels him to know, why the eagerness, why the hurry? She tries to think as he thinks. He stops, turns, looks back towards her. What am I to him? He doesn't know I'm getting old. He doesn't know that Rex left me years ago, and that the anger in me has never faded. He doesn't know that my life, which demands every day an ever greater effort of will, is meaningless.

She loves Perry for not knowing these things, just as she loves him for what he does know. He knows her voice, her tread, her moods, her intentions. If she plans to leave the house without him he knows, she never has to tell him. He creeps to his chair and sits there gazing at her, his eyes reproachful, accepting, uncomprehending. For the blessed truth about Perry is that she is the centre of his existence.

As he runs zigzag down the farm track ahead of her he stops, over and over again, to look back and make sure she is following behind.

There looms the overgrown concrete pillbox. He found its bramble-guarded entrance, disappeared inside. She called to him, afraid there might be broken glass, vagrants sleep there, they leave their bottles. He came springing out, bouncing over the long grass, ears pricked up. Did you call me? Here I am. Is all well with you? Seeing that all was well he ran on down the track, over the cattle grid, through the stand of beech trees, and so out of her sight. Out of her life.

The rector said, 'It's a matter of humility.' Aster Dickinson knows her chosen sin is pride. When Rex left her the grief and the pain were so intense she thought she would die, but she didn't die, and the wounds healed. Only the anger remained: and that was because of her pride. She could not bear to be what she would always be in the eyes of others, the woman whose husband had left her. An object of pity. Out of dread of pity was born rage, and in her rages, unwarranted, unjust, hurtful to others, she was at least not pitiable.

So humility is an unfamiliar virtue to her. She is approaching it cautiously, not sure how far it will bear her weight. But already there has been a reward. She has allowed herself to talk aloud to Perry, to Perry who is gone for ever, and in doing so has found respite from the all-encompassing pain.

So now I'm a mad woman who talks to herself.

Except she doesn't talk to herself. She talks to Perry.

Alone on the farm track re-tracing Perry's last walk, she calls to him as she wishes she had done then, so that it won't be her fault.

'Don't go too far, Perry. You know you're not to chase the sheep. Come back now, Perry. I can't see you. Oh, you bad dog! Perry! Come here at once!'

A charade, of course, but there's no one to hear. He ran on through the trees to the field where the sheep graze, which is a big field, one of the beautiful valley bottoms that lie like bowls at the feet of the Downs. His resting place, more truly than the earth mound in the churchyard. For this is where she found him, a tumble of white in the green, lying so still.

He that believeth in me though he were dead yet shall he live.

Is it as simple as that? Believe, and death is no more? Humility grows more demanding.

She picks her way slowly into the field, the track here now no more than two parallel ruts. The important thing is not to fall. She finds the spot which might be, she can't be sure, where he lay.

'Are you still here, Perry? Can you really hear me? I don't mind you running away, so long as you're safe now. Are you watching me, Perry? Are you looking back to make sure I'm following? I'm afraid I have to go slowly. I have to be so careful not to fall.'

Ridiculous, of course, but who would have thought it could be so reassuring? So liberating? I should have done this before.

'I love you so much, Perry.'

I should have done this with Rex.

'I love you, Rex. I miss you. I hate you.'

She bows her head, pressing her lips tight together, shocked by her own words. Not the thoughts, the thoughts never leave her, but the public utterance. Then the shock passes, and she feels euphoria.

'You bastard, Rex!' she says. 'You bloody bloody bastard!'

Perhaps Rex hears her, somewhere in Maidenhead.

'You selfish cruel bastard! I hope you rot in hell!'

She feels the tingle of her skin, and is suffused with a new vigour. She turns back towards the trees, thinking it's time to go home. The words come of their own volition.

'You always were a useless coward, Rex. You didn't even have the guts to tell me you were leaving.' And this almost thirty years ago. 'You were supposed to love me. Why didn't you love me?'

She's a child again. This isn't Rex she's talking to.

'I didn't know what to do. What did I do wrong? Why didn't you love me?'

Heavens, what must she sound like! An old woman whining in a field because someone or other let her down years and years ago. Only it's not someone or other. It's her mother.

She sees her clearly: those uncomprehending eyes, that tired irritable voice. What is it now, Aster? Must you be so droopy?

She talks to her mother aloud as she follows the track home across the valley bottom.

'You never let me explain. You never listened. Why wouldn't you listen, Mummy? I tried not to be a nuisance. All I wanted was for you to listen.'

This is a revelation. A new marvel. She can talk to anyone she wants. No need to believe, no justification necessary. It's a matter of humility. Who is she to be so afraid of the ridiculous?

I am ridiculous. I have been ridiculous for years.

Whosoever liveth and believeth in me shall never die.

She's reached the trees now. Looking up she sees the cool white of the sky burning through the young green of the beech leaves, a green so fresh and keen and luminous that the canopy could be eternity itself, life for ever renewed. For this is May. She had forgotten about May, the one month in England when every day brings new explosions of glory.

'Lord God in heaven,' she says aloud. 'Don't leave me.'

What kind of prayer is that? Never a believer before, no comfort sought in the cold gloom of the church. But this is what she has it in her to say, to this nothing she has never known. Don't leave me.

And wonder of wonders, her prayer is answered. No voice from the sky, no vision. But all at once there falls on Aster Dickinson an absolute and profound conviction that she is part of something immense. She sees the same bright young leaves on the same branches above; the same soft carpet of beech mast in the wheel-ruts beneath her feet; but now everything is charged with a new meaning. These woods, these fields, this sky are no more than fragments of the immensity. What we see and know is not wrong: it's just inadequate. It's little. There's so much more. How absurd to seek meaning in our own tiny lives. There is meaning, but it's on an entirely different scale. Infinitely large, eternally unfolding.

I am seen. I am heard. I am not abandoned.

This is Aster Dickinson's revelation. She has been touched by the sublime. None of it hidden from view, but to see it takes a kind of innocence. Loss and grief have torn away her protective covers. All around her is a mighty otherness which goes on its serene way, unconcerned by Rex's desertion or by Perry's death.

Of course, she thinks. Now that I see it, it's true that I'll never die. I'm part of it too. I am held in the arms of God.

She walks home in wonder, expecting with every step that the sensation will fade, but it doesn't. Back in her own kitchen she finds she can look at Perry's empty chair without pain. Perry has gone, but it's only as if he's run out into the garden. He's not far away. The only reason she can't see him at present is that she's too small, her eyes are too weak. Those that die are not truly dead. They have entered into the greatness. And she too is part of the greatness. She is in the arms of God, and Perry is in the arms of God, and all is well.

45

Carrying the picnic proves to be quite an operation. Roddy takes charge of the wine so Henry, honour-bound, heaves the enormous picnic cool-bag out of the boot. This dark-green webbed and strapped sarcophagus contains the three courses prepared by Laura's mother Anthea, as well as plates, bowls, cutlery and condiments for six. It is dismayingly heavy. Roddy, in recognition of his lighter load, takes the roll-up table in his other arm. Laura, Diana and Anthea take two folding chairs each. John Kinross, who has a weak back, carries a rug.

'You will be careful, won't you, Henry?' says Anthea. 'The bag has to be kept upright.'

Henry does not answer.

So laden they clamber over the bed of rocks that divides the lines of parked cars, and make their way down the sloping car park to the gardens. Roddy leads, stocky and confident in his mulberry-coloured waistcoat and patent leather shoes. Diana follows, a brightly-coloured bird, walking with Anthea, who pales by her side: Anthea, always elegant, always understated, her long silver hair high on her head to show off her still youthful neck. Then John, a little stooping these days, walking with a stick; Laura by his side, looking ethereal in her new outfit, shimmering and silver-grey, cool as a waterfall, the two folded chairs clanking in her arms.

Henry brings up the rear. His shoulders hurt. He feels sweat form on his brow. A long train of men and women in evening dress, all similarly burdened, runs before him towards the red brick hulk of the opera house. This time of effort, the carrying of the picnic, a rite of passage in the Glyndebourne experience: the males of the tribe dragging the day's kill to the home fires. Or perhaps – a rather different historical echo – they are a stream of refugees fleeing a fallen city,

Paris in 1940, their worldly goods in their battered leather suitcases. And he is in his own way a refugee, fleeing his own life.

Nearer the gardens there are clusters of chauffeurs among the parked cars, smoking and talking in low voices. The chauffeurs do not carry the picnic. The essence of the evening is grandeur at play, formality on the grass, *déjeuner sur l'herbe*. Every time Henry comes here, and courtesy of his parents-in-law he has been many times, he marvels at its magnificent eccentricity. All it takes to complete the absurdity is rain, and rain is forecast.

'Jaysus!' says Roddy, already pink in the face. 'I always forget how far it is.'

Diana stares sternly at the massive lead-clad fly-tower that rises above the opera house.

'I've never understood why they had to make it so ugly.'

'Oh, don't you like it?' John Kinross, the one-time engineer. 'I think it's grand.'

'John admires grain silos,' says Anthea.

'I like things that do their job.' John is unoffended, his self-esteem amiably armoured by the millions for which he sold his company.

The remark is not addressed to Henry, but as he struggles behind with his burden he hears once more Aidan Massey's angry retort: 'You don't know your job.' The failure is not of knowledge, he thinks. The failure is of desire.

Has Laura ever loved me as she loved him? Not the kind of question you can ask.

They troop over the gravel, past the glass-fronted Mildmay Hall. The tables within are already filling up with people securing their places for the long interval.

'They all think it's going to rain,' says Anthea anxiously. 'The terraces will be full.'

By the time they reach the canopied bar Henry is suffering.

'I'll take the lift,' he says.

'But it's so slow, Henry. You'll be there for hours. It's the slowest lift in the world.'

'I don't care. You go ahead.'

He stands in line behind a party of old ladies all of whom are wearing long floral-patterned frocks, like armchairs in the lounge of a provincial hotel. They are talking about bladder control.

'I can cope with Mozart. But Handel — remember, Janet, that *Theodora* with all the funny hand-wagging? — that was very trying.'

'Then don't even think of Wagner.'

By the time he joins the others on the wide brick terrace above the bar they have squeezed a pitch between earlier arrivals and have set up the table and chairs. All round them elaborately-dressed people are struggling with folding furniture and uncorking wine. John Kinross has encountered a friend who shares his back trouble. The friend, a heavily-overweight elderly man, unbuttons his dress-shirt to reveal a species of inner cummerbund.

'Magnetic belt,' he says. 'Trust me. It works.'

'I have a special light-weight support I take on planes.'

'Waste of time. Once your spine is buggered, it's buggered.'

Diana greets Henry with a shrill whine.

'Where have you been, Henry? We're all dying for a drink.'

Henry's bag contains the glasses. They are made of polycarbonate and claim to be unbreakable. Roddy pours champagne. It's half-past four in the afternoon.

Laura whispers to Henry. 'Try to cheer up.'

Henry sips his wine and pretends to cheer up, but he feels detached from the proceedings. It's been coming for days, ever since he stood before the mirror in the bathroom and thought: I'm not living the life I meant to live.

I want you to know that not one day has gone by in which I haven't thought of you. The truth is we have never parted.

He has this sensation he's on the point of falling and there's nothing he can do to stop it. Nor is he sure he wants to stop it. He's watching himself, half-fascinated, half-afraid, to see how far he'll go.

Walking on walls and below only sky.

Their seats are in Row AA, Foyer Circle, Blue side. They command an unimpeded view of the stalls below.

'Wonderful seats, John.'

'They should be.'

John Kinross became a Founder Member when the new opera house was built six years ago, and has bought privileged access for life. Seat prices on top, of course. The tickets for himself and his guests will set him back £780 tonight.

Anthea has her own cushion. The lightly-upholstered blond plywood seats are too hard for her. The programme book has been appropriated by Diana.

'Oh, it's Richard Hudson. We met him at David's, remember, Roddy?'

'No. Who is Richard Hudson?'

'The designer.'

'All David's friends are designers. I can't tell them apart.'

Behind them a man is telling his party in a booming voice, 'John Christie used to say you wear evening dress out of respect for the performers, and when it's over you applaud for *five full minutes!*'

Henry gazes over the sea of heads in the stalls below. Then he looks up at the faces leaning out from the balcony seats, tier upon tier. Right at the top, just under the concrete dome, a closed walkway runs from side to side. How strange it would be to be up there, high above stage and audience, seeing nothing. Suppose you were taken there blindfolded, and left there to listen to the sounds. Would you ever guess where you were?

The lights go down. The conductor takes his stand. The overture begins.

The curtain rises on a pale cream set dominated by a statue of a horse. A giant radiator stands against the rear wall. A tailor's dummy hangs on a cord, wearing a long white dress. A number of wood-framed gauze screens and doorways form insubstantial walls to notional rooms. Figaro and Susanna are in modern dress.

The familiar music, the warmth and darkness of the auditorium, the brilliance of the lit stage, cause Henry's eyelids to droop. He doesn't actually go to sleep, but from time to time he finds his head lolls forward and he has to jerk it up again. He does not achieve full attention until the entry of Cherubino. Cherubino's innocent sexual promiscuity enchants him. Is it because he's young, or is it because the part of a man is played by a woman? When she sings her first aria Henry is gripped.

Ogni donna mi fa palpitar. 'Every woman makes me tremble.'

The overwhelming physical impact of sexual desire.

Then a little later comes the other side of the coin, which is sexual betrayal. The Contessa sings *Porgi, amor.* 'Give me back my loved one or in mercy let me die.' Her loved one is the Count, a calculating and heartless lecher. How can she long for his love? And yet when she sings the emotion is authentic. The music trumps the plot.

Henry glances round at the faces on either side, and sees only placid enjoyment. It strikes him that he alone comprehends the bitter tragedy that is unfolding on stage. This the greatness of opera, the emotions generated by the music broad enough for each listener to appropriate in his own way. The singers' lines, half heard, half understood, snatched from inadequate sur-titles, become passwords to our own secret hopes and fears.

Give me back my loved one or in mercy let me die.

The loved one is Laura. The loved one is myself in love. Give me back a time when I was overwhelmed by love. A time when every woman made me tremble. Give me back the Laura who loved me. Somehow, without knowing it, I have left the room of life. I am on the other side of the pane of glass. I tap on the glass but no one hears.

The lights come up for the long interval. The audience emits a collective sigh and rises and stretches. Ninety minutes of good food and good wine lie ahead. No London nonsense of gobbling at six or starving till ten. The eager shuffle to the dinner table begins.

'What was the radiator about?'

'There was something very odd going on with the costumes.'

'You should have seen Roddy's face when they dressed Cherubino up as a girl. He went all pink.'

'She is a girl, for heaven's sake! She's an Italian mezzo-soprano.'

'My God, those seats are bum killers!'

'I think the idea is the costumes are being created as the opera goes along. Did you see how the coats in Act Two had the tailor's stitches still in them?'

'Yes, but why? I mean, it's so distracting.'

'I loved the gardener.'

'Everyone always loves the gardener.'

'Look, it's not rained after all!'

'Did you see Ted Heath? He was right below us in the stalls.'

'I could murder a glass of red.'

'Maybe we should move the picnic out onto the grass.'

'Are you completely mad? The table's laid on the terrace. We're all starving.'

Roddy turns and says to Henry with an air of sleepy surprise, 'Perky little thing, that Cherubino.'

The first floor terrace is already crowded, picnic tables and chairs squeezed into every space. Some hardy souls have even settled on rugs spread over the brick floor. A bright buzz of voices rises from the bar below.

'This is a '95 Pommard. Should be tasty.'

'We're starting with smoked salmon. Shouldn't we be drinking white?'

'There's more champagne if you want.'

Henry drinks red wine and tries to enter the spirit of the occasion. Just fancy dress really, the trick is to enjoy it. Beautiful people, beautiful music, the green hills of Sussex. Of course it's all absurd, but who am I to sneer?

Like nausea, like car-sickness, the sensation of misery returns.

'The Contessa has the most heavenly voice.'

'Roddy, you're dribbling.'

'Laura, I want to know if Nick's still gorgeous. Does he still do it for you?'

'Oh, Diana. That was all twenty years ago.'

'You remember the Ardmores? You do, Mummy. That dull little man who talked to you about burglar alarms. Well, it turns out he's been poking the nanny.'

'John, you can start cutting up the beef now.'

'Isn't that Billy Holland? My God, he looks terrible.'

'You know Celia left him.'

'That was ages ago. Surely someone's tidied him up by now.'

'Henry, do something with the starter plates, will you?'

The table's unstable, it shudders every time anyone moves, it's far too small for six. Plastic plates, plastic glasses, all part of the uncomfortable picnic experience. At least we don't have to sit on the ground as we used to, now we can perch on little dark-green folding chairs instead, official items from the Glyndebourne shop. These are all social signifiers, the flags of our tribe, and why not? Football fans wear their club colours.

We are the spectators and we are the spectacle.

For Christ's sake cheer up and enjoy it.

'Now come on, Henry. Tell us some dirt. Is Aidan Massey a genuine fuck-bunny?'

'A fuck-bunny?'

'Is he up for it with anyone and everyone? That's what I hear. Serena says she had sex with him standing up in a loo in the BA lounge at Heathrow.'

'He must have stood on the loo seat.'

'Henry!' Diana treasures the flash of malice. 'I shall repeat that.'

So much effort. Clothes bought, jewels uncased, hair sculpted, wines selected, food cooked, furniture hauled across gardens and up stairs, money paid out, time wasted, passion spent. So much effort. A thousand over-dressed men and women holding above their heads a giant mirror-glass sphere in which they see themselves magnified, distorted, swollen-headed. Why not let it fall, smash, shiver to tiny crystals?

But who am I kidding? It's not Glyndebourne, it's me.

Came to see you but you're not here. If you come to see me I'll be there.

The sensation of misery returns. Somewhere along the way I took a wrong turning. This is not the life I meant to live.

'Tell them about Scott, John.'

John Kinross passing round slices of cold pink fillet of beef. Help yourself to the salsa verde, the new potatoes, the French beans. Don't rock the table.

'Ah, the noble Scott. My personal trainer. An individual of sterling virtue.'

'He gives John exercises for his back.'

'Scott never touches alcohol, never watches television, never eats meat, never shops at Tesco. He makes me feel like a spoiled child, which I expect I am. Anyway, to redeem myself in his eyes I told him I'd made a small contribution to charity—'

'Not so small.'

'Inspired by Bob Geldof.'

'Listen to this. This is priceless.'

'Well, Scott positively choked. It turns out he despises Bob Geldof. It seems Geldof provides an escape valve for our guilt.'

'John gave £10,000.'

'To be fair, I didn't tell Scott the sum.'

Henry listens without comment. Is that admirable, to give £10,000 to charity when you're sitting on millions? Diana told Laura that Roddy earned close to a million last year. How can this be? And yet this is today's aristocracy, these are the patrons of the arts, this year's production of *Figaro* made possible by the generosity of Citibank, Salomon Smith Barney, Prudential, EFG Private Bank. They sit round me on folding chairs drinking from polycarbonate glasses, the men whose wives and children don't understand what they do, but we all understand what they get, because what they get makes what we get look stupid, and we feel stupid, and we are stupid, but here we are feeding on the leftovers. Mozart a prestige buy along with the Pommard, the wild salmon, the fillet of beef, the private schools, the flat in town, the house in the country.

Face it, I'm going to have to talk to Laura's father, which means I have to talk to Laura first. Five thousand would cover present needs. God knows John never grudges the money but it embarrasses him, he gets it over with as quickly as possible.

Oh, you know. Money.

'Did you make this, Mummy?'

'Of course I did, darling. The redcurrants may be too tart. That's why I made the crème Chantilly.'

Fuck money. Don't let it poison me. That's not what this is all about. I'm not jealous of John, or Roddy, or Nick for that matter. Wouldn't have their lives if you paid me. But I have my own life and I've taken payment for that.

There's a gap between who I want to be and who I am. Christina got it wrong. I'm not the real thing. Roddy is the real thing. He knows what he wants, and is willing to pay the price to get it. Even Aidan Massey is the real thing. He wants something enough to bully and cheat for it. He's a fuck-bunny who has sex in toilets.

Every woman makes me tremble.

You too, Laura.

And me? I do nothing. I'm on the wrong side of the glass.

'So when will your programme be out, Henry?'

'Some time in the autumn. October, most likely.'

'October! It's amazing how long it takes to make one television programme. So what will you work on after that?'

'Nothing definite yet. Various possibilities.'

'That must be so frustrating. Never knowing when the next job will come up. I know if it was me I'd be wetting myself.'

'You get used to it.'

Thanks to Daddy's money. Or not. Without it this life I lead would evaporate. Maybe that would be better. A terraced house in Lewes, Carrie at the primary down the road, Jack at the comprehensive. It's not as if we'd be badly off, just careful with the money, given that I can't be sure how long I'll ever be between contracts. We're not exactly talking noble poverty, the writer who gives his life for his art. The fix went in long ago. If I've sold myself to television, why not to my father-in-law too? Whose virtue would I be protecting if I dashed that cup from my lips?

'Isn't it wonderful, Mummy? Henry has a programme coming out at last.'

'Actually I think I'll take a walk round the gardens.'

'Don't you want any coffee?'

'No. Wonderful picnic, Anthea. As ever.'

'Wait, Henry. Others may want to stretch their legs too.'

'I'll be by the lake.'

Get out. Tread between the half-eaten dishes of asparagus and poached trout, down the concrete stairs to the bar, out past the Elizabethan mansion onto the double border where the giant alliums brush my face. Down the steps onto the wide lawn that runs to the ha-ha beyond which sheep graze, parodying the rain-defiant picnickers on their rug-islands, most of whom have now reached the stage of after-dinner mints.

Henry is in a dangerous state. He has become separated from the world he inhabits. It's been coming for days, he has fended it off with pressure of work, but now in this oasis of absurdity it has him surrounded. The misery is closing in.

He passes the champagne tent and joins the path round the lake. Here, under cover of trees, he can walk unobserved. At the far end of the lake, by the ornamental bench, he starts to cry.

Give me back my loved one or in mercy let me die.

What right has the music to be so true and the story so false? Fuck Mozart. Why this misery? That letter was written twenty years ago. It's not as if Laura's leaving me. I have all a reasonable man could desire. If I'm fucked up then so is everyone else here. I'm not going down alone. I'm taking you all with me.

Misery morphs into anger. Break something – but what? Kick over the picnics, scatter the opera-goers, stampede them into the lake. Lob grenades onto the double borders, spray the lawns with machine-gun fire. Slaughter in the Urn Garden, blood on the croquet lawn, screams that scare the sheep and shock the green hills.

He returns down the lake path erasing the tears from his cheeks, appalled by his own lack of originality. Got to do better than that, buddy. Not the old shoot-the-rich scene, so 1960s, so Lindsay Anderson. We're all the rich now. Not for us the catharsis of machine-gun fire. Postpone the revolution, there is no golden tomorrow. Only today with its dove-grey sky and a chill in the air.

So here I am in the belly of the joke and the joke is we have it all and we're still not happy. Unhappiness is sin. We have all sinned and fallen short of the glory of God.

This can't go on.

Henry makes his way back across the peopled lawns, and the world he sees no longer makes any sense. The screen on which his life is reflected has broken into bright hurting fragments. A man and a woman are walking towards him. They flicker and dance. Why do they wave their arms? The woman is beautiful, the man is sad. It was ever thus.

Laura? He sees her without recognition, she's wearing garments that are unfamiliar to him, so he responds as he did on the very first day they met. She is unknown and she is beautiful.

'Here you are, Henry.'

The man by her side is Billy Holland.

'Hello, Billy.'

Billy nods. He seems distracted.

'Try to be a bit more sociable,' says Laura. 'Don't spoil it for everyone else.'

She doesn't ask why he went away alone. Because she knows? Because she doesn't want to know? She puts her arm through his and they walk back together, the three of them.

'My father,' Billy tells him, 'turns out to have had some sort of a girlfriend. Laura has traced her. She's still living in the village.'

'Aged ninety,' says Laura.

'I'm thinking of going to see her. I don't know if that's the right thing to do or not.' He seems to be asking Henry's permission. 'There was so much I never knew about my father.'

The first bell goes. All over the lawns ladies in dresses that make it hard for them to walk fast are hurrying to the loos.

Henry says, 'We never do know about other people. Only about ourselves. And not much even then.'

In the dark of the opera house Henry feels as if he is absent from his own body. A wave of well-fed applause greets the return of the conductor, applause for the orchestra, for the singers, for the kindness of the gods: a collective sense of entitlement that Henry can no longer share. The third act proceeds. Infidelities are promised, betrayals are planned, traps are set, secrets revealed. Then out of this flurry of pretty nonsense there rises up once more a moment of pure musical truth. Alone on stage the Contessa sings an aria of fragile haunting beauty. *Dove sono i bei momenti.* 'Where are they now, the happy moments?'

Henry hears that perfect sound, and the memory of all that he has loved and lost strikes him dumb.

Perché ma, se in pianti e in pene
Per me tutto si cangiò
La memoria di quel bene
Dal mio sen non trapasso?

Why if my love had to change to tears and suffering does the memory of that bliss still live in my heart?

46

In bed at last, Laura switches off the bedside light and sinks back on the pillow. The long day has worn her out, for all that she has done nothing. Diana always drains her energy, and Henry was no help at all.

She reaches out her hand beneath the duvet and finds his waiting hand.

'You were in a funny mood. Did you like it?'

'I liked some of it.'

She wants to tell him how irritating it was, having him sulk all through the evening. He knows she finds Diana hard work. All it takes is a little effort. Instead he mooned about like a bored child. But she doesn't tell him. She doesn't tell him because she's afraid it's her own fault.

It's not as if she's done anything wrong. There's nothing to hide. But the fact remains that she has not talked to Henry about Nick.

This is mine. This is me before Henry.

Her own vehemence surprises her. She resents Henry for being someone who might have a claim to be told. She feels guilty, of course, but not conflicted. Whatever is happening with Nick is still happening, there's more to come, and until it has run its course she does not want to be called to account. Her own life has become a performance on which the curtain has not yet fallen.

Is this wrong? Is this infidelity? Is it a betrayal of Henry to want to be again the person who existed before she knew him? To be her own complete and autonomous self?

But maybe it's not quite so abstract, this game she's playing. Maybe it's mere hunger for admiration, the desire to be desired. She learned more from Nick in their walk round the lake at Edenfield Place than in their ten months together; but she has not yet learned it all. What did it cost him, that proud and solitary spirit, to say to her, 'I've thought about you every day from that day to this'? But Laura knows there has to be more. What was broken will not be mended until he gives back what he took from her. The loss has always made itself known to her in physical form, the smell of coffee, the sound of running water; but the true damage is to her idea of herself. She became undesirable on the day he left.

Have you come back to tell me you were wrong, Nick? Telling alone isn't enough. You must make me feel it.

Desire me again.

This is what she's waiting for. This is what she can't share with Henry. More than mere exclusion: for the purposes of this adventure Henry does not exist. She has not met him yet.

His hand comes fumbling against her side. Not expecting it, she gives a start, and then at once feels guilty. She finds his hand with hers, squeezes it in mute apology. His finger traces small caresses on her palm.

No, she thinks. It's been a long day. I'm tired. I want to sleep. But instead of withdrawing her hand she rolls onto her side facing him. He strokes her flank, over the rise of her hip.

This is her private trade. Because of all she's withholding from him she will give her body. There are so many forms of sex: lust sex, comfort sex, consolation sex, pity sex. This is guilt sex.

His hand reaches under her nightdress, and as it moves up her thighs it carries the material with it. She eases her hips up a little to allow it to ride free. His hand circles her breast.

No speech. This is the time of touching. The order of events long rehearsed, long familiar.

She feels for the knotted cord of his pyjamas and tugs it loose. Her hand slips down over the soft secret hair to find his soft secret cock. Long ago and just as wordlessly, this shameless outreach was agreed between them, found to be to his liking, and she in her turn appreciates the slow uncoiling arousal. His hand is on her breasts, on her belly, feeling between her thighs. She squeezes his cock gently, strokes and squeezes, and with her lips she nuzzles at his cheek. A dutiful wife.

Except that it isn't happening.

Always before his cock has grown at her touch, lengthened, lolled heavy in her hand, pushed and plumpened with every squeeze until at last it lies big and hard against his belly and her hand can no longer contain it. Tonight, nothing.

'Too tired?' she murmurs.

'Don't know.'

He sounds far away, as if his own arousal is not his own business. She feels annoyed, then guilty at her annoyance, then annoyed at her guilt.

Is it my fault? Is it because of Nick?

He takes his hand away. Hers remains a moment longer, softly stroking. Then she too withdraws. She wants to say to him, Tell me what to do and I'll do it. Don't make me carry the burden of your unhappiness. But she says nothing.

They lie there side by side, their business unfinished. Someone must speak. Someone must create a bridge over which they can cross from this clumsy silence to mutual forgiveness, and so to sleep. Laura hesitates, not trusting herself to speak without resentment. She does not want her tone to carry the coded message: not my problem.

Of course it's my problem. It's just that there's nothing I can do about it.

Henry lies there, neither moving nor speaking. In the stillness Laura becomes aware of a sound in the passage outside the bedroom door. There's someone there. She can hear the soft breaths. She recognizes the breathing.

'Jack?'

A shuffle from the passage. The door opens, letting in the light from the distant bathroom. Jack comes in, shivering. She takes him in her arms.

'What is it, darling?'

'Can't sleep.'

But it's more than that, he's shaking, he's been crying.

'Did you have a bad dream?'

'Sort of.'

She hugs him close, rocks him, strokes his thin body until the shaking stops.

'Do you want to tell me?'

'Frightened.' His voice muffled, his face pressed to her shoulder.

'Nothing to worry about, my baby. Nothing's going to hurt you. All safe now.'

She wants to say more, wants to say she'll die before anyone hurts him, she'll hold him close for ever, she'll never let him go out into the frightening world. But her duty is to comfort, not to possess.

'Come along. I'll tuck you up in bed.'

They go together to his bedroom and she kneels by his bed for a long time, wanting him to be warm again and calm again before she leaves him on his own.

'I was thinking about dying,' he whispers to her. 'I couldn't stop thinking about it.'

'No need to think about that, darling. Not until you're old as old.'

'It's so frightening.' He grips her hand.

'Maybe it isn't. Maybe it's wonderful. Maybe it's like when we took the train from Paris to Milan, and we went to sleep in cold and rainy France and woke up in sunny Italy.'

'Sunny Italy.'

She can hear from his voice that he thinks she's being silly.

'Do you remember?'

'Carrie fell out of her bunk.'

'That's right. She did.'

She kisses him and feels him let go of her hand.

'Think you can sleep now?'

'Yes. Sorry I woke you.'

'You can always wake me, darling. You know that.'

Back to her own bed. Henry's warmth.

'Is he okay?'

'Yes. Bad dream.'

Jack's night fears have provided all the cover they need. The moment has passed. They are released to seek the discretion of sleep.

So it is sometimes in a marriage. Not every conversation completed. Not every misunderstanding resolved. This is the gift and the curse of a lifelong relationship. It can always wait until tomorrow.

47

Just after eight on Sunday morning, two slices in the toaster, butter out of the fridge, coffee made: and the phone rings.

'Miles? Have you seen the newspapers?'

It's Peter Ansell, the Diocesan Secretary.

'What newspaper?'

'The *Mail on Sunday*. You'd better take a look. It's not good, I'm afraid. Someone's been stirring up the faithful.'

'Oh, Lord.'

'They've probably made it all up. God knows where they got it from. Can you get hold of a copy as soon as possible?'

'Yes, yes. Of course.'

'Call me back. Tell me what's going on. The Bishop's being pestered for a statement.'

Miles takes a sip of his coffee and puts on his outdoor shoes. Outside the village street is quiet. A cool bright spring morning. Family communion at ten, plenty of time. He pads down the pavement to the shop. Of course it's the dog funeral, he should never have spoken to that nice girl. Still, a nation of dog lovers. Surely a forgivable lapse.

Harold Jones is outside the shop filling the display rack with Sunday papers. Tim Critchell in running gear, jogging on the spot, breath puffing out in little clouds, picking up his *Sunday Times*.

'Work out for the heart and lungs,' he says, grinning, 'plus free weight training on the way home.'

He raises the thick wodge of newspaper above his head and pumps it up and down. Then off he bounds up the street to his house.

'If I had his money,' says Harold Jones, 'I'd stay in bed and let me deliver.'

'Do you have a *Mail on Sunday*, Harold?'

'Changing your paper, vicar?'

'Just for today.'

The rector looks at the front page as he returns to his house. A big picture of Tony Blair. 'It was quite a struggle', reads the caption beneath the photograph. A new baby, Leo, born yesterday. Cherie is tired but happy. Tony Blair says, 'He's a gorgeous little boy. The thing you forget is how tiny they are.'

Back in his kitchen, toast and coffee both cold, he lays the newspaper out on the table and turns its pages. The first four are all about baby Leo. Then a page advertising new cars: 'Show off to other X-reg drivers.' Camilla Parker-Bowles not welcome at the General Assembly of the Church of Scotland. A page advertising free internet calls. Woman killed by pigeon disease. Row over spymaster's memoirs. Bishop in call to abolish parish priests.

He reads this last item. The Bishop of Durham wants to halt the decline in churchgoing. He proposes teams of clergy working in 'locality ministries'. Churches with smaller congregations would be abandoned. 'Clergy have become isolated in a failure situation,' the Bishop says.

Then on page 22, on the left-hand side of the left-hand page, above an advertisement for Debenhams ('Spend £100 and get £150 back') he sees a photograph of himself. Just his head and shoulders, beside the head and shoulders of a stone angel. In the photograph he looks dazed, possibly mentally retarded. A news item runs alongside the picture.

STUFF AND NONSENSE!
VILLAGE PROTEST OVER 'BELIEVE WHAT YOU LIKE' VICAR

A village vicar who admits he has no beliefs of his own is facing an angry backlash from his parishioners. Rev Miles Salmon, Rector of St Mary's Edenfield in Sussex, says, 'There's no point in telling anyone they're wrong to believe what they believe. Our beliefs are little more than an accident.'

Churchwarden Joan Huxtable responds: 'Stuff and nonsense! He's supposed to be a Christian, isn't he?'

Rev Salmon has also raised eyebrows in the sleepy Sussex village by conducting a church burial for a dog. 'My job is to give comfort,' he says.

Chairman of the parish council Oliver Hardy was surprised to learn of his parish priest's views. 'He's a good man, but if that's what he thinks then he's not a priest.'

Richard Hayles, author of *The Disappearing Church*, a study of the modern Church of England, says, 'I'm not surprised at all. There are dozens of priests out there who've lost their faith. What's unusual about this case is that he's prepared to go public.'

A spokesman for the Bishop of Chichester confirmed yesterday: 'All parish priests must be believing Christians.'

See Anne Masters on p33

Miles switches on the kettle and makes himself a mug of instant coffee, moving slowly about his small kitchen. Every part of this process is familiar to him, the making as comforting as the drinking. Somewhere just out of sight there is a wide and featureless plain waiting for him. He will turn towards it in due course.

The phone rings. Joan Huxtable.

'I had no idea they were going to put it in the paper like that,' she says. 'This man rang me out of the blue and I just said the first thing that came into my head. It's all too silly for words.'

'Please don't worry about it,' says Miles.

'I hope I haven't got you into any trouble, Miles. That's the last thing I'd want.'

Naturally she's more concerned with her own feelings of guilt than with his difficulties. As is his custom, the rector gives the required comfort.

'You only said what anyone would say in the same situation. What's more, I've no doubt you're perfectly right.'

He drinks his coffee and turns more pages of the newspaper. On page 33 the columnist Anne Masters writes:

At last a country vicar has had the courage to say what we've all long suspected: the Church of England today believes nothing at all. Terrified of offending other faiths, pathetically eager to attract young people, today's church leaders have bent the rules so far that you can believe what you like and still call yourself an Anglican. What's so sad is that now anyone can join, no one's interested. It's the Evangelical churches, where you actually have to believe in the Bible or face damnation, that are packed to the rafters. I wonder why.

He sits at the kitchen table cradling his hot mug in both hands and gazes out of the window at the bronze-red leaves of the climbing rose, and the soft green of the water meadows beyond. A view he has watched as he drinks his coffee every morning for thirty-seven years.

He phones Peter Ansell back.

'Yes,' he says, 'I've read it now.'

'Where on earth did they get it from, Miles?'

'From me, I'm afraid.'

'Did you say all that?'

'I think perhaps I did. They'd found out about the dog funeral. It was supposed to be about that.'

'The dog funeral! Oh, Miles. You are a chump.'

'So it seems.'

'Can we say you've been misquoted? Your words taken out of context, that sort of thing?'

Miles ponders this for a long moment.

'The context, when I was speaking, was certainly very different.' At this same table. Liz Dickinson's attentive gaze, her understanding nods. 'It was a wide-ranging conversation.'

'Well, now we're in damage-limitation mode. You'll most likely get some reporters onto you. My guess is they'll show up at your morning service. You can use that, Miles. Make a strong rebuttal of this story. A ringing affirmation of your Christian faith.'

Miles says nothing.

'Look, Miles, this is serious. You do understand that?'

'Yes, Peter. Yes.'

'I'll do what I can at this end. But you have to help me. And yourself.'

After this Miles unplugs the phone and sits in the armchair in his living room and thinks. From time to time he makes a note. He's not much of a one for long sermons, but he always says a few words from the pulpit on a Sunday morning.

He thinks of the Blairs' new baby, Leo. 'The thing you forget is how tiny they are.' His mind runs back over the babies he has baptized down the years. How many? Must be almost a hundred by now. The first was Dick Waller's boy. He buried him, too, seventeen years later. He baptized Sue Barr, and he baptized Sue's baby Lisa. Now Lisa is sixteen and has a steady boyfriend who works at the North Street Garage in Lewes. Lisa never comes to church but when she has a baby she'll come. Does it really matter what she believes?

Clergy have become isolated in a failure situation.

There must be a public recantation. Can one recant on an absence of belief? A public cantation, perhaps. He must sing for his supper, it seems.

The church is a little fuller than usual, but not much. A few strange faces. Miles has never admired this church with its dark wood and its awkwardly placed side aisle, but he realizes today how much he loves it. Only familiarity, of course, but not to be underestimated for all that. Such deep and rooted bonds take many years to grow.

He climbs up into the pulpit at the assigned time and sees on the faces of the congregation an unusual readiness to hear what he has to say. They remind him of the hounds at a meet, the way they look up at the huntsman, eager for the off. All sports are blood sports; if not actual blood the game calls for conquest and defeat, triumph and humiliation.

His eyes fall on Mrs Huxtable, sitting beside her husband the judge. He remembers their conversation of a few days ago. Words come to his mouth that he has not planned.

'Halloween is a long way off,' he says. 'But I want to say a word about Trick or Treat.'

Mrs Huxtable opens her mouth in surprise, and then shuts it again. The strange faces turn to each other with questioning glances. This is not according to the script.

'I know Trick or Treat is fun for the children, and I don't want to be a killjoy. Dressing up as ghosts and monsters does no harm. Perhaps it even helps children come to terms with their own nightmares. But Trick or Treat – what is that? A threat, and a demand. The children have nothing to give. They come only to take. They don't have a song to sing, like the carol singers who knock on our doors at Christmas time. There's no generosity in it. There's no kindness. So maybe this year, speak to your children. Say to them that the world makes too many demands already. We're beset by threats on all sides. What we lack is kindness. Perhaps kindness seems a small thing to you. It's not even one of the seven virtues. But I rate it very highly, because kindness means wanting to make someone else happy. To do that you have to imagine what it feels like to be them. You have to know them not as you wish them to be, but as they are. That, I believe, is a truly good thing to do. Perhaps it's the only act of true goodness of which we're capable. I have tried to do that for you over these last thirty-seven years. Now I ask that you do it for me. I ask, my dear friends, that we be kind to one another.'

He climbs down from the pulpit in a church that is utterly silent. He has not said what he meant to say. He has said what he believes.

48

If the police come I could tell them the truth but say it was just a joke, which isn't actually the truth, and anyway if it's a crime what difference does it make if you say it was a joke? What's so funny, Jack? Who's laughing? Like Mr Kilmartin asking questions he already knows the answers to so that all you can do is say nothing, then he says, Lost your voice, have you?

Toby says it's not money it's a sign but it looks like money and you can spend it so that's all just stupid. Toby won't go to prison, he'll have some clever way to get out of it. Maybe he'll just stare at the police with those unblinking eyes and say, Nothing to do with me. Prove it. I can't say that. My handwriting on the letter, my fingerprints. But I never had the money. Just asking isn't a crime, you've got to take it, they have to find it on you. Except this is blackmail.

Children don't go to prison. They have special places where they go, not prisons, there's one in Seaford you can see from the Downs, the big white house, it's like a school except you don't go home after lessons. You sleep there and everything for years and years. All the other children are ones who've done crimes too and they make gangs and fight each other. Just boys of course, a different prison for the girls. They don't let you see your parents. And afterwards when they let you out no good school wants to have you and when you grow up you can't get a job because everyone knows you've been in one of those places.

'Jack, aren't you going to eat anything?'

'Not hungry.'

'Henry, make Jack eat something. He's hardly had a thing.'

'I'm not hungry!'

'All right, darling. Just try to have a little.'

Jack bows his head over his untouched plate and wishes it was all a dream. His mouth is dry, there's a bitter taste in his throat, he wants to get up and go somewhere else. They're all looking at him like he's a weirdo and maybe he is a weirdo but he doesn't like all the secret glances that say leave him alone, pretend you haven't noticed.

What if the Dogman doesn't go to the police at all? What if he fetches his gun and comes looking for him himself? Like in the field when he got me, his hand was shaking, I felt it, he's off his head. *You little bastards! You bloody little bastards! I could shoot you!* He's off his head, he could do it too. *Why don't I put you out of your misery now?* Then the gun goes off, louder than anything. The Dogman wouldn't care, he's off his head. Then the lead shot from the cartridge goes into you, into your chest and neck and face and eyes, like what? Stinging? Oh yeah ha ha I don't think so. Like nails banged into your face so you scream with the hurt only one second later the nails are in your brain and you're dead that's you finished all over. Hurt till you scream and all over.

'Where are you going, Jack?'

'Going to the loo.'

'Must you go in the middle of lunch?'

'Gotta go.'

Jack leaves the kitchen and crosses the hall but the downstairs lavatory is too small he doesn't want to be shut in there and in his own bedroom they'll find him, it's the first place they'd look, so he opens the front door really quietly and goes outside. At the bottom of the garden there's a gate into the fields and on the other side of the gate there's a stable, the people who had the house before them had a pony. Carrie wants a pony too but Mummy says she's too young to look after it and she'll end up doing all the mucking out and she hasn't the time. The stable has been empty for years but there's still straw in there on the floor and it's dark and secret. Jack goes there sometimes and plays games there or just does nothing much, it's good sometimes to be somewhere else, to be lost.

The grass is still wet from the night's rain, he leaves dark footprints across the lawn, but there's not much he can do about that except fly. The meadow has sheep in it, they're right down the bottom by the ditch, all huddled together. The door to the stable is stiff. No one's opened it for a while, grass has grown up against it, he has to pull hard. The door has a top part and a bottom part, he closes the bottom part all the way, leaves the top part a little open. There are no windows, the stable is dark, and the darkness comforts him.

He sits on the floor, on the dry dusty straw, and then he lies down, curling himself up tight, knees to his chest. He can hear birds calling, and farther away the drone of traffic on the main road. But mostly he hears nothing.

If the Dogman shoots me he'll go to jail for the rest of his life but I'll still be dead, and what's that like? Like never coming home again, never seeing Mummy and Daddy and Carrie again, never going to sleep in my own room again. Just the worst hurt there can ever be and then nothing for ever.

A sharp pang of love shoots through his body, making him squeeze himself up even tighter. He's crying, tears but no sounds, and twisting his head from side to side, saying no, please no. I love Mummy and Daddy so much, and even Carrie, so much. Don't make me go away. I'll do whatever you tell me to do. I never meant anything. Only a joke. Don't take me away for ever for a joke.

What a baby. What a lot of fuss over nothing. People don't go shooting other people because of a stupid letter. Why should the police care about a kid's game? The Dogman will most likely go to Mr Kilmartin and Mr Kilmartin will call him in and say he's very disappointed and his parents will have to be told, and everyone will be cross for a day or two and then it'll all be forgotten.

Unless the Dogman is mad.

He did look mad, waving his gun, spitting words out of his red face. There are mad people. No good telling them they'll go to prison for the rest of their lives, they're mad, they don't care. He could do it out of mad rage. *You little bastards! You bloody little bastards!* Then the nails bang into my face and then black, and then what? I'm a spirit. I can see Mummy and Daddy but they can't see me or hear me. Calling and calling and they never hear me.

Please no please no let it all go back to the way it was I'll do anything—

Someone coming! Is it the Dogman with his gun?

The stable opens wide. Jack screams, but his scream hardly makes a sound. A man in the bright doorframe.

'Here you are.'

'Daddy!'

Jack throws himself into his father's arms, sobbing and sobbing.

'There now. There now. I guessed you'd be here.'

They sit down side by side on the old straw and Jack feels his father's arms strong and tight round him and his terrors begin to subside. For a while his father says nothing. He just holds him and rocks him, and this is so right.

'Sorry, Daddy. Sorry.'

'Nothing to be sorry for, darling. You wouldn't get like this for no reason. I'm sorry I didn't see it sooner.'

'I'm all right now.'

His father bends his head down and kisses him on the cheek. He feels the cool damp of his father's tears.

'You're crying.'

'I should have found you sooner.'

'Not your fault, Daddy.'

'Yes, it is. But I'm here now. I'll not let anything hurt you now.'

It makes it easier that his father cried. It feels like they're both in it together.

'So you'd better tell me.'

Jack tells about the Dogman letter, and with every word he speaks he feels the fear retreat into the distance.

'So it was blackmail really.'

'Yes,' says Jack.

He can tell from his father's voice that he doesn't think it's all a silly fuss over nothing.

'You could go to prison.'

'Or worse,' says Jack. 'The Dogman has a gun. He's mad, Daddy. Seriously.'

'He could shoot you.'

'Yes.'

'Right. This is serious.'

Oh the bliss of having someone else to talk to about it. Jack clings to his father, nuzzling his cheek against his arm.

'What can we do, Daddy?'

'Well, the first thing is this. I'm not letting him shoot you, okay?'

'Okay.'

'He'll have to shoot me first.'

Thank you for believing me. Thank you for understanding it could really happen. The Dogman might really shoot me. But he won't shoot you, Daddy. So now I'm safe.

'As for the police, that's another matter. But I don't think you'd be sent away for this. You might have to do community service. Or pay a fine.'

'They wouldn't take me away from home?'

'No. Not for a first offence.'

Everything he says is so specific, so sensible. Of course: not for a first offence. Daddy Daddy Daddy I love you so much.

'I'll tell you what I think we should do, Jack. I think we should go round to his house, you and me together, and talk to him.'

'What if he doesn't know it was me who sent the letter?'

'We tell him.'

'Then he'll know for certain!'

'And so will you. Then there'll be no more worrying about what might happen. Because it will have happened.'

'Will you tell him? I don't dare.'

'If you like I'll say everything. You don't have to talk at all if you don't want to.'

'I'll have to say sorry.'

'No. All you have to do is come with me. Nothing else.'

'All right.'

They both get up and brush the straw off their clothes. Jack takes his father's hand in his. They cross the lawn back to the house.

'Do you mind if I tell Mummy what this has all been about?'

'Okay. But not Carrie.'

'I'll have a quiet word. Then we'll go straight into the village.'

49

The cottage door is open. Billy Holland knocks but gets no response. He knocks again and calls.

'Mrs Willis?'

He goes in. The door opens directly into the living room. A barrage of smells: burning firewood, sour milk, urine. The room is dark and dirty, the curtains drawn against the daylight, polystyrene containers of half-eaten food on the floor. Two cats come forward as he enters and rub themselves against his legs. A budgie chirrups in a cage. In the unseen kitchen a tap is dripping.

'Mrs Willis?'

She is sitting asleep in an armchair facing the television. The television is on: motor racing from the Nurburgring in Germany. On the screen a crowd waiting in the rain for the race to start. The voice of the commentator. 'Coulthard has pole position but Michael Schumacher is always happy in the wet, and he's driving in front of a home crowd.'

One of the cats leaves Billy and jumps up onto the old lady's lap. She is dozing with her mouth open, a cup of tea still gripped in one bony hand. Her hair has become thin, her yellowing scalp shows through. Two walking sticks lean against the chair, on either side.

A sudden roar of sound from the television signals the start of the race. Mrs Willis jerks awake. Her watery eyes take in the big man standing uncertainly near the door. She puts down the cold cup of tea.

'So you've come,' she says.

Billy nods, unsure what she means by this.

'I hope I'm not disturbing you.'

'Sit down, then,' says the old lady. 'So you've come.'

'Did the rector tell you I was coming?'

'The rector? Nonsense. She told me.'

'She?'

Mrs Willis wags her head, as if to say they both know the answer
to this question. Billy Holland settles down cautiously on one end of
a sofa. Now he too is partly facing the television. The racing cars are
screaming round the circuit in pouring rain, throwing up blizzards of
spray. Mika Hakkinen has the lead.

'I hope you don't mind me calling on you.'

'Why would I mind? You've been sent.'

'Do you know who I am, Mrs Willis? I'm George Holland's son.
Lord Edenfield's son.'

The old lady stares at him in surprise.

'Are you sure?'

'Yes. I'm sure.'

'And you've come about the whirlwind?'

'No. I've come to ask you about my father. If you don't mind
talking about him.'

'Your father?'

'George Holland.'

'Oh, George.' The old lady wags her head again, this time to aid
her memory. 'That was long ago. What does any of that matter now?'

The crowd at the Nurburgring have their umbrellas up. Cars are
skidding on the wet track, spinning into each other. Coulthard is
in trouble.

'I found some letters my father wrote to you.'

'Letters?'

'He says you made him very happy.'

'George says that?'

'If you'd rather not talk about it, I do understand.'

'There's not much to talk about, dear. I don't really remember.
George, you say?'

'At the big house.'

Comprehension begins to dawn. The deep wrinkles on her face
expand. Her eyes look far away.

'Yes, George,' she murmurs. 'My Georgy.'

'You knew him well.'

'No,' she says, 'no, not well. We suited each other for a while.'

'I think he loved you. He says so in the letters.'

'He gave me a ring.' This comes out quite suddenly, like the click of an opening catch. The discovery pleases her. 'He gave me a ring.'

She starts the long struggle to rise from her chair.

'Can I help?'

'Why don't you look for me, dear? The right-hand drawer of the dresser. A ring with a green stone.'

Billy Holland opens the dresser drawer. Inside is a jumble of small items, a hairbrush, necklaces, a christening spoon. He finds the ring, and gives it to her. A pretty ring, not of any great value.

Mrs Willis sees if it will go on her finger, but her knuckles are swollen with arthritis.

'You knew him well,' Billy Holland says again.

The old lady stares at the television. Hakkinen has pulled in for a pit stop. The crowd is howling in the rain.

'We suited each other,' she says. 'For a while.' She looks at Billy and gives a coquettish smile. 'But that's our secret.'

'What was he like?' says Billy. 'With you, I mean.'

'Georgy? He was soft. He was sweet. So you must be little Billy.' She sounds surprised.

'Yes. I am.'

'You were just a little boy. Your mother was away. She was poorly. Then she died.'

'I know.'

'My guide told me you'd come. None of this matters, you know. All will be destroyed in the coming whirlwind.'

'Mrs Willis, you must tell me if this is none of my business. But I would so much like to know more about my father in those days. I like to think that he had a time of happiness.'

'My guide is a Red Indian, you know. She's the daughter of Sitting Bull. Her name is Standing Holy.'

'Could you tell me a little about those days?'

'She comes to me to warn me. There's going to be a terrible whirlwind. I've told the rector.'

Another roar from the television. Schumacher is overtaking Hakkinen on the inside, down the back straight into the last chicane. 'Schumacher takes the lead!' screams the commentator. 'Could this man be Ferrari's first world champion in twenty-one years?'

Billy reaches out a hand and turns the television off. Mrs Willis frowns, aware that something has changed, without quite identifying what.

'Did you love George?' says Billy.

'Love Georgy?' she replies. 'Oh, yes. He gave me a ring, you know. My Eddie died just after the war. There were the boys. I don't see much of them any more. Gary usually comes round on a Sunday, but he's having trouble with his hip.'

Billy Holland gazes at her in silence. She's ninety years old, it's not fair of him to expect her to have retained the memories he longs to share. He wants to hear tales of his father before he became frozen into the distant figure he himself had known. Billy wants to find out how much happiness his father permitted himself.

His silence, the television's silence, enables the old lady to follow a track of her own.

'I must be true to my heart,' she says. She starts to chuckle, the warm laugh of a girl passed through the dry throat of an old woman. 'Oh, yes, I did love Georgy. We had good times for a while. We did so love to roll about.' She laughs again, far away in her memories of fifty years ago, her visitor forgotten. 'We did so love to tumble. I've not forgotten that. Slow down, Georgy, I told him. Yes, we had good times for a while.'

Her eyes close. She's tired by so much talking. Billy Holland sits in silence. He has learned what he came for. All those years ago, before his mother died, before the monument was erected to her in the chapel, his father had a lover.

I will not burn what remains of the greatest happiness I have ever known.

He rises from the sofa.

'I'll go now, Mrs Willis.'

She does not reply. He wonders whether he should turn the television back on, and decides against it. The cats rub against his legs once more. The old lady's mouth drops open. She seems to be asleep.

Billy Holland departs quietly, leaving the door ajar as he found it. The light of day dazzles him after the shadowed room. He blinks and covers his eyes with one hand.

Driving home, passing through the ornate lodge gates and up the long winding drive, he realizes he's paying no attention to his way. Each bend in the drive, each tree that lines it, is familiar to him. This is where he was born, this is where his father died, and his grandfather before him.

As the big house itself comes into view it's framed by a fine pale blue sky across which high clouds are sailing. The house itself, so proud and prickly, so well guarded by mature trees, has such a commanding air that it seems to belong to this crease of Downs by right. But there was a time when another smaller house stood here, and before that a time when only shepherds came by this valley with their flocks. And before that, no Downs, no valley, and England's chalky southern coast ran dry all the way to Normandy. Things are not as established as they seem.

He drives round the back and enters by the estate workers' door. On his way down the passage to his room he passes the pantry, which does service as the kitchen these days. The house's original kitchen is to be restored to its high Victorian glory for the planned guided tours.

Pat Kelly is sitting at the table reading the *News of the World* and drinking a cup of tea.

'All well, Pat?'

'Well enough,' she says. 'I have a pot just made if you'd like some.'

'Maybe I will.'

He waits in the doorway while she fetches a cup down from the neat dresser.

'Did you see Cherie had her baby? There's a picture of a policeman with a teddy bear. Poor little mite, I feel sorry for him.'

Billy comes into the kitchen to see the policeman with the teddy bear.

'Why do you feel sorry for him, Pat?'

'Oh, they'll never let him alone. Now it's teddy bears, but you wait. It'll be Leo on the booze, Leo on the drugs, Leo with the girls. And will you be having a biscuit with it?'

'What do you have?'

'For your lordship, the plain chocolate digestives.'

She produces the packet with a flourish. Billy smiles with pleasure: his favourite. The cup of tea and the biscuits are on the table, and it seems natural to sit down.

'You know, Pat,' he says, 'I'm over sixty now.'

'What of it?' says Pat scornfully. 'I'm over fifty myself, but I tell you straight, I have a much younger soul. I have a twenty-one-year-old soul.'

'Oh, well, if you're talking souls. Mine must be about seven.'

'Now that is on the youthful side, seven.'

'That's when I went away to boarding school.'

Pat pulls a face. She doesn't approve.

'That's how everyone did it in those days, Pat.'

'Everyone who had too much money to raise their little ones themselves.'

'Yes.' He sighs, remembering his own desolation. 'I expect you're right.'

'Not that I've got any right to go telling others how to live their lives. Look at me, the pride of the clan.'

But even as she mocks herself she smiles so merrily that Billy is comforted.

'You seem to me to enjoy your life, Pat. You never seem to get down.'

'Why be down? Up is better.'

'Much better.'

He eats a biscuit, and then unaware that he is doing so, he eats another.

'I should tell you,' he says, 'I'm thinking of selling the house.'

'Are you, now?'

'You don't seem surprised.'

'It's a fine house for show, but it's no place to live.'

'I used to think I should stay. Keep the house going. After all, my grandfather built it. My father was so proud of it. I made him a sort of promise to keep it in the family. But times change, don't they?'

'Times change, sure enough.'

'You don't mind? I mean, it is your livelihood.'

'Oh, I'll find something. It's not as if I need much.'

'Well, you know, the thing is, nor do I. Once you start to look at it, you realize how little you need. A cottage somewhere. I've always liked the Norfolk coast.'

'A lord in a cottage. It doesn't seem right.'

'Then I won't be a lord. I don't really like being a lord. It gets in the way of things. All I want really is – is—'

He looks at her, furrowing his brow, unable to find the words to tell what he wants. She looks back, and smiles, and understands.

'You want to be easy,' she says.

'Yes. That's right. Easy.'

'And an end to the worrying. And maybe a little company.'

'Yes, Pat.'

'Well, then.' She reaches out one finger and touches his hand lightly with the tip as if to add emphasis to her words. 'That's not too much to ask.'

50

'There,' says Jack, pointing up the overgrown path to the front door. 'I put the letter in there.'

Henry sees at once that this door is not in use. Weeds have grown over the sill.

'We'll go in by the yard.'

Jack stays close by his side but does not hold his hand. Henry feels his fear and wants to tell him he doesn't need to be afraid but they're close now and he doesn't speak. Ever since he understood Jack's terror he's been driven by a simple imperative: he will set his son free. This is a thing he can do.

He knocks on the back door of the house.

'They may be out,' says Jack.

'There are cars in the yard.'

The sound of dogs barking. The door opens. A little girl gazes up at them.

'We got a new baby,' she says.

Behind her a pink-faced man in a multicoloured jersey and jeans is holding a bundle in a white cellular blanket. He greets them with a smile, not because he knows them, but because the happiness in him is overflowing.

'Mr Linton?' says Henry.

'Come in,' he says. 'Come in. I'm Martin Linton. Down, Bess. Down, Sal.'

Another even smaller girl is clinging to his legs.

'Lily, clear the mess off the sofa.'

The girl who opened the door does as she's told. The dogs retreat.

'I'm so sorry to bother you on a Sunday,' Henry says.

'Oh, I don't mind. Is it Sunday? I've lost track of time. This little one only joined us yesterday.' He gazes down at the tiny head just visible at one end of the bundle. 'No, it wasn't yesterday, it was the day before, wasn't it? You're two days old, aren't you, my Rosie?'

Henry and Jack enter the house and are led into the living room. The room is littered with girly things, dolls and doll's house furniture, a rocking horse. Henry introduces himself as a village neighbour, and then comes quickly to the point.

'My son has been playing a game that's got rather out of hand. He sent you a letter.'

'A letter?'

Jack is having difficulty believing that this pink man with the baby is the Dogman. But here are the dogs, now rolling on the rug between the sofas.

'He posted it through the front letter box.'

'Oh, we never use the front door. Lily, my love, go and see if there's a letter in the hall. It'll be behind the draft curtain.'

The girl called Lily, who has been gazing intently at Jack, jumps up at once and goes out to the hall.

'Jack goes to school at Underhill. I think the children there must make nuisances of themselves on your land from time to time.'

'They're little devils, some of them.' He speaks without rancour. 'But it's not my land. I wish it was. I rent it off lordy. Lord Edenfield, I mean. The house, too.'

Lily returns with Jack's letter. Henry puts out his hand and she gives it to him. He glances at Jack, gives him a small smile.

'So what's this letter all about, then?'

'Like I said,' says Henry, 'it was all a silly game. Jack was in your field when that poodle was worrying your sheep. He saw what happened.'

'What poodle?'

Suddenly a change comes over Martin Linton's face. He looks up from his two-day-old baby and all the pink has gone. He fixes his eyes on Jack.

'You saw?'

Jack nods.

Martin Linton looks back down at the baby in his arms.

'Let's see if Mummy's finished her rest.' He says this to the baby, who seems to be asleep.

He leaves the room. The two girls remain, gazing at Henry and Jack in silence.

'So you've got a new baby sister,' says Henry.

They both nod.

'That must be exciting.'

'It was supposed to be a boy,' says Lily. Then after a moment's reflection she adds, 'Daddy says he likes girls better.'

Martin Linton reappears, now without the baby.

'Would you mind if we had a word outside?'

They follow him out into the farmyard, and on into the old flint barn. Inside it's dark and noble, like a church, except instead of worshippers there are cows. Streaks of light fall through cracks in the tiled roof onto the straw-filled pens. The cows stand before the feed-troughs slowly barging each other. Beyond, the dark shapes of old farm machinery.

Martin Linton pushes his hands through his thinning hair.

'The ewes were in lamb,' he says. 'The dog was chasing them, worrying them. It wouldn't stop. You can lose lambs that way, the ewes panic, it's a real problem. I was trying to get the dog to leave them alone, that's all.' He stops and abruptly changes tack, gazing imploringly at Henry. 'Tell me what happened.'

'The poodle died, I'm afraid.'

'Oh, God. Oh, God.'

He looks round at the cows as if for support. Some of them have raised their heads and are peering towards him through the gloom.

'My phone rang,' he says. 'It was Jenny, she'd gone into labour, I was needed. She needed me. I never thought – it went out of my mind – there was the hospital – then the baby—'

'No one's blaming you,' said Henry.

'Oh, but they will.' He gives a bitter laugh. 'You don't know what it's like. They'll go to lordy. I could lose my tenancy over this.'

'Over an accident with a dog?'

'Do you have any idea what it's like being a farmer these days? Sorry, what did you say your name was?'

'Henry Broad.'

'Broad? You bought River Farm.'

'Yes.'

'I'm the only farmer left in the village. Once there were three farming families in Edenfield. Big families, all supported on the land. It's fertile land, this river valley. Fine farming land. But I can barely make a living. My father employed sixteen men. I employ one. That's how times have changed. And on top of that, on top of the daily struggle to feed my family, I get nothing but aggravation from my neighbours. I do my best, but this is a farm. It's not a garden. My tractors hold up their cars in the lanes, and make a noise, and leave mud on the roads, so they hate me. I mean that. I get letters you wouldn't believe! They think I'm poisoning them with the fertilizer I spread on the fields. They hate the smell of slurry even more. They're angry because the footpaths have cowpats on them. They're frightened of my bullocks. They think our cattle are mad and our sheep diseased. People who actually live in the country are convinced that farming is against nature! They shout at me to my face. Profit grubber, land rapist, disease spreader, you name it, I get it. They think farmers are ignorant, brutal and greedy. If they discover I killed some old lady's pet poodle I'll be lynched. I'll be driven out. I'm telling you the truth. It'll be the end of me.'

He falls silent at last, his chest heaving, his head jerking this way and that as if searching for a way out.

'I'm really sorry,' says Henry. 'I had no idea it was so bad.'

'You ask the kids these days. Ask them what farmers do. Farmers pollute the countryside, they'll tell you. Farmers are cruel to animals, they'll tell you. That's all they get told these days.'

He's on the point of tears.

'It's just so bloody hard.'

'Look,' says Henry, 'we don't want to make it any harder. We just wanted to clear up the business of the letter.'

'The letter. Yes.' But he's forgotten all about the letter. 'I never meant to hurt the dog. It was a mistake, that's all.'

Jack speaks for the first time.

'The poodle wouldn't stop yapping,' he says. 'You just wanted it to stop yapping.'

'That's right.' Martin Linton takes Jack in properly. 'I never meant to kill the dog. You saw me. I was just trying to get it to stop worrying the ewes. Then my phone rang. There was Jenny on the phone saying, The baby's coming, the baby's coming. I had to go.'

'That's right,' says Jack. 'That's what I saw.'

For a moment there is silence in the barn.

'Who have you told?' says Martin Linton.

'Only Dad,' says Jack. 'And Toby Clore.'

'Who's he?'

'My friend at school.'

'So I suppose everyone'll know soon.'

'Oh, no. Only us three.'

The farmer looks from Jack to Henry.

'What are you going to do?'

'I don't see that it's any of my business,' says Henry. 'I don't propose to tell anybody.'

'Me neither,' says Jack.

'And this Toby?'

Jack looks uncertain. Henry touches him on the arm.

'Let me and Jack have a private word.'

Martin Linton nods and walks away down the central aisle of the barn. Jack whispers to his father.

'I can't make Toby not talk. Toby won't do what I say.'

'I know,' says Henry. 'But he might.'

'You can never tell with Toby.'

'You could say you'll try.'

'I can't promise.'

'Why don't I say it?'

'Okay.'

Henry goes back to the farmer.

'Jack says he'll talk to Toby. You don't need to worry.'

'You mean that?' His hands are shaking as he grips Henry's arms. 'They'd say things to my girls in school. The other children. Dog murderer. Poodle killer. They do that.'

'Nobody's going to know.'

Still gripping Henry's arms, the farmer bows his head. He seems to be about to burst into tears.

'Thank you,' he says. 'Thank you.'

They part in the farmyard. Martin Linton watches them go, standing like a lost child in his stripy jersey on the broad apron of concrete.

Out in the street Henry says to Jack, 'So that was your Dogman.'

'I feel sorry for him.'

'What will you say to Toby?'

'I don't know.'

Henry pulls the letter out of his pocket. 'Here.'

Jack stuffs it into his own pocket without even looking at it. The letter has lost its power to hurt him.

'He was different,' he says. 'All those little girls.'

'You hungry?'

'Starving.'

'You can have the lunch leftovers when we get home. Or Weetabix.'

Jack says nothing as they get into the car and drive up the village street. Then as they turn into the home lane, he says, 'Dad?'

'Yes, Jack.'

'Do you always know what everyone's thinking?'

'Me?' Henry laughs at the suggestion. 'I hardly even know what I'm thinking myself. I'm useless.'

'No. Really.'

The car pulls into their short drive and they both get out.

'Better?' says Henry.

Jack nods.

'I feel like I'm whizzing.'

The odd thing is that Henry feels like he's whizzing too. They go into the house together and Laura's on the phone to Diana having a post mortem on Glyndebourne. She looks up and meets Henry's eyes. 'Crisis over,' he says. Jack gives her a grin and a little wave of his hand.

Henry settles down to read the Sunday paper but finds his eyes slide over the print without taking in the meaning of the words. Something about the events of the day so far has had a greater effect on him than he can explain. It's not as if his own circumstances have changed. One grows weary of narrow horizons.

Other people's lives. Other people's unending struggles. And yet the images that endure, both real and imagined, are not the ones you expect. A man in a stripy jumper aglow with adoration of his newborn baby girl. Jack walking on walls and below only clouds. Laura coming towards him across the lawns of Glyndebourne, so different and so beautiful.

Where are they now, the happy moments?

The little rector said something so provocative, what was it? Yes. Sin is unhappiness. As if we get a choice in the matter. There's a photograph of Tony Blair on the front page of the *Sunday Times*, he's holding a mug that has a picture of his other three children on it. 'Baby Leo is gorgeous,' says Blair. And further down, these words: 'The thing you forget is how tiny they are.'

Henry tries to remember Jack when he was new born. No picture comes to mind, but he recovers a true feeling. He's holding Jack just as the Dogman held his baby, and he's feeling with overwhelming intensity how fragile this little creature is, and how he will do anything, sacrifice anything, suffer anything to protect him and keep him from harm and make him believe that the world he has so recently entered is a place of kindness.

I should have found you sooner.

Sobbing in the stable in the dark. But that's over now. Whizzing now.

51

Monday morning, and from eight o'clock onwards the filter lane off the main road is solid with cars turning into the school. Mostly the mothers do kiss'n'drop, not even shifting their cars' automatic gears into neutral for the few seconds it takes to disgorge another blue-blazered child into the milling mass. Liz Dickinson, whose little Renault is not automatic, pulls over into a space by the dining hall and parks. Alice spots Alan Strachan over by the school entrance. He's clutching a brown envelope.

'Ask him to come for supper this evening,' Alice says as they get out of the car.

'He won't want to come again so soon.'

'Yes he will.'

Alan Strachan gives them a wave and comes forward to meet them. He holds out the brown envelope. He's blushing.

'My play,' he says. 'Give it a glance if you have time. Don't take it too seriously. It's really all a kind of metaphor.'

'I'll keep that in mind,' says Liz.

'No rush.'

Alice tugs at her arm.

'Go on.'

'Alice wants you to come to supper again.'

She speaks in a low voice because there are children passing near by. This makes it seem like a guilty secret.

'I'd like that,' Alan Strachan replies simply.

'He could come this evening,' says Alice. 'You could, couldn't you, sir?'

'I could if that suits your mother. But just about any evening would do for me.'

'Why not?' says Liz. 'Come round some time after seven. I'll have read this.'

'It's not suitable for children, by the way,' he says. 'Or anyone else, probably.'

Alice goes off to join the others for morning assembly. Liz returns with the brown envelope to her car.

She drives back down the main road thinking of all that she has to do today, knowing that before doing any of it she will read Alan Strachan's play. She made the offer freely, but the truth is she's afraid of reading it. She likes Alan, but may not like his play. What then? Not only the awkward matter of what she says to him; more troubling is how it may change what she thinks of him. Alan Strachan has been occupying a particular place in her mind ever since Friday evening, that place where secret hopes gather and breed. She has done nothing to encourage it, but nor can she stop it. He's so sweet to Alice, of course. But surely he's too young. And more troubling still, too unsure of himself. She compares him in her mind's eyes with Guy, and he looks like a boy. He has none of Guy's self assurance, his savoir-faire—

This is all about sex. She trips over the truth with a little jump of shock. All these adjectives, *young*, *unsure*, they're euphemisms for *unsexy*. She likes Alan Strachan very much, she's grateful to him, but he doesn't excite her. Not in the way that Guy does.

What's wrong with me? Guy's a dead end. There's nothing for me there. He doesn't love me. All he wants me for is sex.

It seems so unfair that the best sex is with the worst men. Or worse than unfair, a sickness in her. But why? Is it that I feel somewhere deep down that I don't deserve pleasure? I can have it, but I have to pay the price in pain. That would be so sick.

She tries to be truthful with herself. Maybe she is a masochist, but it doesn't feel that way, it really doesn't. She'd rather be with a man who loves her and treats her with respect. So why not a sweet boy like Alan Strachan, with his play that's not suitable for children? It's not as if the suitors are lining up outside her bedroom door.

She tries to imagine sex with Alan. She can make the pictures in her head, but she can't make them feel real. In any scenario she creates she finds she's the one who initiates each stage of the proceedings. 'Do you want to stay for coffee, Alan? Do you want to kiss me? Do you want to stay the night?' At no point does Alan take control. Only her imagination, but everything she knows about him so far tells her this is the way it will be. He will seek her permission for every move.

What's wrong with that? For Christ's sake do I want to be raped? What is this caveman shit?

No, not rape. Guy doesn't rape me. He desires me, without hesitation or shame. He puts my hand on his hard cock so I can feel his desire. The choice is mine, I don't have to have sex with him. He just makes me want to. He makes it easy and natural. All I have to do is not resist. Let him carry me away. Surrender.

Surrendering is so fucking sexy.

So there it is. I'm screwed. In the non-physical sense. This is my life choice. Friendly fumbles with nice guys or bang my brains out with bastards. The whole set-up is one big evolutionary error. There's the boys with their Madonna-whore complex, and here am I with the girl version. Nice guy-stud. Be sensitive to me all day and fuck me stupid all night.

Dream on.

As she reaches the Edenfield roundabout she remembers the rector, about whom she has a guilty conscience. She kept meaning to phone him all day yesterday but somehow never got round to it. The piece as it appeared in the *Mail on Sunday* was the usual stitch-up, you had to admire the professionalism, nothing in it untrue, the sure instinct for the guts of a provocative story, but nevertheless a total distortion. It had never occurred to her when she submitted her copy that there was a story in the rector's easygoing views on faith. She had written up the dog funeral, as requested. But some bright spark in Derry Street had spotted the hidden treasure and got to work on the support quotes, and you can't lay a glove on him. Stupid of her to think she could sell a happy pet story. The *Mail* doesn't do happiness, it does anger. That's what they teach their subs to find, to shape, to sharpen: stories that goad their readers into outrage. A vicar who doesn't believe in God feeds the ever-hungry beast.

The rector will be upset by it, of course. Instead of driving on home to Lewes she turns down the Newhaven road and heads into Edenfield. She will seek him out and try to explain what happened. Not just to excuse herself. She owes him some redress.

Then she's passing the church and there he is, his arms full of leaves, entering the open door of the porch.

By the time she's parked he's disappeared inside the church. The dark nave seems at first sight to be empty. Then she sees him in a side aisle, removing flowers from vases, a black bin liner in one hand.

He turns towards her, and for a moment he seems confused. Then he gives a nod of recognition.

'Just replacing the flowers.'

'I came to say sorry about the piece in the paper,' says Liz.

'Well, it did come as something of a surprise.'

'It wasn't what I wrote at all. They changed everything. I feel terrible. I know what these people can do. I should have been more careful.'

The rector picks out fresh cuttings to arrange in the vases.

'These people?' he says, his gaze on the mass of dark leaves.

'Well, me too,' says Liz. He's not angry, he's just puzzled and hurt. 'Will it make things difficult for you?'

'If it does,' says the rector, 'I have only myself to blame for that.'

'Oh no! It's not you. Some creep on the newspaper made the whole thing up. It's a classic bolt-on job.'

'The words they attribute to me are the kind of thing I say. I'm willing to accept that I said them.'

You said them to me, thinks Liz. And I passed them down the line. My contribution to this jewel of British journalism. Befriend and betray.

'I'm really sorry.'

'As I recall, your name wasn't on the article.'

'No, they had that much decency. But I'll be paid. I'll give the money to charity. Whatever charity you like.'

He moves on to the next vase. Liz finds herself looking at the stained-glass window above the altar: Jesus with his arms reached out on either side. In glory, not in crucifixion.

'What is a classic bolt-on job?' he asks.

'It's when you have only one part of a story and you need to build it up. Suppose a politician says he wants to help one-parent families. You don't ring up single mothers and get them to say how great it is that someone wants to help them. That's not a story. You ring up a few well-known pro-marriage lobbyists and get them to say the

politician's failing to help married couples. Then you run the story
as Anger at Attack on the Family.'

'Good heavens.'

'Yes, it is all a bit strange.'

'You mean they actually create a row where there wasn't one?'

'All the time.'

'Why?'

'People love to read this kind of stuff, believe it or not.'

'No, I believe it. The part I don't understand is how they can write
it. It seems to me to be a kind of lie.'

'I know. It's hard to explain. It's something that happens to you
when you work on a newspaper. You want a story so badly you just
lose sight of the fact that you're trampling all over people. And if you
ever do think of it, you tell yourself they deserve it. The politicians,
the celebrities, the crooks.'

'The vicars.'

'Well, that's where it goes wrong.'

'Not really. Whoever wrote that article about me must have thought
I deserved what I was getting. A vicar who doesn't believe in God.
So you see, I don't blame him. Or you. I blame myself.'

'Please. It just makes me feel so much worse when you say that.
Honestly, these people are vermin. They don't deserve your
compassion. Nor do I.'

'Of course you do, my dear. As I deserve yours.'

'Is there anything I can do? I could write my own piece about you.
Say all the things you'd like to have said.'

'No, no. Enough is enough. And anyway, it's too late now.'

'Too late? What do you mean?'

'I've offered my resignation.'

Liz is appalled.

'You can't resign! Not over this! They won't accept it.'

'The Bishop was grateful. He was in a most awkward position. And
I am almost seventy years old. New blood will be an excellent thing.'

'So you're going to go.'

'Yes.'

'What will you do?'

'I shall retire. I shall live with my sister. She has kindly offered me
a room in her flat in Ealing.'

'A room in Ealing?'

'Oh, I think it's for the best, you know. My position in the church has been peculiar for many years now. I described what you journalists do as a kind of lie, but of course it's my life that has been a kind of lie. Now there's no more need for lies. I can be grateful for that.'

He gathers up more flowers and moves away from her, towards the altar. Only they're not flowers, they're leaves. In amongst the leaves are some tiny buds. It strikes Liz then how strange it is, at the height of springtime, to bring plants into the church that are so far from flowering.

'What is it you've picked?'

'Roses,' he says. 'They're from my garden.'

He indicates the front pews. Both pews are piled high with cut rose branches. Far more than could ever be required to decorate a church.

'You must have a big garden.'

'Not very big. This is all of it.'

He looks towards her, and for the briefest instant she sees in his eyes a terrible desolation. She looks down, ashamed to be the witness to his pain; ashamed to have been its cause.

'It doesn't do to become too attached to things,' he says. 'But it seems I have after all become . . .'

He falls silent. Liz looks up. The rector has his head bowed as if in prayer. There comes a soft sighing sound. He takes out a handkerchief and presses it first to one eye, then to the other.

'I think you had better go, my dear.'

'Yes. Yes, of course.'

She wants to say more. She wants forgiveness. And this too shames her, that he is the one in pain, and she the one who seeks comfort. So she goes.

At the end of the aisle she turns and looking back sees the rector illuminated by the coloured light of Christ in glory. The Christ who had to suffer crucifixion to get the glory. This is the lie, she thinks, the great Christian story, that after the suffering comes the redemption. Maybe for Jesus, but not for most. After the suffering comes a room in a flat in Ealing. All the rest is just a classic bolt-on job.

52

All through the first three lessons of the day Jack finds it hard to concentrate. When break comes Toby will want the news. Daddy says tell Toby what happened and he'll get it, but he doesn't know Toby. Toby goes off in ways you can never tell in advance. Maybe he'll say they have to send another letter asking for much more money now they know the Dogman is afraid. I won't do that. Toby can send the letter himself.

Then what? Then I have to go around with fat Dan Chamberlain and barmy Will Guest. The three losers. But at least I won't get sent away to a prison school.

Jack's night of terror has had this benefit: he now knows there are worse things than losing the favour of Toby Clore.

When the bell rings for morning break Jimmy Hall has a random fit and starts shouting at people for no reason. He makes Peter Mackie look for his blazer even though he's looked for it a hundred times, and when Peter Mackie just stands there goggling round him like a zombie Jimmy Hall gets so stressy he actually stamps his foot.

'The rules say you wear your blazer! So you will wear your blazer!'

Then he makes everyone carry chairs to the barn.

'But sir it's our break. It's not fair.'

'Not fair? Who said it was *fair*? Nothing's *fair*, Jason. Justice standeth far off and truth is fallen in the street.'

'Yes sir.'

When at last Jack and Toby and Angus and Richard gather by the tennis courts half the break is gone. Jack bursts straight out with his pre-prepared story.

'I posted the letter but the Dogman saw me so me and my dad went to talk to him and he asked us not to tell about what he did.'

'I still don't know what it is he did,' says Richard Adderley resentfully.

Toby is watching Jack with his cool unmoving eyes.

'And?'

And what? Jack has no idea what to add. So he adds the detail that has lodged most vividly in his memory.

'And he's got a new baby. All he can think about is this new baby. And he's got two little girls too. And this new baby.'

'The Dogman's got a new baby.'

'Yes. Really new. Small.'

Toby absorbs this information in silence.

'Well,' he says at last, speaking slowly, 'I think that's sad. I think babies are sad. What do you think, Angus? Do you like babies?'

'No,' says Angus. 'Who said I did?'

'You don't go round destroying when you've got a baby.'

In some part of Jack's mind he grasps that Toby has no use for a domesticated Dogman.

'He was wearing a woolly jumper,' he says.

'A woolly jumper? What sort of woolly jumper?'

'Striped. In lots of colours.'

Toby Clore shakes his head.

'No,' he says. 'That is so sad it's almost gay.'

His gaze shifts, to reach across the nets to the main terrace. There stands Jimmy Hall, overseeing the morning break, his hands clasped behind his back, his anger still evident in his abrupt changes of posture.

'Justice standeth far off,' says Toby.

'The Dogman doesn't make any money out of his farm.' Jack pursues his advantage. 'He says everyone hates him.'

Instinct guides him. With each additional item of information the Dogman's prestige dwindles. Toby Clore has no interest in persecuting a loser. And as it happens he believes he has found a new prophet in an unlikely form. The mismatch between outward appearance and inner rage appeals to his taste for the unpredictable.

'Behold the true prophet,' he says.

They follow his gaze but can't make out what he means.

'Where, Tobe?'

'The true prophet lives among us but he's in disguise. He's an angel of the Lord. An archangel maybe. What do you think, Jacko?'

Jack is all too willing to play along.

'Lucifer,' he says. 'He was an angel.'

Toby Clore nods his appreciation. He has that look on his face. He's off on one of his jags.

'Lucifer,' says Toby Clore, 'does not have a baby. Lucifer does not wear a woolly jumper. Lucifer does not whine that everybody hates him.'

He sets off across the cricket pitch for the terrace. The others follow.

'Lucifer is filled with righteous anger,' he says as they go. 'We worship and obey.'

Jack laughs out loud. He has followed Toby's mental tracks where the others are still floundering. This one's going to be a cracker.

Toby bounds up onto the terrace.

'Mr Hall sir,' he says. 'Please give us a sign, sir.'

'I'll give you a smack round the head, you cheeky little beggar.'

The sun comes out from behind a cloud and suddenly the terrace is ablaze with light. Shadows sweep over the flanks of the Downs. A crowd of Year Threes come tumbling out of the French windows onto the terrace and chase squealing onto the grass. Jack saunters away with his friends. When they are out of sight round the corner they all burst into laughter.

'We can't worship poor old Jimmy,' says Richard Adderley. 'He's a total reject.'

'That's all you know,' says Toby Clore. 'Me and Jacko know different, don't we, Jacko?'

'He's the angel who fell to earth,' says Jack. 'He's the lord of hell.'

'See, Richard?' says Toby. 'You shouldn't go round assuming you know about people. People aren't the way they look. Are they, Jacko?'

'No,' says Jack. 'People are random.'

53

He's sitting on the stone steps of the hotel warming himself in the sudden sunshine like an orphan. Dressed as he was before, smart shoes, light jacket, his grey-gold hair ruffled by the breeze. He tracks the Volvo with his eyes, the corners crinkling, his mouth acknowledging her punctuality with a wry smile. He doesn't move. As always, everything about Nick Crocker is unemphatic, his attention only granted slowly. But here he is, waiting for her.

'Nick, we're going for a walk. Don't you have any boots?'

'No,' he says, getting into the car.

'You'll ruin your shoes.'

'They'll be okay.'

She swings the car round the gravel sweep and heads back out onto the main road.

'We're lucky. We've got a fine day.'

He says nothing. Looks out at the scenery.

'Where do you want to go?'

'Anywhere,' he says. 'You decide.'

'We'll do the home walk. It starts at one end of the village and goes up to the top, and brings us back down again by the church.'

This is Laura's compromise with herself. She's seeing Nick alone, but seeing him on family territory. No hole-in-corner assignation. Not that there's likely to be anyone else on Edenfield Hill on a Monday afternoon.

She turns off the main road at the roundabout and drives through the village, past the church and the farm and the cricket pitch, to the gates of Edenfield Place.

'We'll leave the car at the back of the big house. There's a path leads up onto the Downs from there.'

When they get out Nick looks at her, studying her in that way he has, taking in her sturdy walking boots and her jeans and her waxed jacket. She tugs a woolly hat out of one jacket pocket and pulls it over her hair.

'It'll be blowy on the top.'

No one can say I dressed up for him. Nothing remotely sexy about a waxed jacket and a woolly hat.

He's holding out an envelope.

'What's this?'

'For you. Put it in a pocket somewhere.'

'Can't I open it?'

'Not yet. I'll tell you when.'

She puts the plump envelope unopened into the inside breast pocket of her jacket, wondering what it can be. Only after they have set off through the little kissing gate onto the steep path does it occur to her that she should not have accepted it. This is some power game of Nick's. He should either give her the letter or withhold it. This giving and not giving is a bait, a lure. But to return it now would make too much of it.

They say little while they climb. The path opens out onto a tractor way, but the going is still hard on the lungs and the thighs. The ground is a mix of chalk and flint, made slippery by recent rains, and once or twice Nick loses his footing. But he doesn't fall.

Laura is setting the pace. Without quite admitting it to herself she wants Nick to have to struggle to keep up, but he's fitter than she supposed. When she pauses to catch her breath he's right behind her.

She points to the four ash trees that line the path, she shows him their low sweeping boughs.

'The children call them the swing trees. They swing on the low boughs.'

Jack and Carrie with her in spirit: her chaperones.

He goes and sits on the sturdiest of the low boughs, his feet touching the ground, and pushes himself gently back and forth.

'Don't you swing too?' he says.

'I'm too big.'

'No, you're not.'

So she sits on the bough next to his and pushes herself back. Lifting her feet, swinging forwards, she feels the sudden swoop of uncontrolled motion, and lets out a little cry. Nick swings too, and as they swing, moving at different speeds, they collide. Her knees bump against his thigh, then they part again.

'It makes me feel giddy.'

She gets off her bough. He remains seated. He's smiling at her.

'What?' she says.

'You're even more beautiful now than you were then.'

'Oh, please.'

'You think I don't mean it?'

For God's sake I'm blushing like a nineteen-year-old. Like I would have blushed when I was nineteen if he'd talked to me this way, which he didn't.

'You're more beautiful now, and you're sexier now, and I want you so much it's killing me.'

Not now, Nick. It's too late.

'So you think a little flattery will do the trick, huh?'

She speaks in a light bantering tone, trying to defuse his intensity and control her own response. But of course flattery does the trick. Married women are exiled from the flattery zone, mothers at any rate, not so many men come on to mothers. It's been a while. Her defences are in a poor state of repair.

'There's no trick,' he says. 'I promised myself I'd say everything. This is part of everything.'

'It doesn't help,' she says helplessly. 'It doesn't go anywhere.'

'Me saying you're beautiful?'

'Yes.'

'It doesn't have to go anywhere. It's here.'

He gives a little lift of his arms that's the beginning of an invitation. Come to me.

Can it be so easy? Can you take what you want and give no thought to the future?

Take what?

A rush of shame. She turns away so he won't see the desire that has taken her unawares. She wants Nick to kiss her.

'We'd better keep going.'

Away from the swing trees, away from Nick, not looking to see if he's following. On up the last stretch of steep track, until the stubby concrete column of the triangulation point comes into view over the brow ahead.

'Soon be at the top.'

Then the brisk wind and the great cloud-charging sky and the view south over tumbling green hills to the sea. To the east the masts of the radio station. To the west the valley of the Ouse. To the north the wide weald where the road and the railway run, and the high spur of Caburn, and the great fertile wooded landscape disappearing into the distance.

My home view. Henry's view.

When they come here with the children he shows them how to find their house, which is hidden by trees. First find the pinched steeple of the church, then imagine you're sitting on its very top and reach out your left arm. There where your fingers are, see, the red-brown roof, the glimpse of white-framed window? That's Jack's bedroom.

Laura stands with Nick Crocker on the South Downs Way, alone in the world.

'Isn't it glorious?' she says.

The wind harries Nick's hair and tugs at his jacket. He's as handsome as he ever was, his high cheekbones lit by the spring sunshine. He spreads his arms as if to embrace the fields and the woods and the villages.

'The English countryside,' he says. 'Please take your litter home with you. Leave this facility as you would like to find it.'

Laura laughs but doesn't understand.

'It's not a park, Nick.'

'Of course it's a park,' he says. 'You didn't think this was real countryside, did you?'

Again she laughs. But it seems he's not joking.

'Who lives in the farmhouses, Laura? Who lives in the farm workers' cottages, and the stables, and the barns?'

'Don't be silly, Nick. There aren't any horses any more, or hayricks, or picturesque peasants.'

'Or farms or farmers or agriculture. Do you know what percentage of the rural English population works in agriculture? Guess.'

'I don't know. I've no idea.'

'Nought point three per cent. One third of one per cent! The English countryside's economy runs on commuters and tourism.'

An edge of real anger in his languid voice. Where's all this coming from?

'Have you been studying rural economics or something?'

'I pick up newspaper reports.'

'Why? What do you care?'

'I care about landscape. You know that.'

'It's because you live in California, isn't it? You're thousands of miles away dreaming of England as it used to be, and it offends you that it's changed. You want it to be all Constable out there, don't you?'

Nick looks over the peaceful scene and doesn't answer. Laura feels irritated. What are they doing arguing about the English countryside, for God's sake?

So what else did I expect us to do alone together?

'The thing is,' says Nick quietly, 'it's fake. It's an image. The final triumph of centuries of mythologizing the rural scene is to turn Arcadia into a consumer product.' He waves at the view. 'It's not countryside any more. It's city life, with the added luxury of space. City people earning city incomes occupying large individual plots of land. It looks like the old countryside because the buildings are still there, and the hedges, and the woodlands. But the country way of life has gone, and the city way of life has taken its place. This is a whole new culture, Laura. This is the suburbs gone to heaven. This is front gardens on steroids. You're living in a fantasy land.'

Now she gets it. Stupid not to have spotted it sooner. This isn't some generalized interest in social change. This is an assault on her chosen way of life. Nick has never raised his voice but she can hear the bitterness, she can feel the need to despise.

'Maybe so,' she says. 'But we like it.'

'I can believe *we* like it,' he retorts. 'I don't believe *you* like it.'

She flushes. He wants to split her from Henry and the children.

'We do and I do,' she says. 'Believe what you please.'

She's angry at him now, offended by his assumption of superiority. And she's angry at herself, because she wanted him to kiss her.

She sets off along the South Downs Way towards the radio masts. Nick falls in beside her. He shows no signs of having registered her anger.

'I know you better than you know yourself, Laura,' he says. 'You can't live a lie.'

'I'm not living a lie.'

'I think you are. Or trying to, at least. I think you've let yourself get trapped in this make-believe world and you've no idea what you're doing here. All you know is, this isn't it. This isn't the life you were meant to live.'

'You have no idea. No idea.'

She walks faster, impelled by her anger and also by dread. He talks on, his soft voice burrowing into her self-belief.

'You knew it once. You felt it once. There is another way of living, where you're alive, truly alive. You've been there, Laura, and so have I. Think of that, and then think of this. How can you tell me this isn't half a life?'

'Shut up,' she says. 'Just shut up.'

'It frightens you. Of course it does. That's because you know I'm right. You know you can't go on like this. You're being suffocated here, Laura. You can hardly breathe. You—'

'Shut up! Shut up!'

'If that's what you want. But you know I'm right.'

They walk in silence. Laura is outraged that he should mount this attack on her current life, about which he knows nothing. And all for his own selfish purposes.

His own selfish purposes.

'Why are you getting at me like this, Nick?'

'I'm not getting at you. I'm trying to save you.'

'Well, I don't need saving, thank you very much.'

She leads them off the high ridge of the Downs onto the long diagonal track that descends towards home. Now in the lee of the wind the sounds of the world change round them. Here in this sculpted hollow they look out as from an amphitheatre at the show that is England in springtime.

'You're wrong, Nick,' she says. 'I love my family, and my home, and my life. You don't know what you're talking about.'

He stops. He has his head down, looking at his shoe as he scuffs the stones of the track.

'Please,' he says.

One word, spoken softly, and everything changes. He's saying, I don't want this argument. This is hurting me. I don't mind being wrong. I mind the distance between us.

'Please.'

He looks up now, his eyes on hers as she has never seen him look before: uncertain, ready to take flight.

'What is it you want, Nick?' she says.

He says, 'Stay.'

The word hangs in the air between them and fades and is gone. She can't speak.

'Stay with me. Come to California with me.'

For a few moments she allows the sleeping ghost of her past self to wake. She is twenty again and he has come back to her as she cried every night for him to come back. He loves her after all, as she knew he must. He needs her as she needs him. They are together again.

'Is that what you came to England to say?'

'Yes,' he says.

'Why now?'

'I don't know. Maybe I'm ready now. Maybe I've come to a fork in the road.'

'You think we can pick up where we left off, after twenty years?'

'No,' he says humbly. 'I just want to be with you, Laura.'

'Why, Nick?'

'Because there's only you. Don't you see? I had no choice but to find you again. There's only you.'

'But I've changed. You don't know me. You think you do, but you don't.'

'People don't change. Not in twenty years. Not in a lifetime. What was true when we were young is true still. We found each other then. That was the real thing. It's still real today.'

Little by little, as she hears him, long-ago shadows are lifting in Laura. She begins to see more clearly. Pain and grief have a way of freezing time. She has preserved her memories of Nick intact through the years, ready for this moment of thaw. And with the thaw comes disintegration.

'I think what I mean,' she says, 'is that you didn't know me then.'

He flinches as if she has struck him.

'Don't say that to me,' he says. 'Tell me you can't leave your children. That I can understand. But don't rewrite history. Don't take from me the one truth of my life.'

'Nick, we were young. We were only just beginning to find out who we were. It wasn't the greatest love affair in history. It was just the first time. For both of us.'

He stares at her, searching her face for a different truth that gives the lie to her words.

'Do you really believe that?'

Down in the valley the little train rattles over the water meadows on its way from Eastbourne calling its cuckoo cry, peep-bo! peep-bo! It crosses the river where Virginia Woolf drowned herself. Stones in her pockets.

Don't look at me like that.

'You're one of life's wanderers, Nick. Go back to California. Write me a letter from time to time.'

He just goes on looking at her.

'Say something.'

'You call me a wanderer. I don't know whether to laugh or cry. If only you knew. I thought you knew.'

'How could I know anything about you, Nick? You walked out of my life. You disappeared.'

'And if your son walked out of your life? If you met him again twenty years later?' The words coming faster now, under pressure. 'Would you not know him? No! You'd take him in your arms and hold him tight and it would be as if you'd never been apart. Time is nothing, Laura! Let a thousand years pass! What we had, what we have, yes, what we have right now, whether you admit it or not, is real and true and rare. That's what I've learned while I've been away from you. How rare it is to love.'

'But to love someone you have to be there for them.'

'I've always been there for you, Laura. I thought you knew. You couldn't see me and I couldn't see you but I was always there. And all the time I knew the day would come when we'd be together again. When you'd be close enough for me to reach out and touch.'

He reaches out one hand and touches her arm. She shivers.

'All I can do is tell you how it is for me,' he says. 'If you doubt me, tell me to go and I'll go. But I'll still be there for you. All you have to do is call me, and I'll come. If I have to wait till Henry dies and you're a widow, I'll wait. I don't mind waiting. I'll be there for you. That's the only way I can show you what I say is true, and always will be.'

Jesus where did he learn this monstrous fidelity? Nick the bolter, Nick the heartbreaker, where are you now?

Wind ruffling his hair, sky shining round him like a halo. Lines on either side of his mouth. His eyes on her, never leaving her, needing her, wanting her. Old lovers are the best, they say. Anxiety shed, mutual desire pre-established, bodies no surprise. Except for the effects of passing time and childbirth and breastfeeding, nothing as firm as it once was. There was a time when she was so proud to hold his naked body in her arms. Her own naked body her gift.

His naked body in my arms.

Look away, Laura. Look away now and never look back.

'We'd better get back.'

'Yes,' he says. 'We'll go now.'

Then he kisses her. This is a non sequitur, she thinks, as she feels his arms pull her close, his lips find her lips. She does not resist or push him away. That would be unkind. And she has in a way invited it.

Oh, this is a kiss. Long time since I've been kissed like it matters. Except now that it's come, it doesn't matter after all.

He holds her in his arms, her head on his shoulder now, and she sees the green playing fields of the school in the valley below. White dots of schoolboys playing cricket. Could be Jack down there.

She feels no guilt because she knows this is an end not a beginning. She's kissing goodbye to her youth, and to the hurt she has hoarded for too long.

So they part, and as she lets him go she feels the hope leave him at last.

They follow the descending path down the flank of the hill.

'I'm sorry,' she says. 'You must have known I could never just walk out on my life.'

'I can do it.'

'You've got less to hold you.'

'I have nothing to hold me.' He throws her a look in which for the first time he allows her to glimpse his desolation. 'Nothing.'

'You've got your work. Your works of art.'

'I buy and sell. That's all.'

'Then do something else.'

He gives a soft laugh.

'This was my something else.'

He has felt the brush of her pity in that kiss as a fatal wound. He makes no more attempts to persuade her. He is withdrawing into whatever fortified place remains within him, for darkness is descending, and with night comes enemy attack. He wants to be gone from her now.

She drives him back to his hotel.

'Don't let it be another twenty years,' she says.

He gives a half smile, a shrug, and turns away. As he goes up the steps into the hotel he raises one hand in a backward wave, but he does not look round.

When Laura takes off her walking jacket in the hall at home she finds the envelope he gave her. Inside the envelope is a plane ticket, a First Class open-dated return flight to Los Angeles, costing $12,600.

54

The animated Coca Cola bottle sails majestic as a space ship above the traffic. As it turns it grows in size, until the droplets can be seen gleaming on its glass flanks, promising cool refreshment to the swarm of people gushing out of the underpasses, bunching at the road crossings, streaming down the pavements. Then when the image can come no closer it dissolves into red lettering, a simple breathtakingly outrageous claim: the Real Thing.

Henry crouches on the pavement at the corner of Regent Street and Piccadilly by the Clydesdale Bank, seeking the exact point at which an approaching pedestrian's head is level with the illuminated advertisement high above. Pale sunlight fails to dim the show of coloured lights.

'This is where we do it,' he says to Christina, who stands behind him notebook at the ready. 'Has Aidan arrived yet?'

'Just got here.'

They walk back together to Jermyn Street, where the crew minibus is parked in a specially reserved space outside Rowley's restaurant. Ray and Oliver are peering in the window of Trumper's, excited by the array of male grooming aids. Aidan Massey is standing by the minibus, watching himself in the tinted window while Rowan works on his hair.

'Yo, Henry,' Aidan says, not taking his eyes off his reflection. 'What's the word on the shirt?'

He's wearing a deep blue open-necked shirt. Henry barely glances at it.

'Looks great, Aidan.'

Ray comes over to him.

'So where's the shot?'

'We're going to do it on the walk.' He continues to Aidan. 'You'll be surrounded by other pedestrians, the bustle of the big city etcetera.'

'Sure, boss. No sweat.'

'Milly'll come and get you when we're ready. Won't be long. Christina, stay here with Aidan while we set up, will you?'

Christina looks a question at Henry: what have I done to deserve this? But Henry's already moving on with Ray and the crew.

Already moving on. A smooth untroubled motion, as if he's floating over the steep-pitched roofs and sharp spires of the world. The events of the weekend, trivial though they may have been, have brought about a change in him. In his heart Henry has resigned from the great game of self-assertion. His anomalous position no longer has the power to hurt him. He performs his duties today solely as a courtesy.

Remarkable the power you accrue when you stop caring. With power comes tolerance. Let Aidan Massey primp his hair, seek admiration from car windows. I smile and move on. I'm out of here, brother. I'm not at your service any more.

His gaze lingers on the people in the street. So many of them wear the expression he knows so well, the empty faces made featureless by the unending succession of unrewarded days. They do their best work for the glory of others. Afraid, they sell themselves as cloak-bearers to follow in the train of those few who dare to demand lives of their own. But what they fear is less terrible than what they have.

Let me be real.

'Set up here, Mo. On the deck. You're lining up Aidan with the Coke ad.'

'I'll radio mike him,' says Oliver, 'but it's going to be guide track only. You're going to have to post-synch it.'

'Let's see what we get, okay? It's only a short piece.'

The crew sets up the camera. Henry crosses the bus lane and walks back to the camera several times so that they can mark the focus points.

'You'll want cover,' says Ray.

Henry nods to Milly to fetch Aidan. He stands looking down Regent Street at the stumpy silhouette of a tower in the distance. To his surprise he realizes it must be the Houses of Parliament on the far side of St James Park.

A lanky youth accosts him.

'What you filming then?'

'Educational video.'

The youth drifts off.

Aidan joins them, murmuring his lines under his breath. Henry explains the shot, demonstrates the start and finish spots, both of which have been marked on the pavement by Mo in yellow camera tape. Aidan stands for a moment gazing across Piccadilly Circus at the animated Coke ad, and sees its message flash up. He nods in appreciation.

'Nice one, Henry.'

They rehearse twice, then they shoot.

'Images have the power to create reality,' Aidan Massey declaims to the faraway camera as he strides through the crowd of pedestrians. 'Images trigger responses we can't always control. Desire. Envy. Anger. Do we really want to be manipulated like this? Maybe we should rise up against the images, tear down the advertisements, smash the glowing screens, sweep the visual pollution from our streets. If you find yourself nodding as you listen to me, then you're an iconoclast. In the seventeenth century you'd have been smashing stained-glass windows.'

Inevitably there are glitches. On the first take Aidan is obscured by a man with a child on his back. On the second take Aidan mistakes his cue, and by the time the camera has completed its pull from the Coke ad he has already started his walk. The third take is acceptable, but Aidan believes he can do better. The fourth take also dissatisfies him.

'It's fine,' says Henry.

'Why would I want fine when I can get brilliant? Where's your fucking ambition, Henry?'

He speaks without aggression, but also without the slightest concern for Henry's feelings. He has not reckoned on the change in Henry.

'Your show, Aidan. Your glory. Why should I give a fuck?'

This too spoken in the same easy tone. Aidan is amazed, then outraged.

'If you don't give a fuck, what the fuck are you doing here?'

'Christ knows. Inertia, I suppose.'

'That is not sodding good enough!' Aidan's rage is growing positively religious. 'We're making a top-quality show here and I expect total professionalism!'

The crew stand round with their eyes on the ground, savouring every word. Christina tries to intervene, but Aidan Massey brushes her aside.

'No, Christina, this is serious. How am I supposed to have confidence in a director who tells me he doesn't give a fuck?'

'He doesn't mean it, Aidan.'

'Then he'd better convince me,' says Aidan, staring at Henry, breathing hard.

'Or what, Aidan?'

'Or I ask for you to be replaced.'

'Then what?'

'Then you're fucking history, boyo.'

'Then I'm history.' Henry grins at that. 'Sounds good to me.'

He turns on his heel and strides away from them across Piccadilly Circus. He hears the beating of drums, he hears the singing of angels. He's walking on air. He's whizzing.

As he reaches Shaftesbury Avenue, moving fast, no idea where he's going other than away, he hears footsteps pounding up behind him, and there's Aidan Massey.

'Slow down,' he says, panting.

'It's okay, Aidan. You win. I'm gone.'

'We need to talk.'

'Barry'll sort something out. You'll be fine.'

'You know the Bar Italia? Best coffee in London.'

It's a traditional old-style Italian bar on Frith Street. Three or four metal tables outside with people drinking coffee in the pale sunlight. A long narrow room inside, mirrored all down the wall facing the bar. Henry has no desire for a coffee, but Aidan Massey won't take no for an answer. He herds him into the bar and orders two double espressos and sits them down on two high leatherette stools by the mirror wall. There's a narrow Formica shelf for the coffees.

'Okay,' says Aidan Massey. 'I'm an asshole.' He says it the American way. 'You think I don't know it? There's nothing you could tell me about myself, *nothing*, that I don't already know.'

'Aidan, you don't have to justify yourself to me.'

'I know I don't have to. But I want to. Ask me why.'

'Why?'

'Because you're good. Because you're so good you make me good. Because I don't want to lose you.'

'You said in front of the entire crew that you could do my job better than me.'

'I was pissed off. I'm no director. To tell the truth, you're not that hot as a director either. What you are is an amazingly talented writer. You think subtle and you write plain. That's rare, Henry. I try to do it. Sometimes I manage it. But you – you're a natural.'

Henry hears him with astonishment. This is not the Aidan Massey he knows. The shock is not the late rush of praise: it's the revelation of Aidan's self-knowledge.

'So,' Aidan goes on, 'big surprise, I want to steal your stuff. Why wouldn't I? It's great stuff. And, big surprise, you don't like that. But we can sort this fucker out. We can do a deal.'

'Jesus, Aidan, I wish you'd talked like this before.'

'Why would I? If I can get it easy, why bleed for it? You think I like telling you this shit? I tell this to nobody. How's the coffee?'

'It's good.'

'Best coffee in London. Listen to me, Henry. I don't know what you think I am, but whatever it is, I'm not that guy. Here's who I am. I'm my own act of fucking will. I'm one-hundred-per cent self-invention. My dad sold greetings cards. We lived on a Wimpey estate. I'm not even working class for Christ's sake, just low-achieving, high-conforming, medi-fucking-ocrity. Then one day I decided I was clever enough to read on my own, and I spent the next twenty years in libraries. On my own. Now I teach at Yale, I teach at Cambridge, I write books, I do television programmes, I review, I give opinions, I sit on committees – I do every fucking thing I'm asked to do, because it was a long lonely time coming. I take on too much, I cut corners, I trample on people, you think I don't know? But that's my life now. That's how it works. If you don't like it you're free to cut me loose. I can understand that. But there's something else you can do. You can do a deal with me. You can use me to get what you want.'

He pauses. He fixes Henry with his intent gaze.

'That is, if you know what you want.'

Henry stares back in silence.

'Do you know what you want?'

'God knows.' Henry finds himself impelled to tell the truth. 'I know some of it. I know I don't want it to be like this.'

'So how do you want it to be?'

'I don't know that I want to be a director. But I like history. I'd like to go on working in the field.'

He listens to himself talking, like a schoolboy to a careers master. But he has no way to say the real words. People don't have that conversation. How can he say that for months now, maybe years, he's felt like he's on the point of falling?

'So you want to write.'

'Maybe.'

'Come on, Henry. Help me here. Write what? Articles in learned journals? Books?'

'Anything.'

'You know what you'd be paid for an article? A hundred if you're lucky.'

'I know.'

'A book – you could write a bestseller, you've got the talent. But I'm not sure that's the kind of book you want to write. And anyway you'd have to live while you're working on it. An advance of maybe £20,000 to see you through maybe three years.'

'I know.'

'Is that the plan? Holy poverty?'

'There's no plan.'

'Okay. I get the picture. So let me tell you my favourite story. It's a true story, about Gandhi. You know Gandhi came from a prosperous middle class background, he went to the best schools, he trained as a barrister, he got married, he had a son. Then he changed. He became the Mahatma. He gave up everything, out of pure idealism, and led a life of true poverty. He sent his son to the village school, which was quite incapable of giving the boy the kind of education Gandhi himself had had. Then one of Gandhi's wealthy followers offered to pay all the school fees to give the boy the best education money could buy. Gandhi accepted. His son was very excited. But when the time came for the boy to leave and go to his fine new school, Gandhi picked out a poor village kid and sent him in his son's place. His son hated him for that. He determined from that day on to reject everything his father believed in. He became a drunkard, he visited brothels, he was a parasite, a burden, a bum. His father died a martyr, mourned by the whole nation. His son died only six months later. For days his body lay unrecognized and unclaimed among the nameless street corpses.'

He taps the sand-coloured Formica shelf with his index finger to drum in his story's moral.

'Don't get me wrong,' he says. 'I think Gandhi was a great man. But he didn't have to do that. He could have reached a deal.'

'Like you have.'

'Fucking right. Like I do every day. I'm dealing all the time, getting a little of what I want, giving a little I'd just as soon not give. That's called living in the real world.'

'The real thing.'

Aidan Massey laughs his rich laugh.

'Coke isn't the real thing. But a world where marketing men can make you value Coke by calling it the real thing – that's the real thing. We crave authenticity. So they use that craving. It's not ironic, Henry. Irony's just one of our ways of dodging reality.'

'I'm with you there.'

'So do a deal.'

'What do you have in mind?'

'Go on working with me. Go on writing lines for me. That way you get paid, you get out of the house, you get status. Okay, so I get all the credit. But right now that's the way the cards are dealt. You want to be the star, get down to work. When you're not working with me, you work for yourself. Take all that energy you expend on resenting me and pour it into becoming you.'

'I have a family too.'

'So get up early. Work late. The day is longer than you think. No one said it was easy.'

Henry shakes his head. Against all expectations he's warming to Aidan Massey.

'You may be right.'

'Look, no one gets the life they want. Not me, not anyone. But if you're lucky you get good times along the way. Be grateful, brother. Enjoy the parade. It's going to pass on by, believe me.'

'Do you enjoy the parade?'

'You bet I do.'

Henry shakes his head again. He means this gesture as an acknowledgement of Aidan Massey's powerful vitality, but the star misunderstands him.

'You think I'm fooling myself, don't you? You think I'm somewhat ridiculous. But you know what? I don't care.'

'I don't think you're ridiculous at all. If anything, I envy you. I wish I had your energy.'

'You have got my energy. Everyone's got energy. But most people's energy is all used up by their anxieties. People are far crazier than we ever guess.'

'Don't you have anxieties?'

'No,' says Aidan. 'But I'm an asshole.'

'You say that like an American.'

'Like I said, I'm one-hundred-per cent self-invention. I'm still working on it. I'm a work in progress.'

'Me too.'

Aidan reaches out his hand for Henry to shake.

'Deal?'

'Okay. Deal. For now.'

They shake. Then they walk back to Piccadilly Circus without speaking. They walk side by side, in step, newly bonded. For Henry everything to do with his job has changed.

The crew are on the island photographing Eros.

'Got you some cover,' says Ray.

Christina looks at Henry with concern.

'You okay?'

'Yes,' he says. 'I'm fine. Sorry to go off like that. But now that Aidan's explained to me that he just can't help being a prick, I've got over it.'

All eyes turn to Aidan Massey.

'What can I say?' He spreads his arms and grins. 'I'm a prick. Let's do the piece to camera again.'

55

Is she reading it now? Is she raising her eyebrows at the language, or is she yawning, rolling her eyes? Reading it beginning to end, or putting it down, doing other things, fitting it into her day like an unloved chore? In the school hall, rehearsing his Year Eight actors, Alan Strachan prompts the thin high voices as they struggle with Shakespeare's verse, his mind on his own lines. He sees her brown eyes scanning the black type, her fingers turning the next page. And feeling what?

James Shaw can't stop swinging his arms as he speaks.

> 'One turf shall serve as pillow for us both;
> One heart, one bed, two bosoms and one troth.'

Snorts of suppressed laughter greet the eagerly-awaited line. Alan wonders yet again if he was foolish not to cut it. On the other hand you could say that through this one line Shakespeare has entered the every day speech of these privileged but illiterate children. 'Sir, Harry has two bosoms, sir, I've seen them.' The chief target of the jibe is Mrs Digby, who is now widely known as Two Bosoms.

Alan is playing the scene for comedy in the crudest possible way. Katie Beale shuffles sideways two steps with each line, heel-toe, heel-toe.

> 'Nay, good Lysander, for my sake, my dear,
> Lie further off yet, do not lie so near.'

'Now go after her, James. Heel toe, heel toe. Keep facing the audience.'

Shakespeare as slapstick. But it works. Even in rehearsal they get a laugh. Nothing like laughter to boost a performer's confidence.

'For God's sake keep your arms still, James. I'm going to tie them down.'

'Sorry sir.'

'Why do you do it?'

'Don't know sir.'

'Here. Hold this.'

He throws the boy a cushion.

'Now do it again.'

They're not bad kids. At least they find it funny. No one's told them yet that Shakespeare's educational.

She must have read it by now. Her gaze swept the forty-three pages like a searchlight exposing them to pitiless scrutiny. In this form no one but himself has read it, it has lived all its life in a warm dark room, protected from the bright lights and the keen stripping winds beyond the door. Now his baby has been thrust naked into the world.

An adolescent attempt to shock. The plot only too predictable. The characters mere posturing stereotypes. Not that she'll say any of it. Really liked your play, Alan. No, really. It's so unusual. Never read anything like it before. Don't really know what I think. It's different.

Oh, fuck. Why did I ever give it to her? Nice going, Alan. First you blub in front of her then you give her your crap play to read.

Only it's not crap. This is the madness with which Alan lives all the time these days. He's a genius tied to a fool, back to back, elbows to elbows, shins to shins. However many times he spins about the genius can never see the fool, but nor can he escape him. Sometimes in the mirror of his solitude he catches the wry smile of the genius, sometimes the vacant mouthing of the fool.

This play is startlingly original, vital, funny and heartbreaking. A central device of powerful simplicity, an hour in the disintegration of a love affair interwoven with, counterpointed by, an hour of sexual foreplay. The final breach between the lovers coincides with the release of orgasm. This is highly charged work, no?

Yamma yamma yamma says the fool. It's a brain-wank, buddy. You're living in la-la land.

Christ she's called Elizabeth. She'll think I named my heroine after her. I'm this sad loser with sick fantasies of what I want to do to her. She won't even let me in the house.

Just tell me I'm not insane. Tell me I can write.

Why do I want this so much if it's all a delusion? Why does the act of forming the lines in my head excite me so much that my bowels melt and I have to run to the lavatory unbuckling my belt as I go? Don't tell me that's not the real thing.

> 'But, gentle friend, for love and courtesy
> Lie further off—'

The bell rings.

'Good, Katie. I like the little push. Next time try giving him a good hard shove. Thank you, James. You can let go of the cushion now. Same time Wednesday, everyone.'

His actors clatter out of the hall, laughing and jostling. Alan replaces the cushion, moves the lectern back to mid-stage for tomorrow morning's assembly, switches out lights.

Shakespeare had it made. His own company of actors, a theatre to fill, no time to fuck about. Write, rehearse, perform. Imagine Shakespeare wetting himself because some girl he fancied was reading a play of his. Who cares what she thinks? His actors are already learning their lines, he's halfway through the play after next, the show goes on. If it doesn't work, fix it. Listen to the audience, follow the tears and the laughter. That's the way to write. Not this lonely terror.

So like love. The fear of being without talent so like the fear of never being loved. The one a surrogate for the other, no doubt. The hunger for genius a hunger for love.

Just say good things about my play. But mean what you say, lady. I don't want pity. Only totally sincere awestruck admiration will do. Is that too much to ask? Oh, and let me fuck you afterwards. An awestruck fuck, that would truly be the cherry on the cake.

Yamma yamma yamma. Dream on.

He weaves his way between the slow-moving procession of parents' cars to the main school. Jimmy Hall is on pick-up duty.

'Hello, Jimmy. How's things?'

'Not so good, Alan. Actually, since you ask, I'm bloody livid.'

The last thing Alan wants to do is listen to Jimmy Hall's catalogue of disappointments in life, given that to all young male teachers in the school Jimmy Hall represents a hideous warning of what they might themselves one day become. But a moment or two is only polite.

'What's got you going, Jimmy?'

'You know I do work from time to time for the local rag? Well, I turned in a piece on Saturday that was something special. You know, though I say it myself, it had a touch of true artistry. The editor loved it. And what happens? The nationals nick my story! The big boys come barging in and re-work it and get it all wrong needless to say, and my little piece is left to die the death.'

'I'm sorry, Jimmy. It's a tough world.'

'They're killers,' says Jimmy Hall bitterly. 'They're vampires.'

Alan collects his work bag from his classroom and leaves for the staff car park by the library door. He doesn't want to meet Liz Dickinson picking up Alice. She expects him some time after seven. The short exchange with Jimmy Hall has depressed him. Easy to laugh at his sad little dreams of journalistic glory, but why should his own dreams be any different?

Though I say it myself it had a touch of true artistry.

Jimmy Hall says it himself because there's no one else to say it. Just like me. Though Liz may be kind. Except kind has no value. Only true has value. But hey, I'll settle for kind.

As always it takes a long time to make the turning out of the school lane onto the main road. At this time of day the A27 is a ceaseless flow of home-going commuters, and it's a rare driver who slows and flashes his lights to let waiting cars in from side roads. Alan turns on the radio and someone on the PM programme is talking about paternity leave. Tony Blair has decided to take two weeks off to help look after his new baby son, and John Prescott is to be in charge. The Downing Street website has published the first pictures of baby Leo and has crashed under the massive demand.

Why? All the newspapers will carry the pictures tomorrow. You look at a picture of a baby and then what? People are strange.

Onto the main road at last and into the ever-flowing river of human desolation. Not that I know they're all miserable. They may be happy as Larry in their cars, singing all the way home. The driver behind is right on my tail. What am I supposed to do, buddy? Ram the car in front?

Gentle friend for love and courtesy lie further off.

She won't be reading it now. She'll be driving Alice home. She's read it by now or not at all. Off the main road at last and up the lane to Glynde.

Fucking typical. There's a car parked in his customary parking space. In fact, a police car. As he goes to his front door a policeman appears from his neighbour's house.

'Has something happened to Mrs Temple-Morris?' says Alan.

'Did you know her, sir?'

'No, not really. Just as a neighbour.'

'When did you last see her?'

'On Friday. What's happened to her?

'Bad news, I'm afraid. She passed away.'

'Good God! I didn't even know she was ill.'

'The newspaper boy raised the alarm.' The policeman gives a shrug. 'The newspapers were jamming up inside.'

'She seemed fine when I saw her.' Then he realizes she was not fine at all. 'What did she do? Take an overdose?'

'Something like that. We'll know more when the coroner submits his report.'

'Has her husband been told?'

'Husband, sir? There's no husband.'

'No husband?'

'Never been married, sir. We've been checking next of kin. Turns out that was just her little story. Would you be available tomorrow, sir? Just for a short statement.'

'Yes. Of course.'

Alan goes on into his house, profoundly shaken. Not grief at his neighbour's death: shock at how little he knew her. He sees her now, bathed in the flattering light of his own over-easy assumptions, an ageing woman with too much make-up on her face and not enough to fill her day. The husband she had invented. The smile she synthesized. The over-cheerful voice she faked. All to avoid the shame of being exposed as a lonely, unwanted, fearful, fragile human being.

God in his mercy lend her grace.

Where's that from? Tennyson, 'The Lady of Shalott'. Another suicide.

On either side the river lie

Long fields of barley and of rye

Funny how some lines stick in your mind for ever. Singing in her song she died. Not an overdose, then. More like a fairy curse. Go on seeing the world in your shadowy mirror, lady. If you turn round and look at the real thing, you die. So maybe that's what she did. Maybe

Mrs Temple-Morris took one look at the real world, the world in which she had no husband and no reason to smile, and not liking what she saw chose to leave by the nearest exit.

I can use that, he thinks, the structure of a new play already forming in his mind. A modern Lady of Shalott. A lonely death unredeemed by iambic tetrameters.

He showers and changes, preparing for the coming evening, in the course of which the world's opinion – which is to say all that is not inside his own mind and under his own control – will pronounce judgement on his play. On his aspirations to be a writer. On his estimation of himself.

My aspiration to be a writer. Which is to say my aspiration to live. My act of engagement with life. To be a writer is to live fully, to be an explorer, to be one of the few who are awake in a world of sleepwalkers. And yet all the time, separated from me by a few inches of wood and plaster, a life has been ending in solitude and silence.

This is the source of his shame. He knew nothing. He never tried to know. He bought the fiction she created, out of pity and laziness.

That was just her little story.

Mrs Temple-Morris a writer too, in her way. Her early work an entertainment for the neighbours, a conventional tale in the comic mode. Her mature work an unheard cry of despair, a tragedy.

Come round some time after seven. Five past? Ten past? He forces himself not to leave his house until seven o'clock. From Glynde to Lewes is barely three miles and by now the traffic will have eased on the A27 so he'll be there in no time. He takes a bottle of red wine from his modest store.

The house next door is closed and silent. The police car long gone. Alan drives away with a line from 'The Lady of Shalott' running in his head.

All in the blue unclouded weather

I'll know as soon as I see her face if she's read it. I'll know what she thinks of it. She won't tell me the truth but I'll know.

Lewes is quiet, the shops long closed. He leaves his car in the half empty car park behind the Cliffe, and walks up past All Saints and the Friends Meeting House. He sees Alice's face at the downstairs front window of her house, looking out for him. She knows he'll be punctual. He sees her run to open the door.

'I've had my supper already,' she tells him. 'It's school tomorrow so I have to be in bed by eight.'

'Quite right.' He enters the narrow hallway.

Liz appears from the kitchen holding a broad-bladed kitchen knife. She looks pleased to see him. Beyond that, contrary to his expectations, her face tells him absolutely nothing.

'Come on in. I'm chopping onions. Only pasta.'

'Great,' says Alan. He holds out his bottle of wine. 'A contribution.'

'I'll do that,' says Alice. 'I'm good at opening wine.'

Liz turns back into the kitchen, saying as she goes, 'I loved your play. We'll talk about it after Alice has gone up.'

'Why?' says Alice.

'Because you wouldn't understand it, and because I say so.'

'Is it at all like *Friends*?'

'No, not really,' says Alan. 'It's about a couple breaking up.'

'That happens in *Friends*. Ross and Rachel broke up.'

'This isn't funny.'

'Ross and Rachel breaking up wasn't funny. It was awful. I still think they shouldn't have broken up, they just go so well together. I just know they'll get back together in the end. They just have to.'

Alan is re-running Liz's words, trying to discover from her tone of voice the true opinion that lies behind them. *I loved your play.* Once again he finds he can be sure of nothing.

'A terrible thing,' he says. 'My neighbour in Glynde, the woman who lives right next door, took an overdose.'

'That is so sad,' says Liz, her eyes stinging from the onions.

'I didn't know her. But I still feel terrible that I had so little idea.'

'You said terrible before,' says Alice.

'And the other thing I didn't know was that she lived alone. She pretended to be married. She used to talk to me about her husband. But he was just made up.'

'Oh, the poor woman,' says Liz.

Alice is fascinated.

'She just made up a husband? And everyone believed her?'

'Well, I did. I suppose I never really bothered to think much about it. You don't expect people to invent husbands.'

'I think that is so cool.'

When Liz goes upstairs to tuck Alice up for the night Alan prowls round the living room looking for the copy of his play. He fails to find it. There's the latest *Vogue* and last month's *Harpers*. Then he catches sight of himself reflected in the mirror over the fireplace. Christ what a scarecrow. He pushes down his unruly hair, tucks in his escaping shirt.

Liz appears.

'Alice says good night.'

He follows her into the kitchen.

'Your play. It really is something else.' She busies herself over the pan of now-boiling water. 'Totally, totally not what I was expecting. It's fantastically rude, but it's brilliant. I don't claim to understand it all, but really, it's brilliant.'

O sweet Liz, bringer of joy. Comfort of angels, bread of heaven. Don't stop. Say more. Pour balm on my soul.

'You think so?'

'It's sharp, it's funny, it's shocking. God knows if it could ever be put on. Wasn't there a play not so long ago where a guy had a sex chat online, pretending to be a girl?'

'Yes. It was called *Closer*.'

'I like yours better. It's got such a great climax.' She giggles. 'Oh, God. Ending, I mean.'

'The pun is deliberate. If you can call it a pun.'

'Yes, of course. It's a brilliant idea. I've never heard of a play that ends with an orgasm.'

She turns round to smile at him as he sits by the table, rolling his wine glass between his hands.

'And you a school teacher, too.'

'I know. I'm a disgrace.'

The bottle of red wine is now finished so she produces one of her own. Alan needs no more alcohol to be intoxicated.

'Have you shown it to anyone else?' she asks him.

'Not in this form, no. I sent an earlier version to Radio Four, but they didn't want it.'

'Radio Four! You must be off your rocker!'

'It didn't have all the sex phone call stuff. I added that.'

'Oh, okay. That would make quite a difference.'

'So you like it?'

'I am trying to give you that impression, Alan. But maybe I'm not making myself clear when I use words like brilliant.'

'You could try saying it all again.'

He grins at her, filled with a great and perfect love.

'It's brilliant,' she says. 'Your play's fucking brilliant. And let me tell you, I do not use that word lightly.'

'Brilliant?'

'Fucking.'

O sweet Liz fuck me now. I love you for ever.

'The thing is,' he says, 'so few people have read anything of mine. What you say is really rather important.'

'Just as well I like it then, isn't it?'

'So you do like it?'

'It's fucking brilliant.'

They're like two little children, conspirators in naughtiness.

She serves out the pasta and they finish the second bottle of wine with the food.

'I have a question,' she says, her wide mouth twitching with suppressed laughter. 'The sex phone call. Is that really what they're like, or did you make it up?'

'No, it's real. I edited it here and there, but mostly it's just the way I heard it.'

'So anyone can phone a number and hear all that?'

'Sure. But it costs a pound a minute.'

'And people phone these numbers?'

'It's big business. There's a lot of them about.'

'Where?' she says, blushing a little. 'I've never seen any. I suppose in men's porn magazines.'

'They're everywhere. Even in local papers.'

He looks round the kitchen and his eyes fall on a copy of *Friday Ad*. He reaches for it, flicks through the pages of flats to rent, cars for sale. There's an Adult section at the back.

'See.'

'*Friday Ad*! My God!'

Liz takes it from him and runs her eyes down the little black-and-white ads. Unzip and relax. Quick relief. Lay back and climax. Sluts at home. Filthy phone sex.

'It's a whole other world.'

'But you knew it was there, didn't you?'

'Yes, I suppose so.'

He can see that she's really curious.

'Why not try it? If you don't mind the cost.'

'How does it work?'

'Well, it's really quite a complex operation. You dial the number, and – er – you listen.'

She smacks his arm.

'No, I mean, what do you have to say to the person on the other end?'

'Nothing. There is no person on the other end. It's a recording.'

'I wouldn't know what to say if it was a real person.'

'There's no one there. See, it says it here, in the ad. Don't talk, just listen.'

She looks at him with bright eyes, wanting to be persuaded. He glances round for the phone.

'I'll do it. I'll dial for you.'

'What if Alice hears?'

'Does Alice listen in on your phone calls on another extension?'

'No.'

'Then she won't hear.'

He dials the number. The first recording, as ever, is the age and contents warning. He waits for it to end before handing her the cordless phone.

'Just listen.'

He watches her face as she listens. At first she giggles and her eyes open very wide, but after a few moments she just sits there listening intently. Then she gets up and goes through to the living room, still listening, and sits down on the deep sofa. He follows. She pats the sofa by her side. He sits down beside her. Now her eyes are on him as the phone whispers dirty secrets into her ear. She seems to have forgotten the time.

He raises his watch and turns it towards her, concerned about the mounting cost. She nods, but her mind is elsewhere.

Alan is enchanted.

She likes my play. She loves my play. It's brilliant, sharp, funny, shocking. That's more than politeness, she's not the polite type, look at her, she's the real thing. Lorraine Jones would never dial up a sex line.

Tread softly, you tread on my dreams. Touch softly. Stroke softly. Kiss softly.

She pulls the phone from her ear at last and hits the end button.

'Jesus!' she says. 'You could end up spending twenty quid on that stuff!'

'People do.'

'I never even got to the end.'

'But it was fun?'

'She made him lie back on a desk, then she knelt on top of him so that he couldn't move his arms and made him — I can't say it. I don't know you well enough.'

'I can imagine.'

She wriggles in the deep soft cushions.

'God help me,' she says. 'If Alice wasn't asleep upstairs I think I'd be taking advantage of your good nature.'

He smiles at her, too brimming with happiness to mind that she's telling him there'll be no sex tonight. But she likes his play.

Suddenly she leans towards him, presses her face onto his chest.

'You shouldn't have let me do that.'

He puts his arms round her. His right hand rests on her hip. She takes it and puts it between her thighs.

'Unfinished business,' she whispers.

'Then let me get closer.'

She unzips her jeans, pulls down denim and cotton, sinks back onto the sofa. His hand returns, his finger feeling for the soft folds. Her hand joins his, guides his, makes his finger press on the perfect spot. Her pelvis moves, pushing back, chafing. Then it's her finger alone between her thighs, flying up and down, while she twists and turns silently in his arms.

Just before she comes she goes still. Then she shudders and folds up on herself, and rolls against him. For a long moment she remains like this, clinging to him tightly. Then she lets go.

'Thank you.'

'My pleasure.'

'But it wasn't.'

She feels the ridge of his cock, hard beneath his trousers.

'Do you want to do something about it?'

'I'd rather do it properly.'

'I can't. I'd be too worried Alice would hear.'

'Some other time.'

'Oh, yes, I think so. I owe you now.'

She cuddles up against him. He bends his head down and kisses her brow. She looks up at him. He kisses her lips.

'You're gorgeous,' he says. 'And sexy. And highly intelligent.'

'And an excellent judge of contemporary drama.'

'The best.'

They kiss again.

The phone rings. She reaches about for it, finding it at last on the floor.

'Yes? Oh, it's you.'

Alan lets himself sink back into the sofa cushions, feeling his erection soften and dwindle.

All in the blue unclouded weather

'I can't, Guy. I just can't. I've got too much on. Tell me your plans for Alice's birthday. Okay, okay, I'm only asking. Just make sure you call her on the day. No, sorry. Don't go on about it, Guy. I've got company, okay? Just company. Sure. You do that. Bye.'

She puts the phone back down on the floor and zips up her jeans.

'Alice's father,' she says. 'One of my many errors of judgement.'

He looks at her. He has nothing to say. Nothing would make this time more perfect. Let it go on for ever.

She feels his approval and his happiness.

'You know what makes you very unusual,' she says. 'You write about sex as if you like it.'

'Doesn't everyone?'

'No. Not at all. Most writers make a joke of it, or make it creepy and disgusting, or sad. They don't want to do pornography and they don't want to do bodice-rippers so they put on this superior tone about sex, as if they're not part of it. But they are part of it. We're all part of it. Well, I am.'

'Me too.'

'I could work from home tomorrow. I could make some time tomorrow afternoon.'

'What's tomorrow? Tuesday.' He shuts his eyes, mentally scanning his timetable. 'I've got a gap between two-fifteen and three.'

'That's enough, isn't it?'

He opens his eyes and there she is, smiling at him.

'Yes. It's enough.'

56

Break something.

Ah, those iconoclasts. They thought they were breaking images, but they were breaking patterns. Not the great pattern, not the framework that sustains daily life, that would be more than iconoclasm, that would be revolution. We're talking small ruptures in the fabric of habit. But through these rips comes new air, bearing new smells.

Window down in the car. Sussex on a May evening, the hawthorn in scented bloom. A land saturated with new life. Darkness coming, but it's never fully dark, even when there's no moon. The one true darkness is in death, which is coming too, but not yet, not yet. The poplars on the corner have such a respectable way of standing there, as if there was never a time when they did not mark the junction of the lanes, and yet they too were once seeds, were once shoots.

Anything is possible once you learn to endure disappointment. Hopes are dashed, plans miscarry, but next May the leaves will unfold once more, each year's leaves are a new creation, a reprise of joy. And how many more Mays will I live to see? Forty if I'm lucky. A finite number, inexorably ticking down to zero.

Let Laura be alive when I get home. Let Jack and Carrie be alive. Let all be well.

Laura is in the kitchen when she hears Henry's car pull up outside. She hears his footsteps on the gravel, his key in the lock. The rattle of the closing door, the clunk of his bag onto the hall table. Then silence.

In this time, she knows, she sees without seeing, he bends down and unlaces his shoes. He eases them off, pushes them under the hall bench, finds his slippers, shuffles his feet into their home embrace.

He loves to get out of his shoes at the end of the day. He wears leather heel-less slippers, she buys them for him, they make a soft flop-clack sound as he walks.

Flop-clack, flop-clack. His face in the doorway.

'Carrie still up?'

She gives him a nod and off he goes up the stairs. She can't speak because she's overwhelmed by the realization of how well she knows him. She knows him even in his silences.

Carrie is in bed, curtains drawn, her light not yet out. She tells Henry of the latest turn in her turbulent relationship with Naomi Truscott.

'She wasn't there in the lunch queue and no one had seen her and I was really hungry so I went on into lunch, I did wait, I waited lots, but she didn't come. What was I supposed to do? Miss lunch? How was I to know she was looking for her clarinet? But she got so stressy as if I'd deliberately abandoned her or something.'

Henry sits on the side of her bed, nodding gravely. He's watching her hands, seeing how perfect they are, how pale the skin, though she does bite her finger-nails. He remembers her when she was born, a quick birth, much quicker than Jack. The way she gazed at him, almost suspiciously. 'That one's nobody's fool,' the midwife said. My little girl. My girl.

Only the bedside reading lamp is on, throwing a pool of soft light onto the crumpled pink flowers of the duvet.

'Maybe she's frightened you'll make best friends with one of the others.'

'Well I won't. Except if she carries on like this then I will. Tessa says she's a retard.'

The cruellest truth: we only give our love to those who have no need of it. But later the need grows. Or another kind of love. A historical love, love with a history.

'Maybe you've outgrown each other. Maybe it's time for new friends.'

'Oh, Daddy I couldn't. We've been best friends for ever.'

This offer and her rejection of it brings to an end her inner agitation as effectively as if she had talked it over with Naomi herself. The unfairness of Naomi's accusations against her neutralized by her own generosity.

'Do you want me to tuck you up now?'

She nods and puts away her book.

'Tuesday tomorrow. I like Tuesdays. Tuesday's a good day.'

He leans down to kiss her.

'Love you, darling.'

By the door he looks back and sees her fuzzy head framed by the white pillow in the pool of lamplight. The lamp stays on until Laura comes up for the final phase of the night-time ritual.

Descending the stairs he recalls a time when for him too different days had different colours, different tastes. Monday always the worst. Monday the return of struggle and dread. And yet today is a Monday.

'She's ready for you,' he tells Laura.

Jack is in the living room watching a television programme about spiders. Henry watches with him in silence for a few moments. He is shown a close-up of a funnel-web spider's fangs oozing venom.

'One bite and you're dead,' says Jack. 'But they only live in Australia.'

'How was Toby Clore today?'

'Toby's okay.'

The crisis has passed. The extraordinary immediacy of life to a child. The wave of terror rises and falls and is forgotten. There's something he's been meaning to ask Jack for days. What is it?

'Oh, yes.' Pausing in the living room doorway as he leaves the room. 'That composition you wrote at school about a dream. Was it really a dream you had?'

'I think so. Probably.'

'About walking on walls. Clouds below.'

'Don't really remember.'

'You didn't ever fall? In your dream.'

'Don't think so.'

'So was it a happy dream?'

'Don't really remember.'

Henry goes on to the kitchen, swept by his own thoughts. He's thinking of the unimaginable otherness of other people. We each live in our own world, and our worlds collide, but all we get is a little dented. A little bruised. These bruises our only chance of understanding those who are not ourselves. The precious ache of understanding.

He pours himself a glass of red wine. Laura comes down from kissing Carrie goodnight.

'Drink?' he says.

'Definitely.'

He pours more wine and considers how much to tell her of his day. Not all: she can never know it all. There are limits to intimacy. But he feels the need to narrow the gap. Every day the gap widens, and every evening, no, not every evening, but most evenings, they bridge it anew.

'I had a talk with Aidan Massey today. A real talk.'

'That's a first.'

Laura moves back and forth between the table and the stove, making dinner.

'His father was a greetings card salesman.'

She turns and reads his expression.

'You've stopped minding.'

As quickly as that. Must be my tone of voice.

'As a matter of fact I walked out today. But then I walked back.'

It sounds ridiculous. It is ridiculous. He grins.

'As far as I'm concerned,' says Laura, 'you can walk out any time you like. You know that.'

'Maybe tomorrow.'

'Ah, the famous tomorrow.'

'I just thought, what the hell. I like the people.'

And the money, and the status, and the somewhere to go where demands are made, and coming home tired at the end of the day. Not the end result after all, but the doing of the thing.

'That's what I miss most,' says Laura. 'The people.'

'You could go back.'

'I don't know if they'd even have me back.'

'Or somewhere else. If that's what you want.'

He's thinking how beautiful she is. Just like when he saw her by the lake at Glyndebourne. *Dove sono*. Where are they now, the happy moments?

'If that's what I want,' she says. She stops doing what she's doing and looks at him in the way she looks when she's thinking. 'I'm not sure it really matters what any of us want.'

Then her face smoothes out and she gives a laugh, laughing at herself.

'Stupid thing to say.'

Henry understands. It's not stupid at all.

'No, you're right.' Then he adds, 'Just don't die, please. Ever.'

'All right. I won't.'

Now as good a time as any. Make a joke of it.

'I need your money.'

'Our money. The family's money.' This her way of making him believe he's not a beggar. 'You want me to have a word with Daddy?'

'The funds are a bit on the low side.'

She puts down what she's doing and goes to where he sits, in the kitchen's only armchair. She drops down on her knees so that her face is on a level with his. She takes his hands in hers.

'If you want, we'll sell the house. I don't care. I really don't. It's just that Daddy's got so much and he loves to help us and I think, why not? But you hate it, don't you?'

'No. I don't hate it. I have a bit of a struggle from time to time, that's all.'

'I don't want money to make you sad, Henry.'

'You'd rather we were poor but happy.' Teasing her.

'Any day.'

She kisses his hands. It strikes him that she's more overtly affectionate than usual.

'What have I done to deserve this?'

'Nothing special,' she says. 'Sometimes I think I take you for granted. But I don't really.'

She leans forward and kisses his lips. Then she gets up and goes back to making dinner.

'It's all just pride,' he says. 'Stupid male pride. I'm getting better about it.'

There's the true modern idolatry: the worship of the self. The pursuit of self-fulfilment. Each of us makes our own idol in our own image.

'You have been a bit down lately,' she says, her back turned.

'Yes.'

'Anything I'm doing?'

'No. Just life. Growing older.'

He watches his wife with love and gratitude. Feels her soft kiss still lingering on his lips.

'I want you to be happy, Laura.'

'How happy?' she says.

There it is. Two words: the simple impossible question. How happy am I supposed to be? When am I entitled to complain and ask for more? Absurd to expect perfection, but how far short are we to allow ourselves to fall?

Where's your fucking ambition, Henry?

'That is the question, isn't it?'

'I went for a walk on the Downs with Nick Crocker,' she says. She's ladling risotto from the pan onto dinner plates.

'Is he still around?'

'Not any more.'

'What's he doing with his life these days?'

'He sells works of art. He seems to be doing very well. Cotman, Turner, big-ticket stuff. Come and eat.'

As they eat, Laura tells him about Nick Crocker.

'He came up with this tremendous rant about the countryside. He thinks we're all living fake lives in a fake landscape and the real countryside has gone for ever.'

'He's probably right.'

'No, he isn't right. My life isn't fake. I'm building a home and raising my children and making as much sense of my life as I can. What's fake about that?'

'I just meant about the countryside changing.'

'The countryside's always changing. You're the historian.'

'Of course.'

'I bet the first thing Iron Age man said when Bronze Age man came along was, There goes the countryside.'

Henry grins. He likes that.

'What right has Nick to sneer at us?' Laura speaks with the energy of anger. 'Maybe we're not farmers, but we're people, aren't we? It's just sentimentalism. I refuse to be told I'm not real.'

The real thing, for ever out of reach. But somehow it doesn't matter any more. Watching his wife across the table, her familiar beautiful face animated as she speaks, he thinks: of course she's real. And I'm real. Maybe we're not living the life we meant to live when we were young, but who's to say we were right back then? No one gets it all. Accidents happen.

So Laura was in love with Nick when she was young. The story's no secret. She gave him her whole heart, it proved too burdensome a gift, he dropped it and it broke. Ever since, she has had many parts of her broken heart to give: some to him, some to Jack, some to Carrie, and so on. Is that a diminution of love or an enrichment?

'So he's gone now, is he?'

'Back to California.'

'Do you ever wonder what it would have been like if you and Nick had stayed together?'

She doesn't answer for a moment.

'Yes,' she says. 'It's been strange seeing him again after all these years. I'm trying to be honest. The odd thing is, he hasn't changed. And he should have changed. I've changed. But somehow he's got himself stuck. And that's just really sad.'

Neither of them speaks for a moment. Then,

'I read your letter,' Henry says. 'The one you wrote to him, years ago.'

'My letter?'

'I was looking for Jack's composition. In your desk drawer.'

'Oh, God. I wish you hadn't.'

'I didn't mean to.'

She's blushing, not looking at him.

'It's all such nonsense,' she says. 'Nick never made me happy. Never.'

'But you were in love with him.'

'Yes. That's something different.'

'Different from what?'

'Different from love.'

Did I tell Henry the truth? Not all of it, not everything, but it's not possible to tell everything. Not even desirable. There's a courtesy of restraint even between wife and husband. For example, I've never told him how I calculated the pros and cons of marrying him, weeks before he asked me, knowing he would ask me. One column for lover, one for father, one for provider, one for friend. My talent for cataloguing. Now if I were to draw up the lists again I'd add a new one that doesn't have a public name: call it memories, or life together, or maybe history. That's the part that Nick understands so little because he's never had it in his life, he's kept himself apart. Children the external evidence of this life together, but it's there in me too, my fifteen years with Henry, it's changed me. Who knows, perhaps it would have been better if I'd gone through the same process with Nick, all that matters is I didn't. Now it's Henry who's woven into me. You couldn't pull him out without tearing me. And the bonds grow stronger with each passing day.

Jack said, 'Daddy was brilliant.'

Laura feels a surge of gratitude, because of Jack and because of Nick and because of history. She recalls again how she heard his silence in the hall and knew what he was doing. That's love, isn't it? The knowledge that allows us to escape the prison cell where each of us lives in solitary confinement, to discover we're not alone after all.

In bed at night, his hand reaching for hers. She holds his hand, strokes his fingers.

'You know what I was remembering today?' she says.

'What?'

'How you proposed to me.'

'Oh, God.'

'You said, We could get married if you'd like that. Like you were asking if I wanted to go to see some film.'

'I was nervous.'

'You knew I'd say yes.'

'I didn't. I thought you'd say let's give it time.'

'Well. I knew you'd ask me.'

And wanted you to ask me. I've thought about you every day from that day to this.

Later they make love.

'I want to be slow tonight,' she says.

Henry feels how there are shivers all down his long body. Every woman makes me tremble.

'You know when you came and found me by the lake. I didn't recognize you. I thought, Who's this beautiful woman?'

'No you didn't. You never notice me any more.'

'Well, that's true too. But I did think that.'

She eases her legs apart so that he can stroke her. Her hand on his cock, which is already hard. No problems this time. But she wants to go slow.

'Something else I was remembering today,' she says. 'I was thinking how it was with Nick all those years ago.' She means making love with Nick, but she's too shy to say so, even with Henry's cock in her hand. Or too considerate. 'I remember wanting it to be good for Nick, and worrying about if it was good enough, and if I should be doing more, I don't know what. I was always thinking he'd get bored. But what I have no memory of at all is what it was like for me.'

Her hips move, pushing against his probing fingers.

'You certainly should have done more,' he says, sweetly mocking. 'I'm sure he got bored.'

'Do you mind me talking about him?'

'No.'

'Why not?'

'I don't know why not. I suppose he doesn't seem all that real to me.'

'He isn't real. He's a ghost.'

'Whatever I feel about him is what you choose to let me feel.'

'Yes. I suppose that's true.'

She pulls him gently over her, guiding his cock between her thighs. 'Slow, remember?'

'Would you rather I was jealous?'

'No. You're fine the way you are.'

His cock easing in, slowly, slowly.

'Oh, I do like this,' says Laura.

'I was thinking about the Swanborough walk. Over the Downs to the secret valley.'

Now he's all the way in, home at last. His naked body in my arms.

'I want to go there again,' he says. 'You and me and Jack and Carrie.'

'Then we'll go there again.'

'There's a monument there to a man who died in the valley. I've often wondered why he died.'

A long slow fuck. She knows very well why he's talking about a valley in the Downs as he pulls slowly back and pushes slowly in again. He doesn't want to come too soon.

Desire me again, my darling. I will not burn what remains of the greatest happiness I have ever known.